DOGS OF WAR

BY **SHEILA KEENAN**   ILLUSTRATED BY **NATHAN FOX**

COLOR FOR *BOOTS* AND *LOKI* BY **RICO RENZI**

COLOR FOR *SHEBA* BY **GUY MAJOR**

graphix

An Imprint of

■SCHOLASTIC

To all those who have served, sacrificed, and suffered, and to the peacemakers who are trying to put an end to that suffering.

Many thanks to David Saylor for seeing the merits of this book; to Ken Wright for shepherding it through; to Lisa Sandell, an outstanding editor; to Phil Falco, the guy with the design eye; to Jody Corbett and Jennifer Ung for editorial support; and to Rico Renzi and Guy Major for the great color palette.

Major thanks to Nathan Fox for bringing the visual power and glory to these stories!

Above all, thank you, Kevin, for everything.

— S.K.

This book has been a labor of love, an engaging challenge, education, and a flat-out personal joy to be a part of, to say the least. My sincerest thanks to Phil Falco, David Saylor, and Lisa Sandell for making this book possible and their patience, collaboration, and unyielding support throughout it all, and to Sheila Keenan for the opportunity to bring her words, characters, and these great stories to life. And most important, to Jennifer and our daughters — for inspiration, support, and putting up with the late hours, unending talk about dogs, pages to go, and deadlines — all my love. Thank you.

As a young boy, my best friends and pseudo brothers-in-imaginary-arms were a shepherd collie named Stormy and a mutt named Odie. My fondest memories and backyard adventures with them and throughout my youth was with my father. Growing up, he taught me how to respect, train, and care for our dogs, and through the good times and the bad, he and those dogs were always there when I needed them the most. Now, as a father myself with our first puppy (Mr. Truffles), I understand the joy and fun he must have had playing and teaching me those lessons. So to my father and to all of the parents and four-legged best friends out there, and to those whom we have loved and lost, given their lives and service to protect us — I humbly dedicate this book to you. You have and continue to inspire us in more ways than words could ever accomplish — thank you.

— N.F.

Text and compilation copyright © 2013 by Sheila Keenan
Art copyright © 2013 by Nathan Fox

Library of Congress Cataloging-in-Publication Data Available

ISBN 978-0-545-12887-2 (hardcover)
ISBN 978-0-545-12888-9 (paperback)

10 9 8 7 6 5 4   14 15 16 17

First edition, November 2013
Lettering by John Green
Colorists: *BOOTS* and *LOKI* by Rico Renzi; *SHEBA* by Guy Major
Book Design by Phil Falco
Edited by Lisa Sandell
Creative Director: David Saylor
Printed in China   38

TABLE OF
CONTENTS

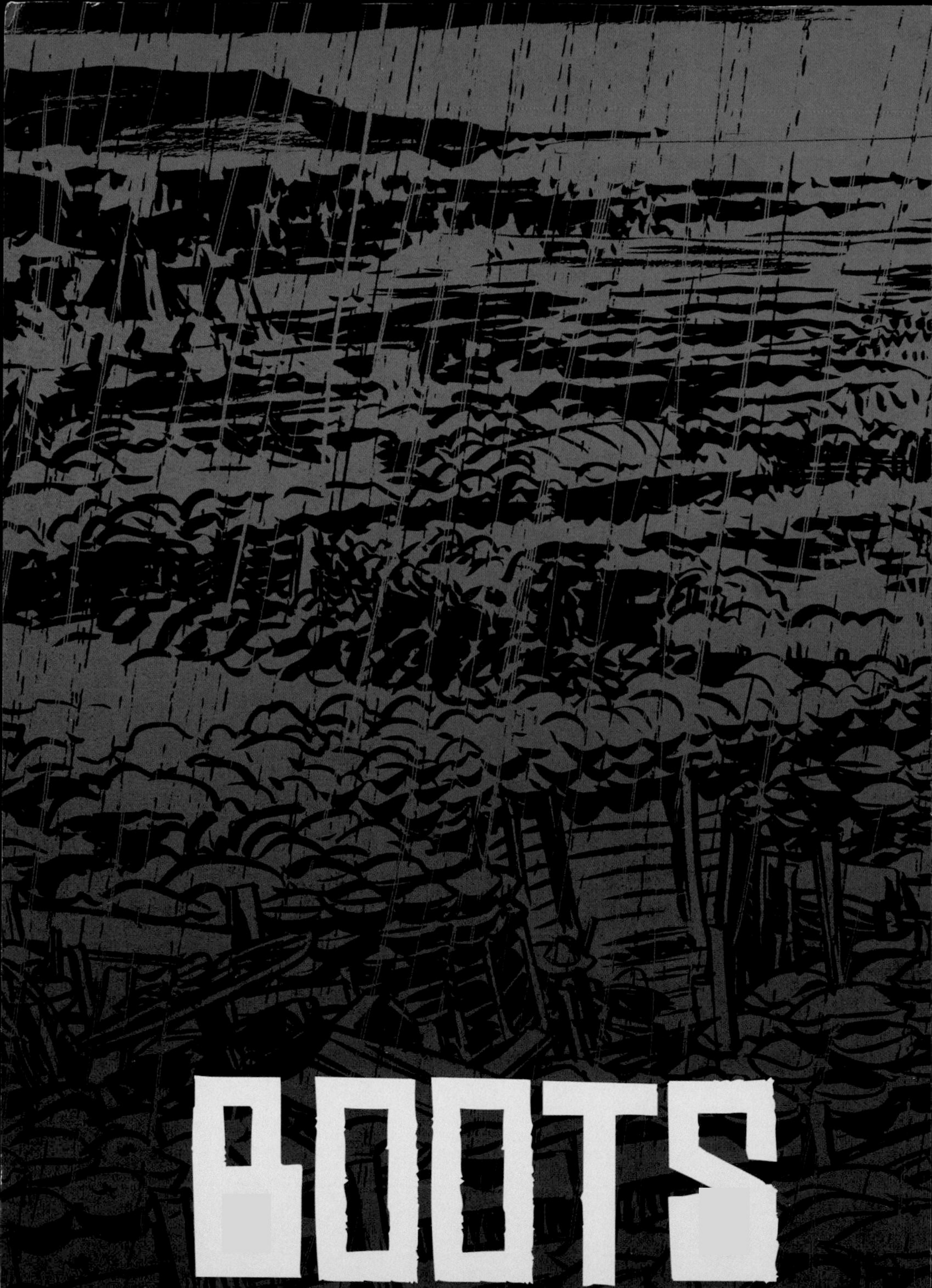
BOOTS

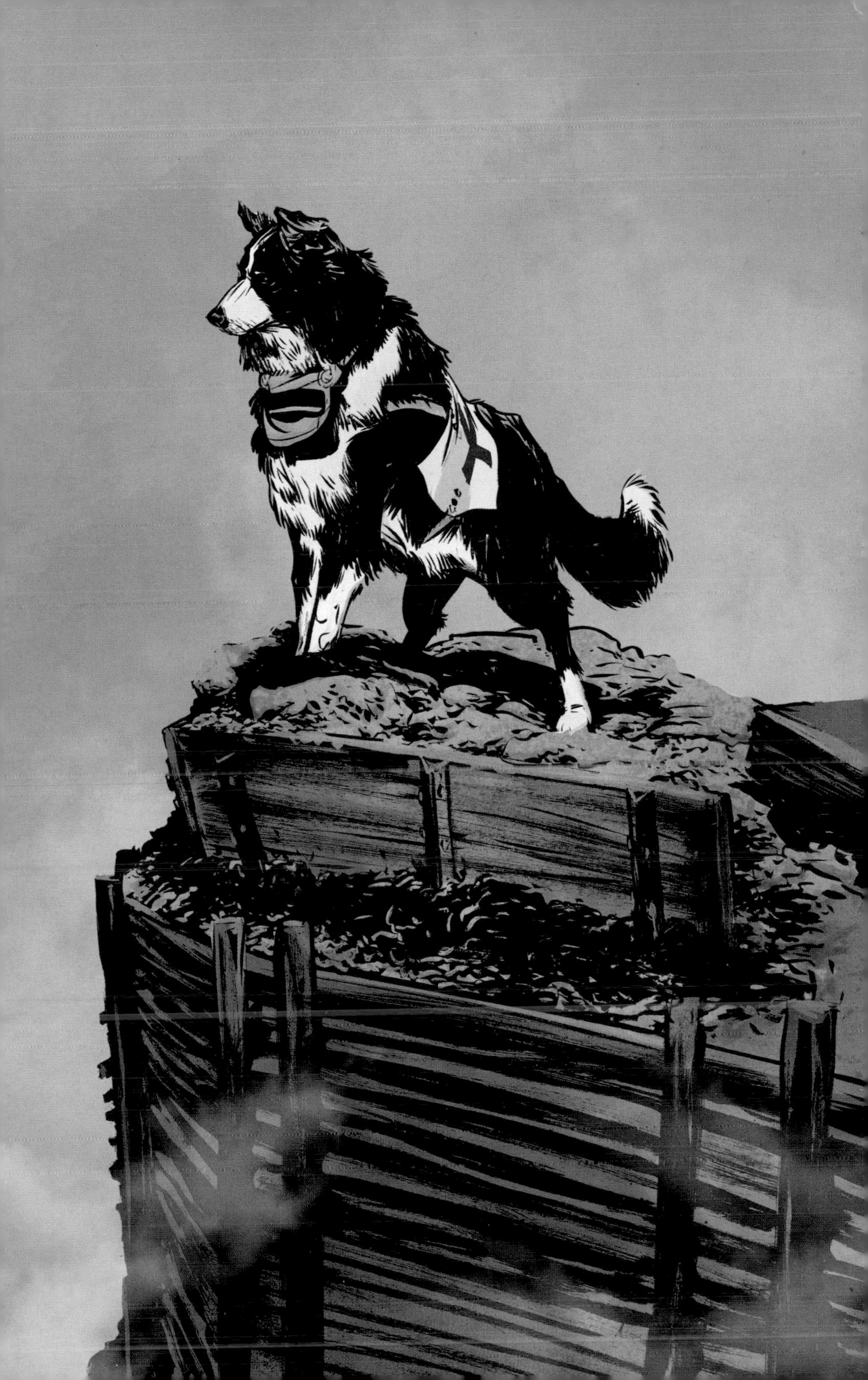

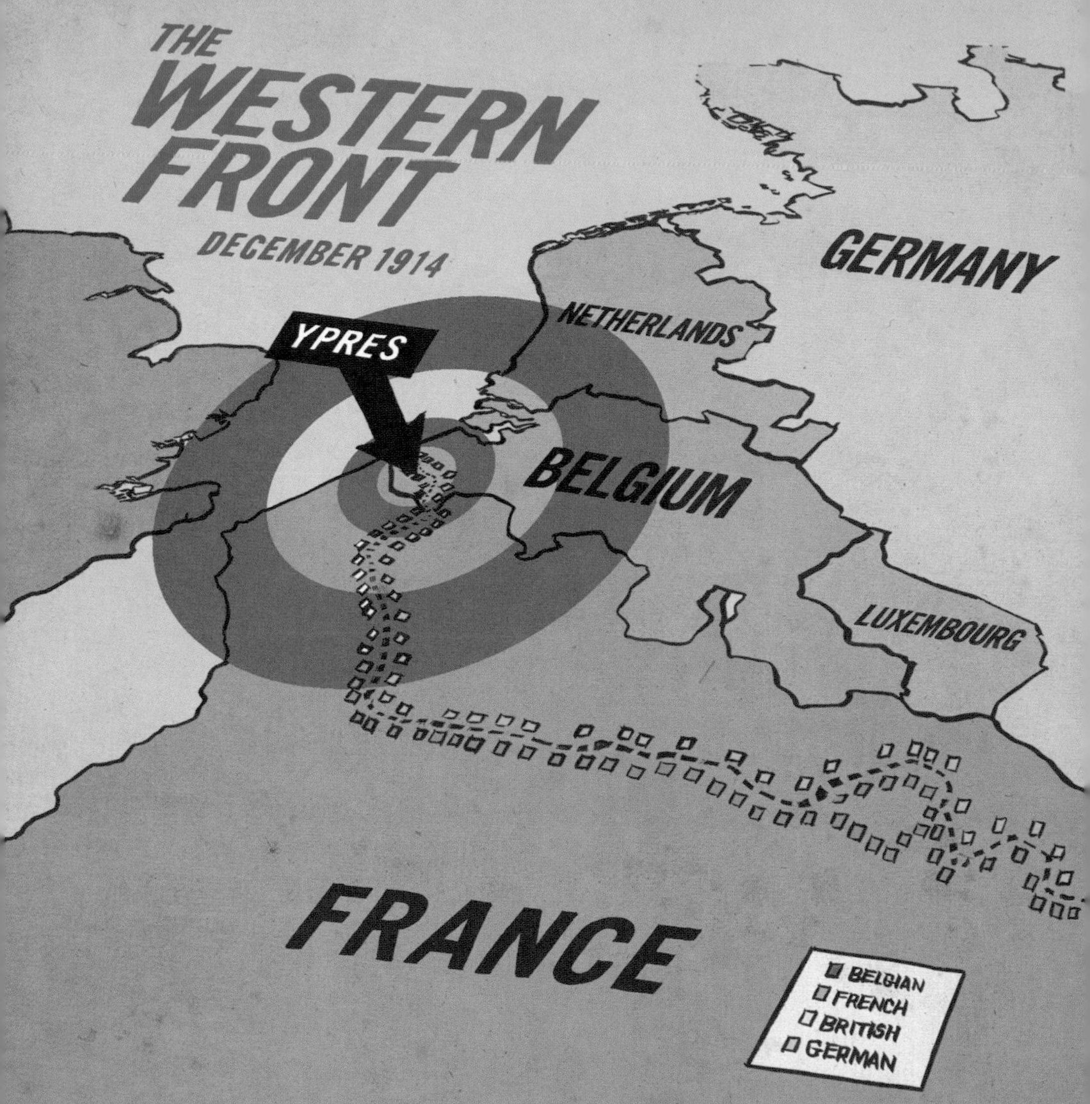
THE WESTERN FRONT
DECEMBER 1914
GERMANY
NETHERLANDS
YPRES
BELGIUM
LUXEMBOURG
FRANCE
BELGIAN
FRENCH
BRITISH
GERMAN

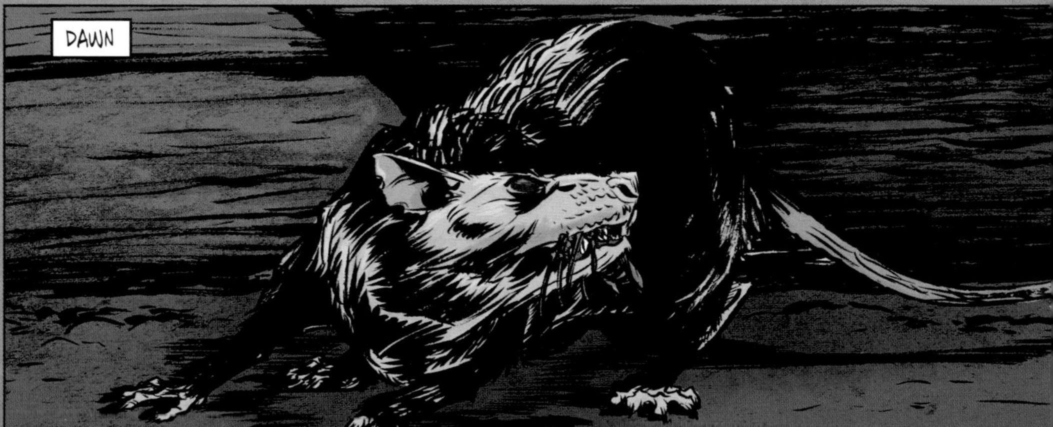
DAWN

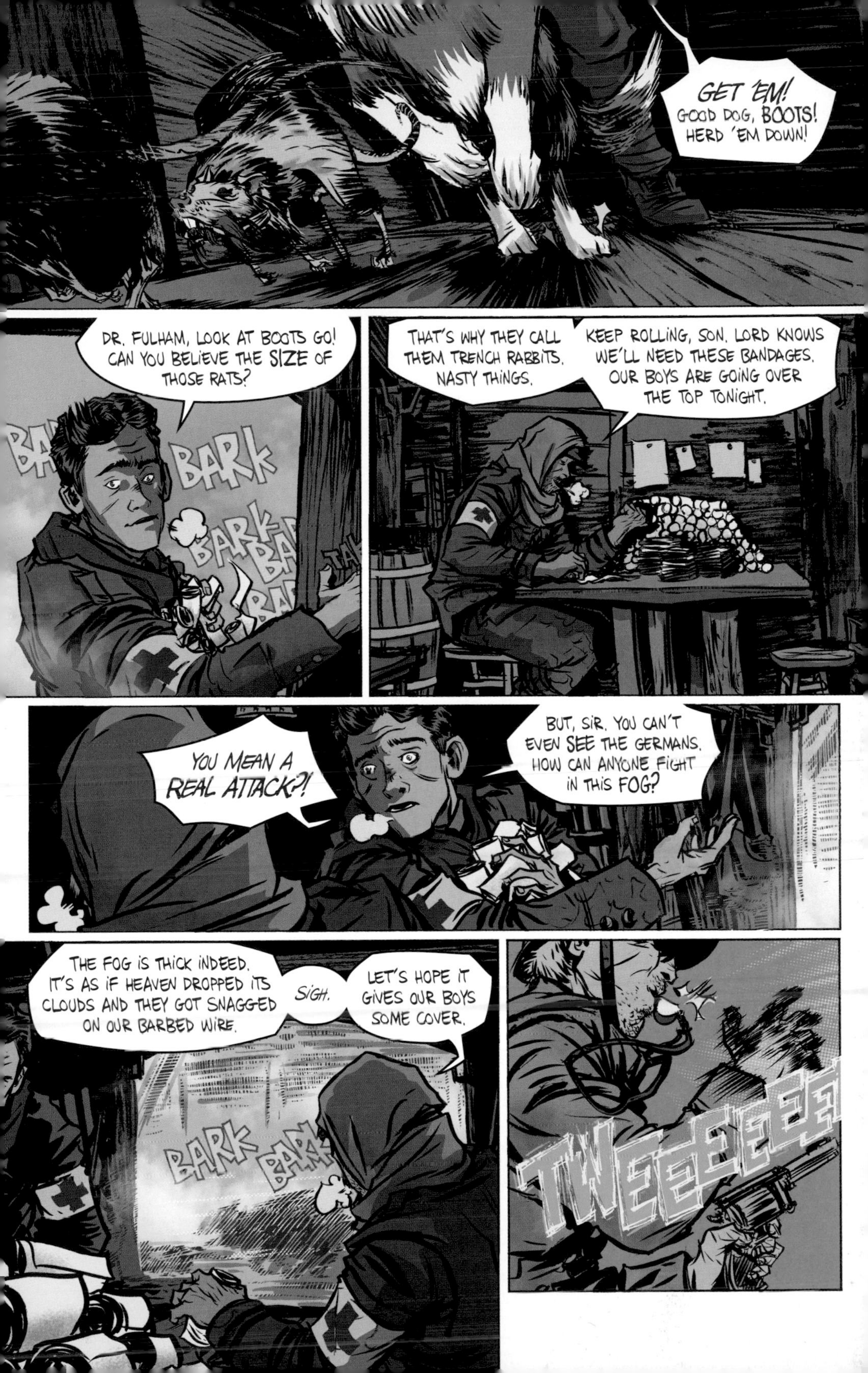
GET 'EM! GOOD DOG, BOOTS! HERD 'EM DOWN!
DR. FULHAM, LOOK AT BOOTS GO! CAN YOU BELIEVE THE SIZE OF THOSE RATS?
BARK
BARK
THAT'S WHY THEY CALL THEM TRENCH RABBITS. NASTY THINGS.
KEEP ROLLING, SON. LORD KNOWS WE'LL NEED THESE BANDAGES. OUR BOYS ARE GOING OVER THE TOP TONIGHT.
YOU MEAN A REAL ATTACK?!
BUT, SIR. YOU CAN'T EVEN SEE THE GERMANS. HOW CAN ANYONE FIGHT IN THIS FOG?
THE FOG IS THICK INDEED. IT'S AS IF HEAVEN DROPPED ITS CLOUDS AND THEY GOT SNAGGED ON OUR BARBED WIRE.
SIGH.
LET'S HOPE IT GIVES OUR BOYS SOME COVER.
BARK
TWEEEEEE

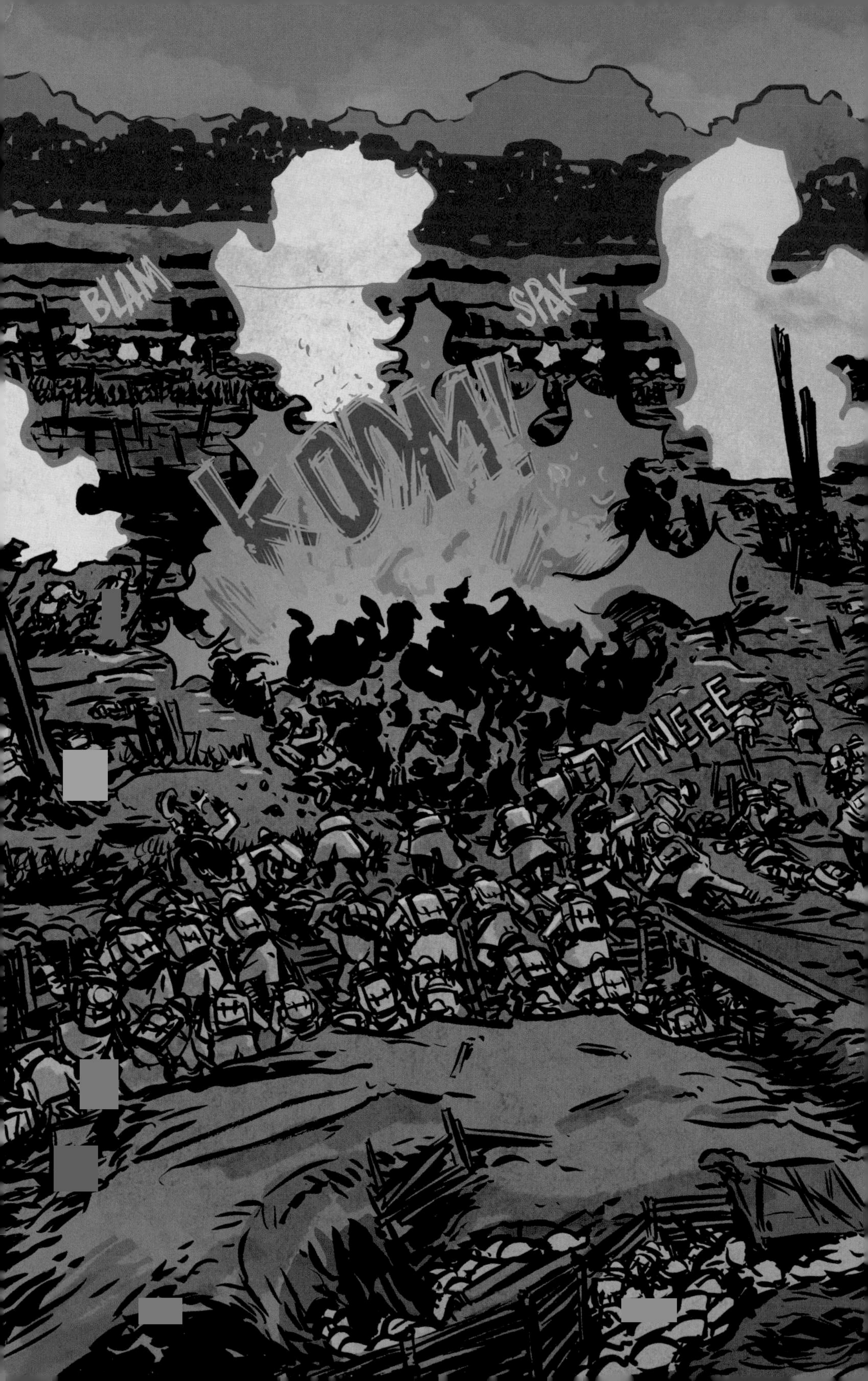
BLAM
SPAK
KOOM!
TWEEE

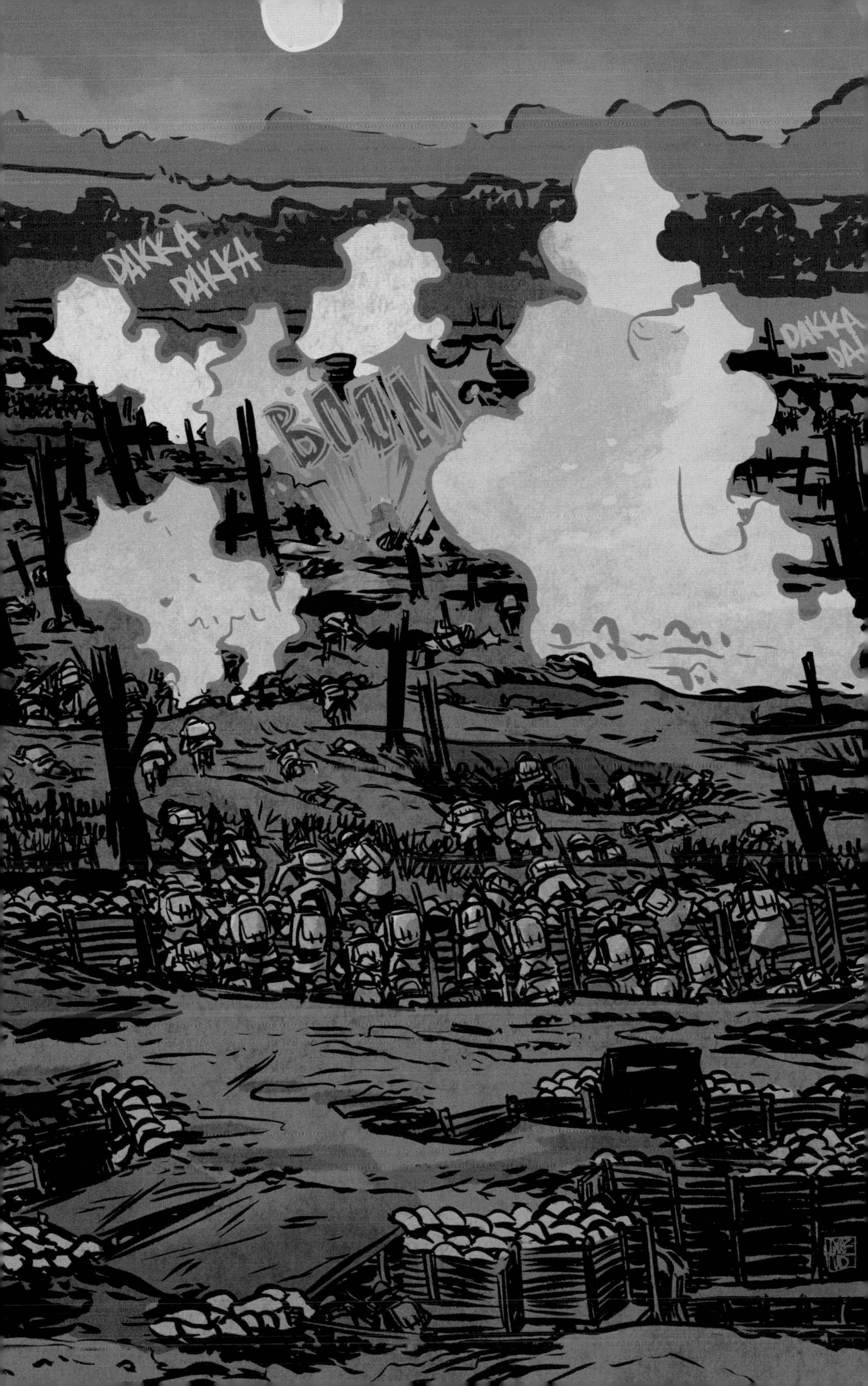
DAKKA DAKKA
BOOM
DAKKA DA

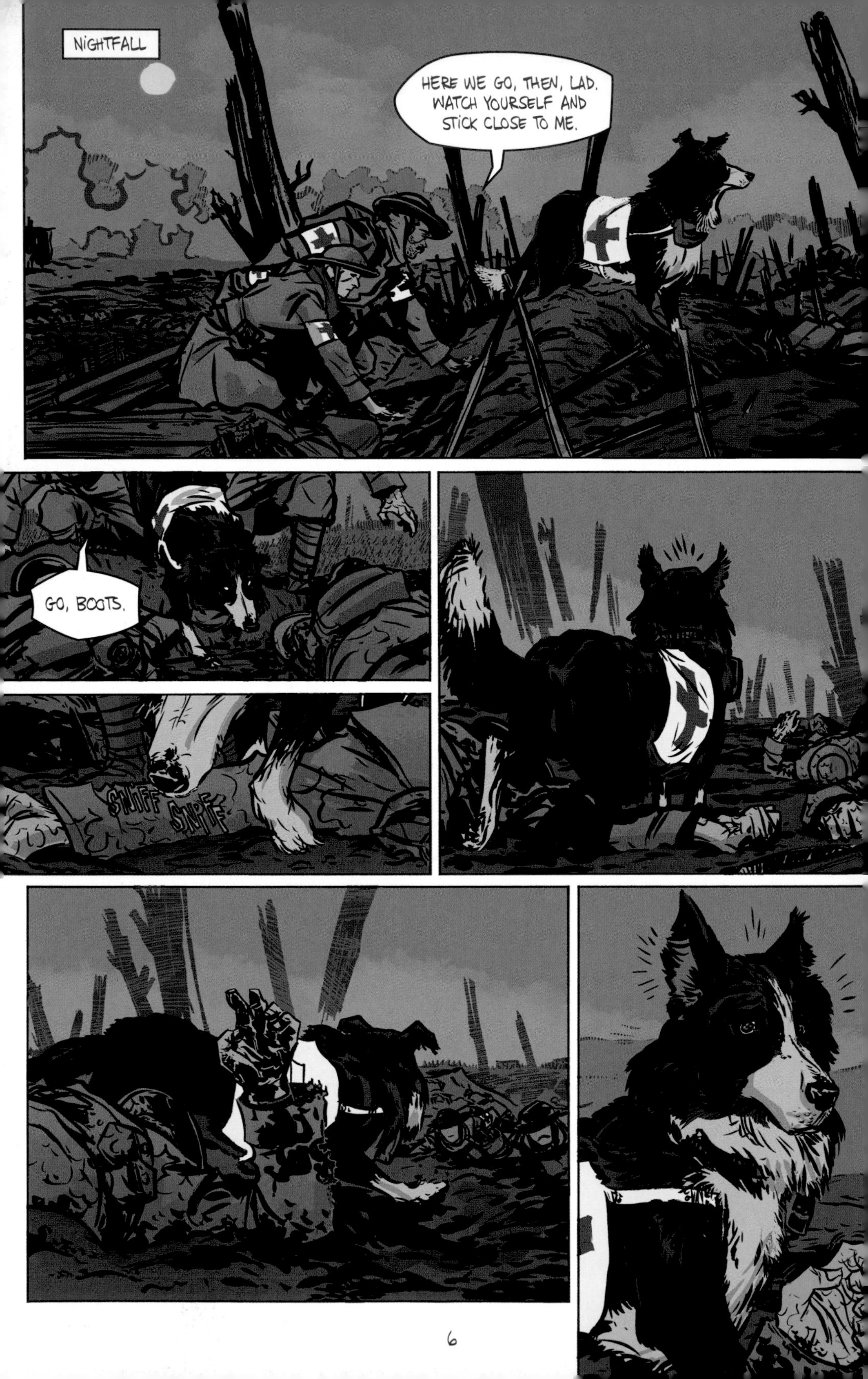
NIGHTFALL
HERE WE GO, THEN, LAD. WATCH YOURSELF AND STICK CLOSE TO ME.
GO, BOOTS.
SNIFF SNIFF

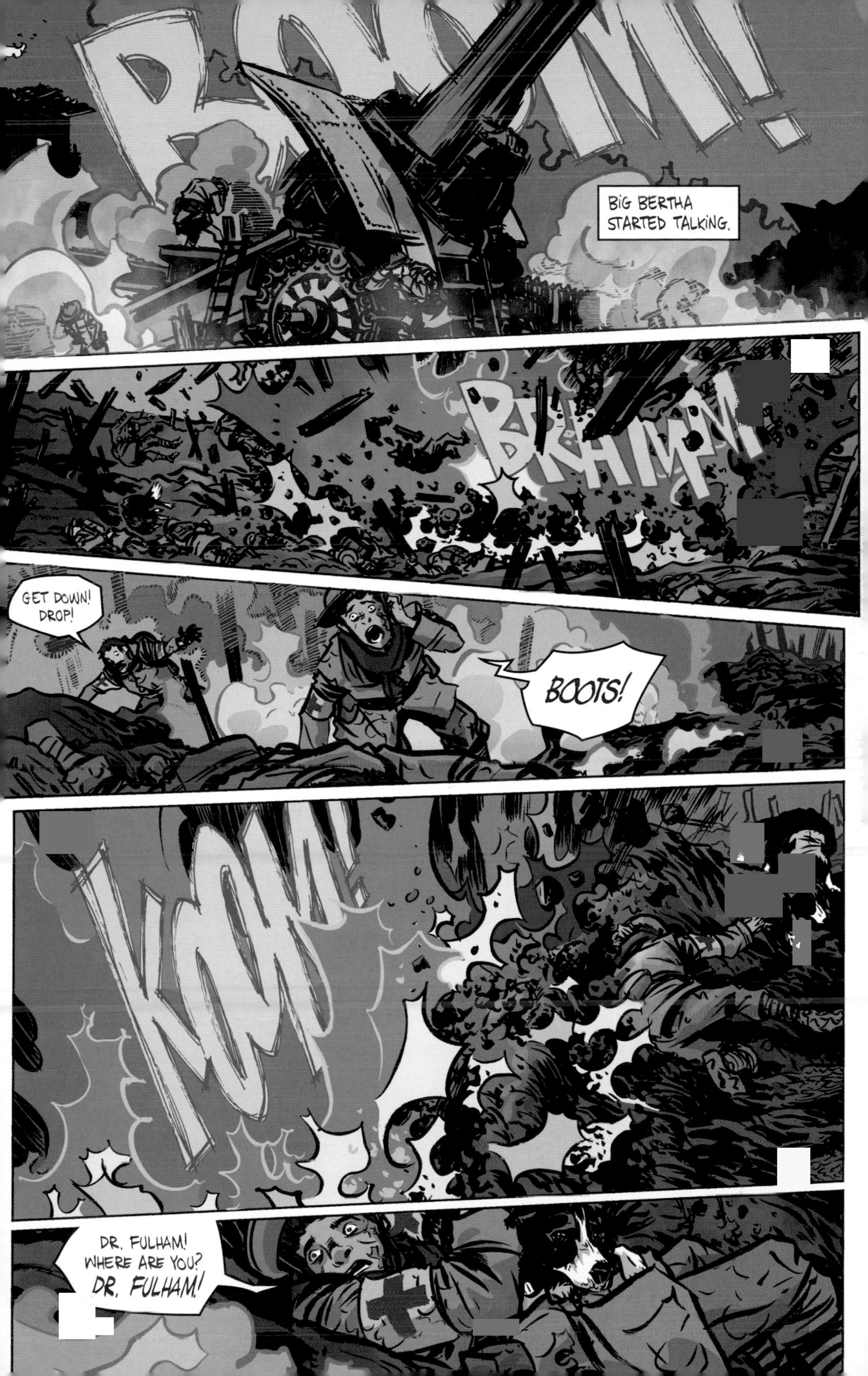

BIG BERTHA STARTED TALKING.
GET DOWN! DROP!
BOOTS!
DR. FULHAM! WHERE ARE YOU? DR. FULHAM!

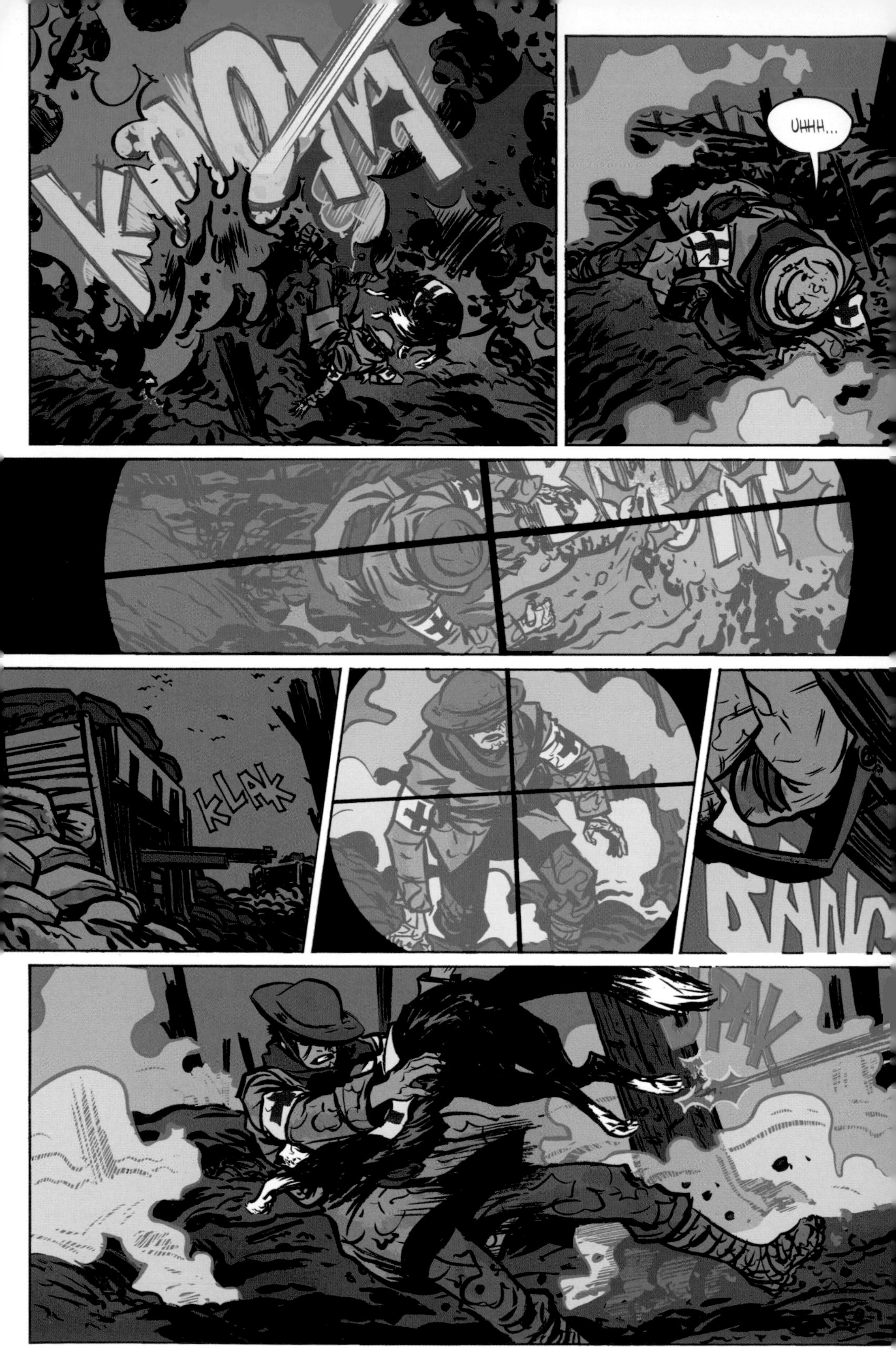
KADOOM
UHHH...
KLAK
PAK

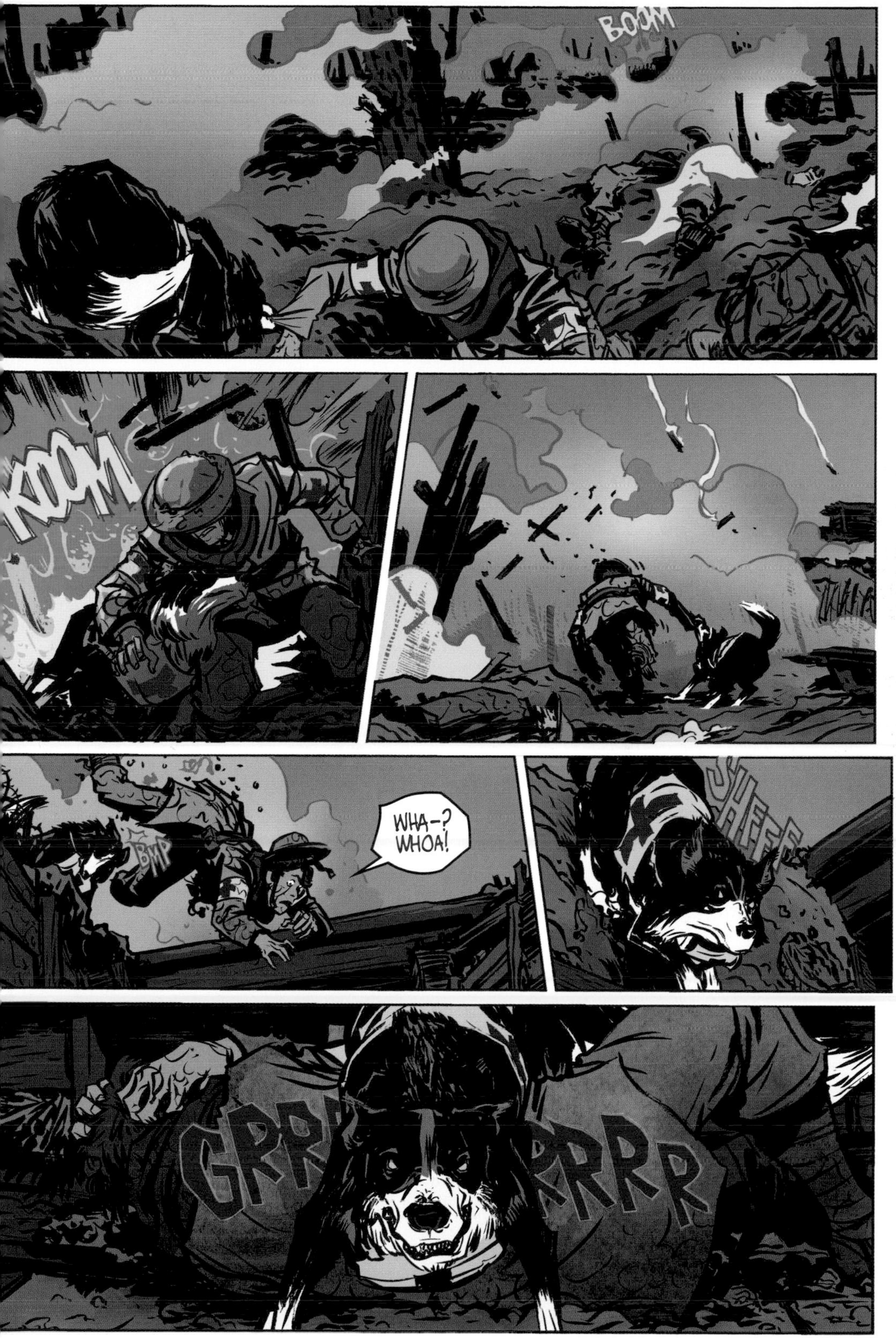
BOOM
KOOM
WHA-?
WHOA!
BMP
SHFF
GRRRRRR

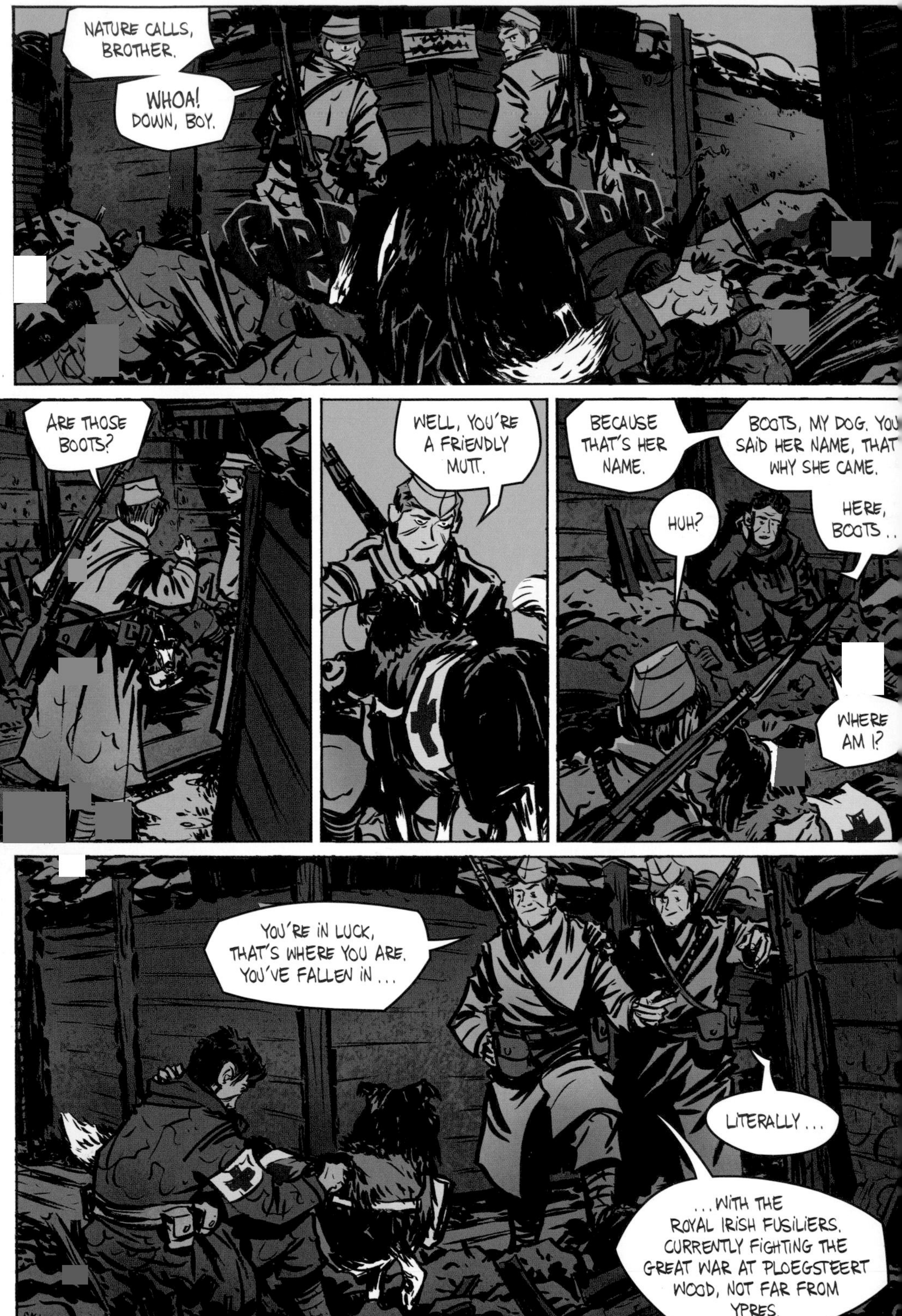
NATURE CALLS, BROTHER.
WHOA! DOWN, BOY.
ARE THOSE BOOTS?
WELL, YOU'RE A FRIENDLY MUTT.
BECAUSE THAT'S HER NAME.
BOOTS, MY DOG. YOU SAID HER NAME, THAT WHY SHE CAME.
HUH?
HERE, BOOTS . .
WHERE AM I?
YOU'RE IN LUCK, THAT'S WHERE YOU ARE. YOU'VE FALLEN IN . . .
LITERALLY . . .
. . . WITH THE ROYAL IRISH FUSILIERS. CURRENTLY FIGHTING THE GREAT WAR AT PLOEGSTEERT WOOD, NOT FAR FROM YPRES.

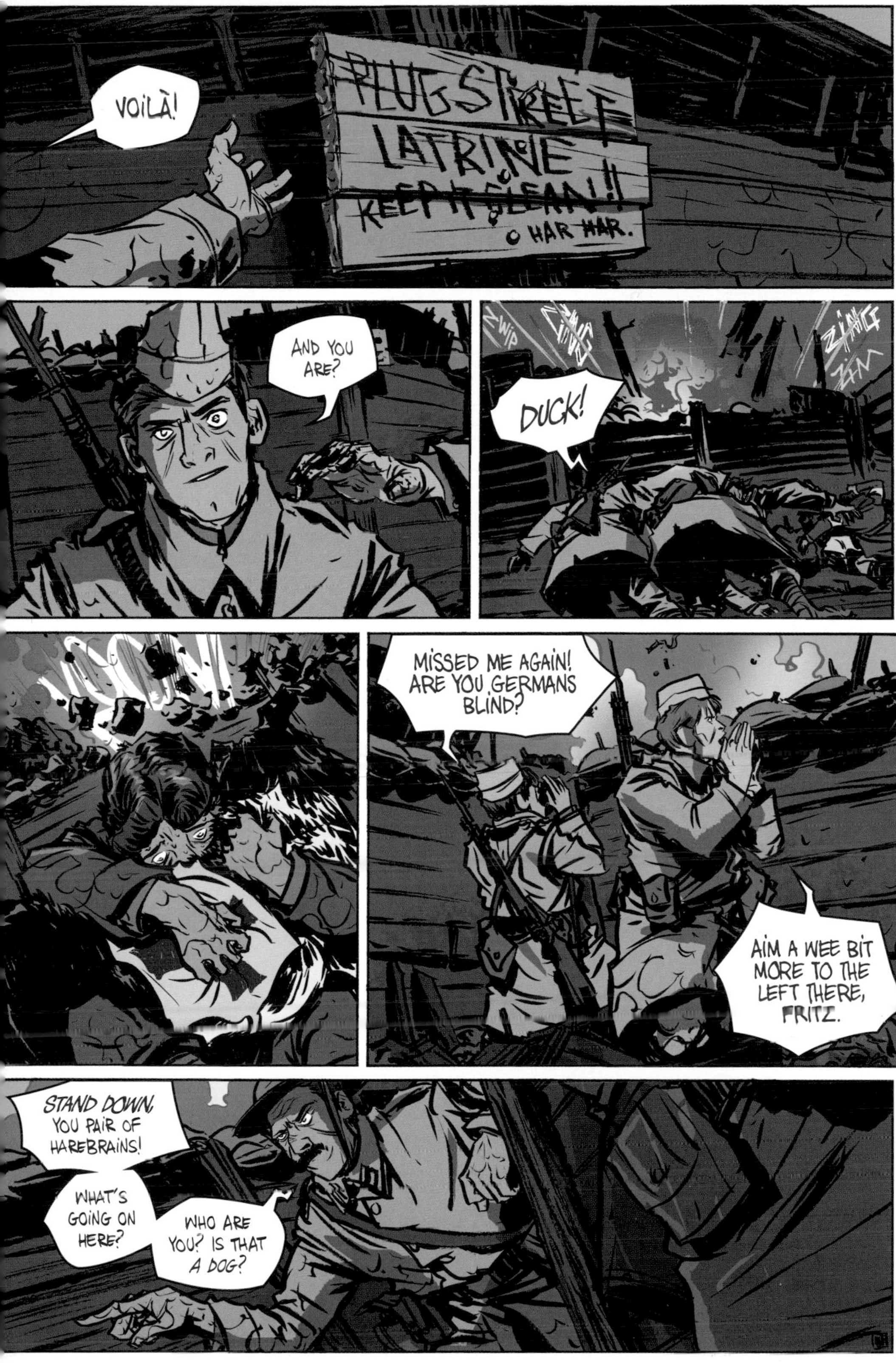
VOILÀ!
PLUG STREET LATRINE KEEP IT CLEAN!!
HAR HAR.
AND YOU ARE?
Z-WIP
ZING
DUCK!
ZING
ZIM
MISSED ME AGAIN! ARE YOU GERMANS BLIND?
AIM A WEE BIT MORE TO THE LEFT THERE, FRITZ.
STAND DOWN, YOU PAIR OF HAREBRAINS!
WHAT'S GOING ON HERE?
WHO ARE YOU? IS THAT A DOG?

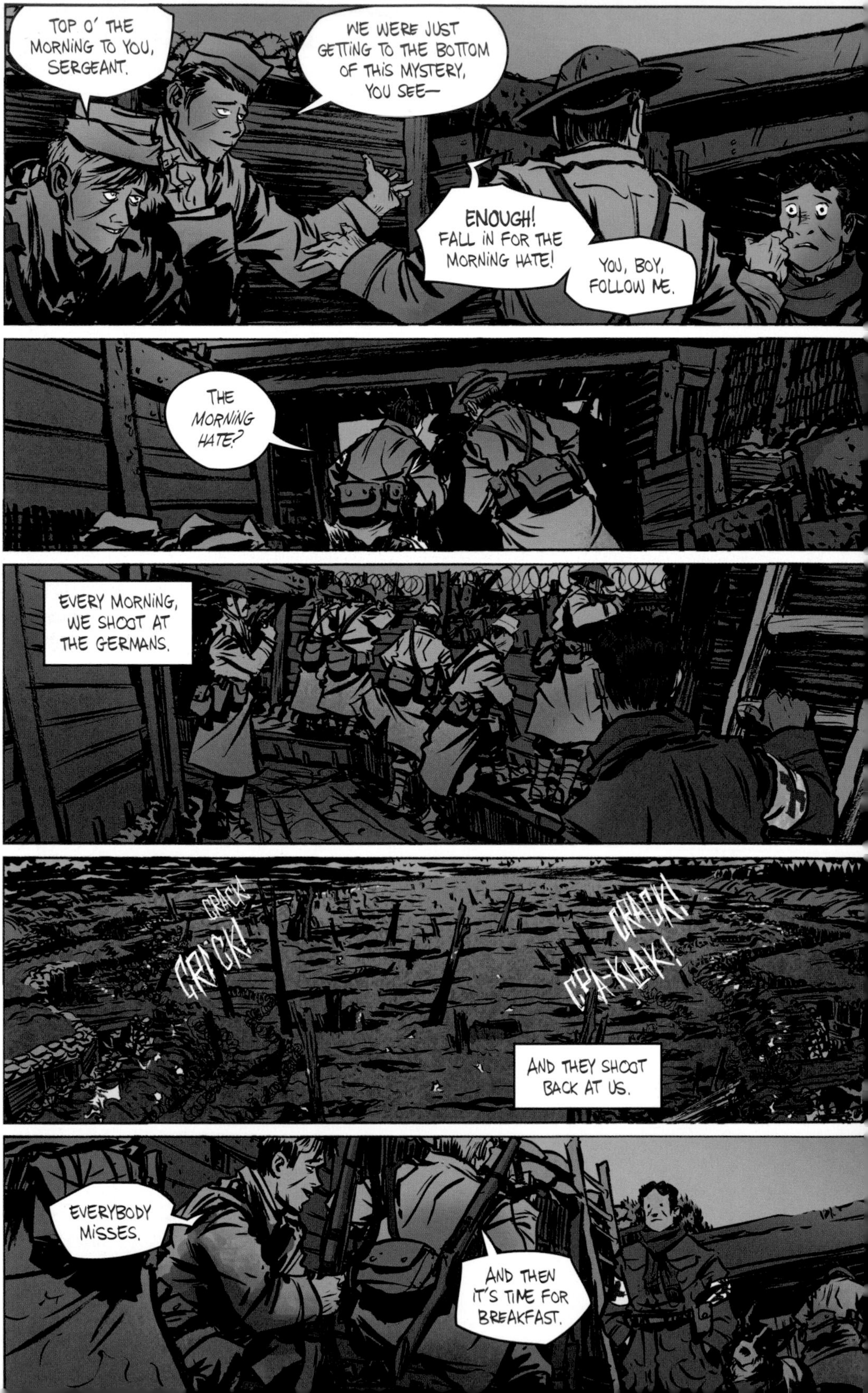
TOP O' THE MORNING TO YOU, SERGEANT.
WE WERE JUST GETTING TO THE BOTTOM OF THIS MYSTERY, YOU SEE—
ENOUGH! FALL IN FOR THE MORNING HATE!
YOU, BOY, FOLLOW ME.
THE *MORNING HATE?*
EVERY MORNING, WE SHOOT AT THE GERMANS.
CRACK!
CRACK!
CRACK!
CRA-KLAK!
AND THEY SHOOT BACK AT US.
EVERYBODY MISSES.
AND THEN IT'S TIME FOR BREAKFAST.

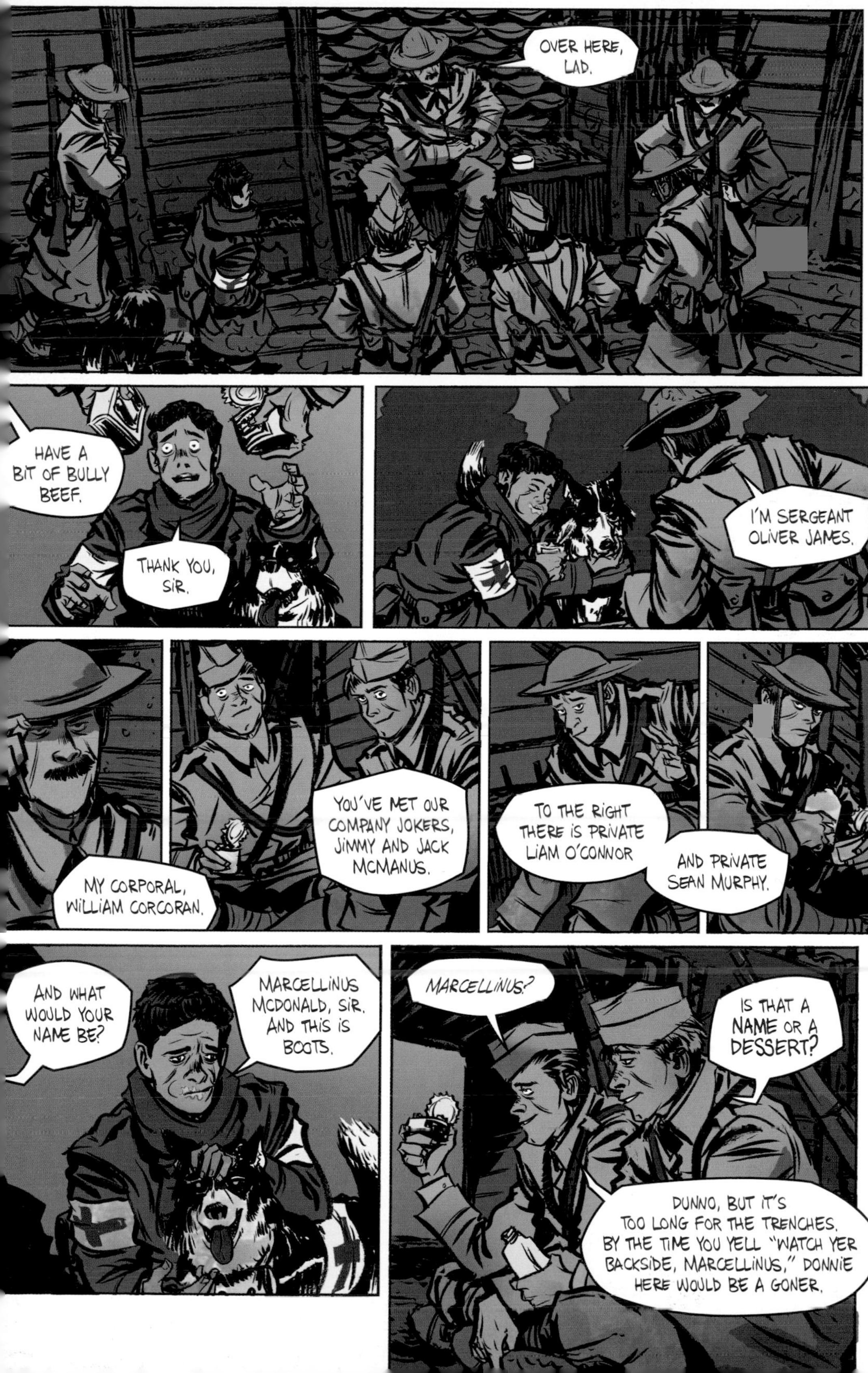
OVER HERE, LAD.
HAVE A BIT OF BULLY BEEF.
THANK YOU, SIR.
I'M SERGEANT OLIVER JAMES.
MY CORPORAL, WILLIAM CORCORAN.
YOU'VE MET OUR COMPANY JOKERS, JIMMY AND JACK MCMANUS.
TO THE RIGHT THERE IS PRIVATE LIAM O'CONNOR
AND PRIVATE SEAN MURPHY.
AND WHAT WOULD YOUR NAME BE?
MARCELLINUS MCDONALD, SIR. AND THIS IS BOOTS.
MARCELLINUS?
IS THAT A NAME OR A DESSERT?
DUNNO, BUT IT'S TOO LONG FOR THE TRENCHES. BY THE TIME YOU YELL "WATCH YER BACKSIDE, MARCELLINUS," DONNIE HERE WOULD BE A GONER.

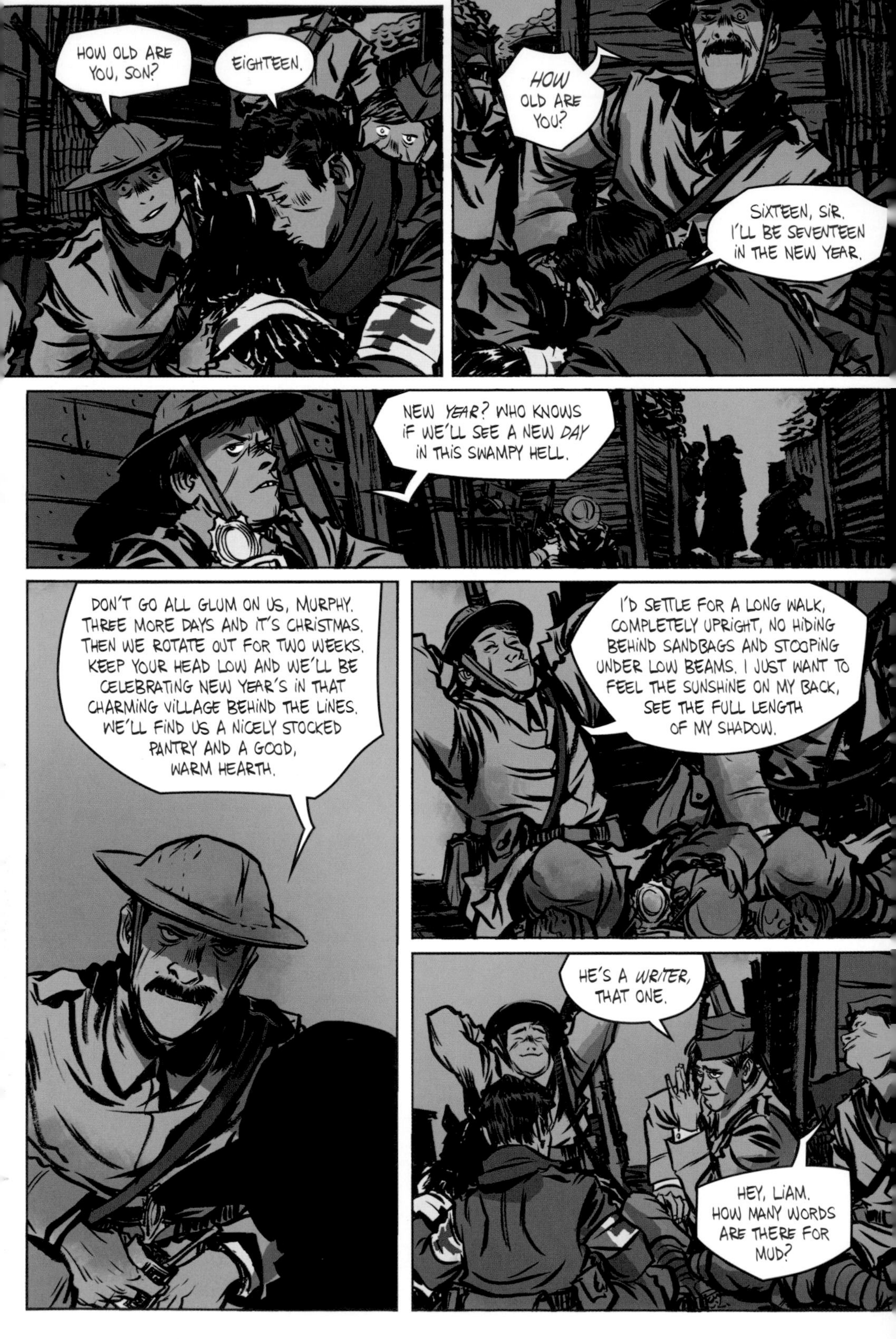
HOW OLD ARE YOU, SON?
EIGHTEEN.
HOW OLD ARE YOU?
SIXTEEN, SIR. I'LL BE SEVENTEEN IN THE NEW YEAR.
NEW YEAR? WHO KNOWS IF WE'LL SEE A NEW DAY IN THIS SWAMPY HELL.
DON'T GO ALL GLUM ON US, MURPHY. THREE MORE DAYS AND IT'S CHRISTMAS. THEN WE ROTATE OUT FOR TWO WEEKS. KEEP YOUR HEAD LOW AND WE'LL BE CELEBRATING NEW YEAR'S IN THAT CHARMING VILLAGE BEHIND THE LINES. WE'LL FIND US A NICELY STOCKED PANTRY AND A GOOD, WARM HEARTH.
I'D SETTLE FOR A LONG WALK, COMPLETELY UPRIGHT, NO HIDING BEHIND SANDBAGS AND STOOPING UNDER LOW BEAMS. I JUST WANT TO FEEL THE SUNSHINE ON MY BACK, SEE THE FULL LENGTH OF MY SHADOW.
HE'S A WRITER, THAT ONE.
HEY, LIAM. HOW MANY WORDS ARE THERE FOR MUD?

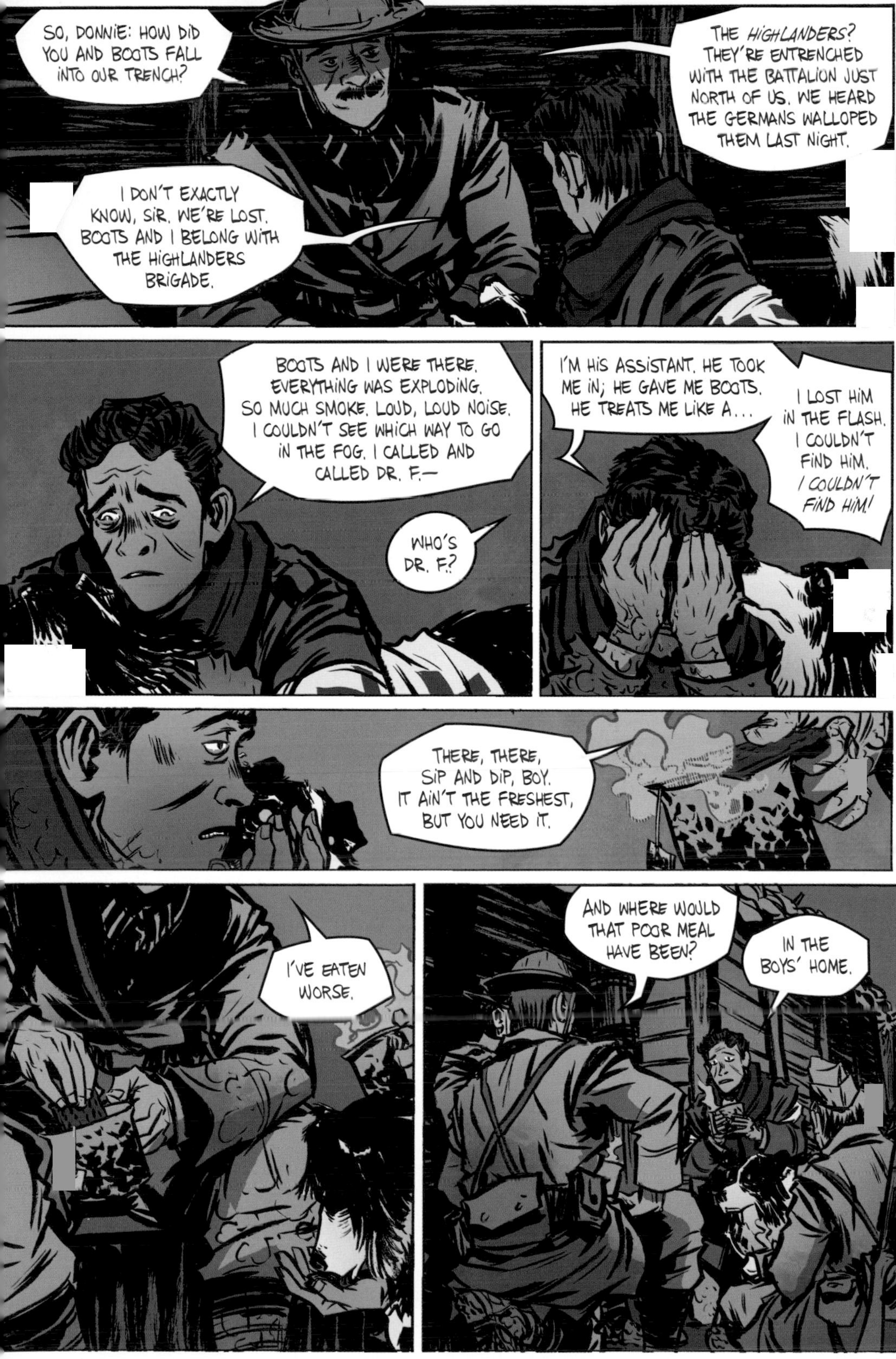
SO, DONNIE: HOW DID YOU AND BOOTS FALL INTO OUR TRENCH?
THE *HIGHLANDERS*? THEY'RE ENTRENCHED WITH THE BATTALION JUST NORTH OF US. WE HEARD THE GERMANS WALLOPED THEM LAST NIGHT.
I DON'T EXACTLY KNOW, SIR. WE'RE LOST. BOOTS AND I BELONG WITH THE HIGHLANDERS BRIGADE.
BOOTS AND I WERE THERE. EVERYTHING WAS EXPLODING. SO MUCH SMOKE. LOUD, LOUD NOISE. I COULDN'T SEE WHICH WAY TO GO IN THE FOG. I CALLED AND CALLED DR. F.—
WHO'S DR. F.?
I'M HIS ASSISTANT. HE TOOK ME IN; HE GAVE ME BOOTS. HE TREATS ME LIKE A...
I LOST HIM IN THE FLASH. I COULDN'T FIND HIM. *I COULDN'T FIND HIM!*
THERE, THERE, SIP AND DIP, BOY. IT AIN'T THE FRESHEST, BUT YOU NEED IT.
I'VE EATEN WORSE.
AND WHERE WOULD THAT POOR MEAL HAVE BEEN?
IN THE BOYS' HOME.

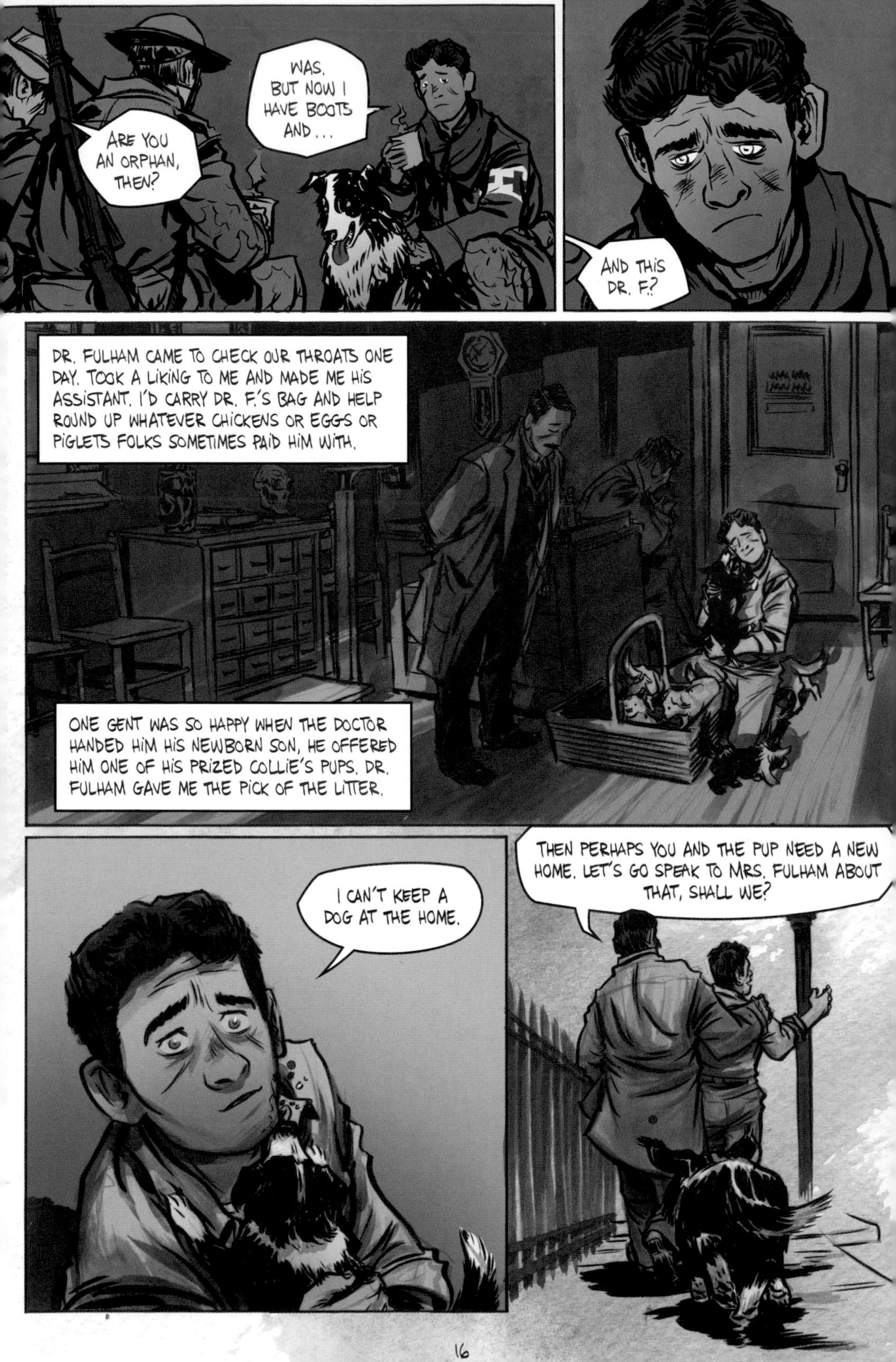
WAS. BUT NOW I HAVE BOOTS AND...
ARE YOU AN ORPHAN, THEN?
AND THIS DR. F.?
DR. FULHAM CAME TO CHECK OUR THROATS ONE DAY. TOOK A LIKING TO ME AND MADE ME HIS ASSISTANT. I'D CARRY DR. F.'S BAG AND HELP ROUND UP WHATEVER CHICKENS OR EGGS OR PIGLETS FOLKS SOMETIMES PAID HIM WITH.
ONE GENT WAS SO HAPPY WHEN THE DOCTOR HANDED HIM HIS NEWBORN SON, HE OFFERED HIM ONE OF HIS PRIZED COLLIE'S PUPS. DR. FULHAM GAVE ME THE PICK OF THE LITTER.
I CAN'T KEEP A DOG AT THE HOME.
THEN PERHAPS YOU AND THE PUP NEED A NEW HOME. LET'S GO SPEAK TO MRS. FULHAM ABOUT THAT, SHALL WE?

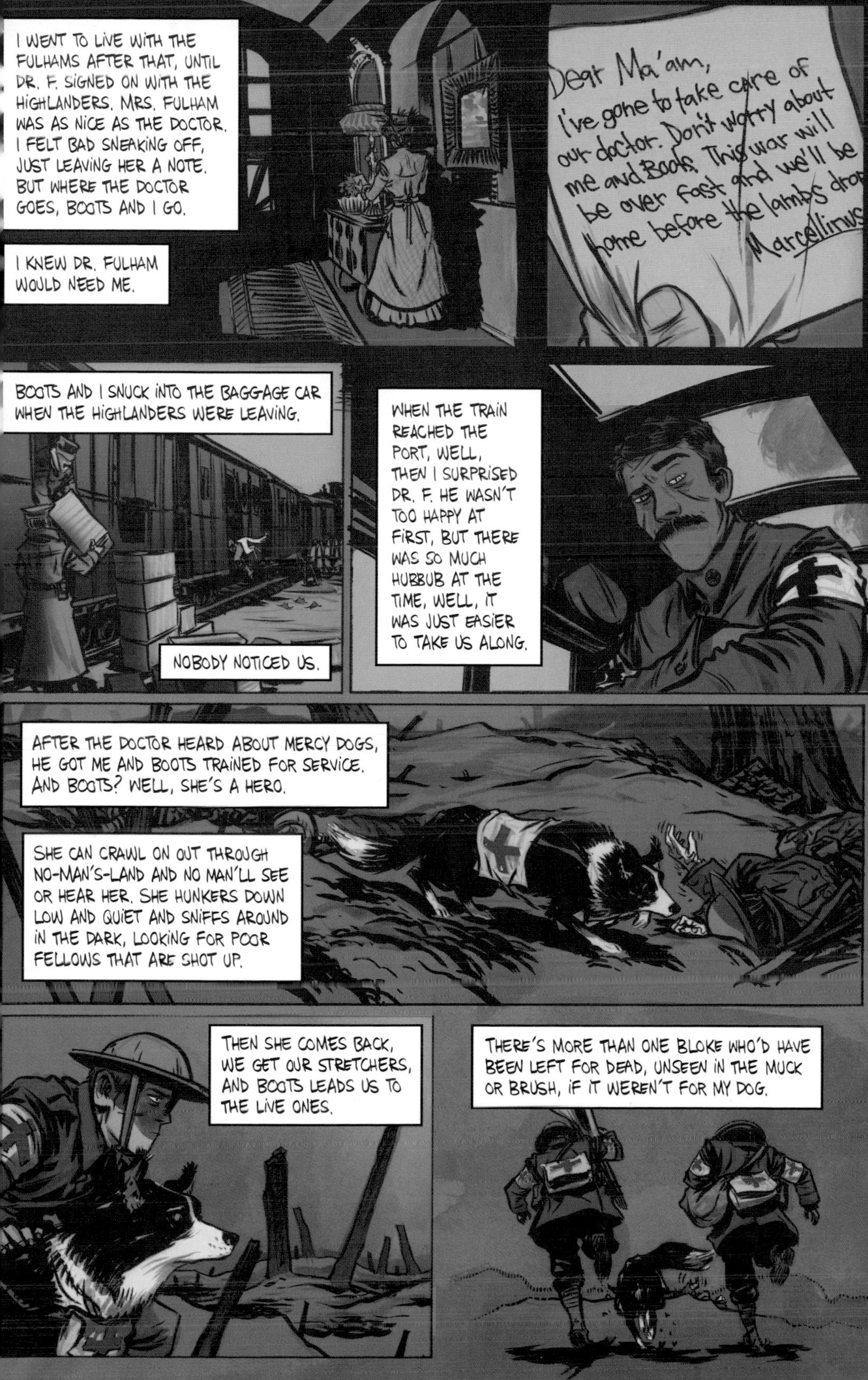
I WENT TO LIVE WITH THE FULHAMS AFTER THAT, UNTIL DR. F. SIGNED ON WITH THE HIGHLANDERS. MRS. FULHAM WAS AS NICE AS THE DOCTOR. I FELT BAD SNEAKING OFF, JUST LEAVING HER A NOTE. BUT WHERE THE DOCTOR GOES, BOOTS AND I GO.
I KNEW DR. FULHAM WOULD NEED ME.
Dear Ma'am,
I've gone to take care of our doctor. Don't worry about me and Boots. This war will be over fast and we'll be home before the lambs drop
Marcellinus
BOOTS AND I SNUCK INTO THE BAGGAGE CAR WHEN THE HIGHLANDERS WERE LEAVING.
NOBODY NOTICED US.
WHEN THE TRAIN REACHED THE PORT, WELL, THEN I SURPRISED DR. F. HE WASN'T TOO HAPPY AT FIRST, BUT THERE WAS SO MUCH HUBBUB AT THE TIME, WELL, IT WAS JUST EASIER TO TAKE US ALONG.
AFTER THE DOCTOR HEARD ABOUT MERCY DOGS, HE GOT ME AND BOOTS TRAINED FOR SERVICE. AND BOOTS? WELL, SHE'S A HERO.
SHE CAN CRAWL ON OUT THROUGH NO-MAN'S-LAND AND NO MAN'LL SEE OR HEAR HER. SHE HUNKERS DOWN LOW AND QUIET AND SNIFFS AROUND IN THE DARK, LOOKING FOR POOR FELLOWS THAT ARE SHOT UP.
THEN SHE COMES BACK, WE GET OUR STRETCHERS, AND BOOTS LEADS US TO THE LIVE ONES.
THERE'S MORE THAN ONE BLOKE WHO'D HAVE BEEN LEFT FOR DEAD, UNSEEN IN THE MUCK OR BRUSH, IF IT WEREN'T FOR MY DOG.

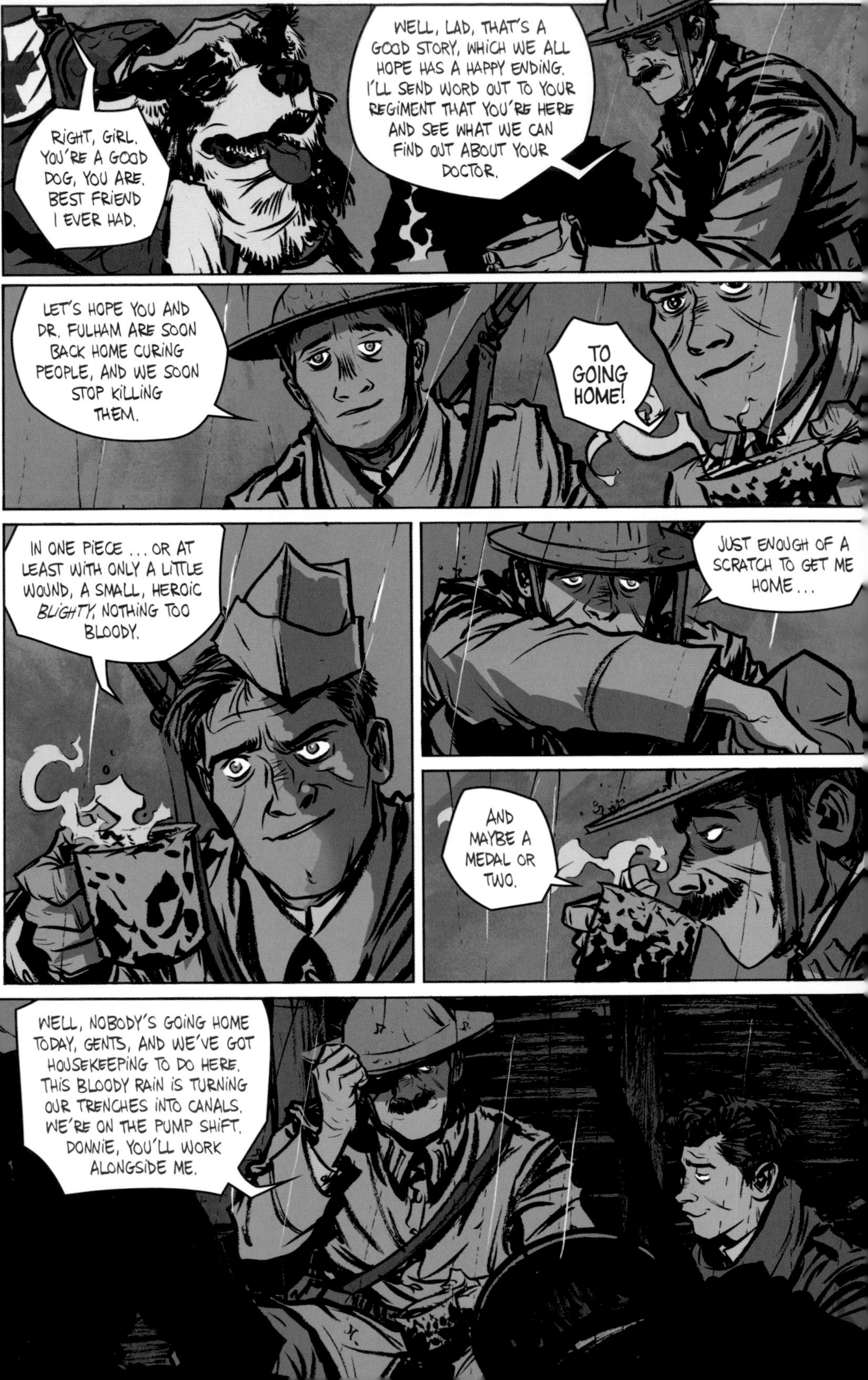
RIGHT, GIRL. YOU'RE A GOOD DOG, YOU ARE. BEST FRIEND I EVER HAD.
WELL, LAD, THAT'S A GOOD STORY, WHICH WE ALL HOPE HAS A HAPPY ENDING. I'LL SEND WORD OUT TO YOUR REGIMENT THAT YOU'RE HERE AND SEE WHAT WE CAN FIND OUT ABOUT YOUR DOCTOR.
LET'S HOPE YOU AND DR. FULHAM ARE SOON BACK HOME CURING PEOPLE, AND WE SOON STOP KILLING THEM.
TO GOING HOME!
IN ONE PIECE . . . OR AT LEAST WITH ONLY A LITTLE WOUND, A SMALL, HEROIC *BLIGHTY*, NOTHING TOO BLOODY.
JUST ENOUGH OF A SCRATCH TO GET ME HOME . . .
AND MAYBE A MEDAL OR TWO.
WELL, NOBODY'S GOING HOME TODAY, GENTS, AND WE'VE GOT HOUSEKEEPING TO DO HERE. THIS BLOODY RAIN IS TURNING OUR TRENCHES INTO CANALS. WE'RE ON THE PUMP SHIFT. DONNIE, YOU'LL WORK ALONGSIDE ME.

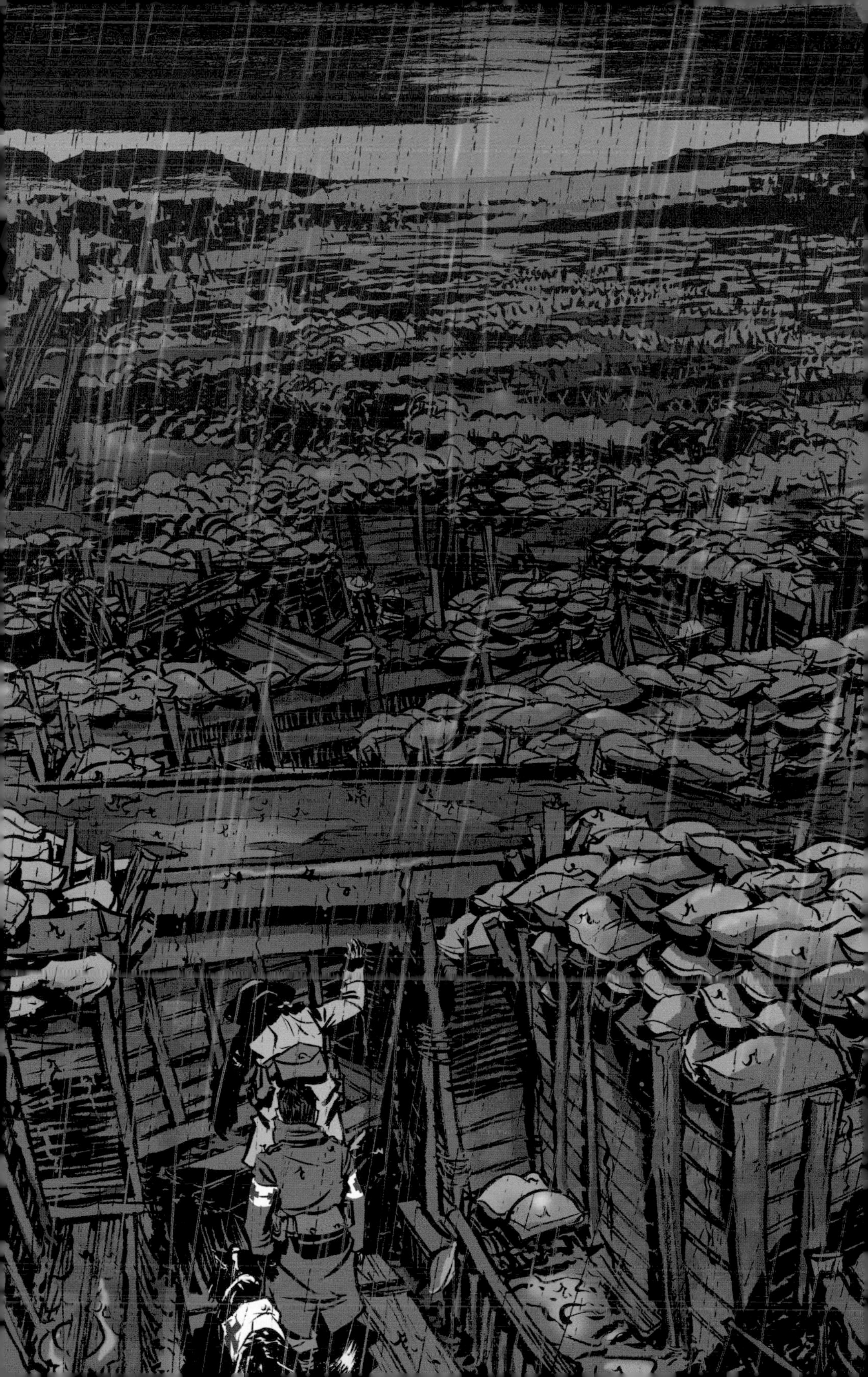

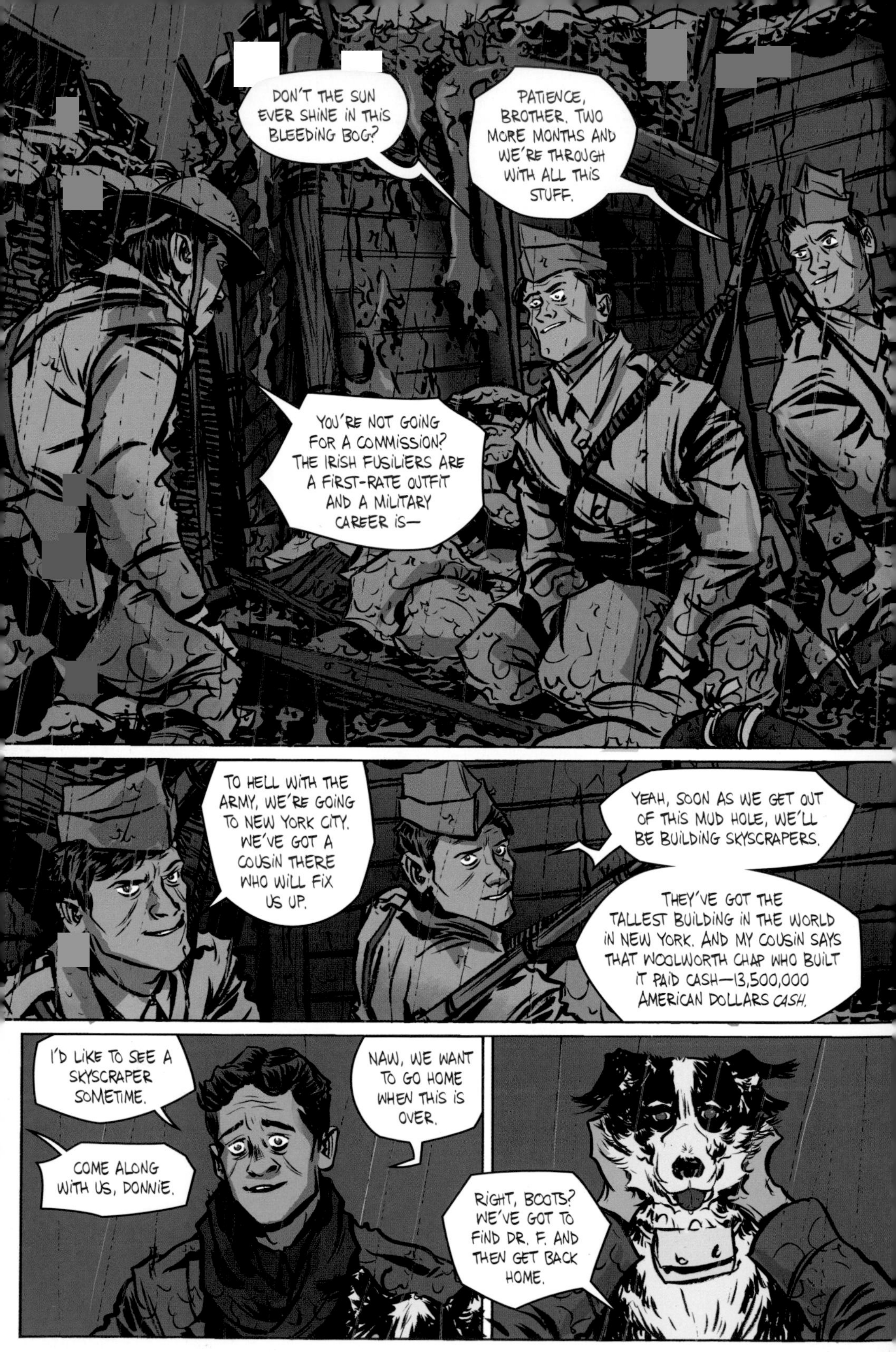
DON'T THE SUN EVER SHINE IN THIS BLEEDING BOG?
PATIENCE, BROTHER. TWO MORE MONTHS AND WE'RE THROUGH WITH ALL THIS STUFF.
YOU'RE NOT GOING FOR A COMMISSION? THE IRISH FUSILIERS ARE A FIRST-RATE OUTFIT AND A MILITARY CAREER IS—
TO HELL WITH THE ARMY, WE'RE GOING TO NEW YORK CITY. WE'VE GOT A COUSIN THERE WHO WILL FIX US UP.
YEAH, SOON AS WE GET OUT OF THIS MUD HOLE, WE'LL BE BUILDING SKYSCRAPERS.
THEY'VE GOT THE TALLEST BUILDING IN THE WORLD IN NEW YORK. AND MY COUSIN SAYS THAT WOOLWORTH CHAP WHO BUILT IT PAID CASH—13,500,000 AMERICAN DOLLARS *CASH*.
I'D LIKE TO SEE A SKYSCRAPER SOMETIME.
COME ALONG WITH US, DONNIE.
NAW, WE WANT TO GO HOME WHEN THIS IS OVER.
RIGHT, BOOTS? WE'VE GOT TO FIND DR. F. AND THEN GET BACK HOME.

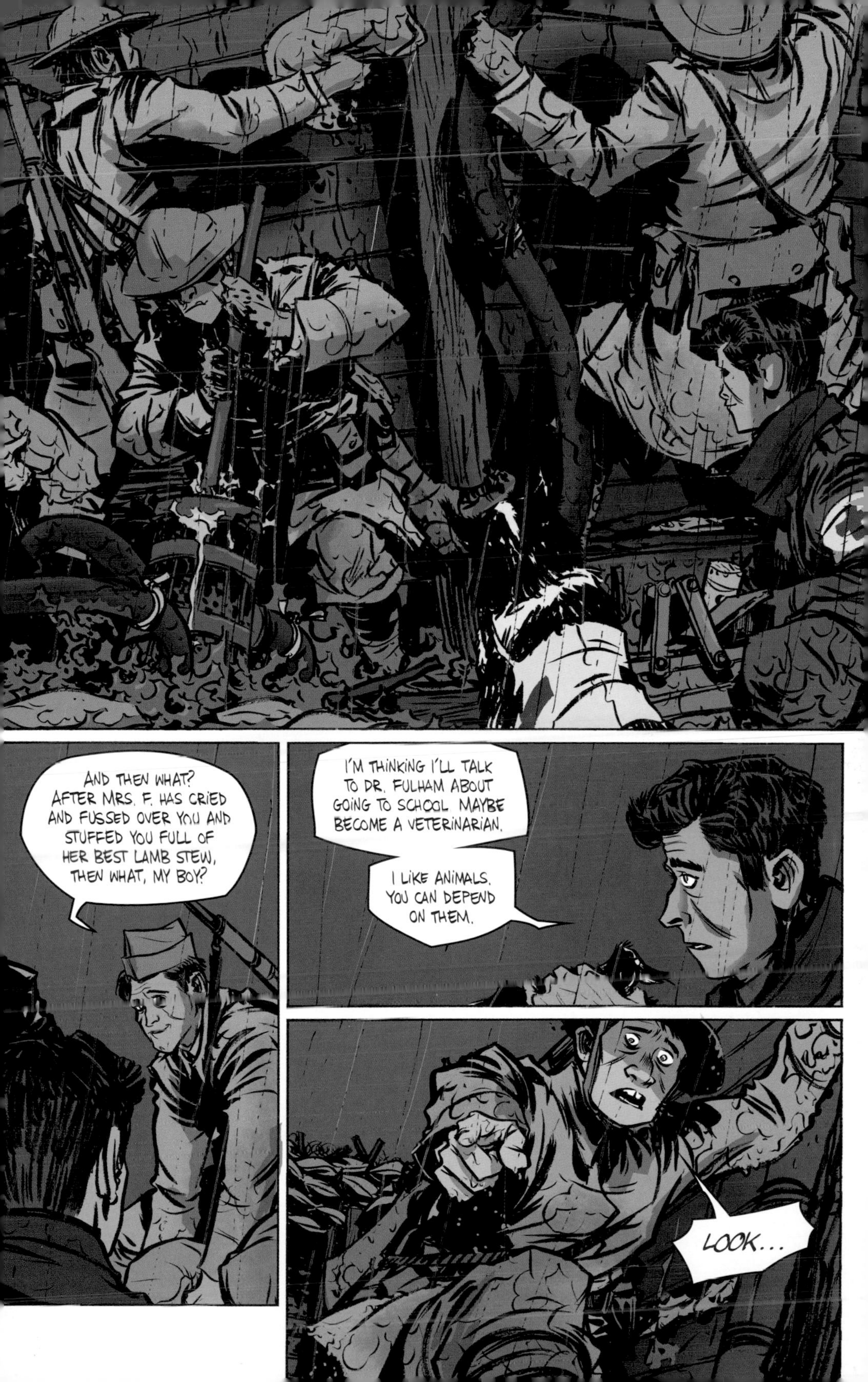
AND THEN WHAT? AFTER MRS. F. HAS CRIED AND FUSSED OVER YOU AND STUFFED YOU FULL OF HER BEST LAMB STEW, THEN WHAT, MY BOY?
I'M THINKING I'LL TALK TO DR. FULHAM ABOUT GOING TO SCHOOL. MAYBE BECOME A VETERINARIAN.
I LIKE ANIMALS. YOU CAN DEPEND ON THEM.
LOOK...

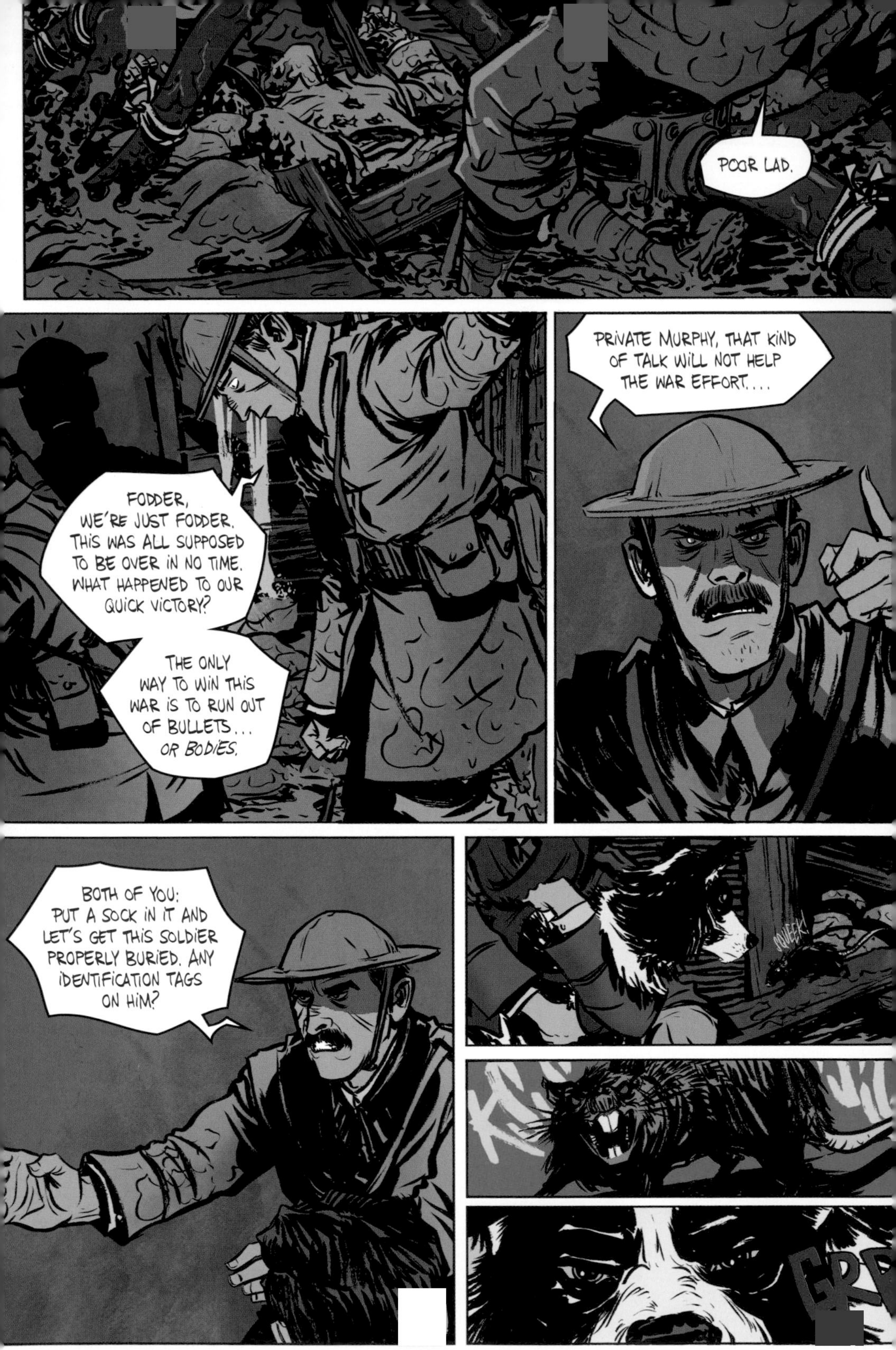
POOR LAD.
FODDER, WE'RE JUST FODDER. THIS WAS ALL SUPPOSED TO BE OVER IN NO TIME. WHAT HAPPENED TO OUR QUICK VICTORY?
THE ONLY WAY TO WIN THIS WAR IS TO RUN OUT OF BULLETS... OR *BODIES*.
PRIVATE MURPHY, THAT KIND OF TALK WILL NOT HELP THE WAR EFFORT....
BOTH OF YOU: PUT A SOCK IN IT AND LET'S GET THIS SOLDIER PROPERLY BURIED. ANY IDENTIFICATION TAGS ON HIM?
SQUEEK!

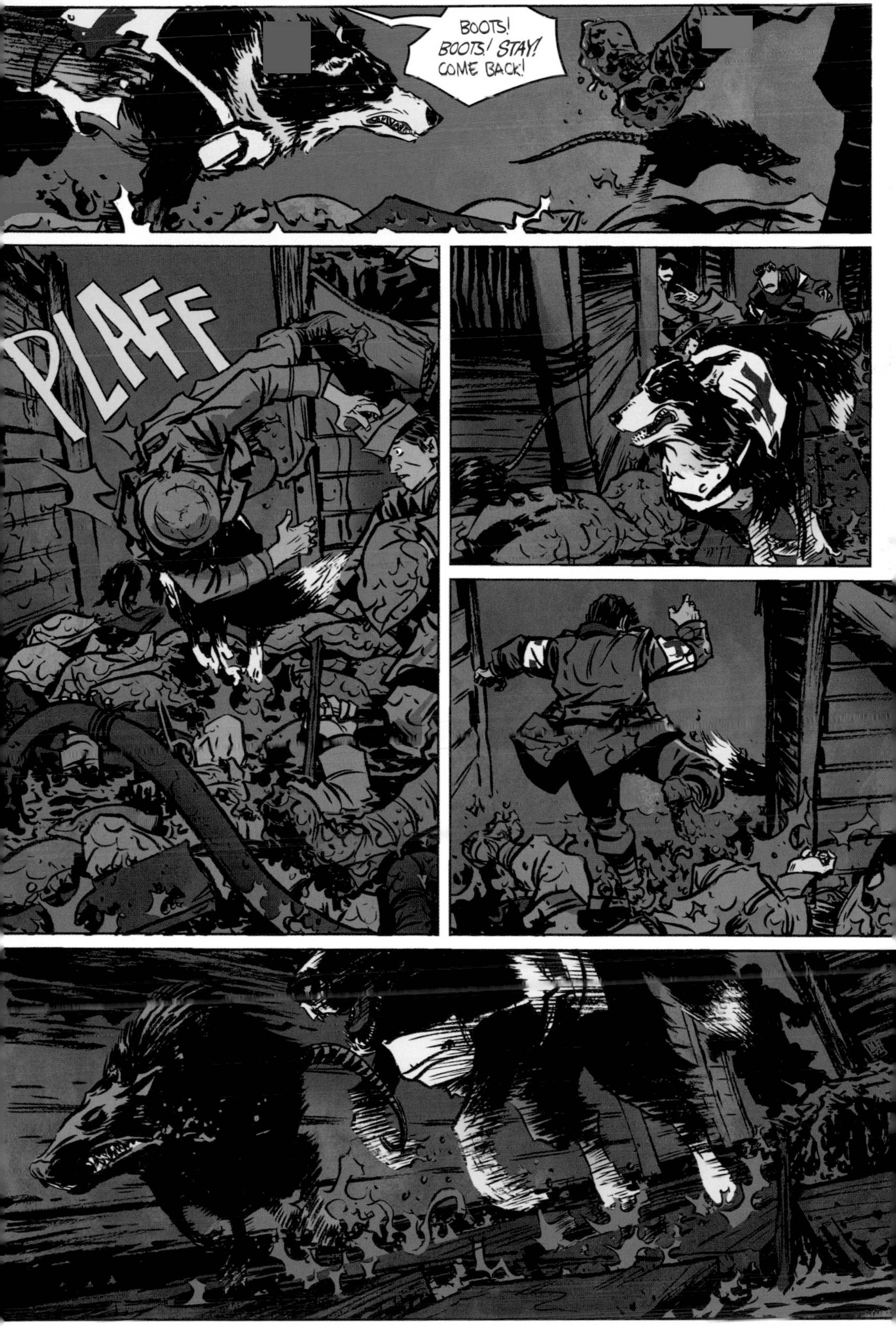
BOOTS!
BOOTS! STAY!
COME BACK!
PLAFF

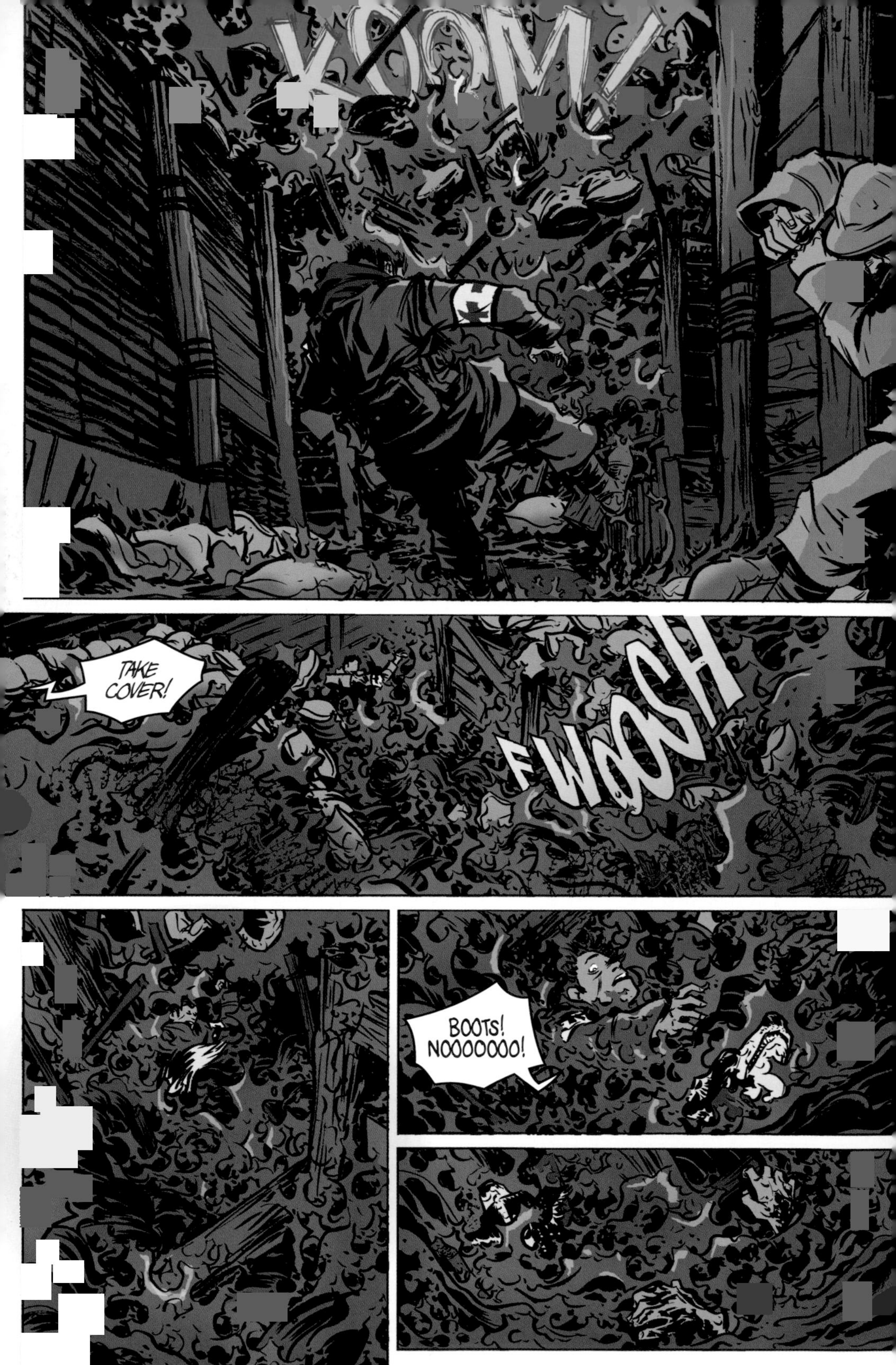
KOOM!
TAKE COVER!
FWOOSH
BOOTS! NOOOOOOO!

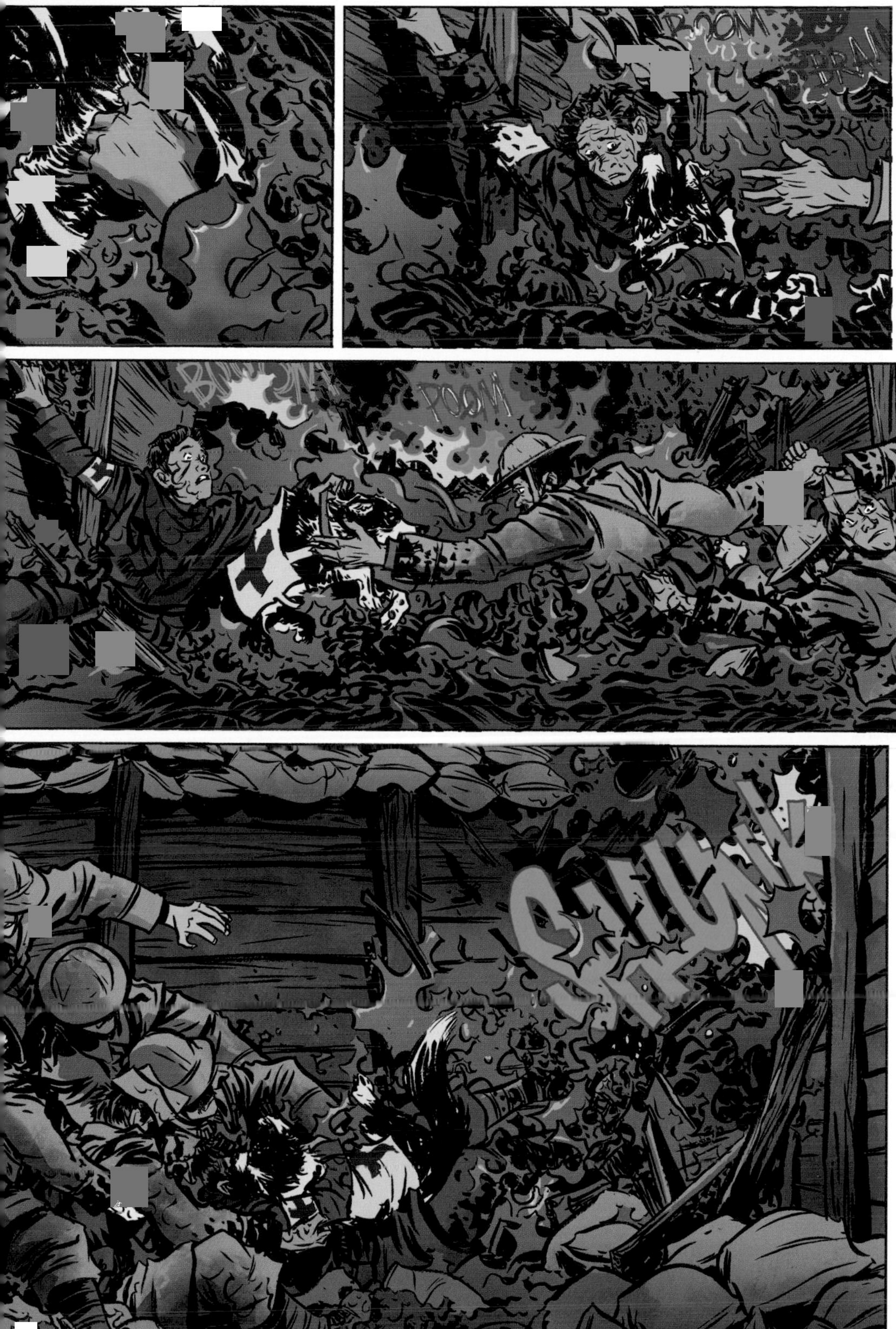
BOOM
BRAM
POOM
CHUNK

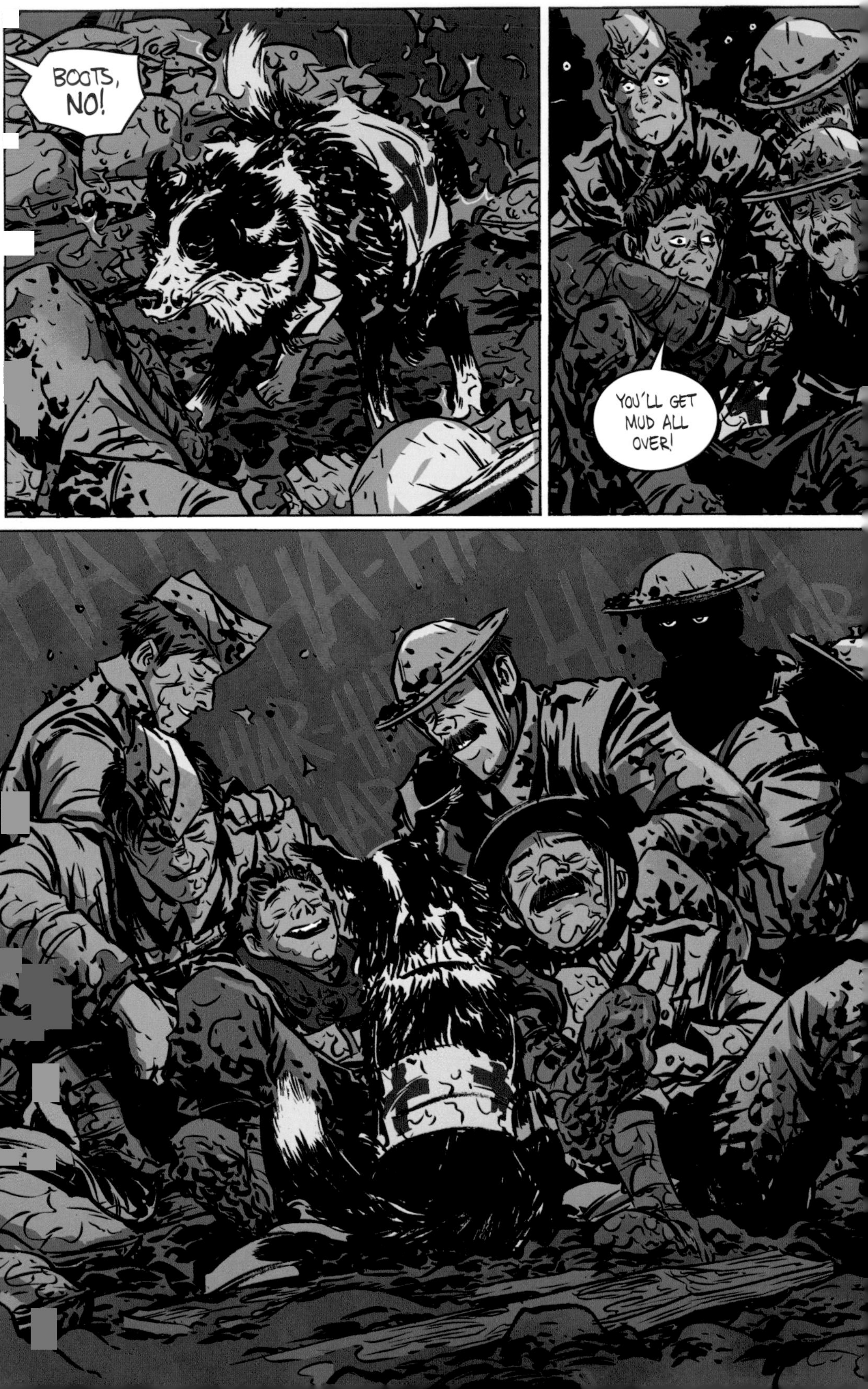
BOOTS, NO!
YOU'LL GET MUD ALL OVER!

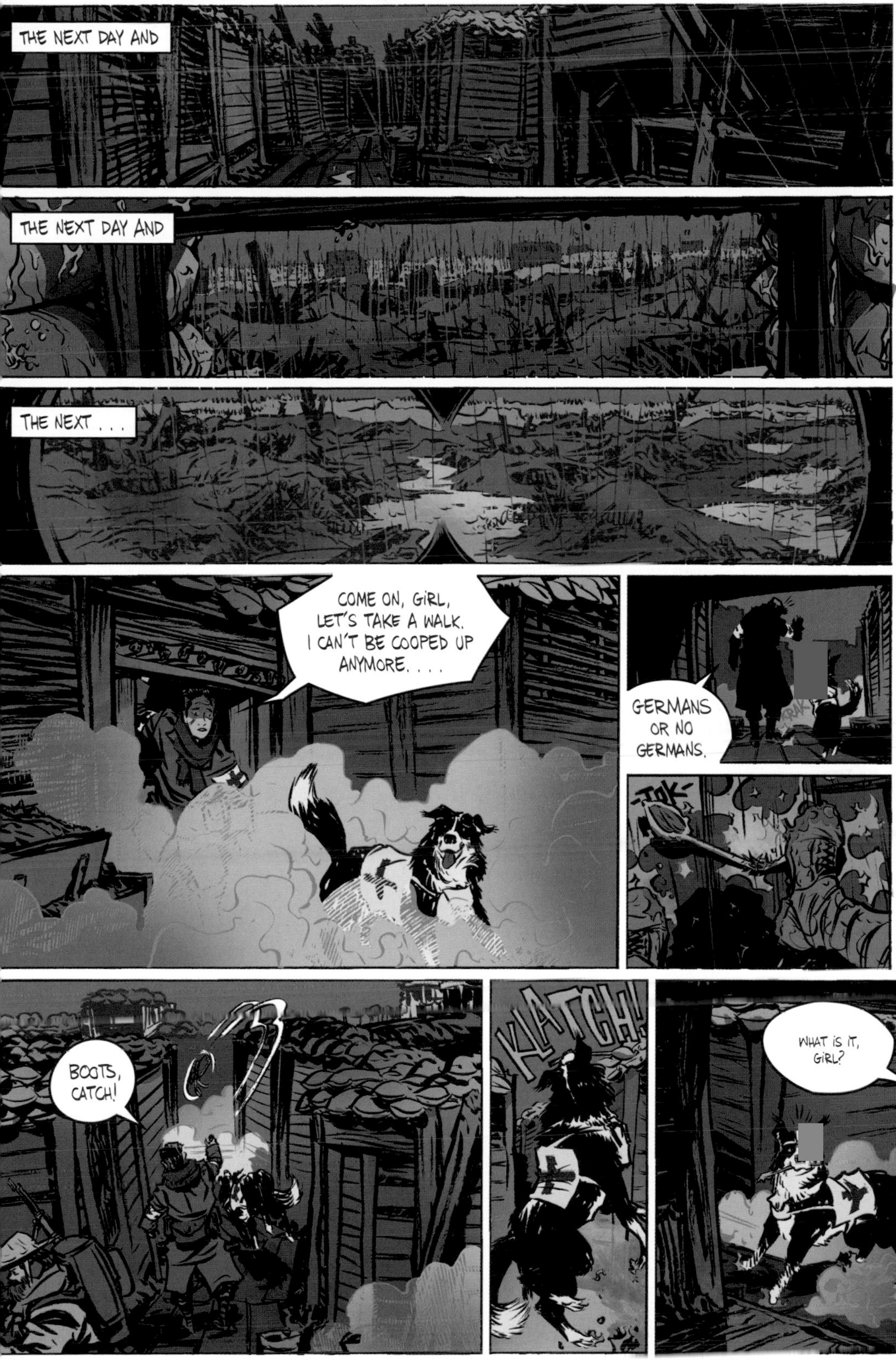
THE NEXT DAY AND
THE NEXT DAY AND
THE NEXT . . .
COME ON, GIRL, LET'S TAKE A WALK. I CAN'T BE COOPED UP ANYMORE. . . .
GERMANS OR NO GERMANS.
BOOTS, CATCH!
KATCH!
WHAT IS IT, GIRL?

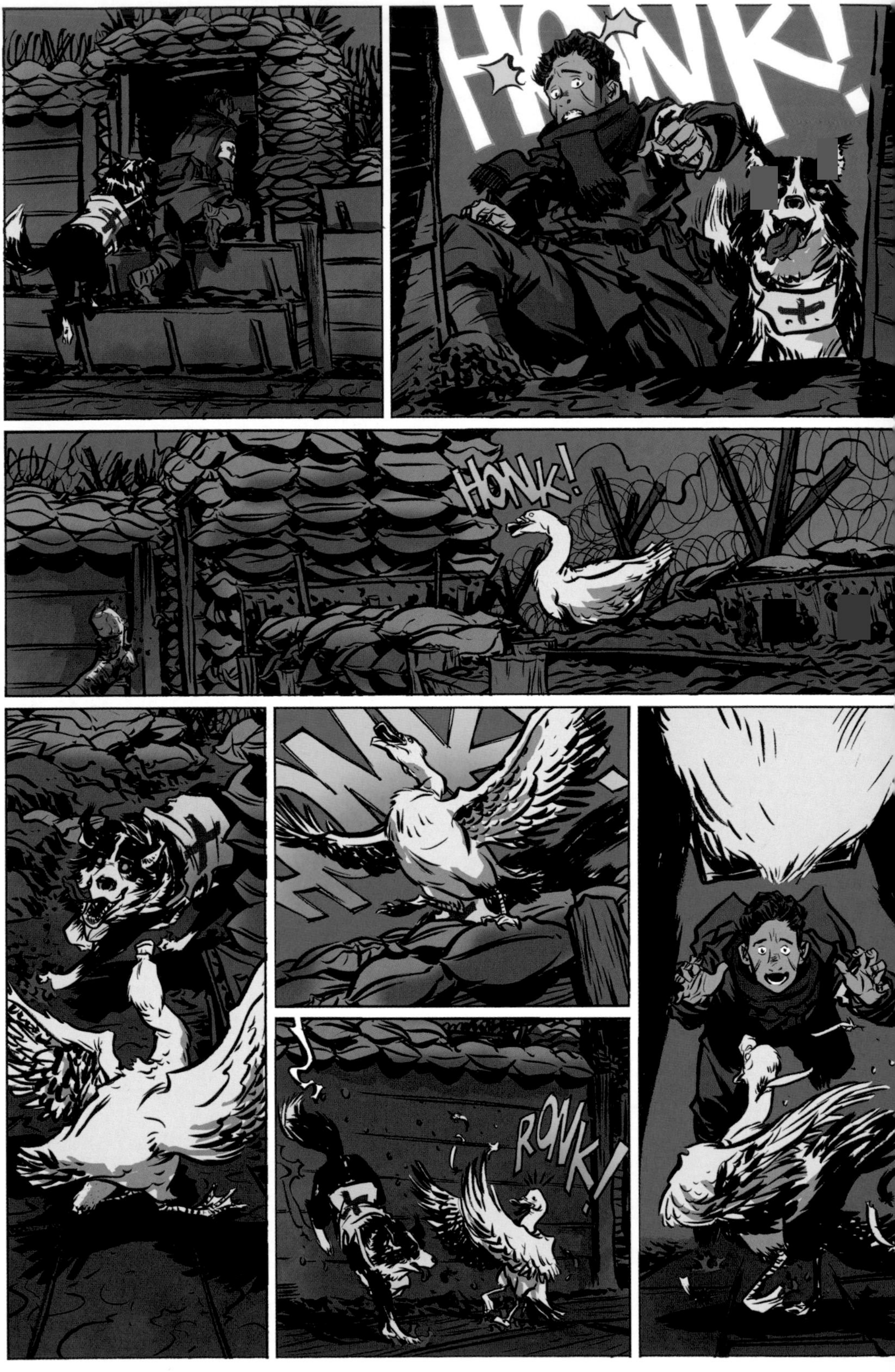
HONK!
HONK!
RONK!

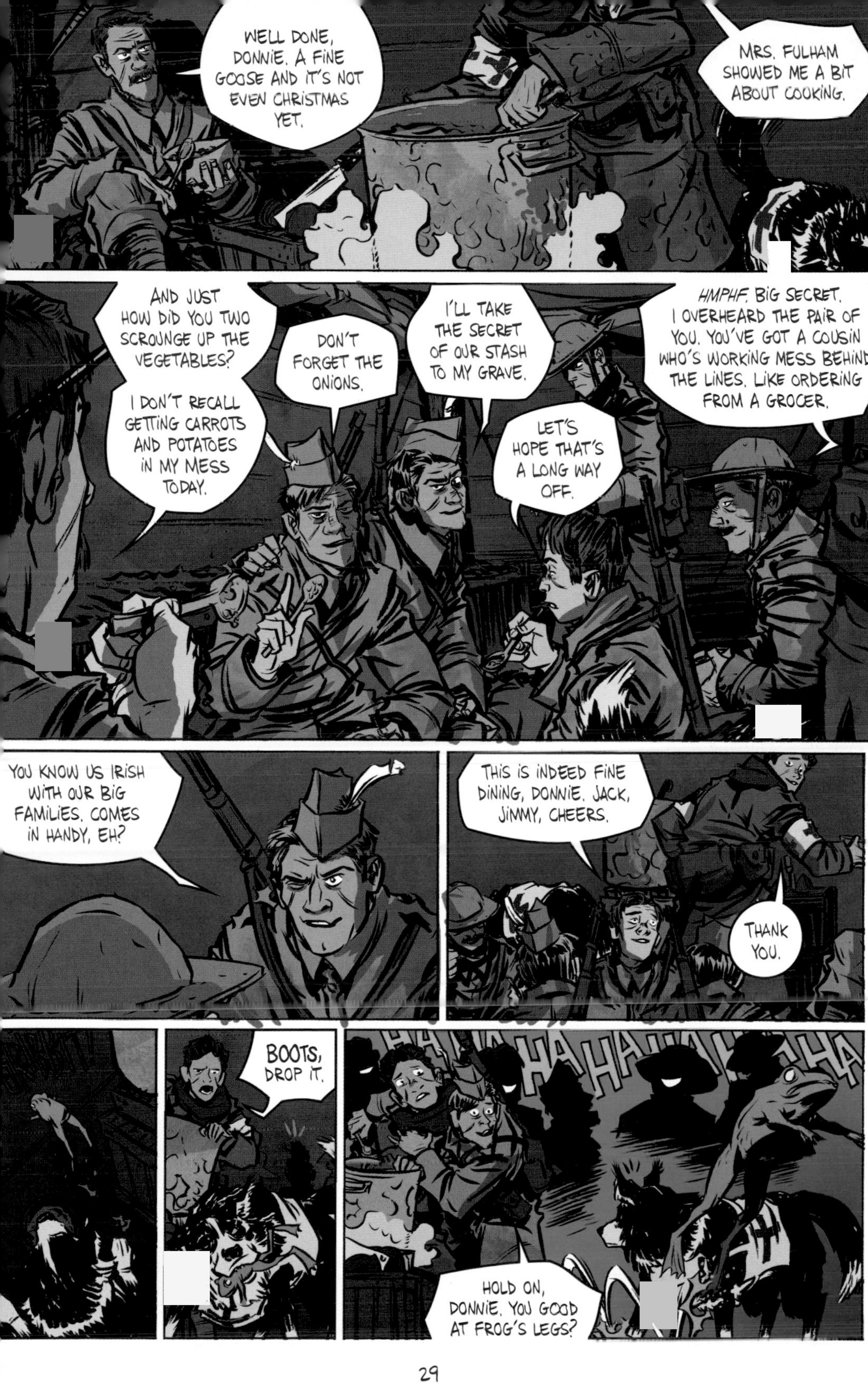
WELL DONE, DONNIE. A FINE GOOSE AND IT'S NOT EVEN CHRISTMAS YET.
MRS. FULHAM SHOWED ME A BIT ABOUT COOKING.
AND JUST HOW DID YOU TWO SCROUNGE UP THE VEGETABLES?
I DON'T RECALL GETTING CARROTS AND POTATOES IN MY MESS TODAY.
DON'T FORGET THE ONIONS.
I'LL TAKE THE SECRET OF OUR STASH TO MY GRAVE.
LET'S HOPE THAT'S A LONG WAY OFF.
HMPHF. BIG SECRET. I OVERHEARD THE PAIR OF YOU. YOU'VE GOT A COUSIN WHO'S WORKING MESS BEHIND THE LINES. LIKE ORDERING FROM A GROCER.
YOU KNOW US IRISH WITH OUR BIG FAMILIES. COMES IN HANDY, EH?
THIS IS INDEED FINE DINING, DONNIE. JACK, JIMMY, CHEERS.
THANK YOU.
BOOTS, DROP IT.
HAHAHAHAHA
HOLD ON, DONNIE. YOU GOOD AT FROG'S LEGS?

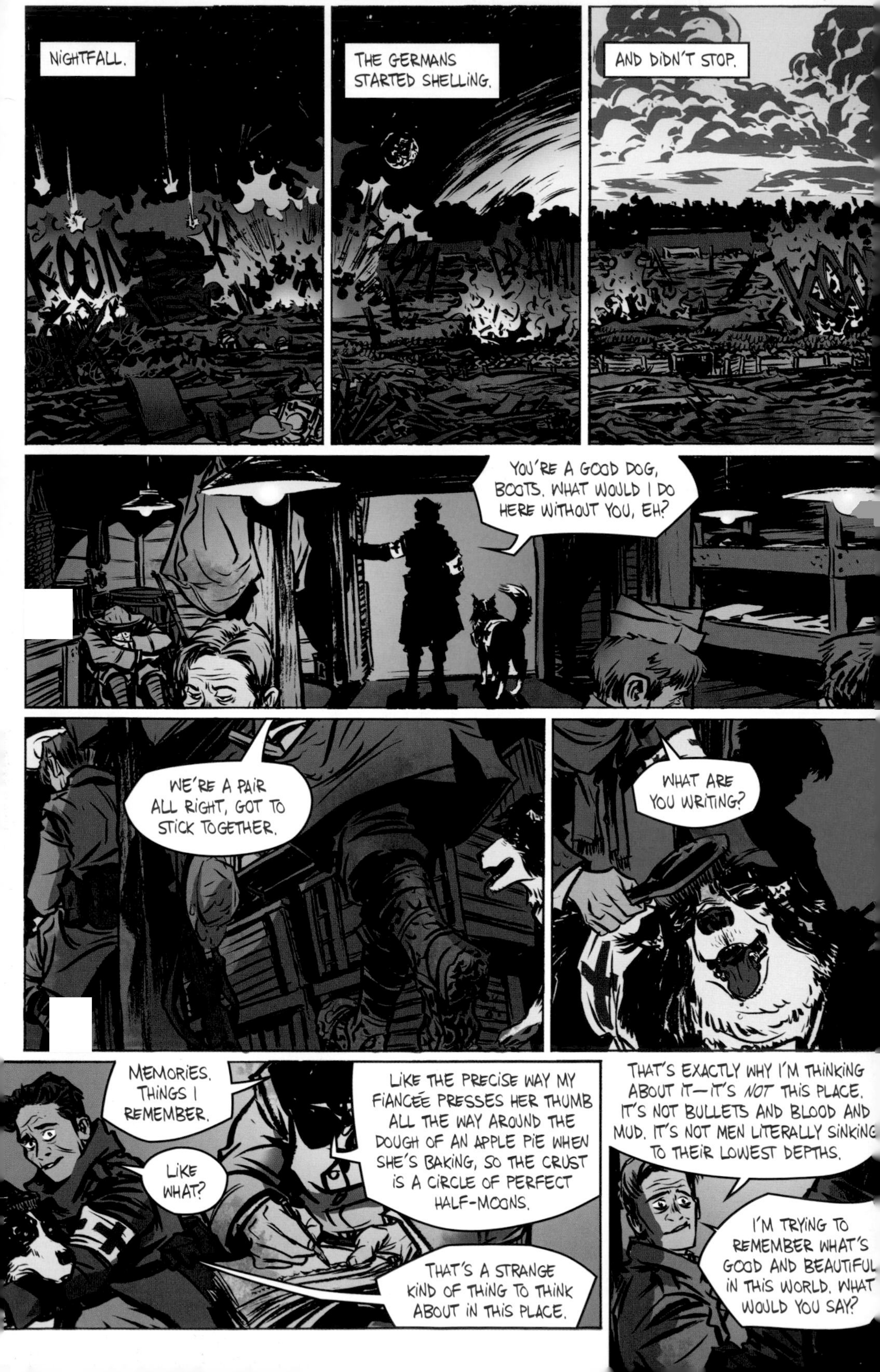
NIGHTFALL.
KOOM
THE GERMANS STARTED SHELLING.
AND DIDN'T STOP.
YOU'RE A GOOD DOG, BOOTS. WHAT WOULD I DO HERE WITHOUT YOU, EH?
WE'RE A PAIR ALL RIGHT, GOT TO STICK TOGETHER.
WHAT ARE YOU WRITING?
MEMORIES. THINGS I REMEMBER.
LIKE WHAT?
LIKE THE PRECISE WAY MY FIANCÉE PRESSES HER THUMB ALL THE WAY AROUND THE DOUGH OF AN APPLE PIE WHEN SHE'S BAKING, SO THE CRUST IS A CIRCLE OF PERFECT HALF-MOONS.
THAT'S A STRANGE KIND OF THING TO THINK ABOUT IN THIS PLACE.
THAT'S EXACTLY WHY I'M THINKING ABOUT IT—IT'S *NOT* THIS PLACE. IT'S NOT BULLETS AND BLOOD AND MUD. IT'S NOT MEN LITERALLY SINKING TO THEIR LOWEST DEPTHS.
I'M TRYING TO REMEMBER WHAT'S GOOD AND BEAUTIFUL IN THIS WORLD. WHAT WOULD YOU SAY?

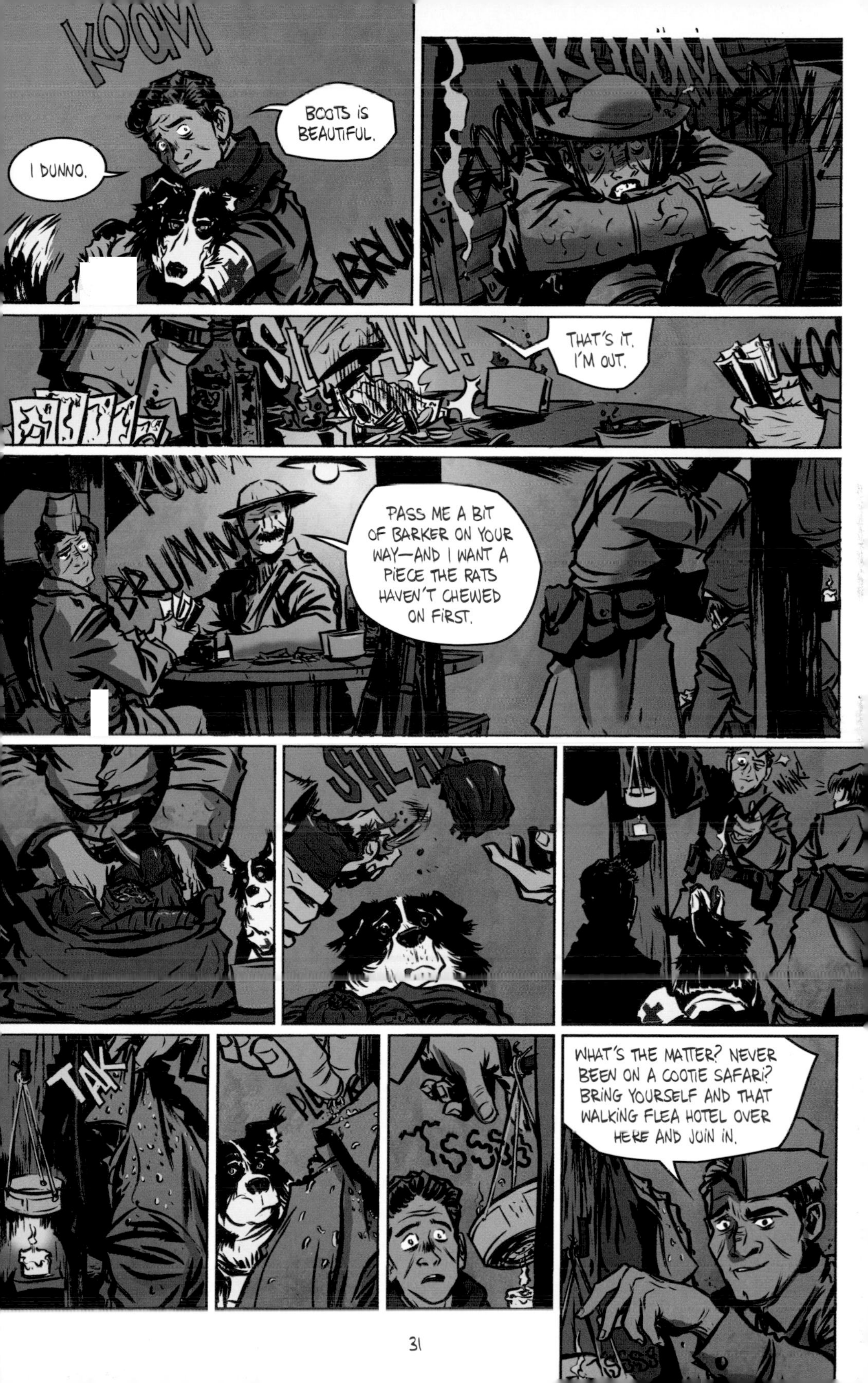
KOOM
I DUNNO.
BOOTS IS BEAUTIFUL.
BRUM
KOOOM
SLAM!
THAT'S IT. I'M OUT.
PASS ME A BIT OF BARKER ON YOUR WAY—AND I WANT A PIECE THE RATS HAVEN'T CHEWED ON FIRST.
BRUMM
SHLAK!
WINK!
TAK
WHAT'S THE MATTER? NEVER BEEN ON A COOTIE SAFARI? BRING YOURSELF AND THAT WALKING FLEA HOTEL OVER HERE AND JOIN IN.

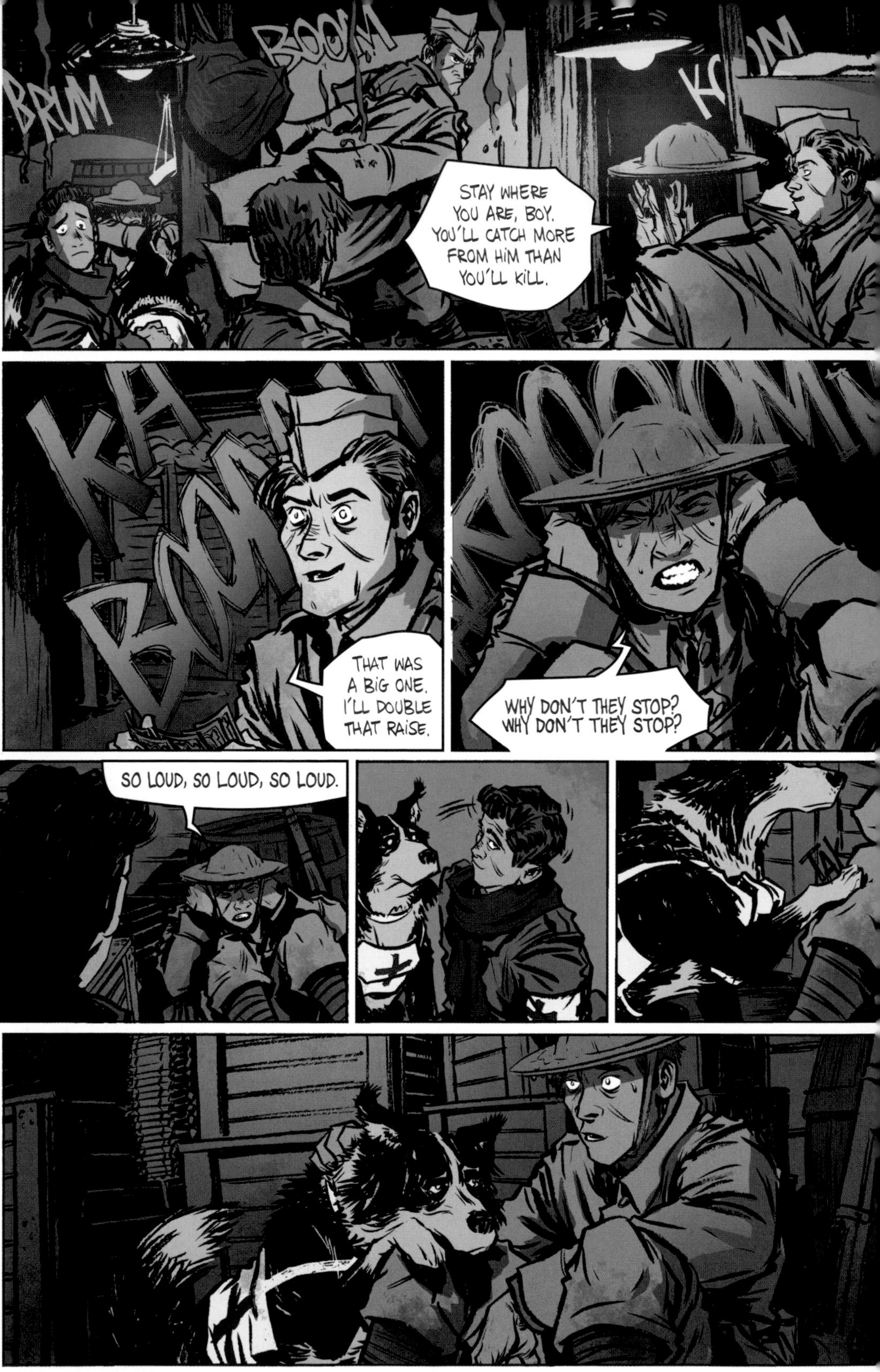
BRUM
BOOM
KOOM
STAY WHERE YOU ARE, BOY. YOU'LL CATCH MORE FROM HIM THAN YOU'LL KILL.
KA BOOM
THAT WAS A BIG ONE. I'LL DOUBLE THAT RAISE.
WHY DON'T THEY STOP? WHY DON'T THEY STOP?
SO LOUD, SO LOUD, SO LOUD.

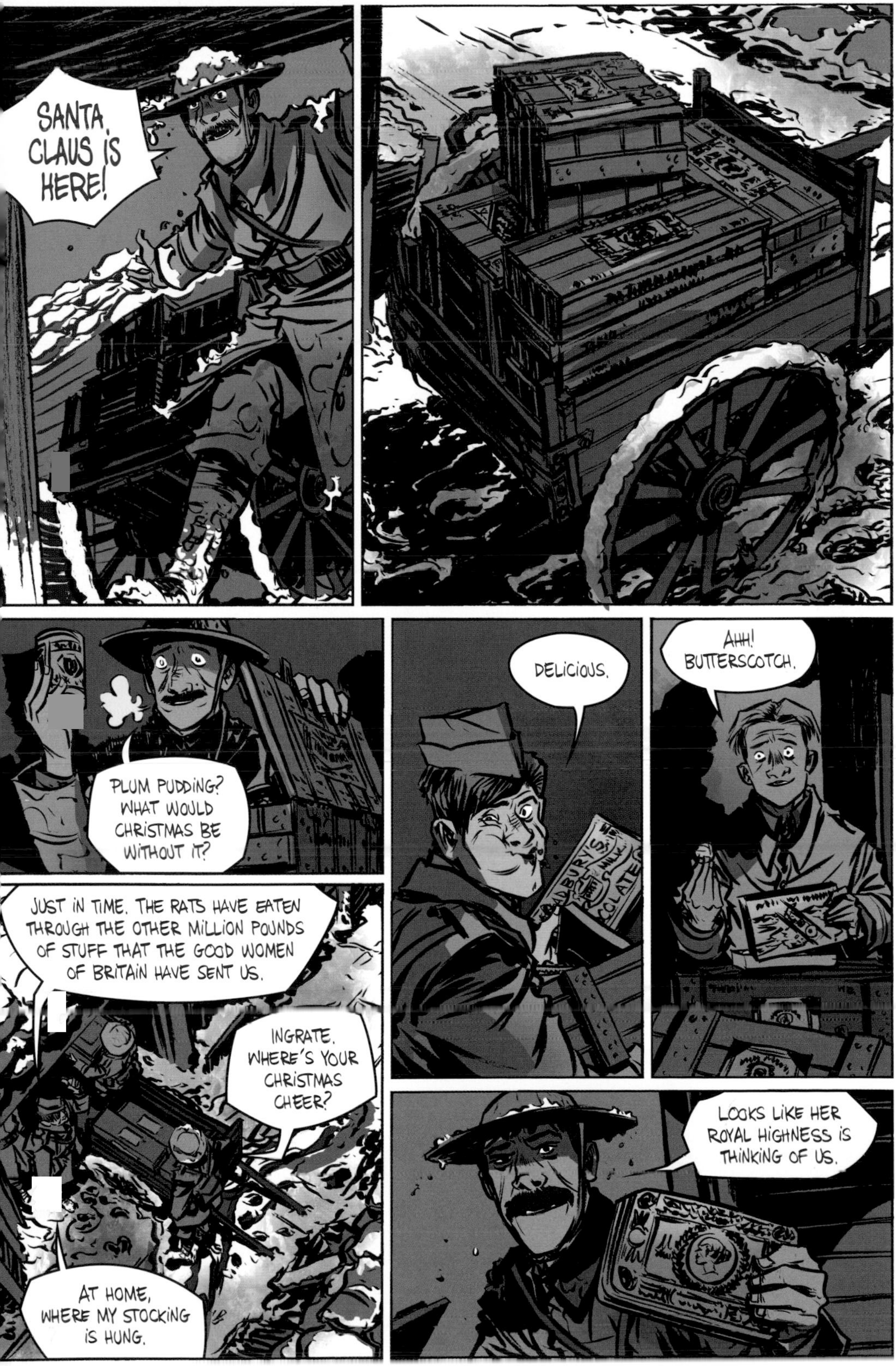
SANTA CLAUS IS HERE!
PLUM PUDDING? WHAT WOULD CHRISTMAS BE WITHOUT IT?
DELICIOUS.
AHH! BUTTERSCOTCH.
JUST IN TIME. THE RATS HAVE EATEN THROUGH THE OTHER MILLION POUNDS OF STUFF THAT THE GOOD WOMEN OF BRITAIN HAVE SENT US.
INGRATE. WHERE'S YOUR CHRISTMAS CHEER?
AT HOME, WHERE MY STOCKING IS HUNG.
LOOKS LIKE HER ROYAL HIGHNESS IS THINKING OF US.

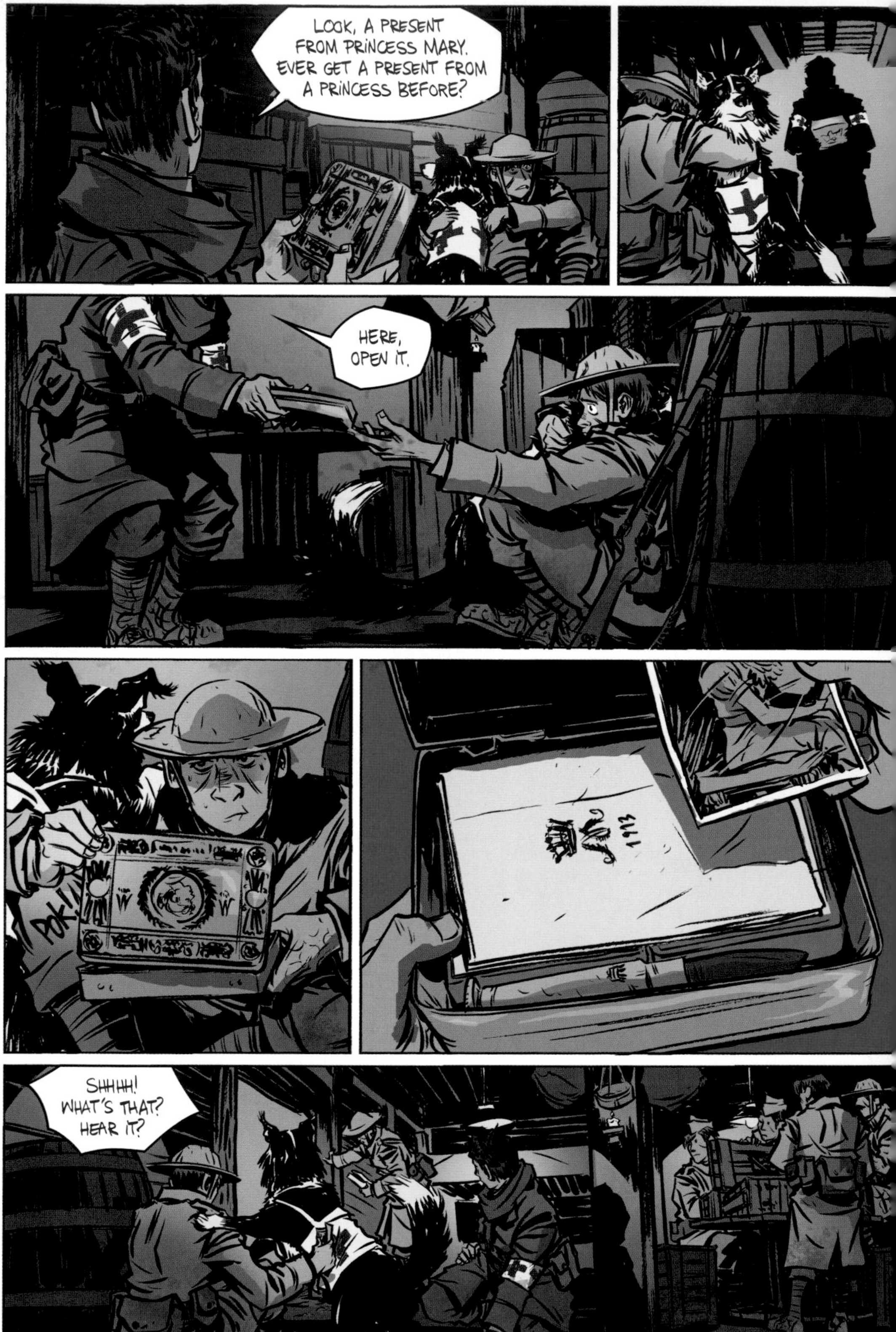
LOOK, A PRESENT FROM PRINCESS MARY. EVER GET A PRESENT FROM A PRINCESS BEFORE?
HERE, OPEN IT.
POK!
1913
SHHHH! WHAT'S THAT? HEAR IT?

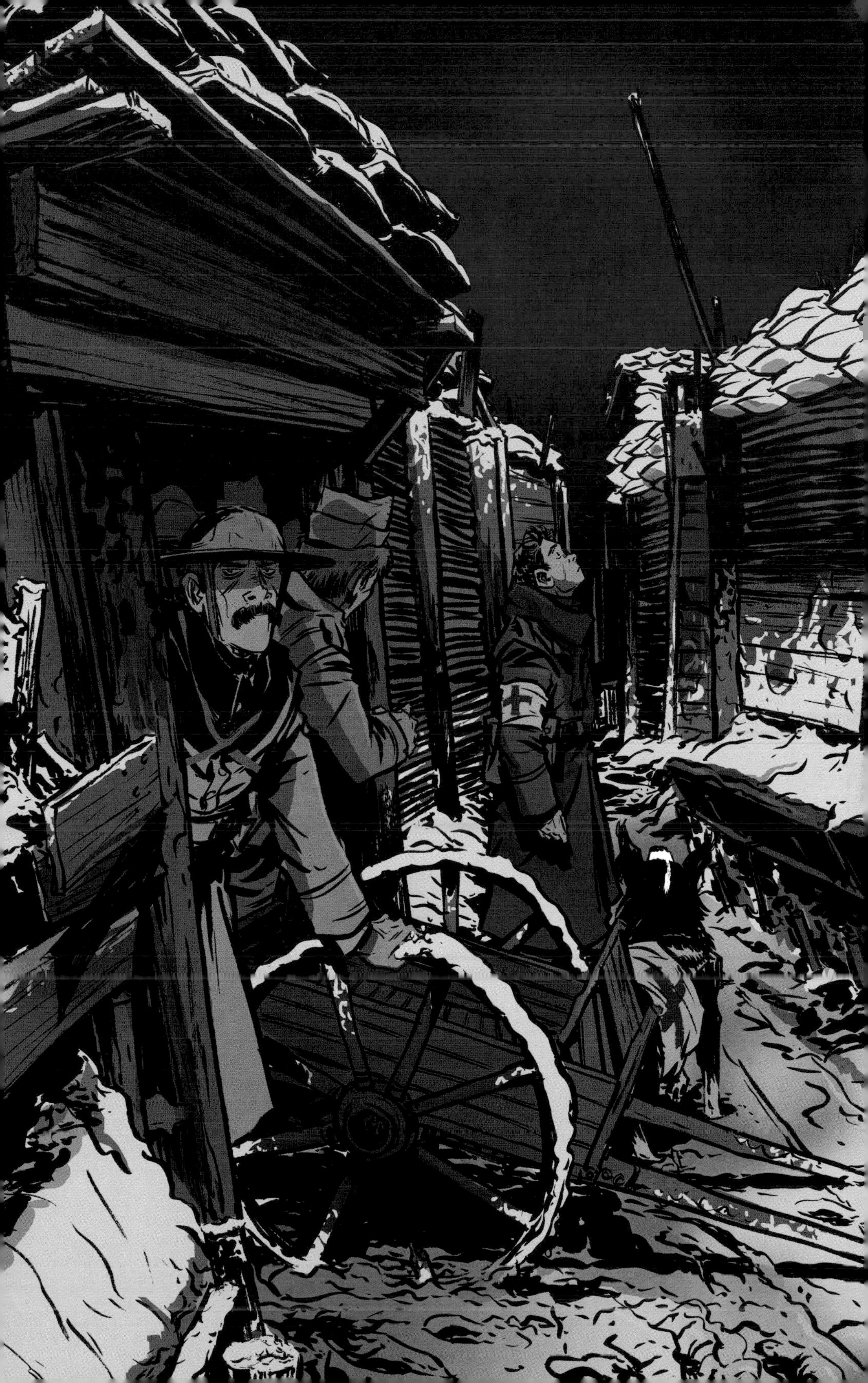

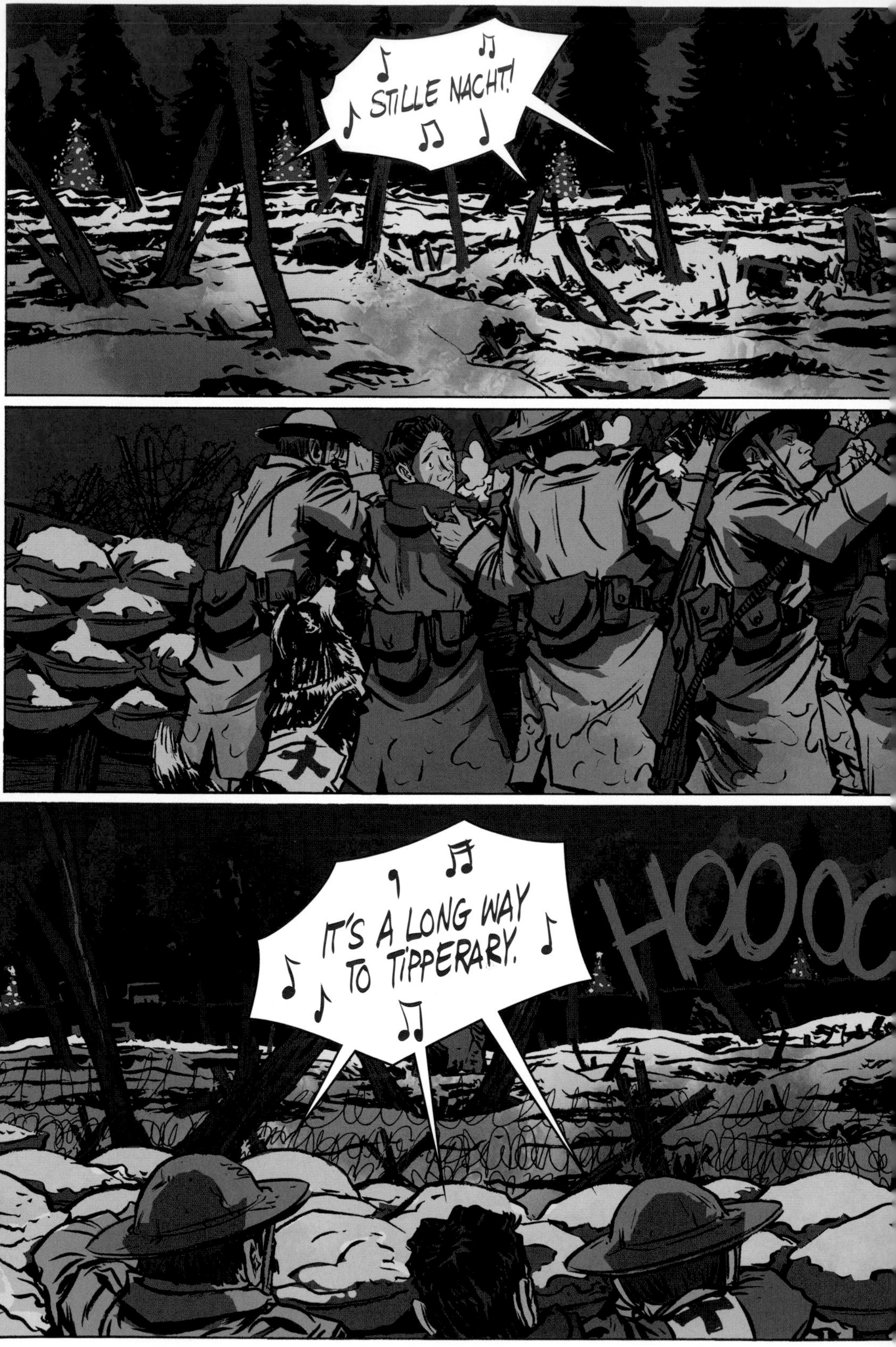
STILLE NACHT!
IT'S A LONG WAY TO TIPPERARY.
HOOOO

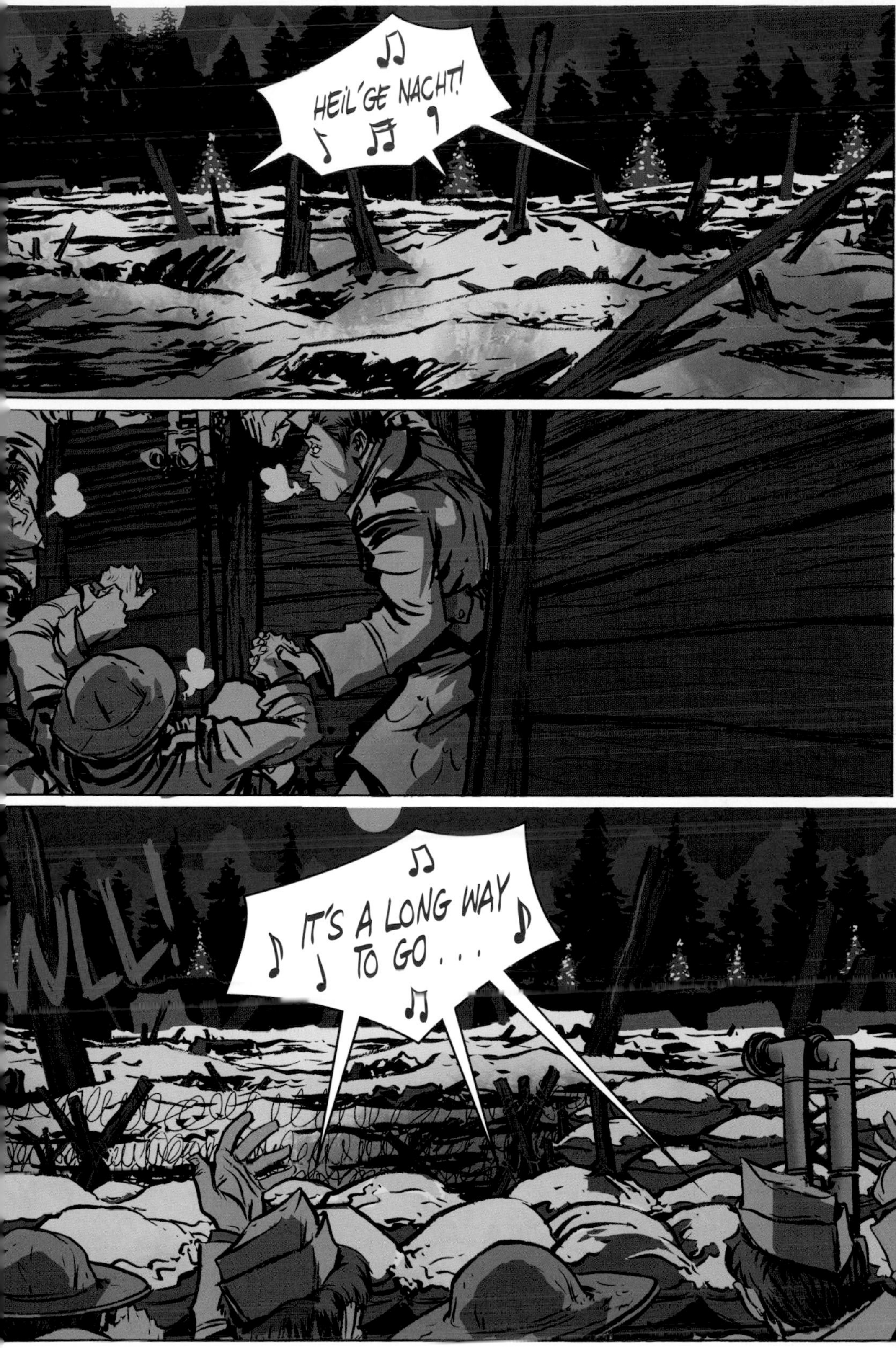
HEIL´GE NACHT!
IT'S A LONG WAY TO GO . . .

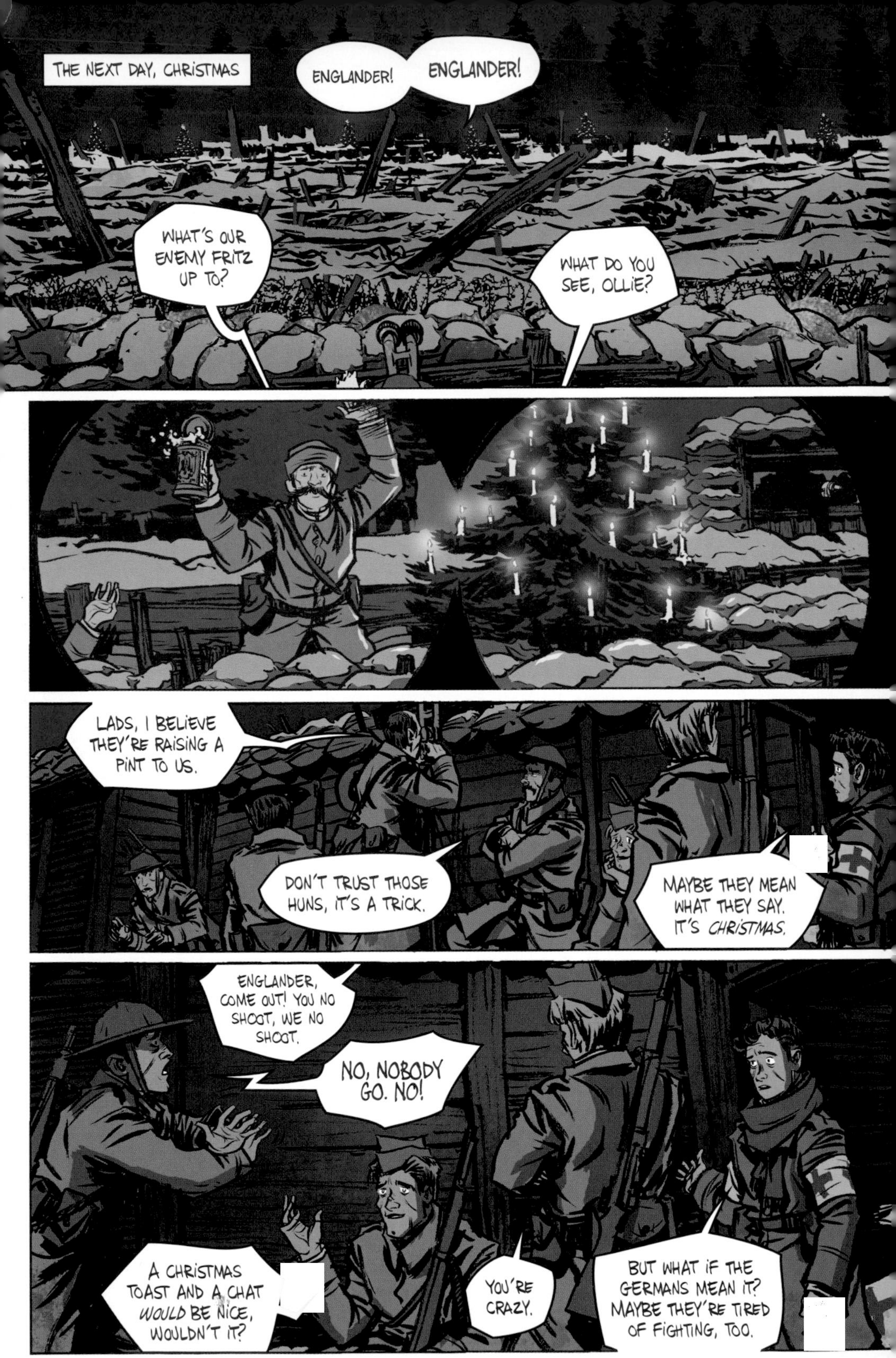
THE NEXT DAY, CHRISTMAS
ENGLANDER!
ENGLANDER!
WHAT'S OUR ENEMY FRITZ UP TO?
WHAT DO YOU SEE, OLLIE?
LADS, I BELIEVE THEY'RE RAISING A PINT TO US.
DON'T TRUST THOSE HUNS, IT'S A TRICK.
MAYBE THEY MEAN WHAT THEY SAY. IT'S *CHRISTMAS*.
ENGLANDER, COME OUT! YOU NO SHOOT, WE NO SHOOT.
NO, NOBODY GO. NO!
A CHRISTMAS TOAST AND A CHAT *WOULD* BE NICE, WOULDN'T IT?
YOU'RE CRAZY.
BUT WHAT IF THE GERMANS MEAN IT? MAYBE THEY'RE TIRED OF FIGHTING, TOO.

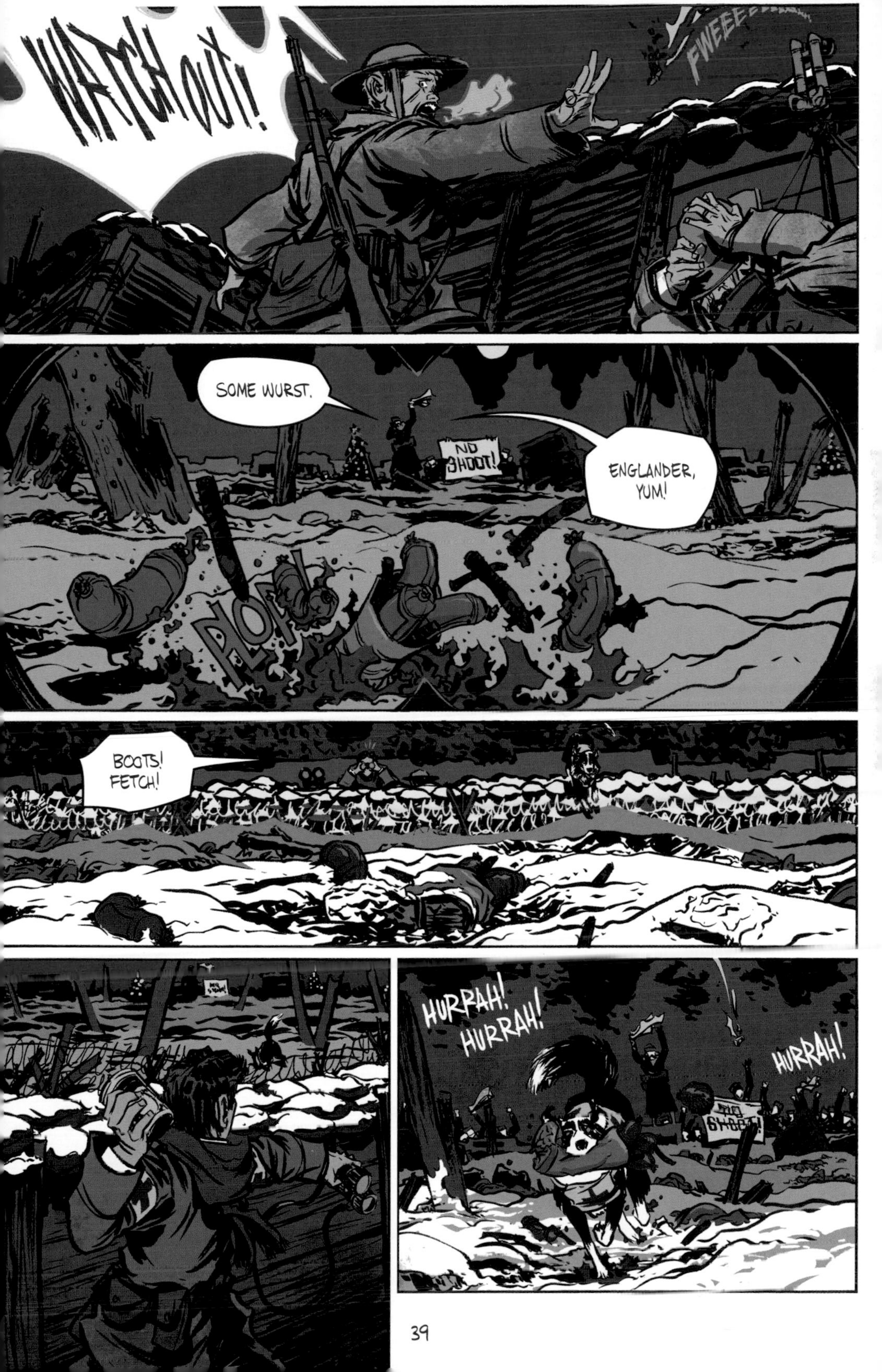
WATCH OUT!
FWEEE
SOME WURST.
NO SHOOT!
ENGLANDER, YUM!
PLOP
BOOTS! FETCH!
HURRAH! HURRAH!
HURRAH!

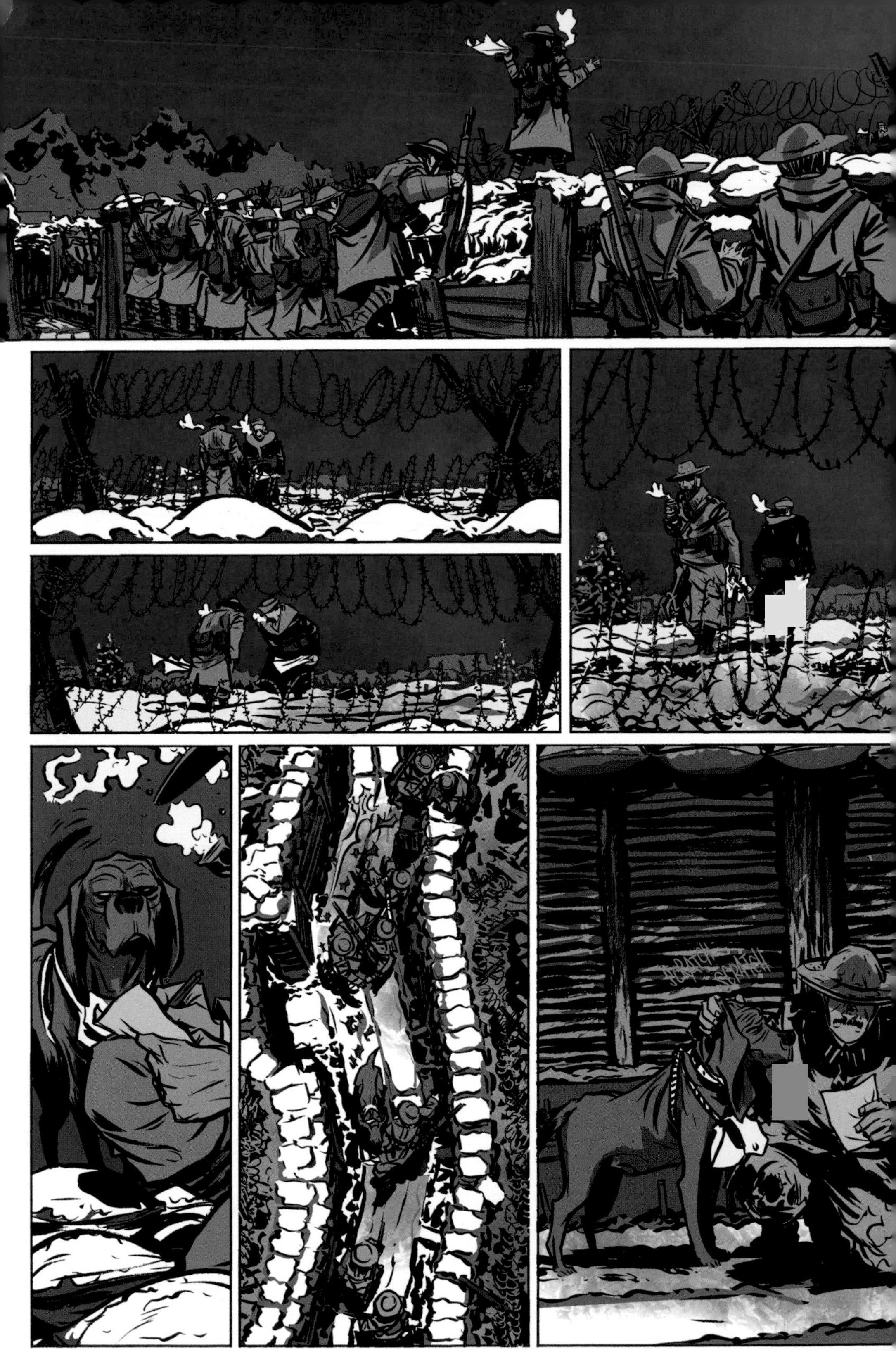
SCRATCH SCRATCH

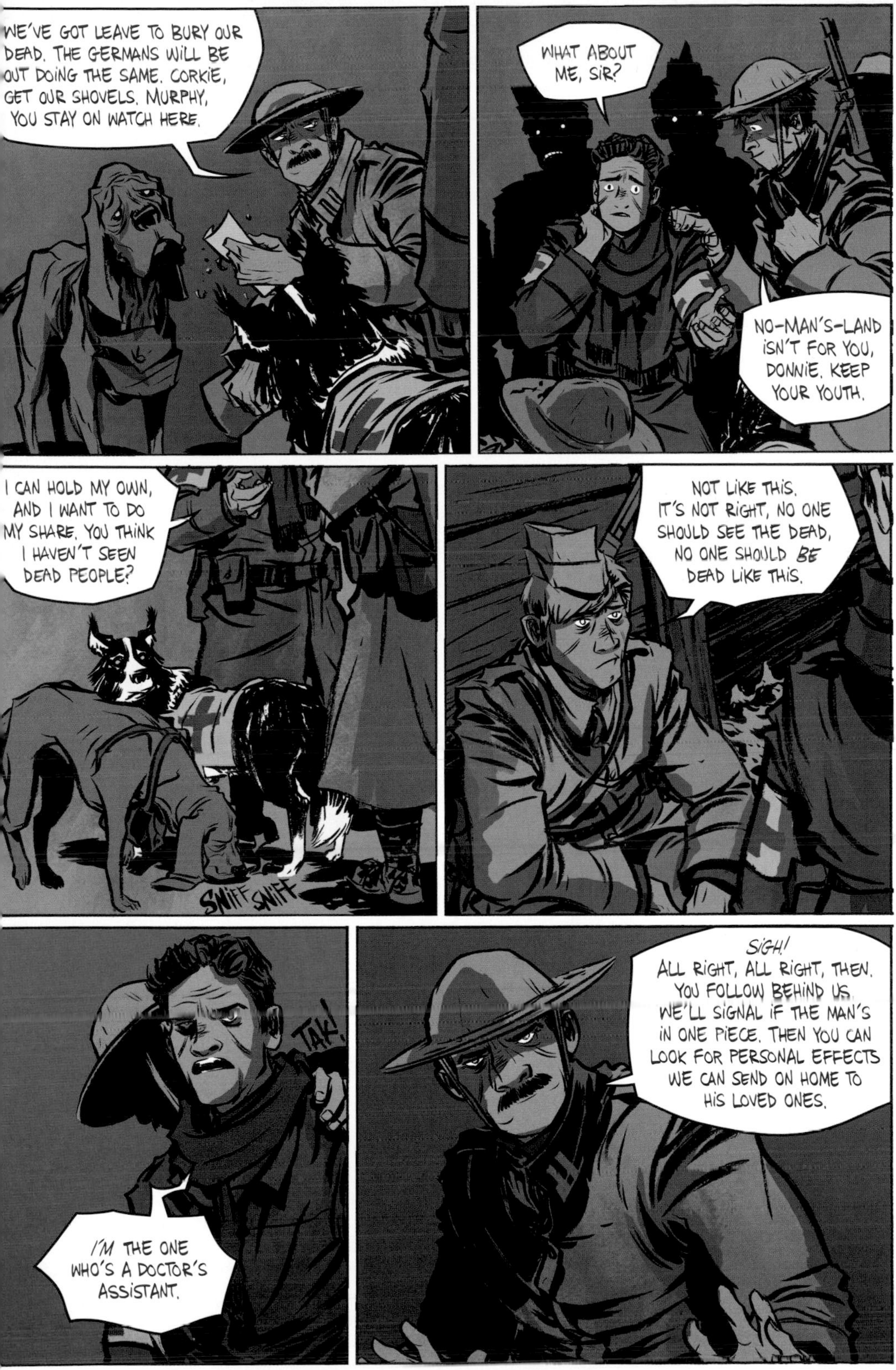
WE'VE GOT LEAVE TO BURY OUR DEAD. THE GERMANS WILL BE OUT DOING THE SAME. CORKIE, GET OUR SHOVELS. MURPHY, YOU STAY ON WATCH HERE.
WHAT ABOUT ME, SIR?
NO-MAN'S-LAND ISN'T FOR YOU, DONNIE. KEEP YOUR YOUTH.
I CAN HOLD MY OWN, AND I WANT TO DO MY SHARE. YOU THINK I HAVEN'T SEEN DEAD PEOPLE?
SNIFF SNIFF
NOT LIKE THIS. IT'S NOT RIGHT, NO ONE SHOULD SEE THE DEAD, NO ONE SHOULD *BE* DEAD LIKE THIS.
TAK!
I'M THE ONE WHO'S A DOCTOR'S ASSISTANT.
SIGH!
ALL RIGHT, ALL RIGHT, THEN. YOU FOLLOW BEHIND US. WE'LL SIGNAL IF THE MAN'S IN ONE PIECE. THEN YOU CAN LOOK FOR PERSONAL EFFECTS WE CAN SEND ON HOME TO HIS LOVED ONES.

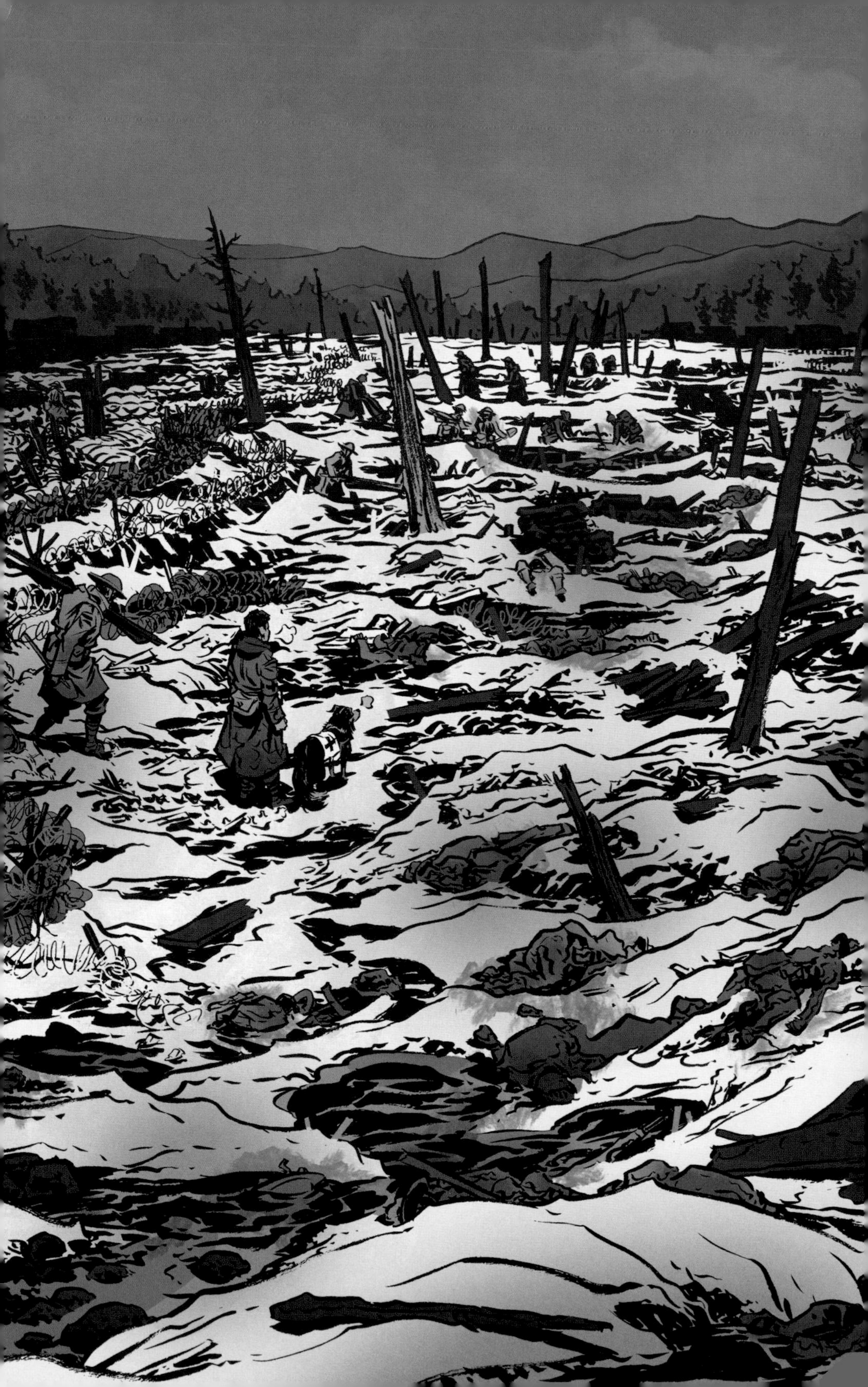

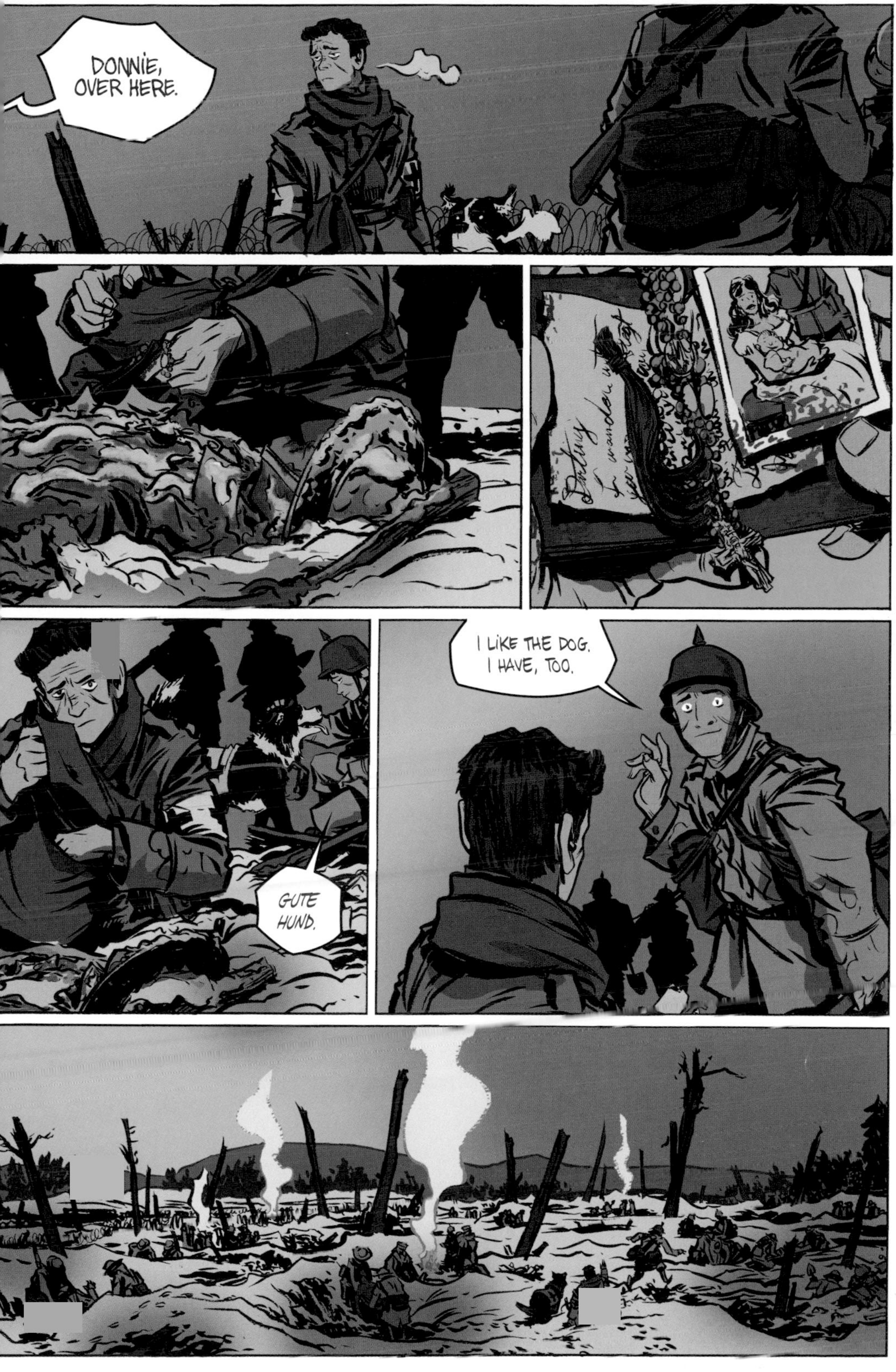
DONNIE, OVER HERE.
GUTE HUND.
I LIKE THE DOG. I HAVE, TOO.

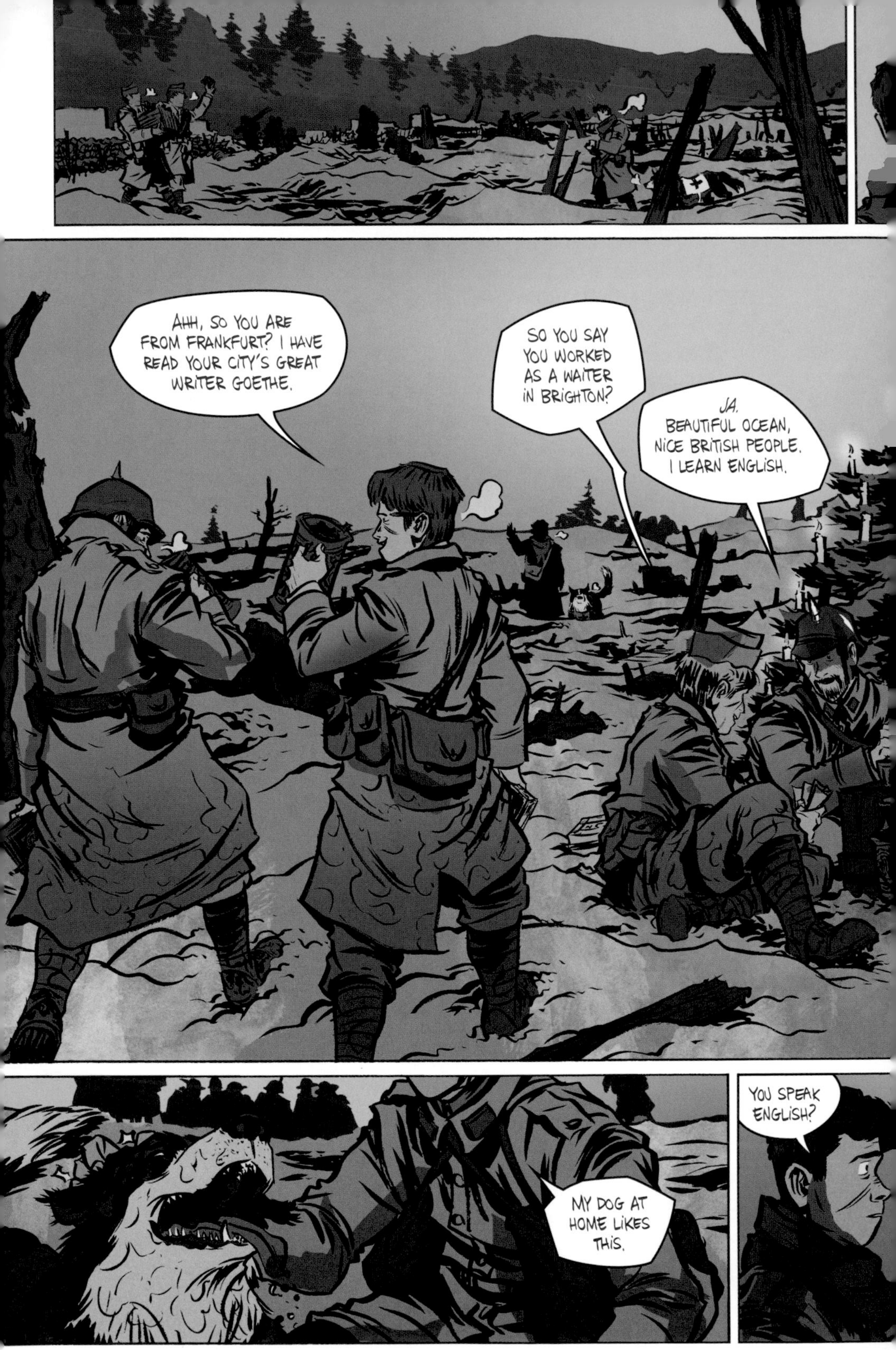
AHH, SO YOU ARE FROM FRANKFURT? I HAVE READ YOUR CITY'S GREAT WRITER GOETHE.
SO YOU SAY YOU WORKED AS A WAITER IN BRIGHTON?
JA. BEAUTIFUL OCEAN, NICE BRITISH PEOPLE. I LEARN ENGLISH.
MY DOG AT HOME LIKES THIS.
YOU SPEAK ENGLISH?

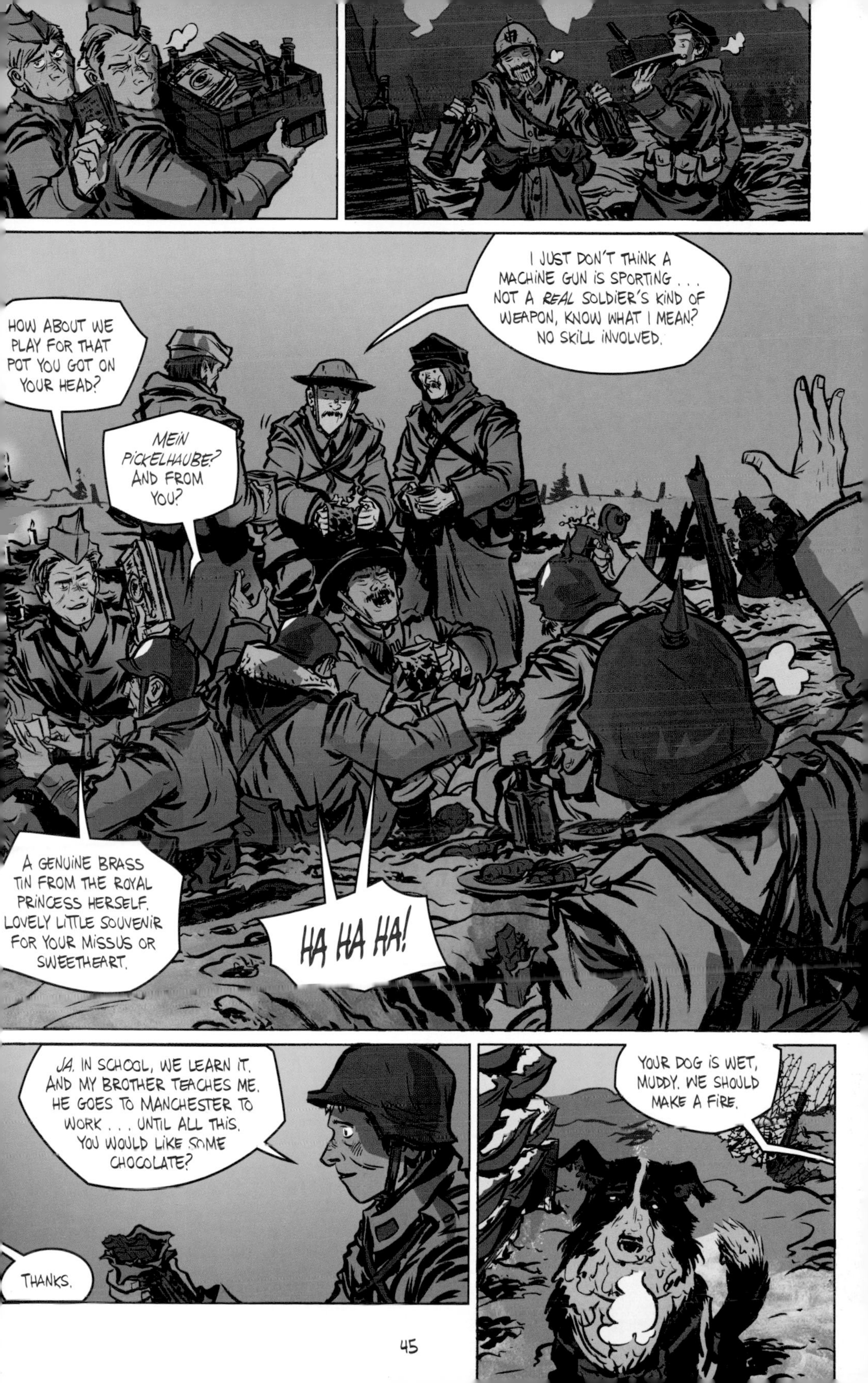
HOW ABOUT WE PLAY FOR THAT POT YOU GOT ON YOUR HEAD?
I JUST DON'T THINK A MACHINE GUN IS SPORTING . . . NOT A *REAL* SOLDIER'S KIND OF WEAPON, KNOW WHAT I MEAN? NO SKILL INVOLVED.
MEIN PICKELHAUBE? AND FROM YOU?
A GENUINE BRASS TIN FROM THE ROYAL PRINCESS HERSELF. LOVELY LITTLE SOUVENIR FOR YOUR MISSUS OR SWEETHEART.
HA HA HA!
JA. IN SCHOOL, WE LEARN IT. AND MY BROTHER TEACHES ME. HE GOES TO MANCHESTER TO WORK . . . UNTIL ALL THIS. YOU WOULD LIKE SOME CHOCOLATE?
THANKS.
YOUR DOG IS WET, MUDDY. WE SHOULD MAKE A FIRE.

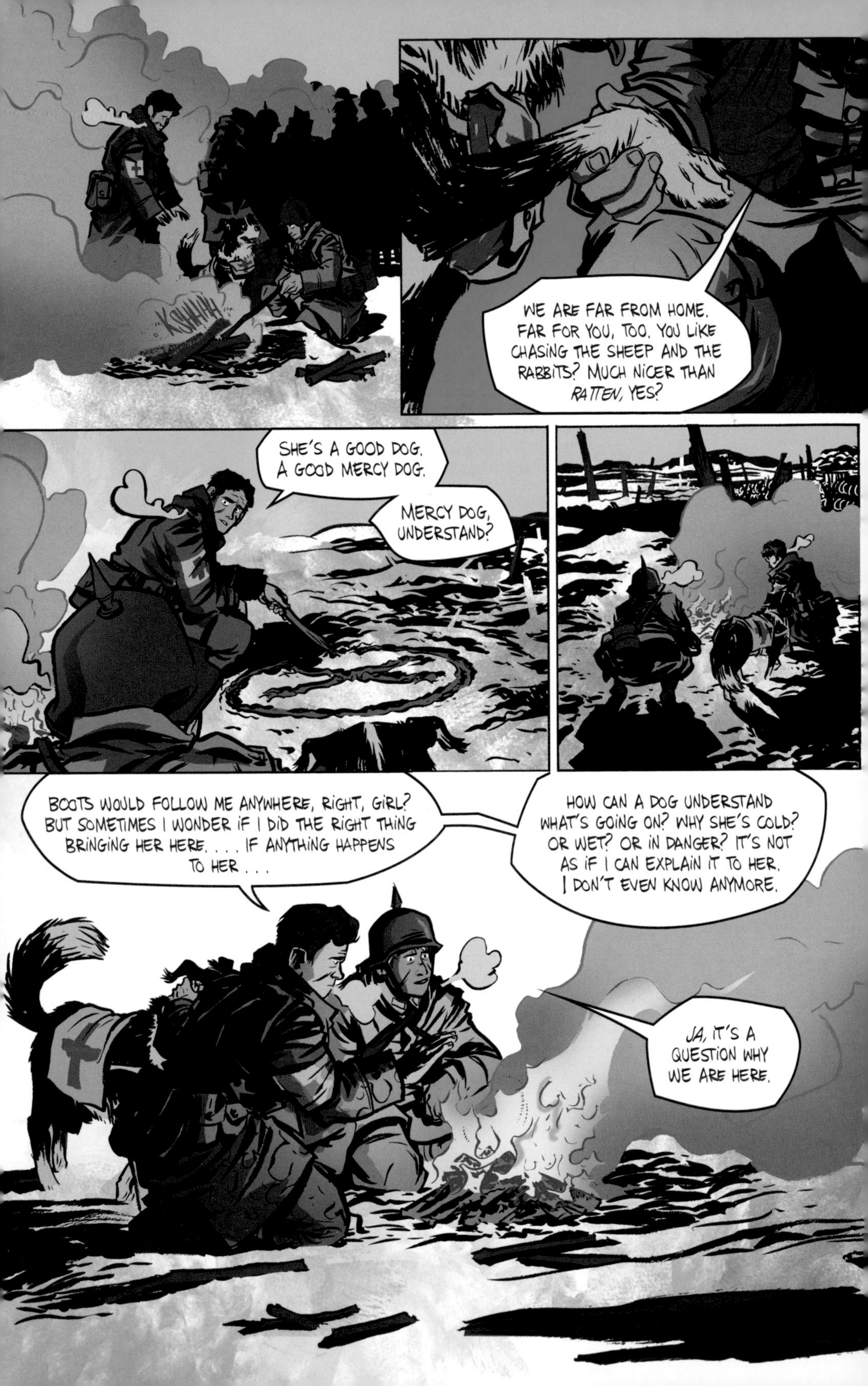
KSHHHH
WE ARE FAR FROM HOME. FAR FOR YOU, TOO. YOU LIKE CHASING THE SHEEP AND THE RABBITS? MUCH NICER THAN *RATTEN*, YES?
SHE'S A GOOD DOG. A GOOD MERCY DOG.
MERCY DOG, UNDERSTAND?
BOOTS WOULD FOLLOW ME ANYWHERE, RIGHT, GIRL? BUT SOMETIMES I WONDER IF I DID THE RIGHT THING BRINGING HER HERE. . . . IF ANYTHING HAPPENS TO HER . . .
HOW CAN A DOG UNDERSTAND WHAT'S GOING ON? WHY SHE'S COLD? OR WET? OR IN DANGER? IT'S NOT AS IF I CAN EXPLAIN IT TO HER. I DON'T EVEN KNOW ANYMORE.
JA, IT'S A QUESTION WHY WE ARE HERE.

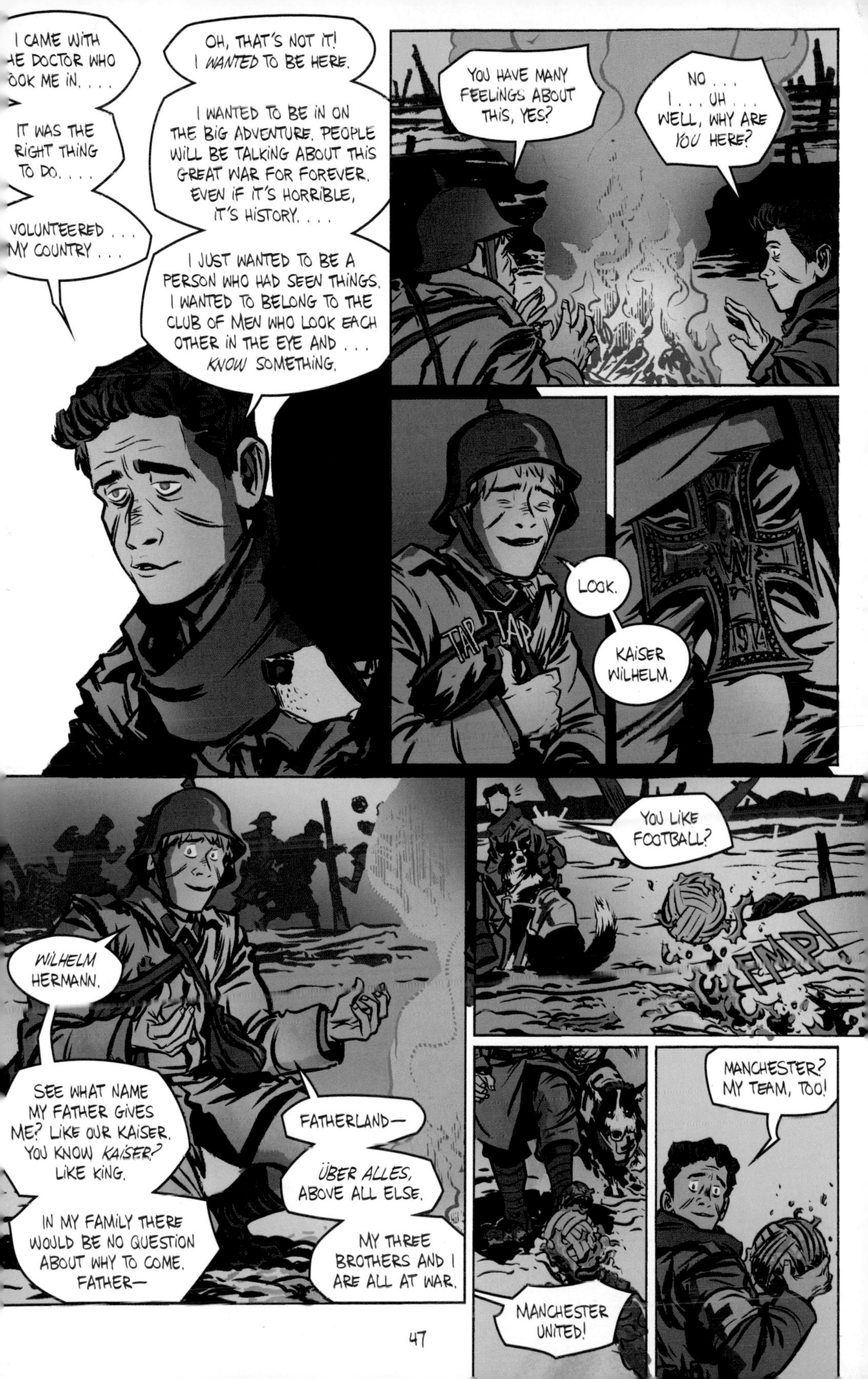
I CAME WITH
HE DOCTOR WHO
OOK ME IN. . . .
IT WAS THE RIGHT THING TO DO. . . .
VOLUNTEERED . . . MY COUNTRY . . .
OH, THAT'S NOT IT! I WANTED TO BE HERE.
I WANTED TO BE IN ON THE BIG ADVENTURE. PEOPLE WILL BE TALKING ABOUT THIS GREAT WAR FOR FOREVER. EVEN IF IT'S HORRIBLE, IT'S HISTORY. . . .
I JUST WANTED TO BE A PERSON WHO HAD SEEN THINGS. I WANTED TO BELONG TO THE CLUB OF MEN WHO LOOK EACH OTHER IN THE EYE AND . . . KNOW SOMETHING.
YOU HAVE MANY FEELINGS ABOUT THIS, YES?
NO . . . I . . . UH . . . WELL, WHY ARE YOU HERE?
TAP TAP
LOOK.
KAISER WILHELM.
WILHELM HERMANN.
SEE WHAT NAME MY FATHER GIVES ME? LIKE OUR KAISER. YOU KNOW KAISER? LIKE KING.
IN MY FAMILY THERE WOULD BE NO QUESTION ABOUT WHY TO COME. FATHER—
FATHERLAND—
ÜBER ALLES, ABOVE ALL ELSE.
MY THREE BROTHERS AND I ARE ALL AT WAR.
YOU LIKE FOOTBALL?
FMP!
MANCHESTER UNITED!
MANCHESTER? MY TEAM, TOO!

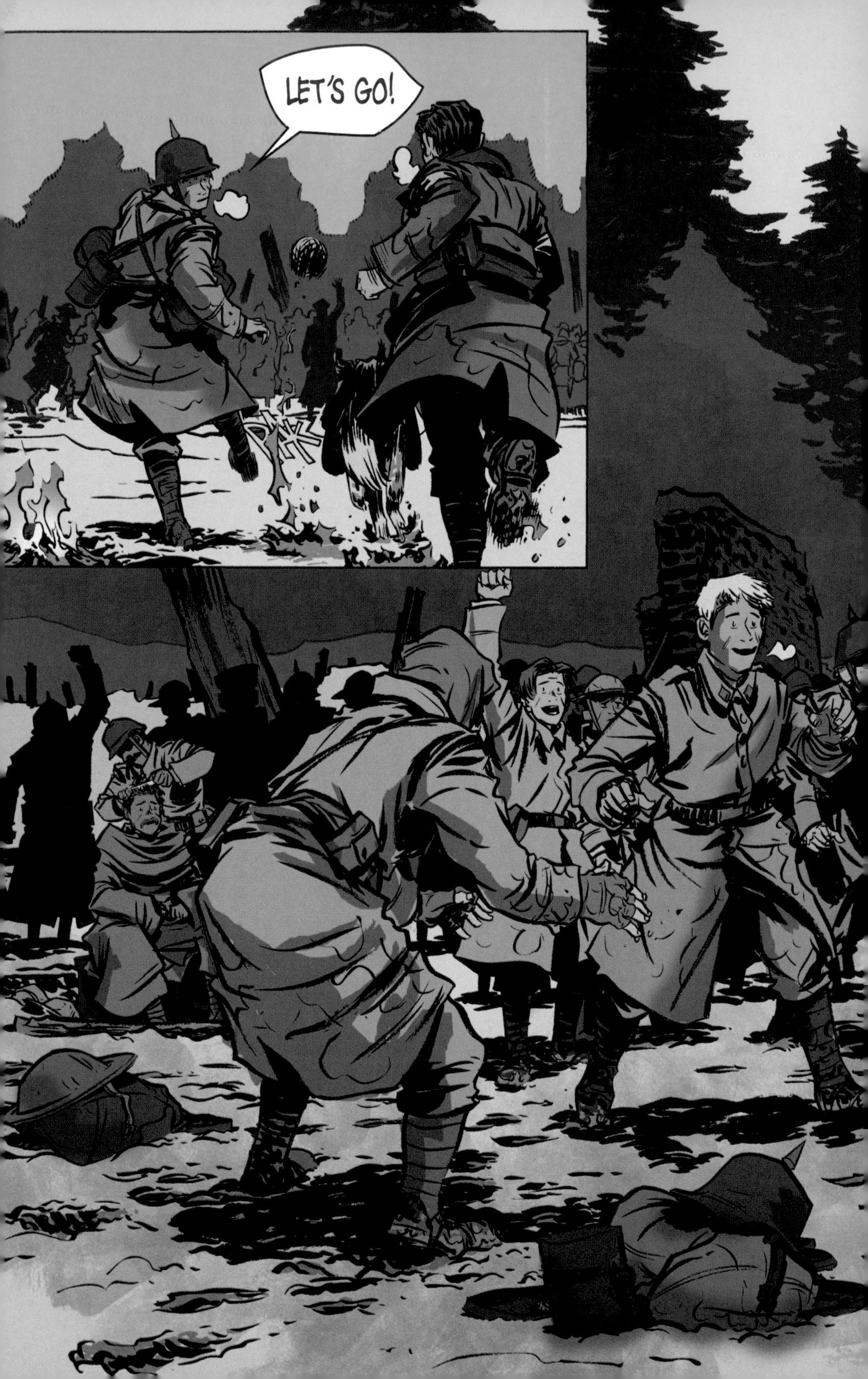
LET'S GO!

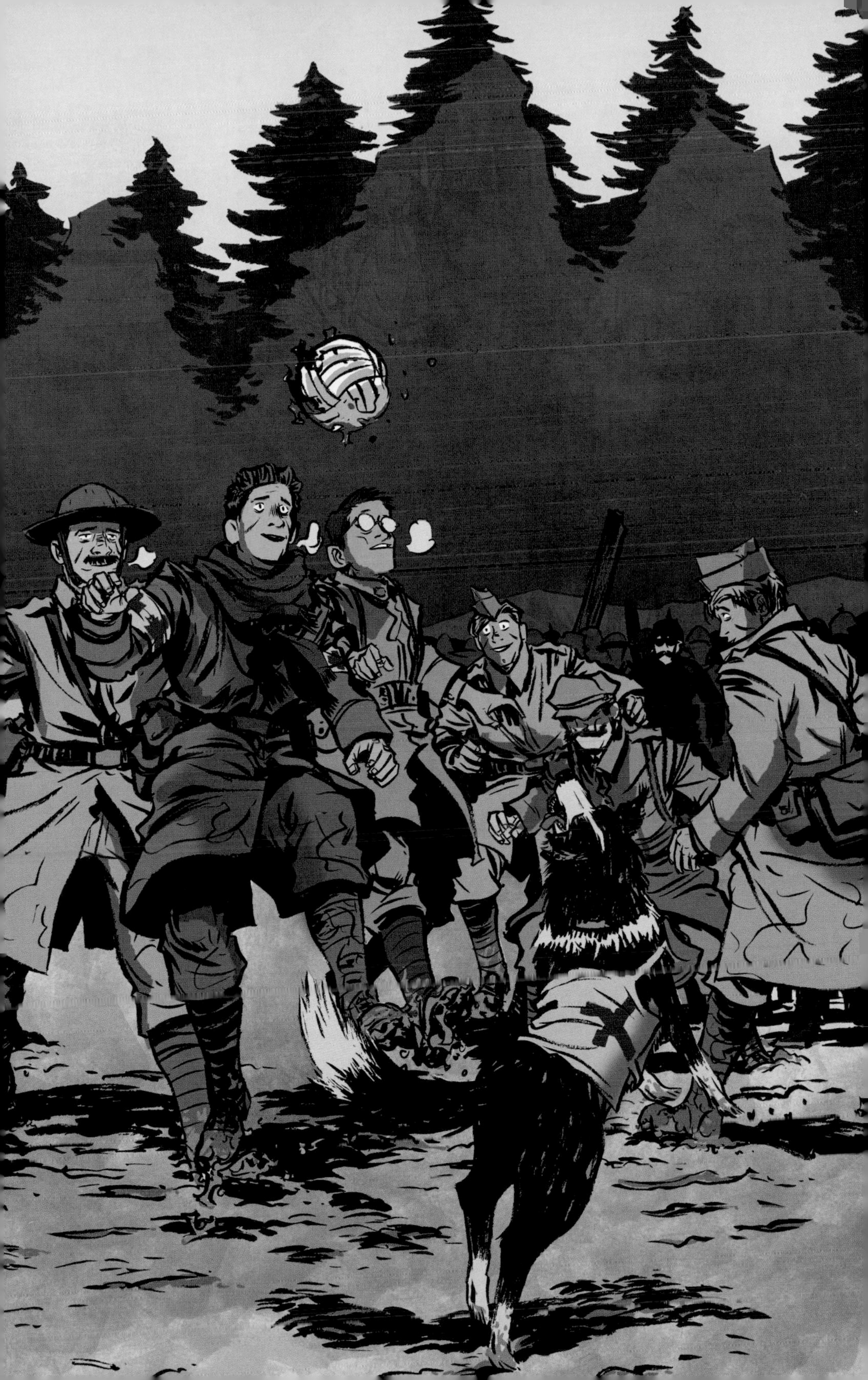

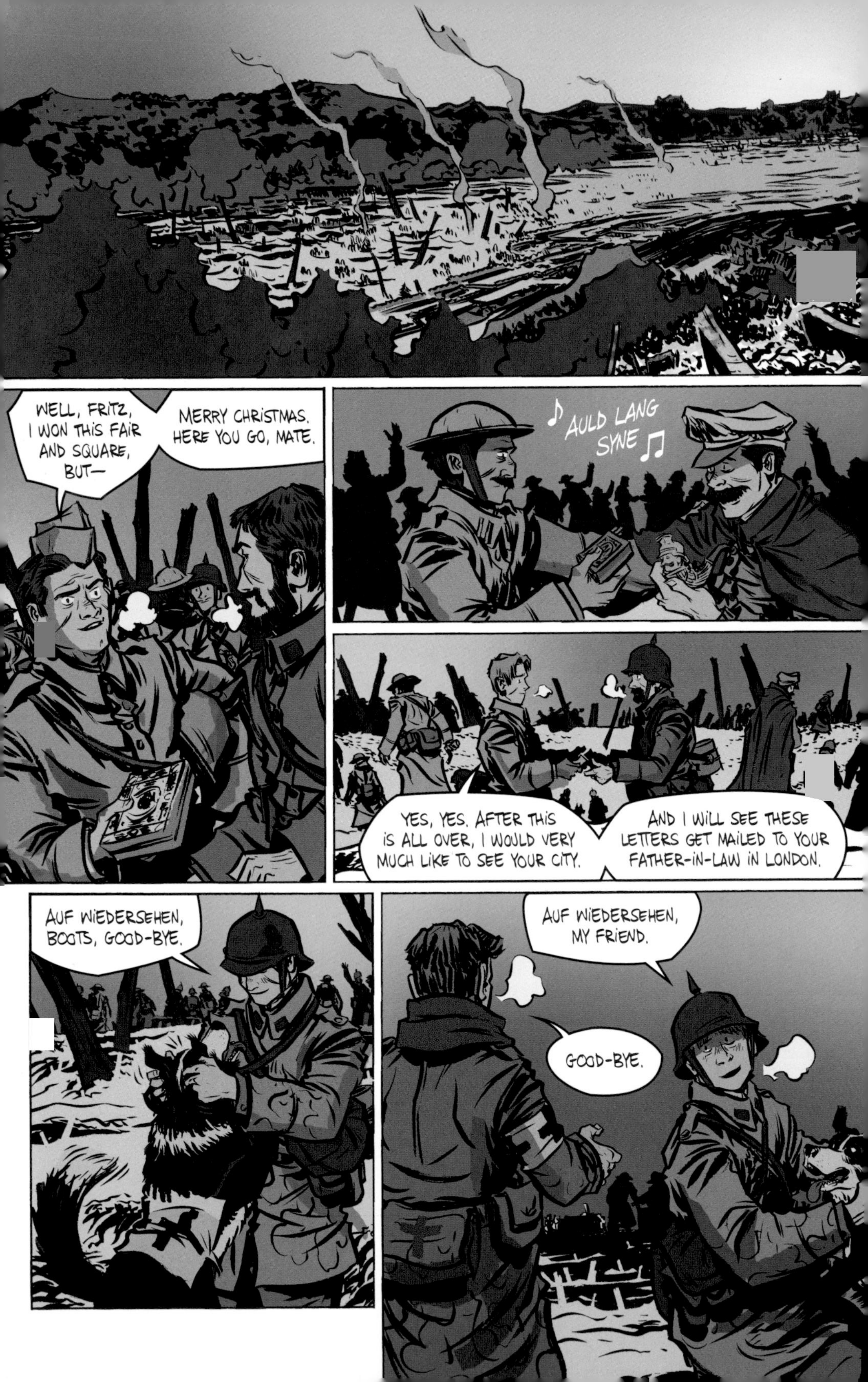
WELL, FRITZ, I WON THIS FAIR AND SQUARE, BUT—
MERRY CHRISTMAS. HERE YOU GO, MATE.
AULD LANG SYNE
YES, YES. AFTER THIS IS ALL OVER, I WOULD VERY MUCH LIKE TO SEE YOUR CITY.
AND I WILL SEE THESE LETTERS GET MAILED TO YOUR FATHER-IN-LAW IN LONDON.
AUF WIEDERSEHEN, BOOTS, GOOD-BYE.
AUF WIEDERSEHEN, MY FRIEND.
GOOD-BYE.

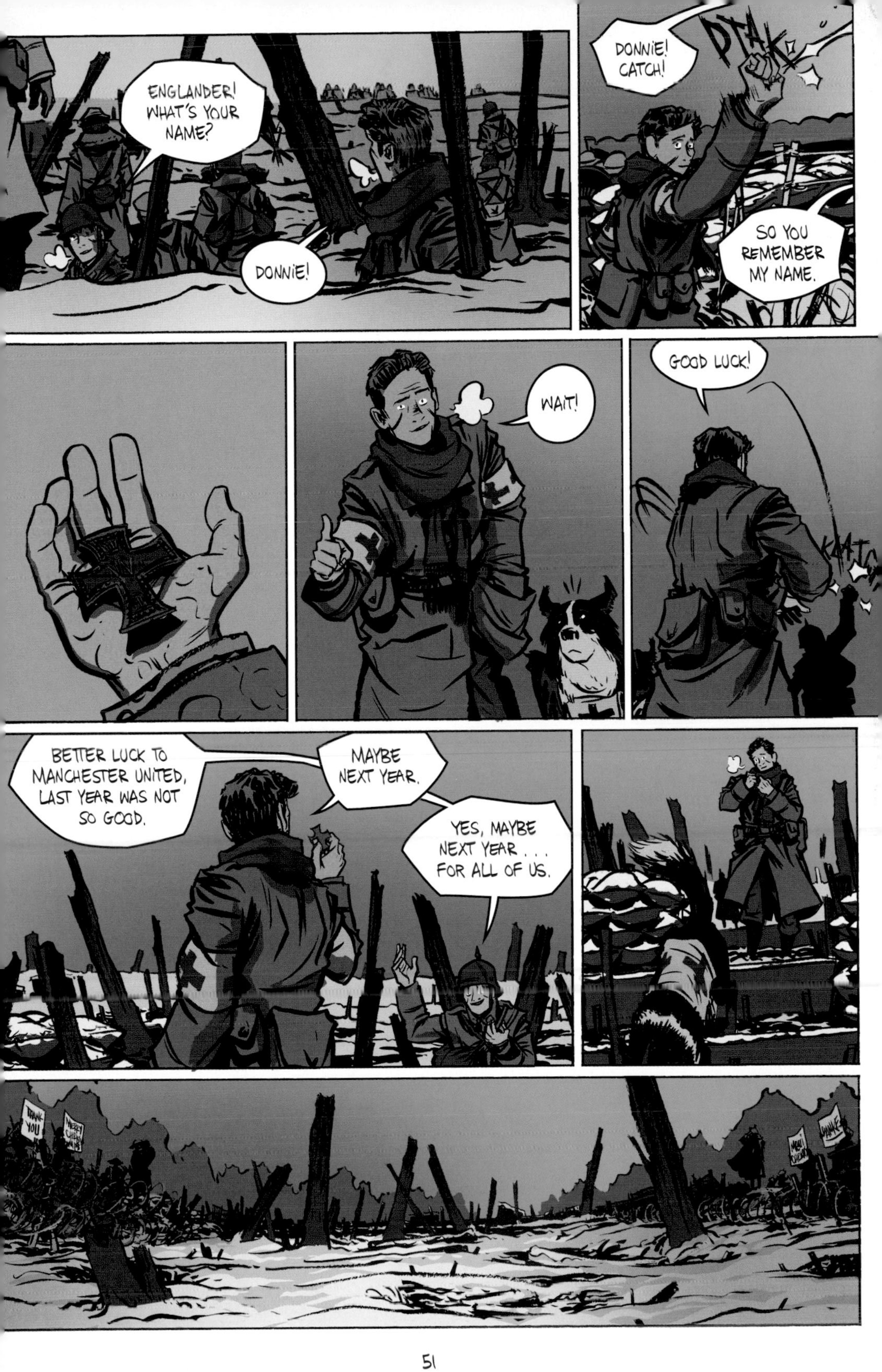
ENGLANDER! WHAT'S YOUR NAME?
DONNIE!
DONNIE! CATCH!
PTAK
SO YOU REMEMBER MY NAME.
WAIT!
GOOD LUCK!
BETTER LUCK TO MANCHESTER UNITED, LAST YEAR WAS NOT SO GOOD.
MAYBE NEXT YEAR.
YES, MAYBE NEXT YEAR . . . FOR ALL OF US.
THANK YOU

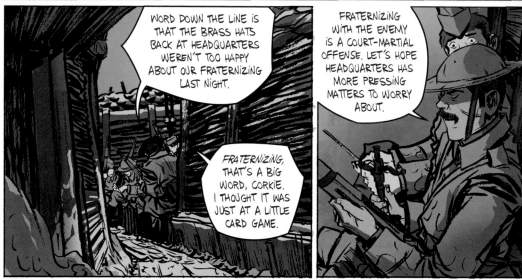

WORD DOWN THE LINE IS THAT THE BRASS HATS BACK AT HEADQUARTERS WEREN'T TOO HAPPY ABOUT OUR FRATERNIZING LAST NIGHT.

FRATERNIZING WITH THE ENEMY IS A COURT-MARTIAL OFFENSE. LET'S HOPE HEADQUARTERS HAS MORE PRESSING MATTERS TO WORRY ABOUT.

FRATERNIZING, THAT'S A BIG WORD, CORKIE. I THOUGHT IT WAS JUST A LITTLE CARD GAME.

SEEMS THAT THEY DO. I JUST GOT ORDERS THAT WE'RE INVITED TO A WIRING PARTY TONIGHT.

I'M BUSY.

I'M AFRAID OF THE DARK!

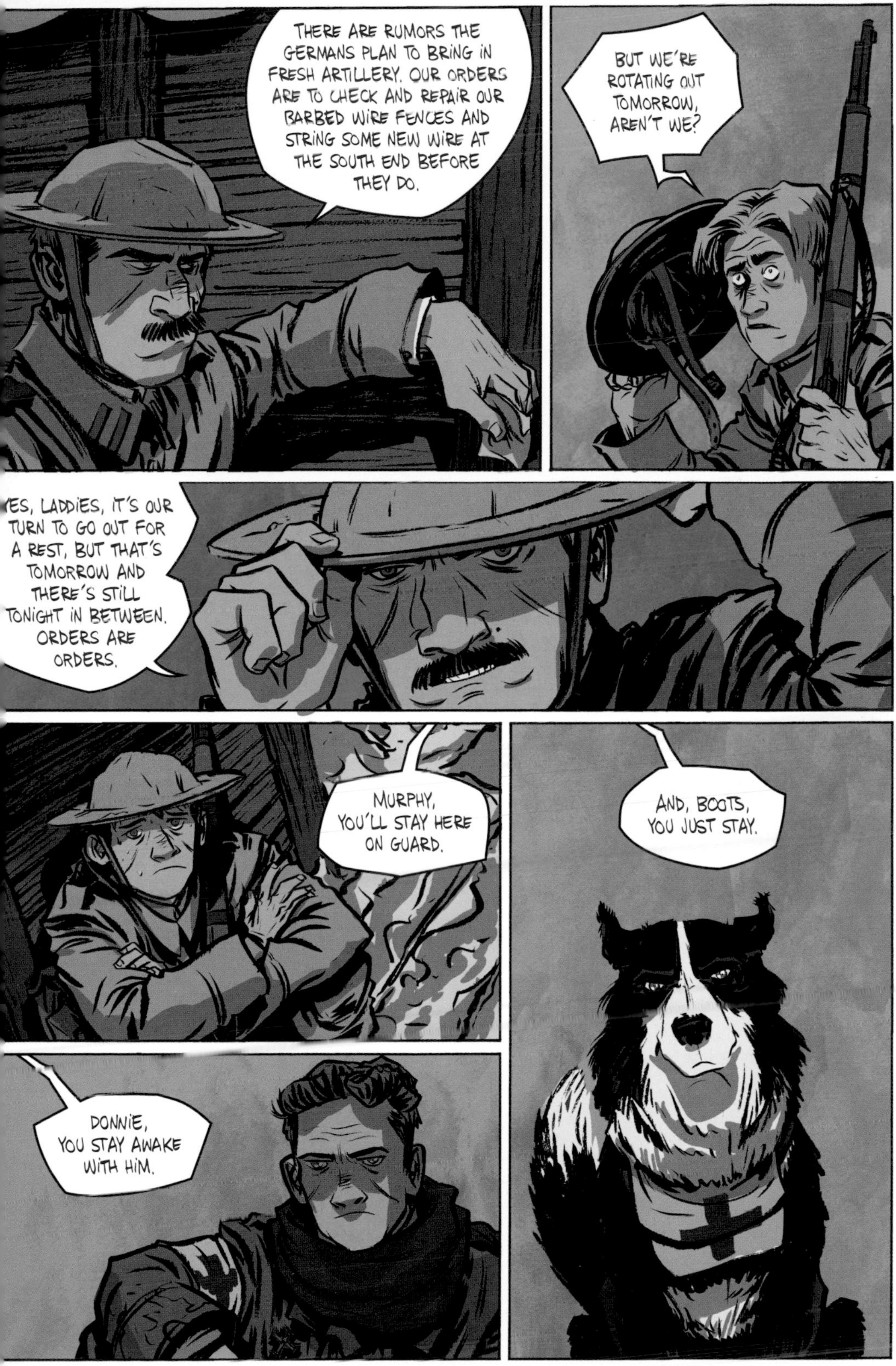
THERE ARE RUMORS THE GERMANS PLAN TO BRING IN FRESH ARTILLERY. OUR ORDERS ARE TO CHECK AND REPAIR OUR BARBED WIRE FENCES AND STRING SOME NEW WIRE AT THE SOUTH END BEFORE THEY DO.
BUT WE'RE ROTATING OUT TOMORROW, AREN'T WE?
YES, LADDIES, IT'S OUR TURN TO GO OUT FOR A REST, BUT THAT'S TOMORROW AND THERE'S STILL TONIGHT IN BETWEEN. ORDERS ARE ORDERS.
MURPHY, YOU'LL STAY HERE ON GUARD.
DONNIE, YOU STAY AWAKE WITH HIM.
AND, BOOTS, YOU JUST STAY.

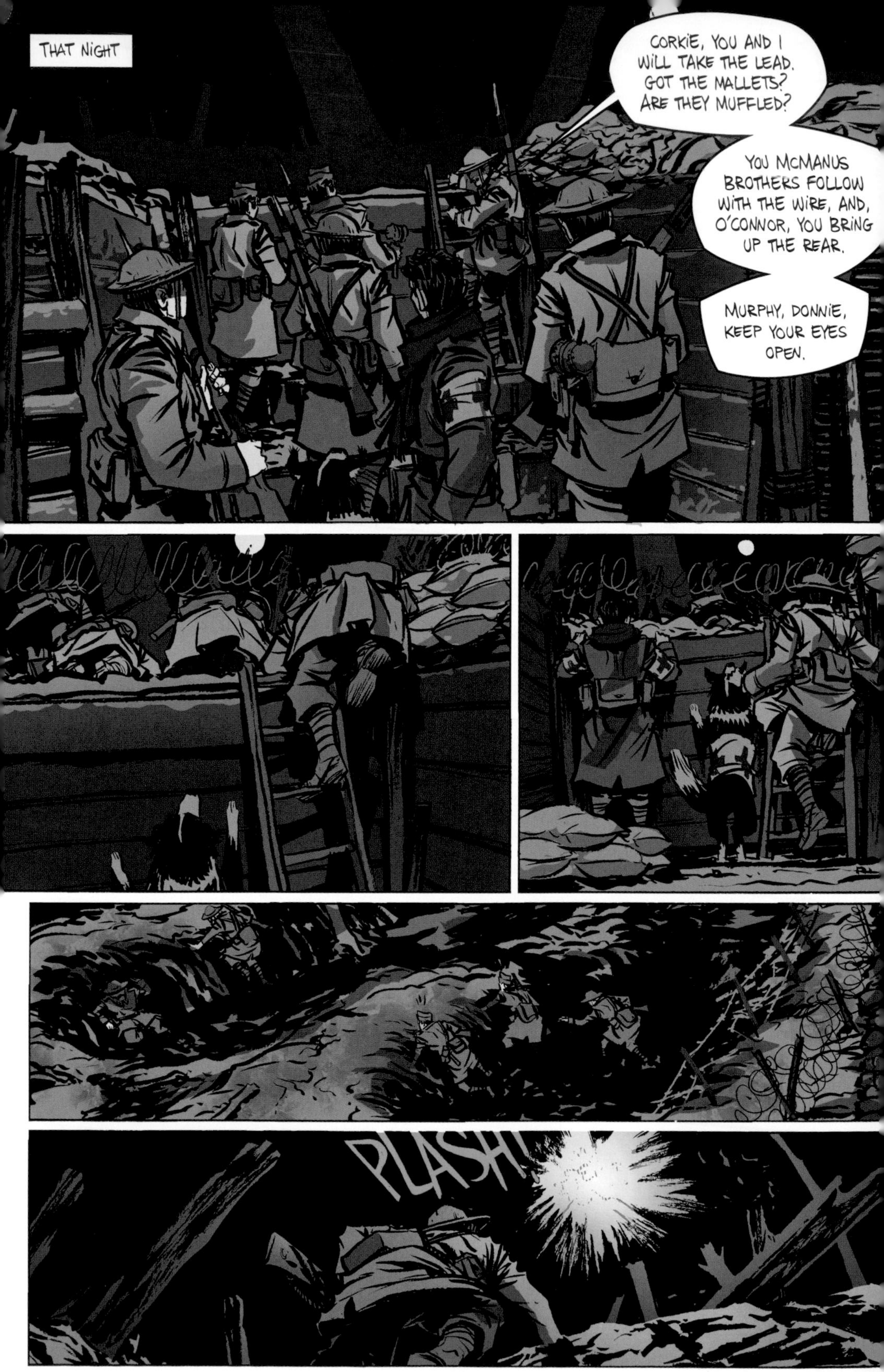
THAT NIGHT
CORKIE, YOU AND I WILL TAKE THE LEAD. GOT THE MALLETS? ARE THEY MUFFLED?
YOU McMANUS BROTHERS FOLLOW WITH THE WIRE, AND, O'CONNOR, YOU BRING UP THE REAR.
MURPHY, DONNIE, KEEP YOUR EYES OPEN.
PLASH!

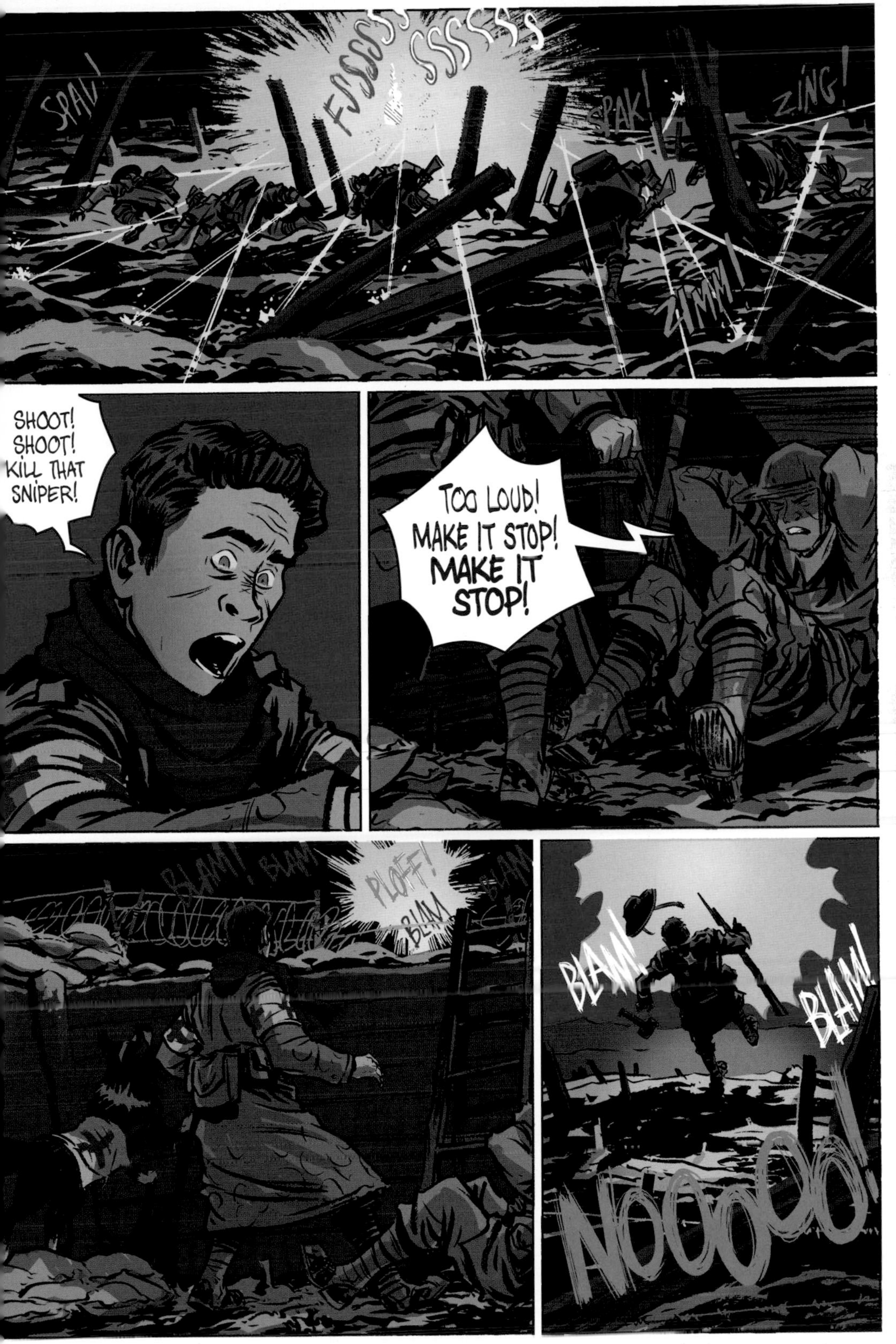
SPAK!
FSSSSSS SSSSSSS
SPAK!
ZING!
ZIMM!
SHOOT! SHOOT! KILL THAT SNIPER!
TOO LOUD! MAKE IT STOP! MAKE IT STOP!
BLAM! BLAM
PLOFF!
BLAM
BLAM!
BLAM!
NOOOOO!

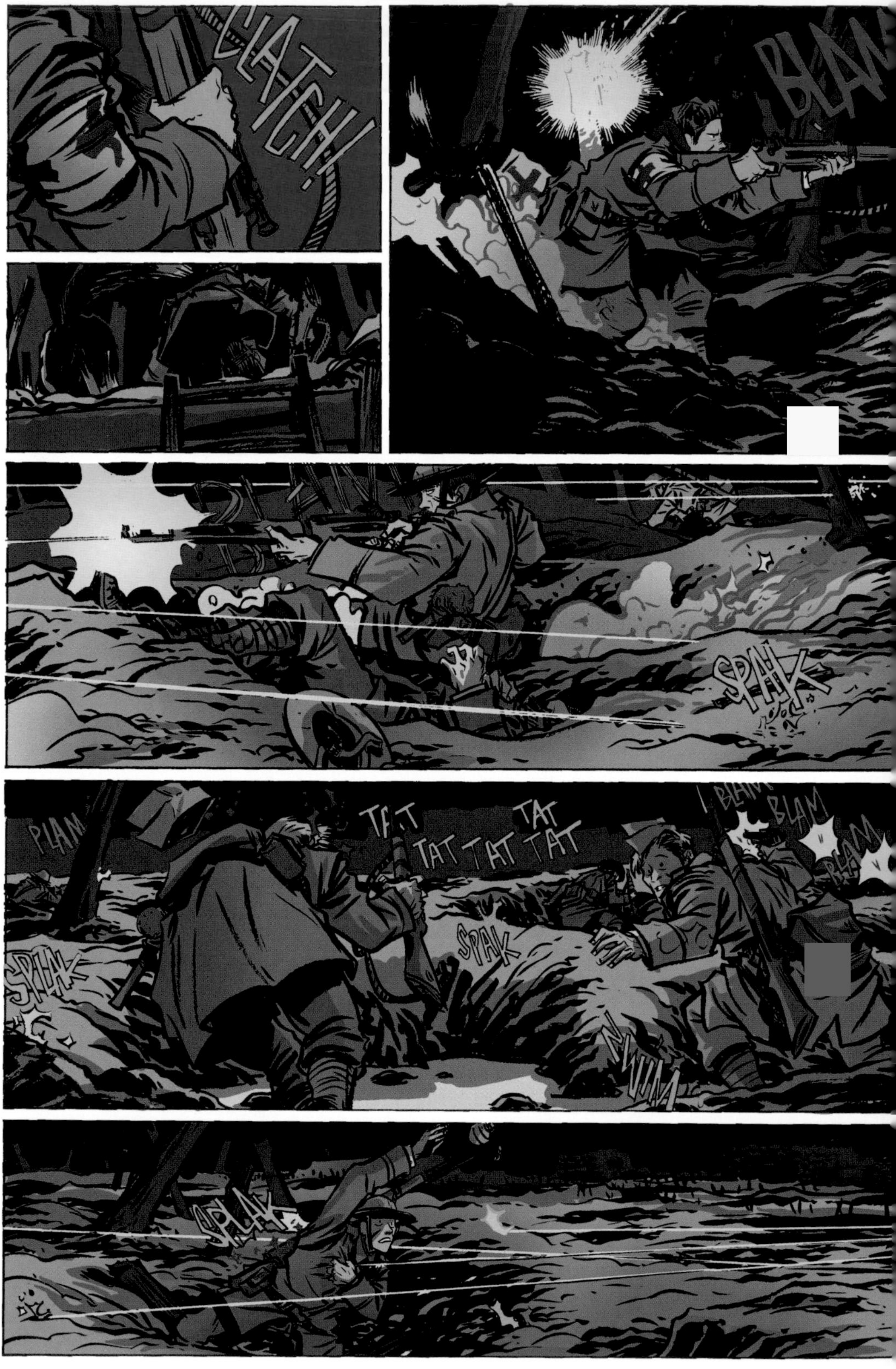
CLATCH!!
SPAK
PLAM
TAT TAT TAT TAT TAT TAT
BLAM BLAM BLAM
SPAK
SPAK
SPLAK

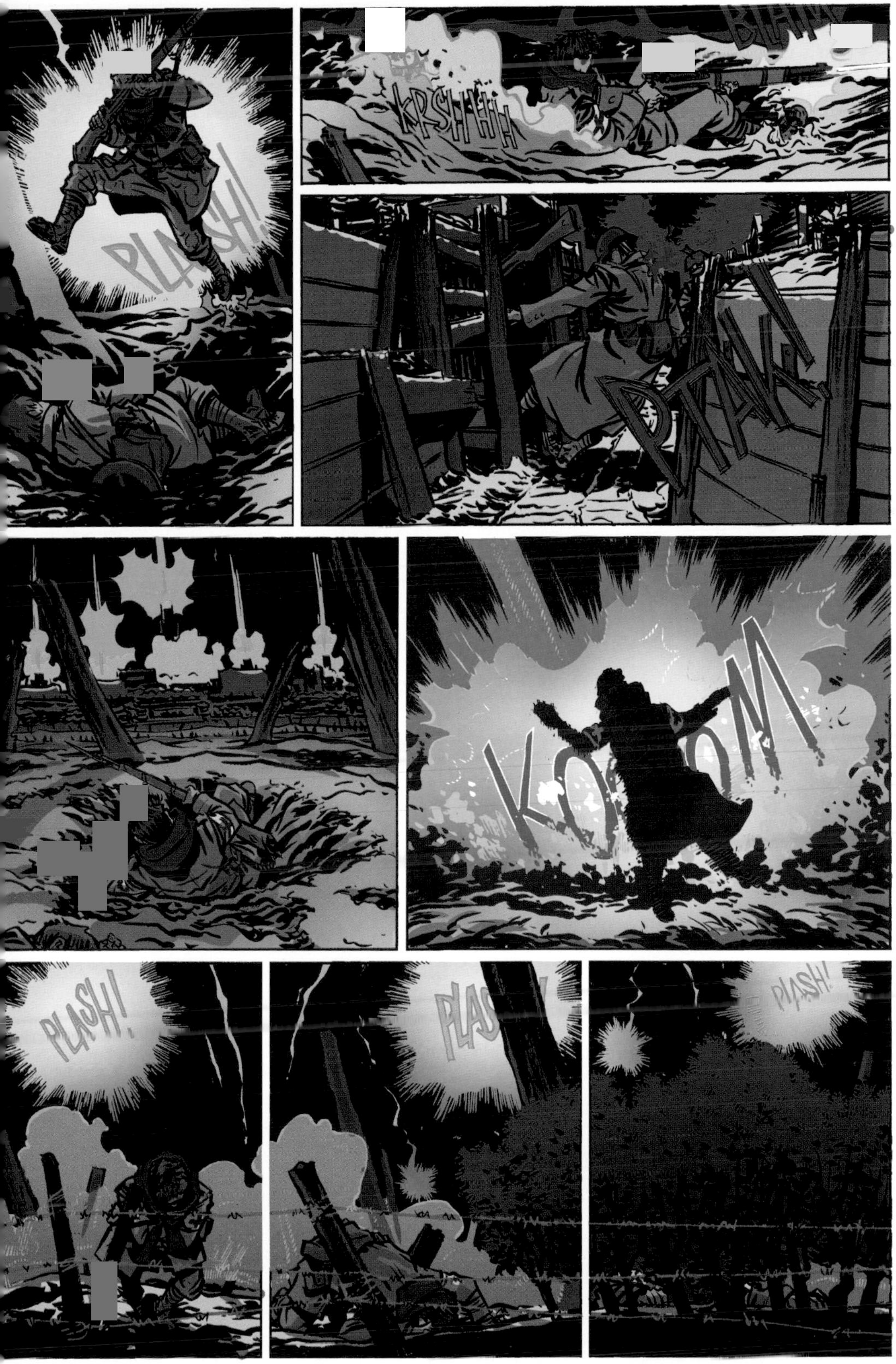
PLASH!
KRSHHHH
PTAK!
PLASH!
PLASH!

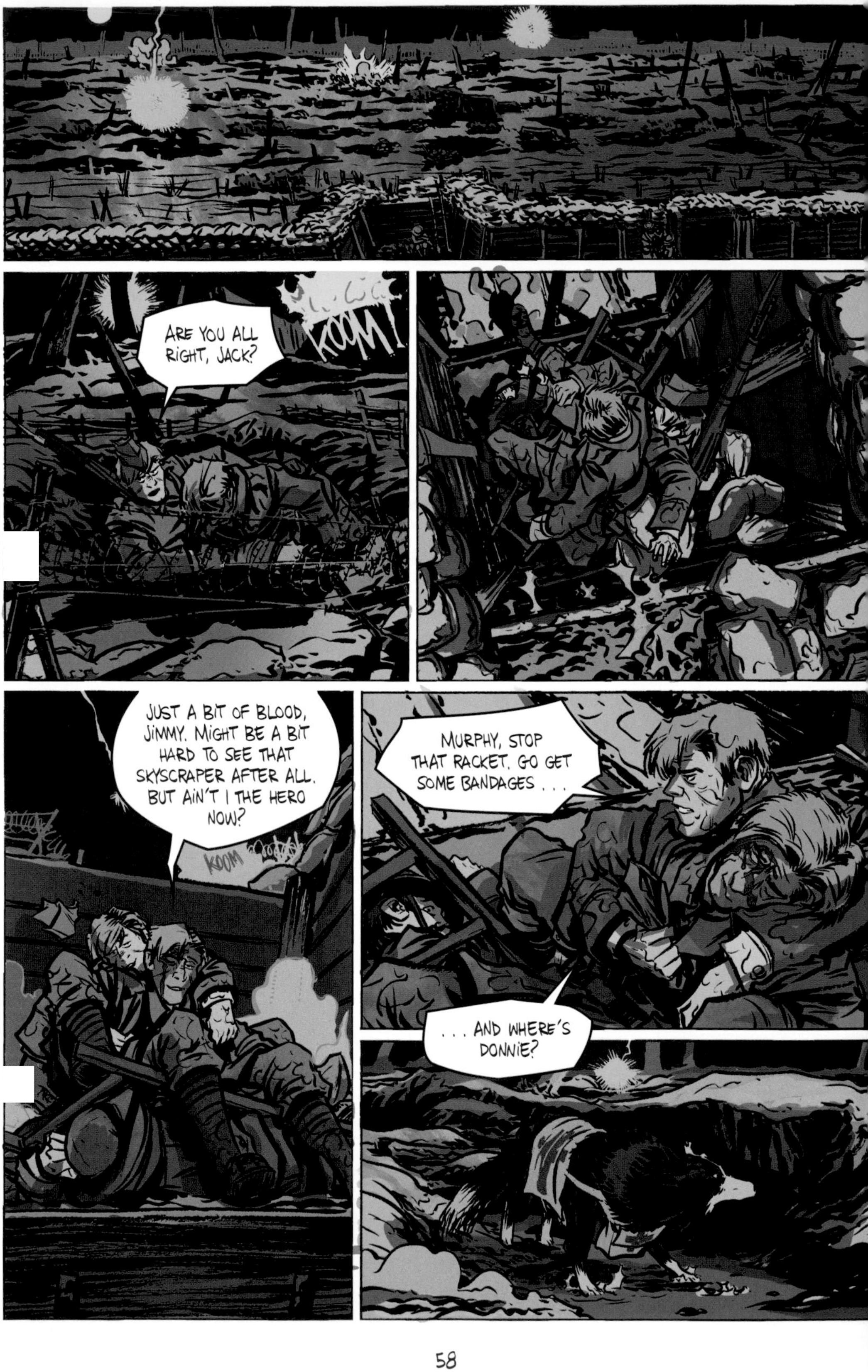
ARE YOU ALL RIGHT, JACK?
KOOM!
JUST A BIT OF BLOOD, JIMMY. MIGHT BE A BIT HARD TO SEE THAT SKYSCRAPER AFTER ALL. BUT AIN'T I THE HERO NOW?
KOOM
MURPHY, STOP THAT RACKET. GO GET SOME BANDAGES . . .
. . . AND WHERE'S DONNIE?

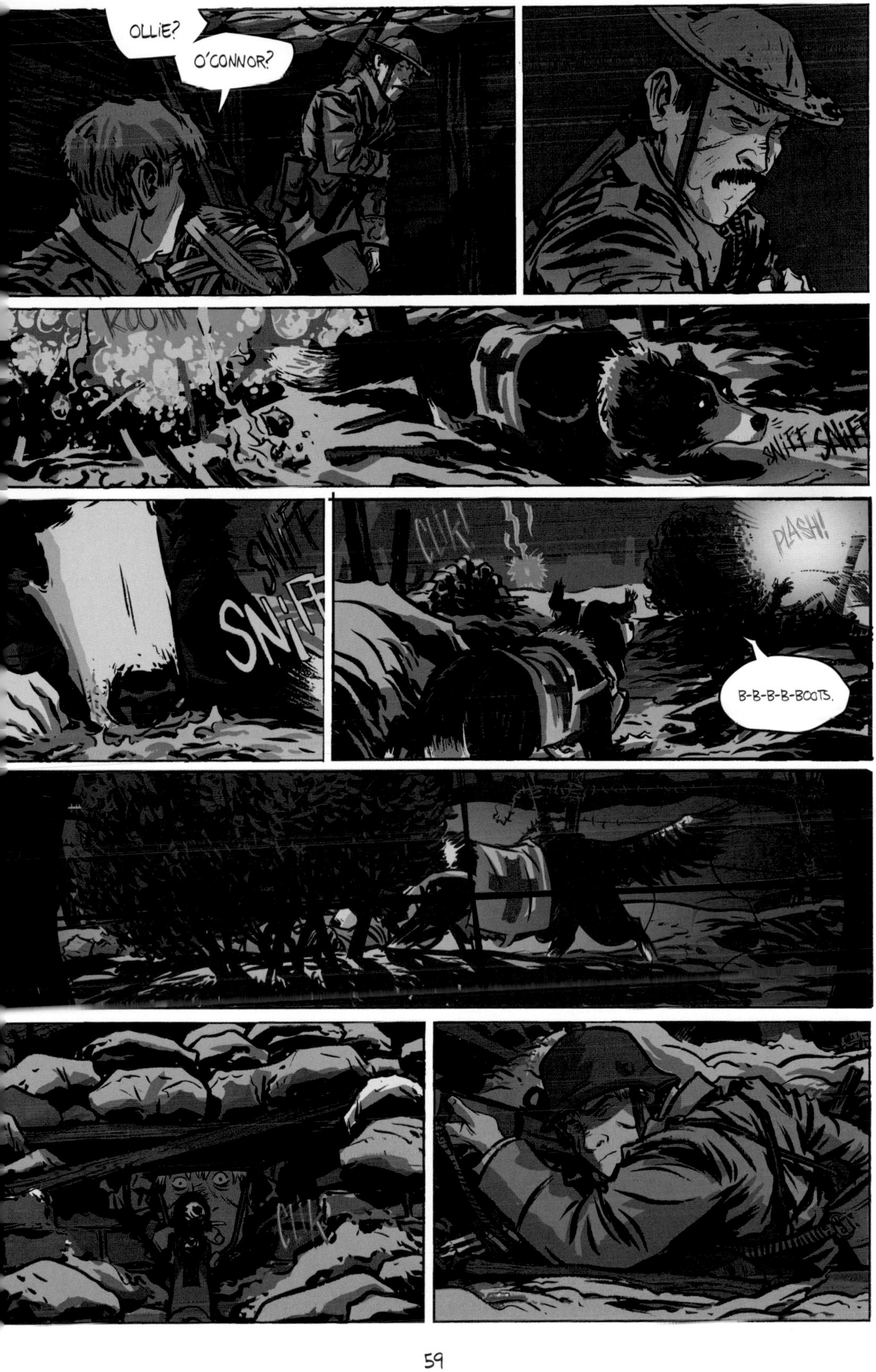
OLLIE?
O'CONNOR?
SNIFF SNIFF
SNIFF
SNIFF
CLIK!
PLASH!
B-B-B-B-BOOTS.
CLIK

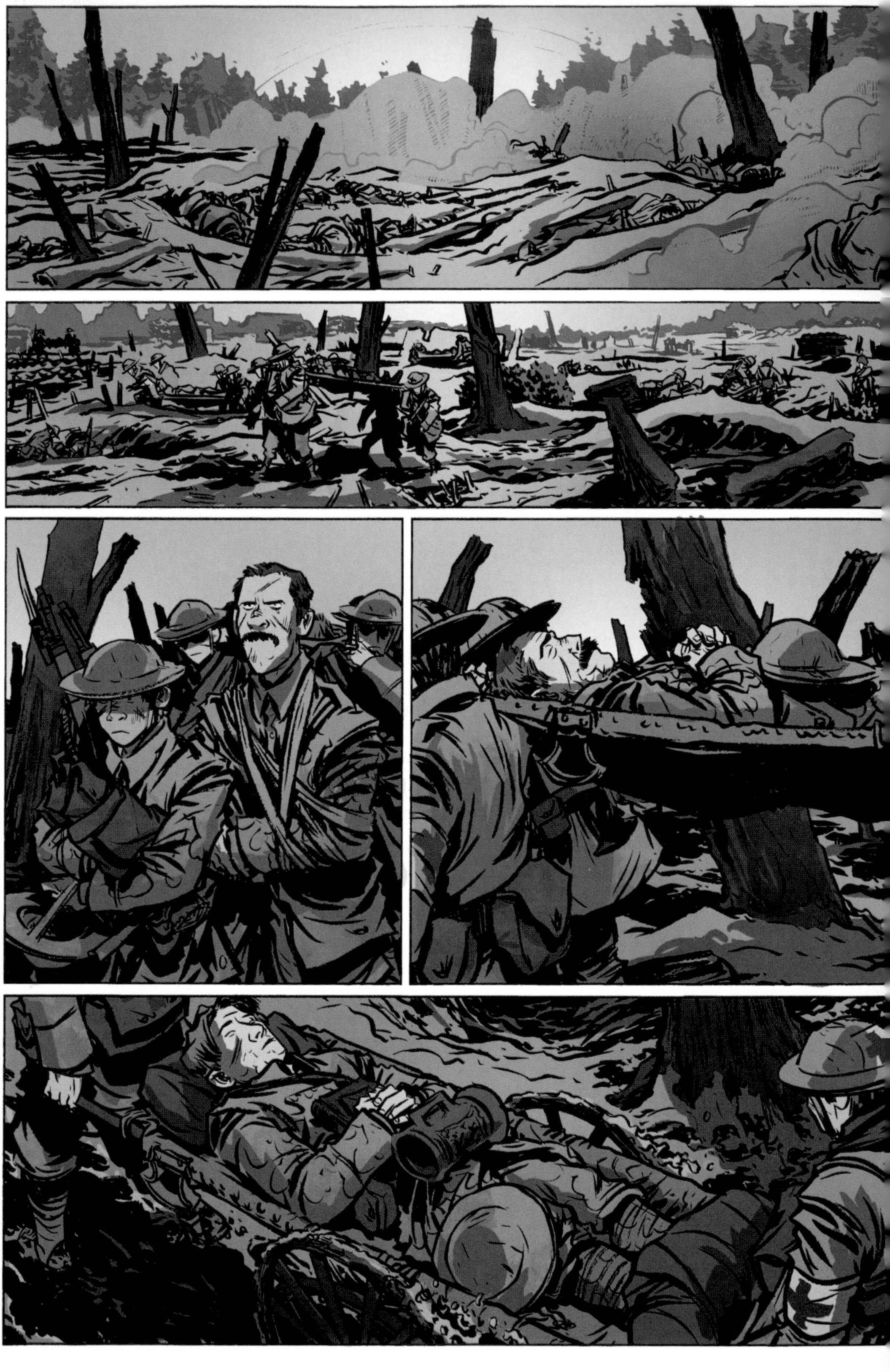

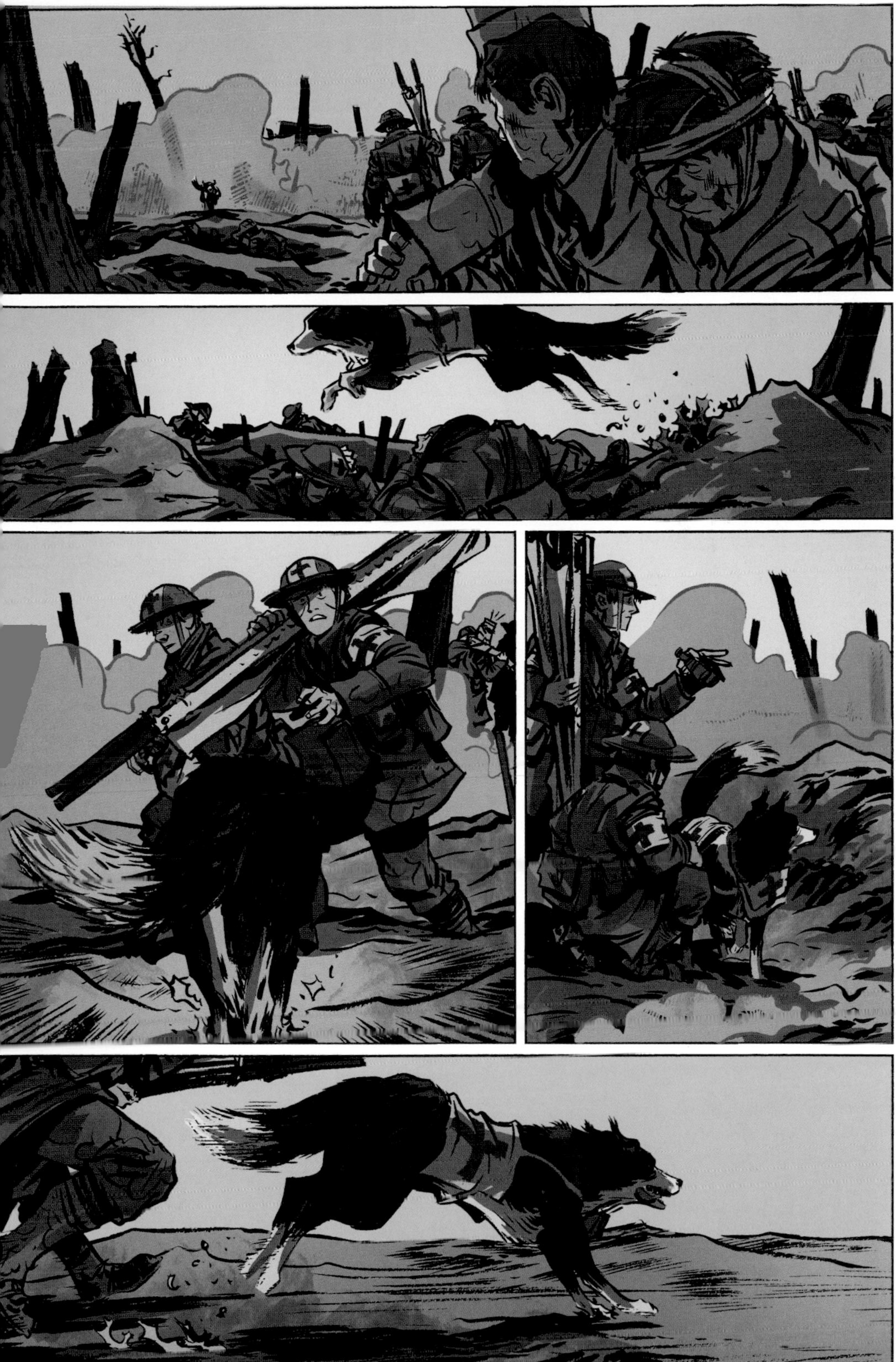

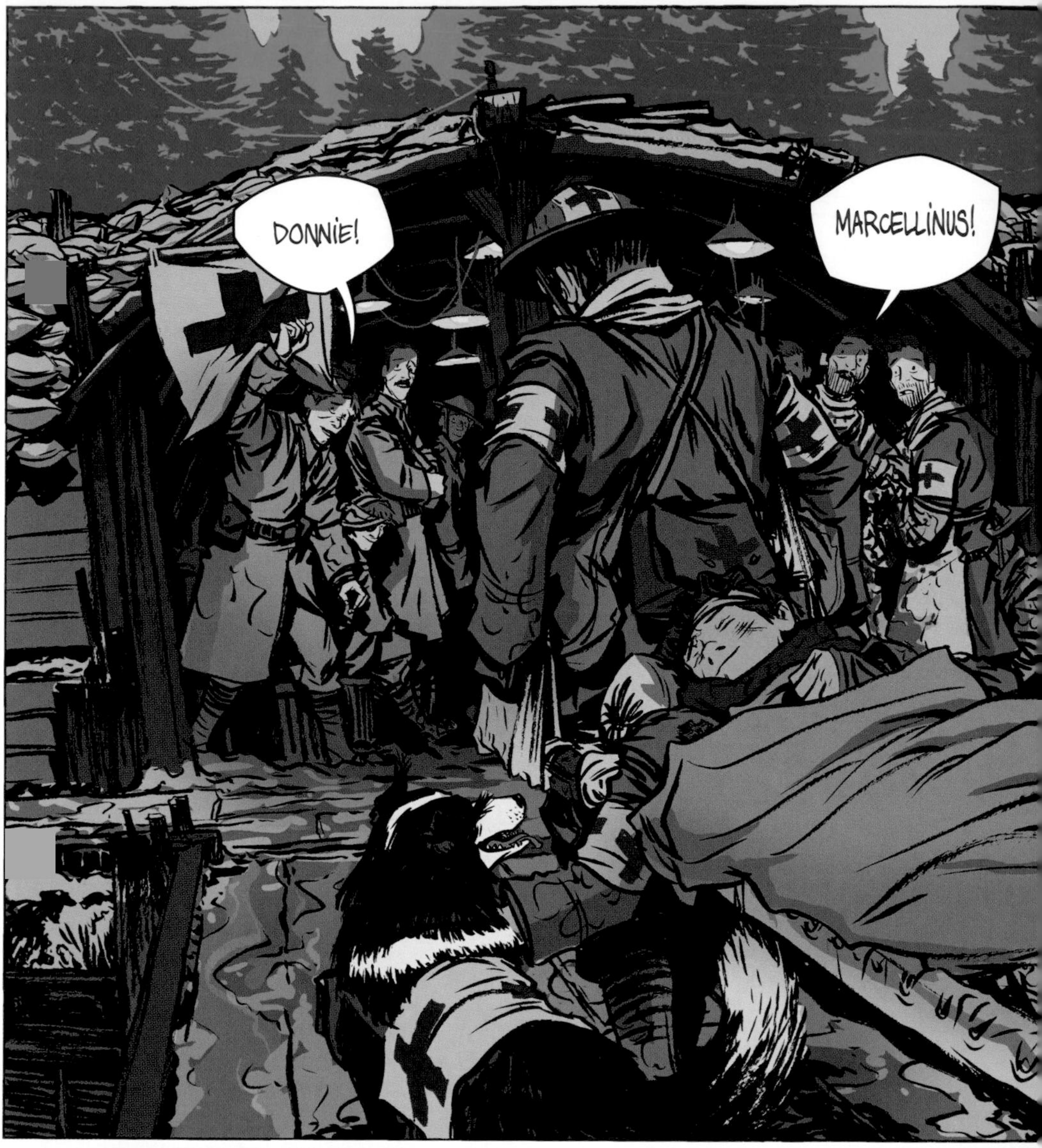
DONNIE!
MARCELLINUS!

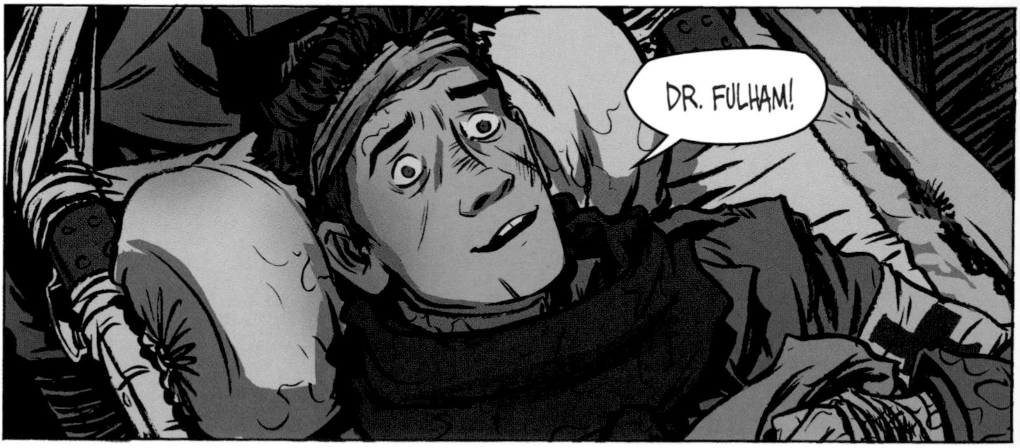
DR. FULHAM!

FLIP
MANCHESTER

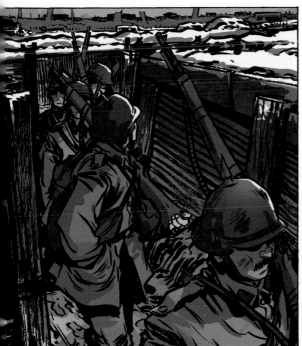

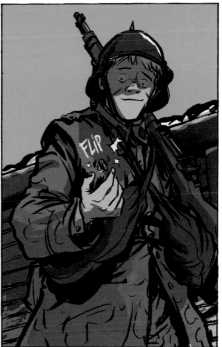

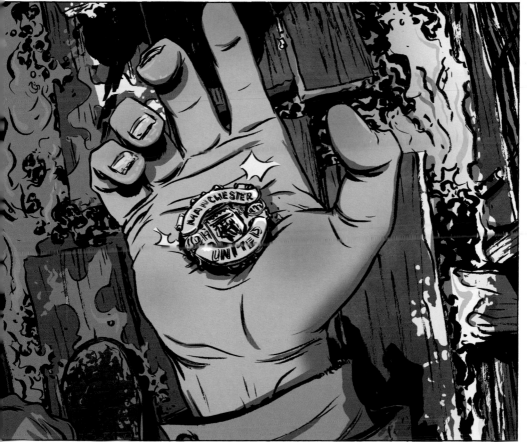

THE END

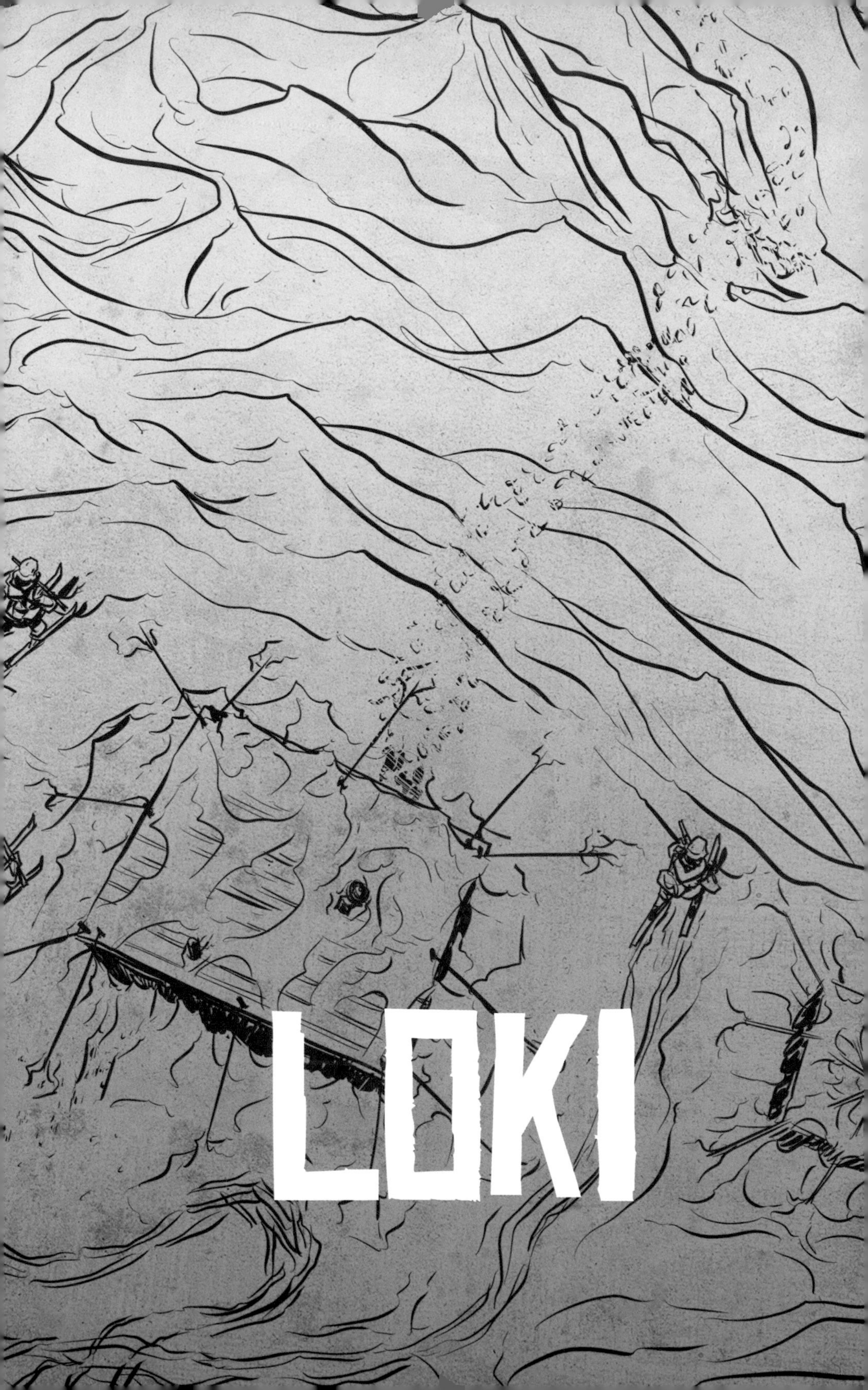
LOKI

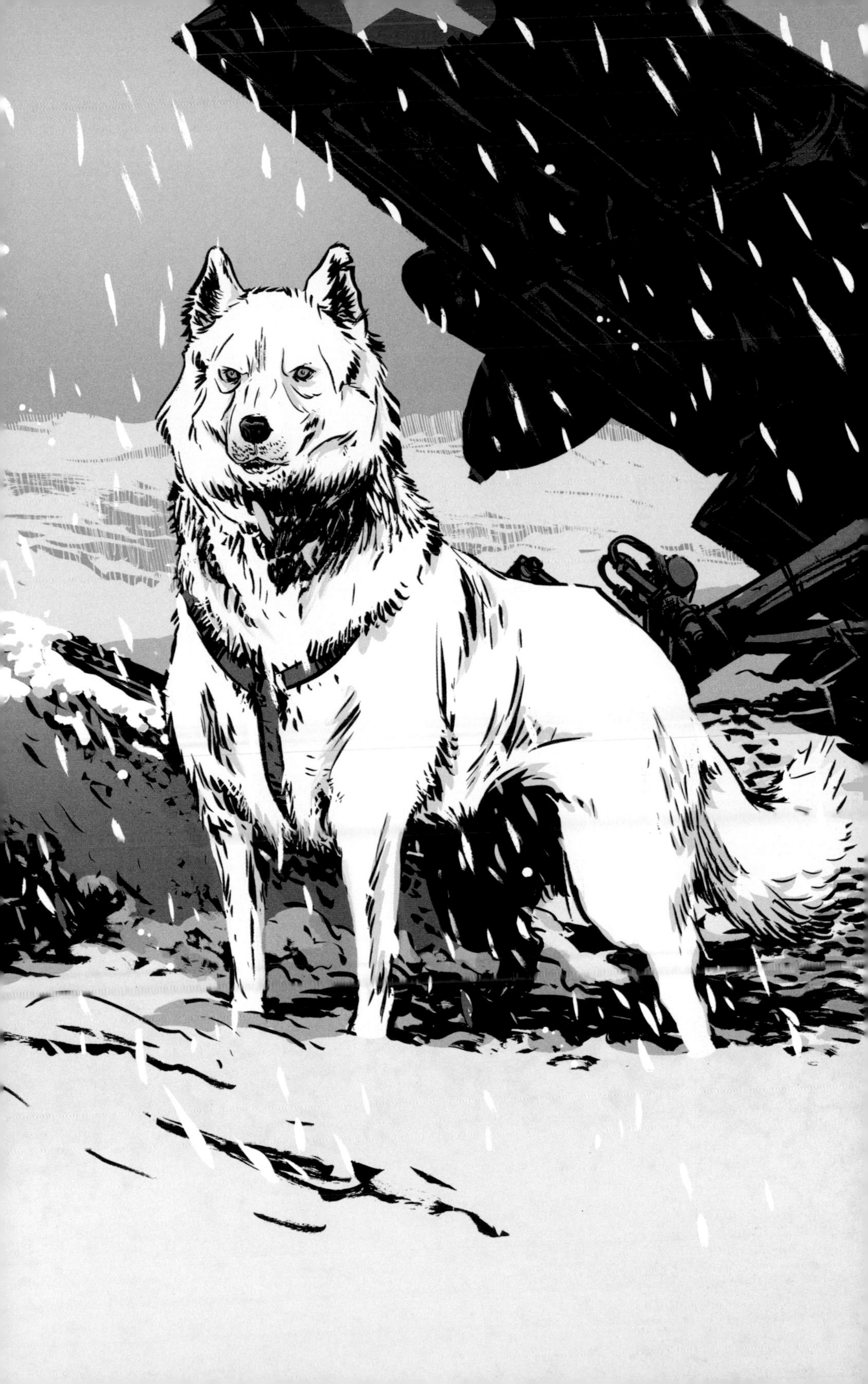

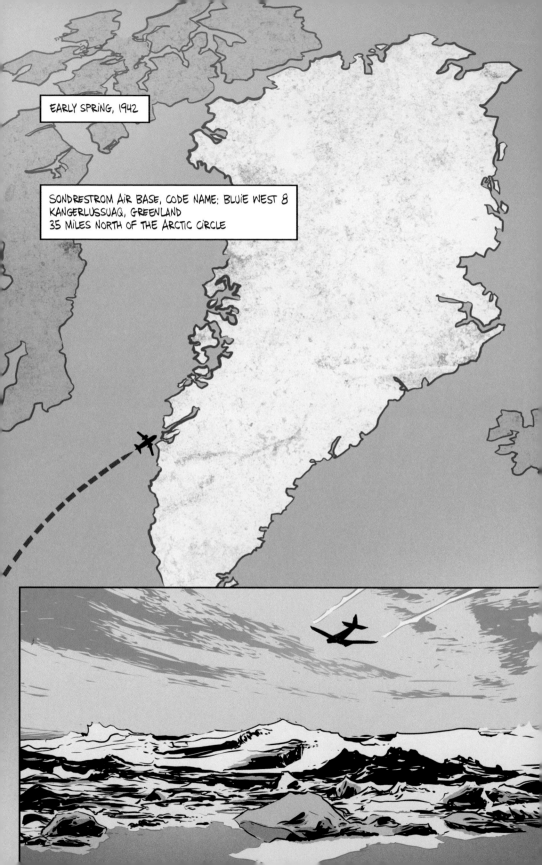

EARLY SPRING, 1942

SONDRESTROM AIR BASE, CODE NAME: BLUIE WEST 8
KANGERLUSSUAQ, GREENLAND
35 MILES NORTH OF THE ARCTIC CIRCLE

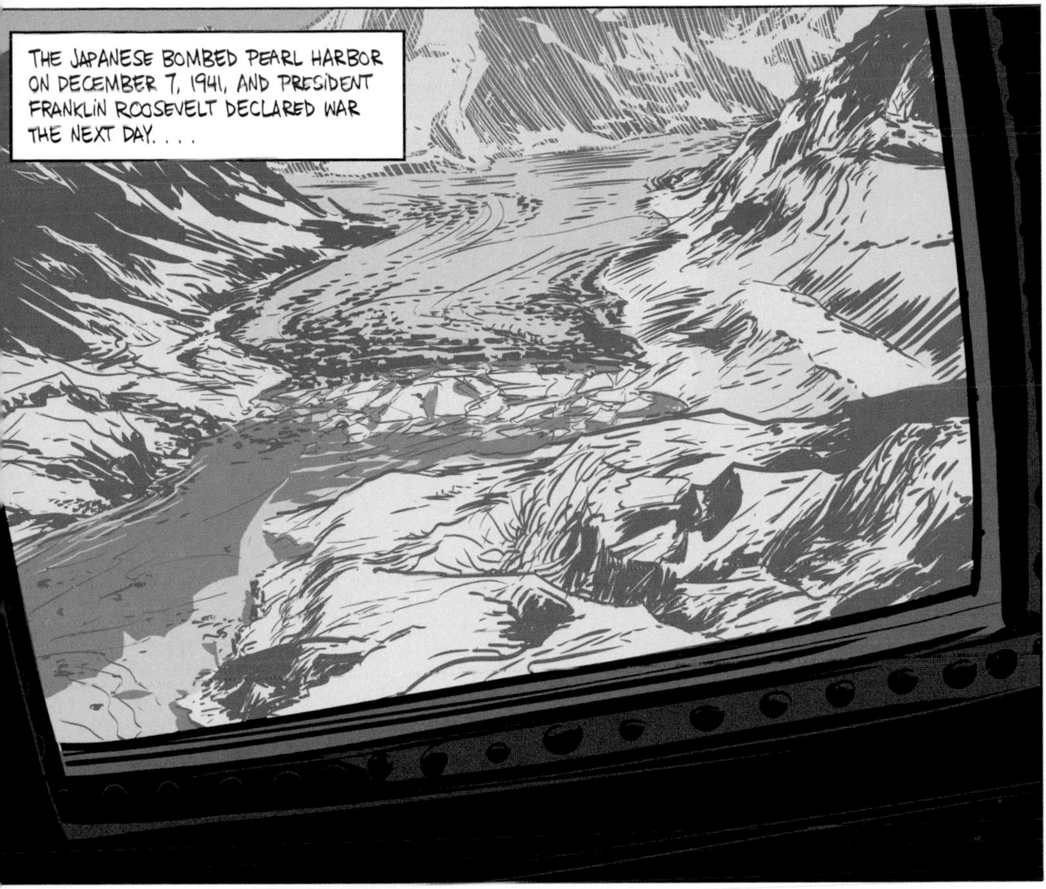
THE JAPANESE BOMBED PEARL HARBOR ON DECEMBER 7, 1941, AND PRESIDENT FRANKLIN ROOSEVELT DECLARED WAR THE NEXT DAY. . . .

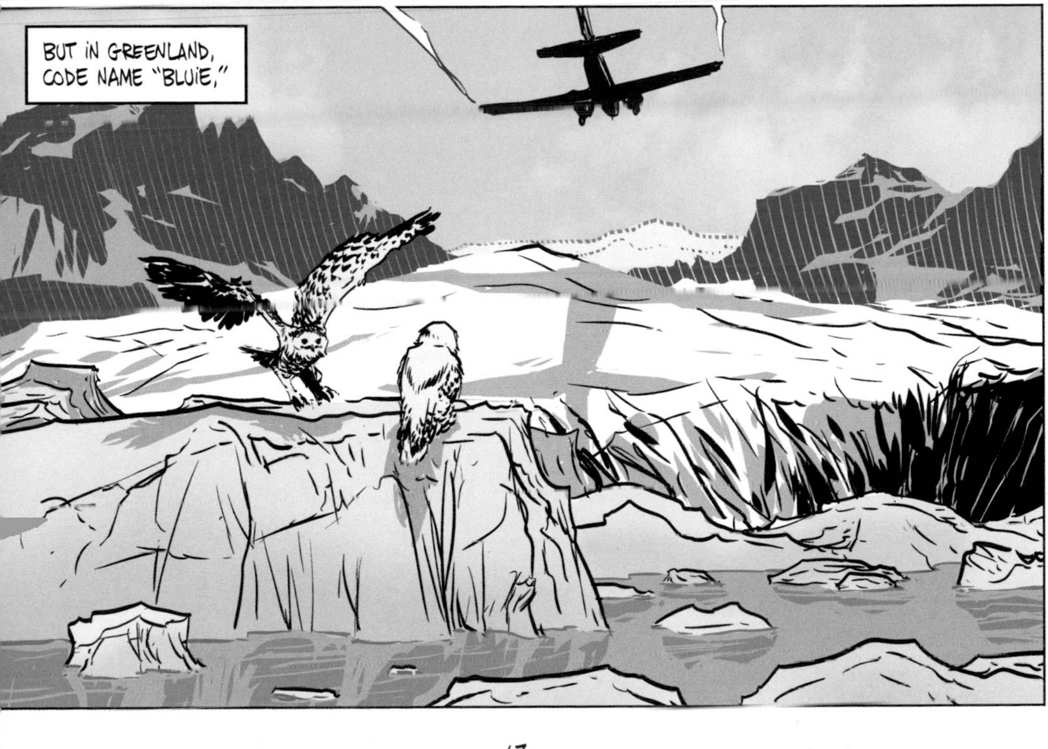
BUT IN GREENLAND, CODE NAME "BLUIE,"

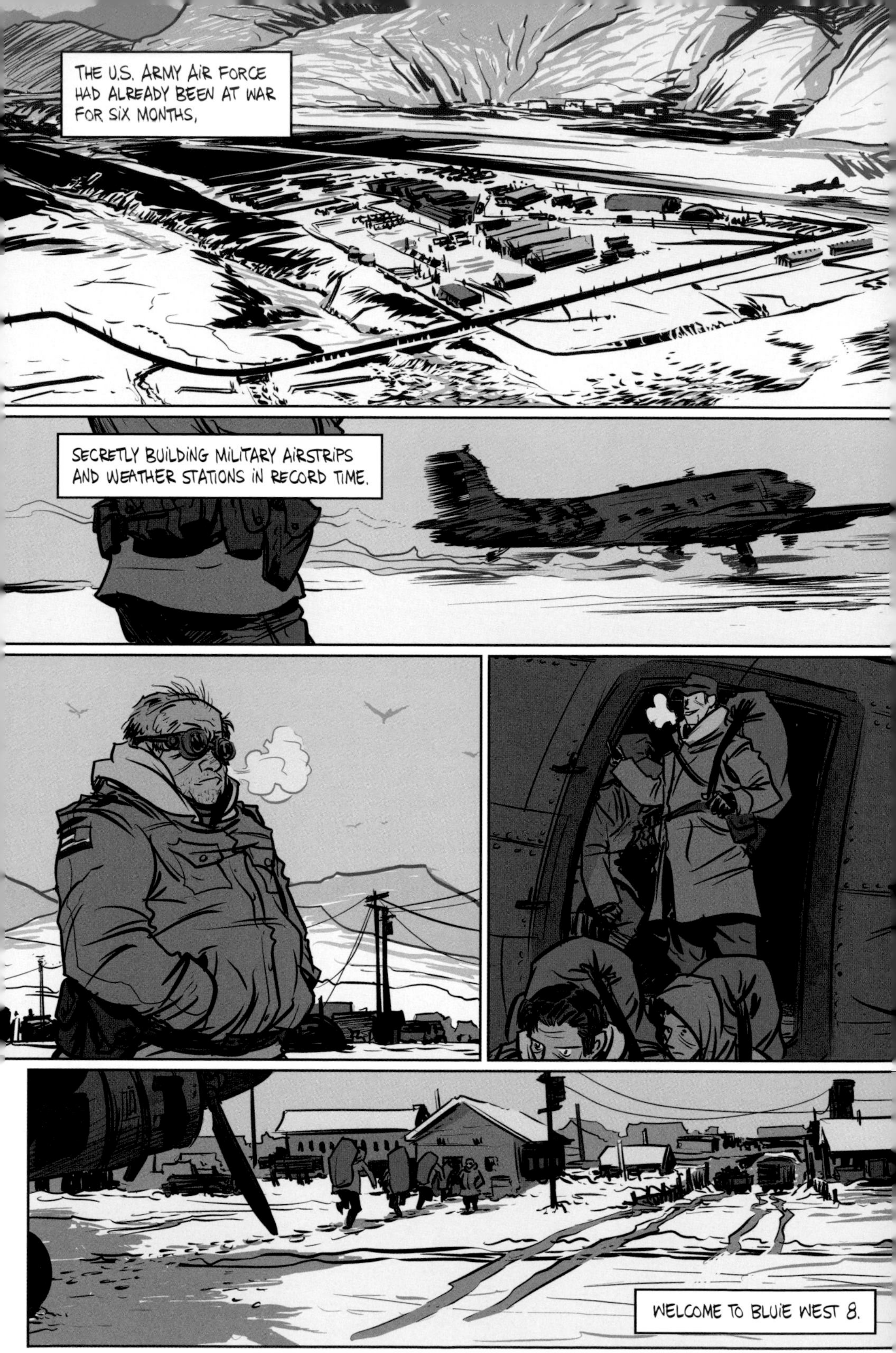
THE U.S. ARMY AIR FORCE HAD ALREADY BEEN AT WAR FOR SIX MONTHS,
SECRETLY BUILDING MILITARY AIRSTRIPS AND WEATHER STATIONS IN RECORD TIME.
WELCOME TO BLUIE WEST 8.

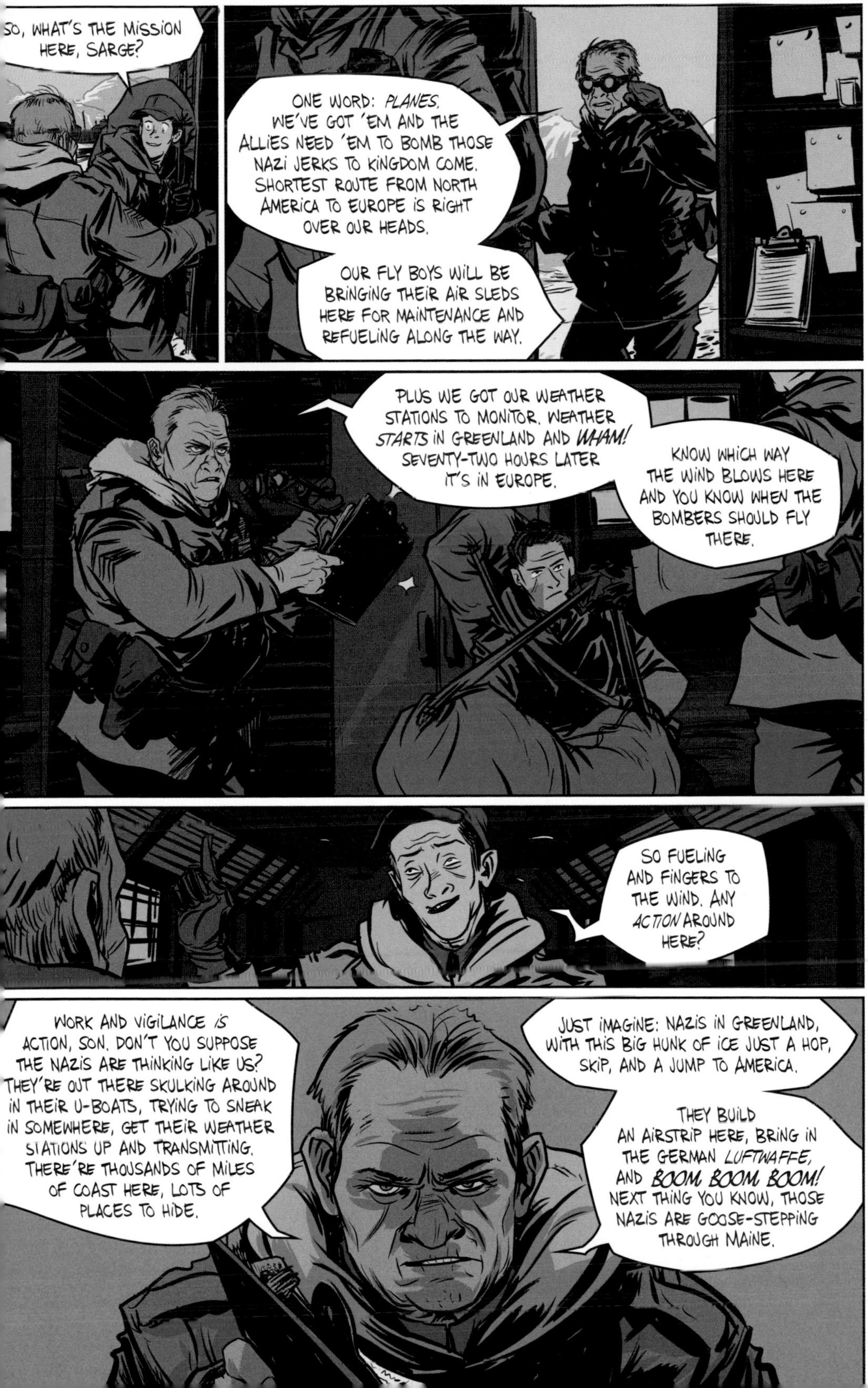
SO, WHAT'S THE MISSION HERE, SARGE?
ONE WORD: *PLANES.* WE'VE GOT 'EM AND THE ALLIES NEED 'EM TO BOMB THOSE NAZI JERKS TO KINGDOM COME. SHORTEST ROUTE FROM NORTH AMERICA TO EUROPE IS RIGHT OVER OUR HEADS.
OUR FLY BOYS WILL BE BRINGING THEIR AIR SLEDS HERE FOR MAINTENANCE AND REFUELING ALONG THE WAY.
PLUS WE GOT OUR WEATHER STATIONS TO MONITOR. WEATHER *STARTS* IN GREENLAND AND *WHAM!* SEVENTY-TWO HOURS LATER IT'S IN EUROPE.
KNOW WHICH WAY THE WIND BLOWS HERE AND YOU KNOW WHEN THE BOMBERS SHOULD FLY THERE.
SO FUELING AND FINGERS TO THE WIND. ANY *ACTION* AROUND HERE?
WORK AND VIGILANCE *IS* ACTION, SON. DON'T YOU SUPPOSE THE NAZIS ARE THINKING LIKE US? THEY'RE OUT THERE SKULKING AROUND IN THEIR U-BOATS, TRYING TO SNEAK IN SOMEWHERE, GET THEIR WEATHER STATIONS UP AND TRANSMITTING. THERE'RE THOUSANDS OF MILES OF COAST HERE, LOTS OF PLACES TO HIDE.
JUST IMAGINE: NAZIS IN GREENLAND, WITH THIS BIG HUNK OF ICE JUST A HOP, SKIP, AND A JUMP TO AMERICA.
THEY BUILD AN AIRSTRIP HERE, BRING IN THE GERMAN *LUFTWAFFE,* AND *BOOM BOOM BOOM!* NEXT THING YOU KNOW, THOSE NAZIS ARE GOOSE-STEPPING THROUGH MAINE.

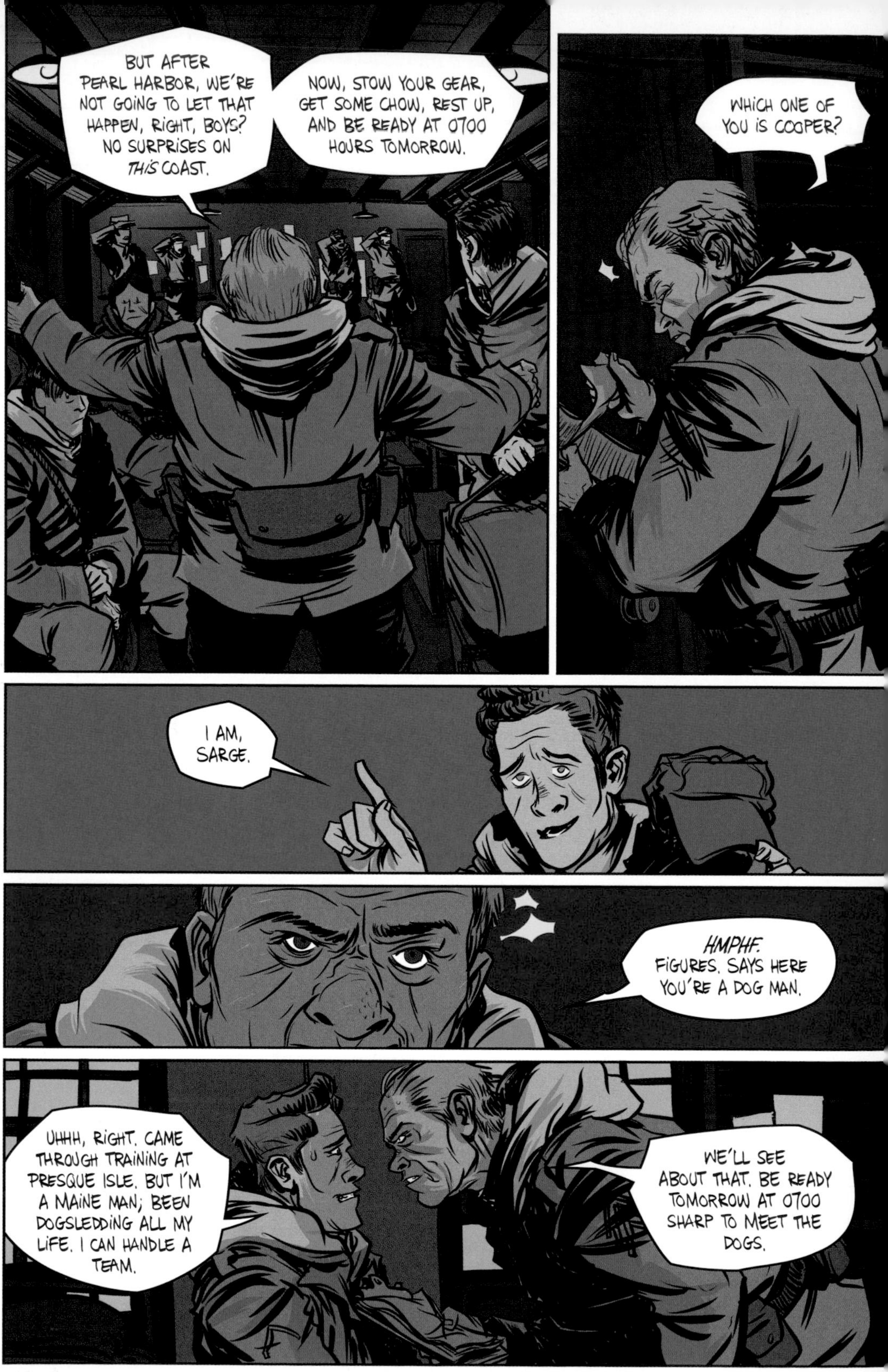
BUT AFTER PEARL HARBOR, WE'RE NOT GOING TO LET THAT HAPPEN, RIGHT, BOYS? NO SURPRISES ON *THIS* COAST.
NOW, STOW YOUR GEAR, GET SOME CHOW, REST UP, AND BE READY AT 0700 HOURS TOMORROW.
WHICH ONE OF YOU IS COOPER?
I AM, SARGE.
HMPHF. FIGURES. SAYS HERE YOU'RE A DOG MAN.
UHHH, RIGHT. CAME THROUGH TRAINING AT PRESQUE ISLE. BUT I'M A MAINE MAN; BEEN DOGSLEDDING ALL MY LIFE. I CAN HANDLE A TEAM.
WE'LL SEE ABOUT THAT. BE READY TOMORROW AT 0700 SHARP TO MEET THE DOGS.

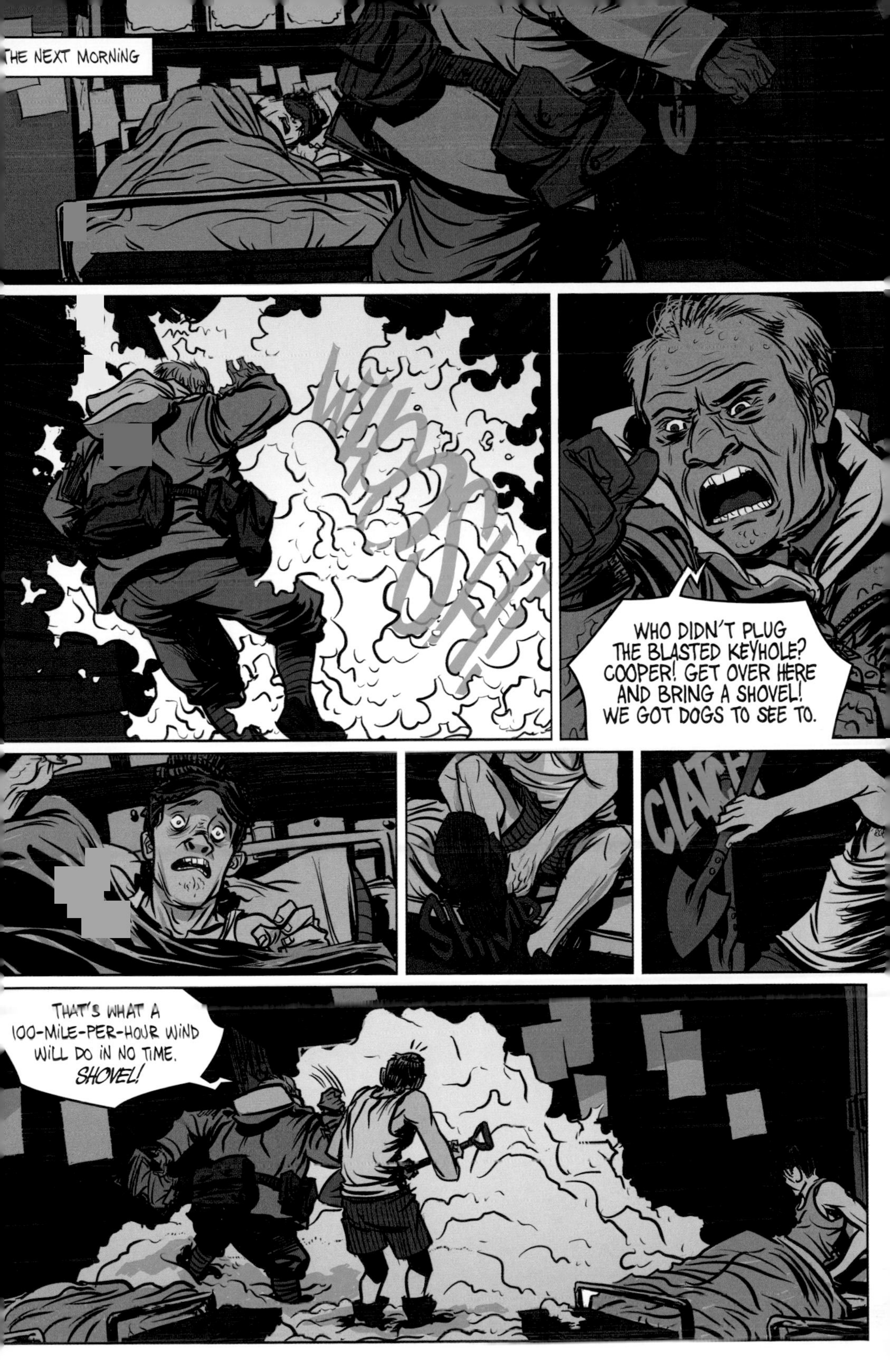
THE NEXT MORNING
WHO DIDN'T PLUG THE BLASTED KEYHOLE? COOPER! GET OVER HERE AND BRING A SHOVEL! WE GOT DOGS TO SEE TO.
THAT'S WHAT A 100-MILE-PER-HOUR WIND WILL DO IN NO TIME. SHOVEL!

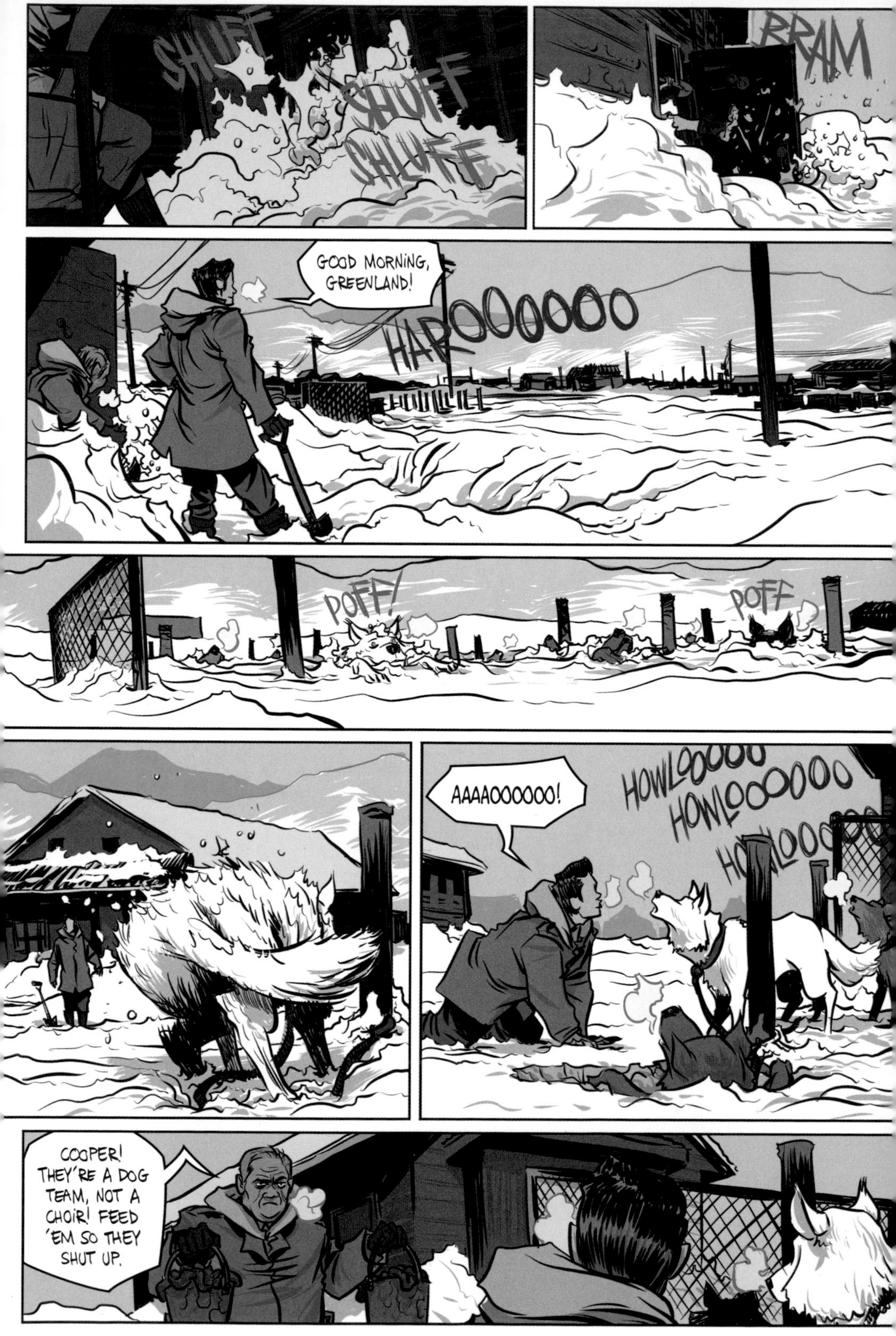
SHUFF
SHUFF
SHUFF
BRAM
GOOD MORNING, GREENLAND!
HAROOOOOOO
POFF!
POFF
AAAAOOOOOO!
HOWLOOOOO
HOWLOOOOOO
HOWLOOO
COOPER! THEY'RE A DOG TEAM, NOT A CHOIR! FEED 'EM SO THEY SHUT UP.

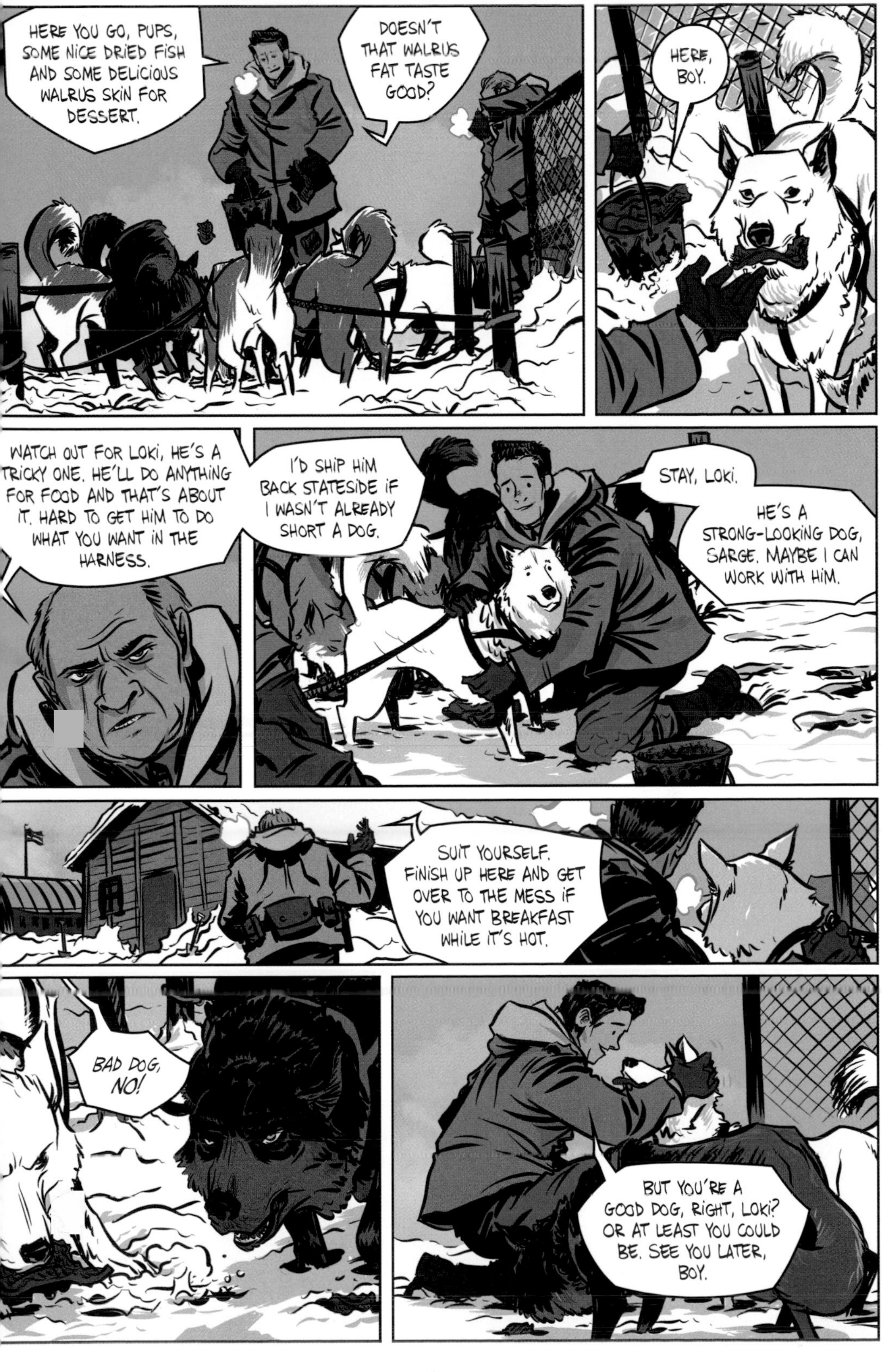
HERE YOU GO, PUPS, SOME NICE DRIED FISH AND SOME DELICIOUS WALRUS SKIN FOR DESSERT.
DOESN'T THAT WALRUS FAT TASTE GOOD?
HERE, BOY.
WATCH OUT FOR LOKI, HE'S A TRICKY ONE. HE'LL DO ANYTHING FOR FOOD AND THAT'S ABOUT IT. HARD TO GET HIM TO DO WHAT YOU WANT IN THE HARNESS.
I'D SHIP HIM BACK STATESIDE IF I WASN'T ALREADY SHORT A DOG.
STAY, LOKI.
HE'S A STRONG-LOOKING DOG, SARGE. MAYBE I CAN WORK WITH HIM.
SUIT YOURSELF. FINISH UP HERE AND GET OVER TO THE MESS IF YOU WANT BREAKFAST WHILE IT'S HOT.
BAD DOG, NO!
BUT YOU'RE A GOOD DOG, RIGHT, LOKI? OR AT LEAST YOU COULD BE. SEE YOU LATER, BOY.

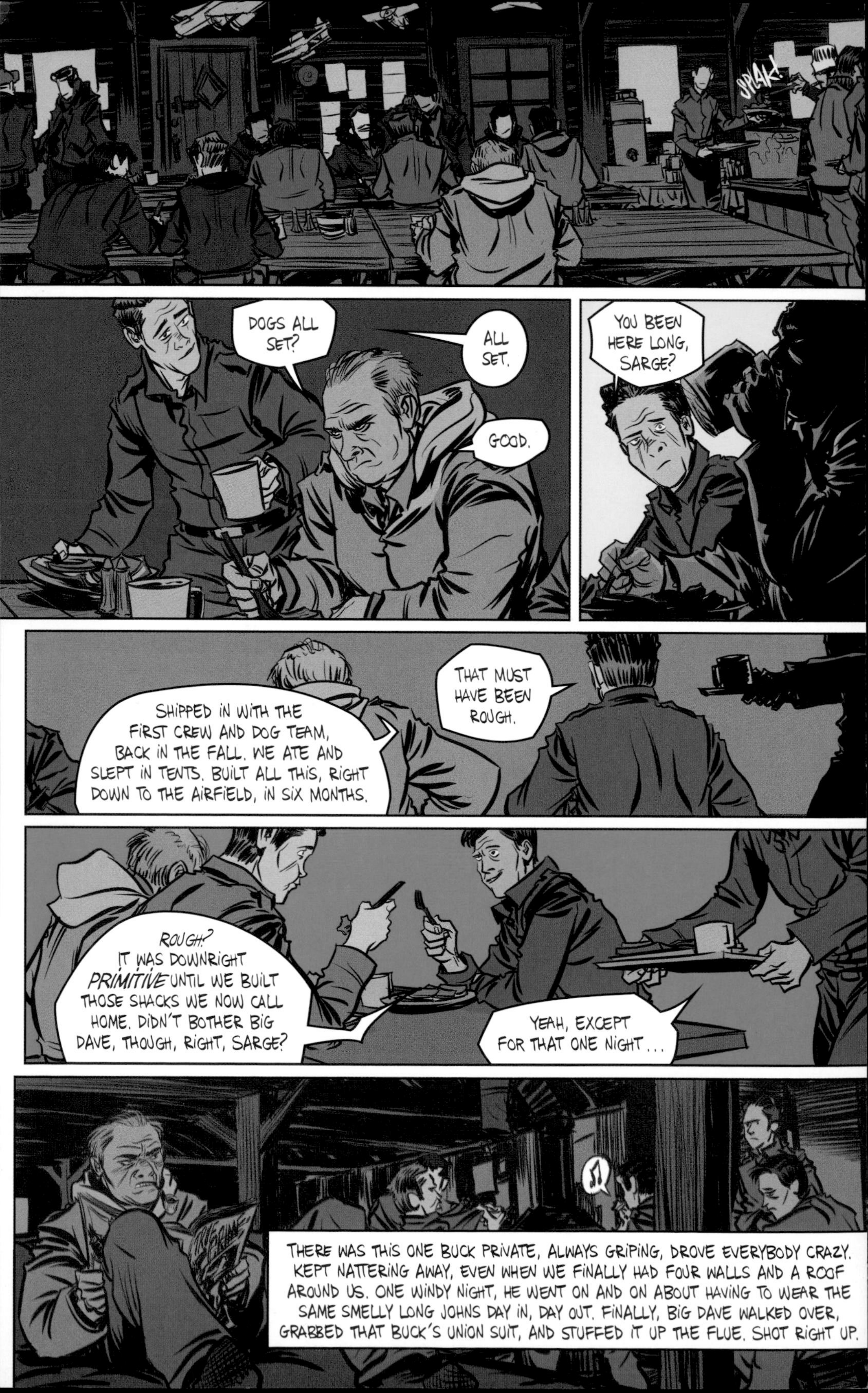
SPLAK!
DOGS ALL SET?
ALL SET.
GOOD.
YOU BEEN HERE LONG, SARGE?
SHIPPED IN WITH THE FIRST CREW AND DOG TEAM, BACK IN THE FALL. WE ATE AND SLEPT IN TENTS. BUILT ALL THIS, RIGHT DOWN TO THE AIRFIELD, IN SIX MONTHS.
THAT MUST HAVE BEEN ROUGH.
ROUGH? IT WAS DOWNRIGHT PRIMITIVE UNTIL WE BUILT THOSE SHACKS WE NOW CALL HOME. DIDN'T BOTHER BIG DAVE, THOUGH, RIGHT, SARGE?
YEAH, EXCEPT FOR THAT ONE NIGHT . . .
THERE WAS THIS ONE BUCK PRIVATE, ALWAYS GRIPING, DROVE EVERYBODY CRAZY. KEPT NATTERING AWAY, EVEN WHEN WE FINALLY HAD FOUR WALLS AND A ROOF AROUND US. ONE WINDY NIGHT, HE WENT ON AND ON ABOUT HAVING TO WEAR THE SAME SMELLY LONG JOHNS DAY IN, DAY OUT. FINALLY, BIG DAVE WALKED OVER, GRABBED THAT BUCK'S UNION SUIT, AND STUFFED IT UP THE FLUE. SHOT RIGHT UP.

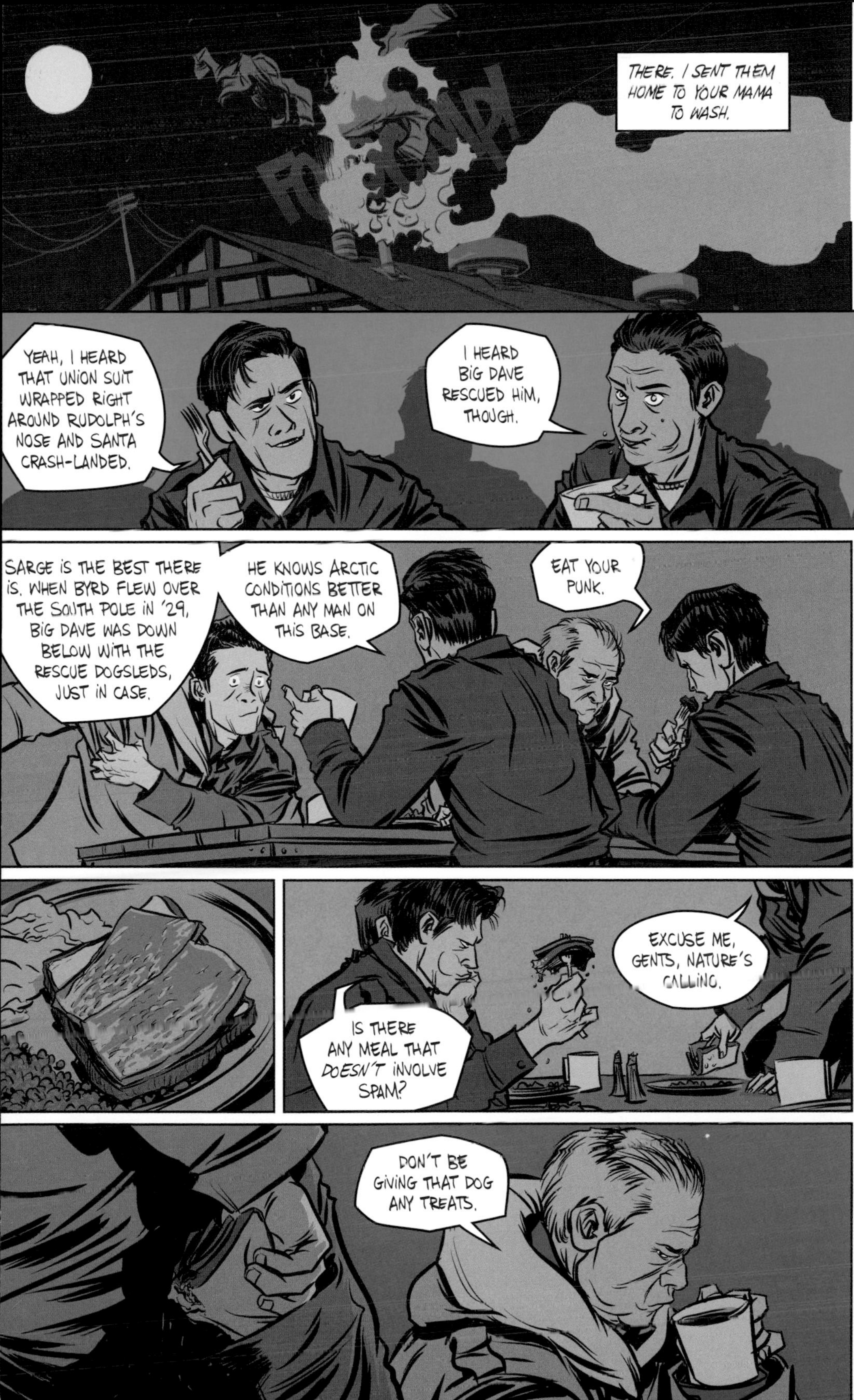
THERE. I SENT THEM HOME TO YOUR MAMA TO WASH.
FOOMP
YEAH, I HEARD THAT UNION SUIT WRAPPED RIGHT AROUND RUDOLPH'S NOSE AND SANTA CRASH-LANDED.
I HEARD BIG DAVE RESCUED HIM, THOUGH.
SARGE IS THE BEST THERE IS. WHEN BYRD FLEW OVER THE SOUTH POLE IN '29, BIG DAVE WAS DOWN BELOW WITH THE RESCUE DOGSLEDS, JUST IN CASE.
HE KNOWS ARCTIC CONDITIONS BETTER THAN ANY MAN ON THIS BASE.
EAT YOUR PUNK.
IS THERE ANY MEAL THAT DOESN'T INVOLVE SPAM?
EXCUSE ME, GENTS, NATURE'S CALLING.
DON'T BE GIVING THAT DOG ANY TREATS.

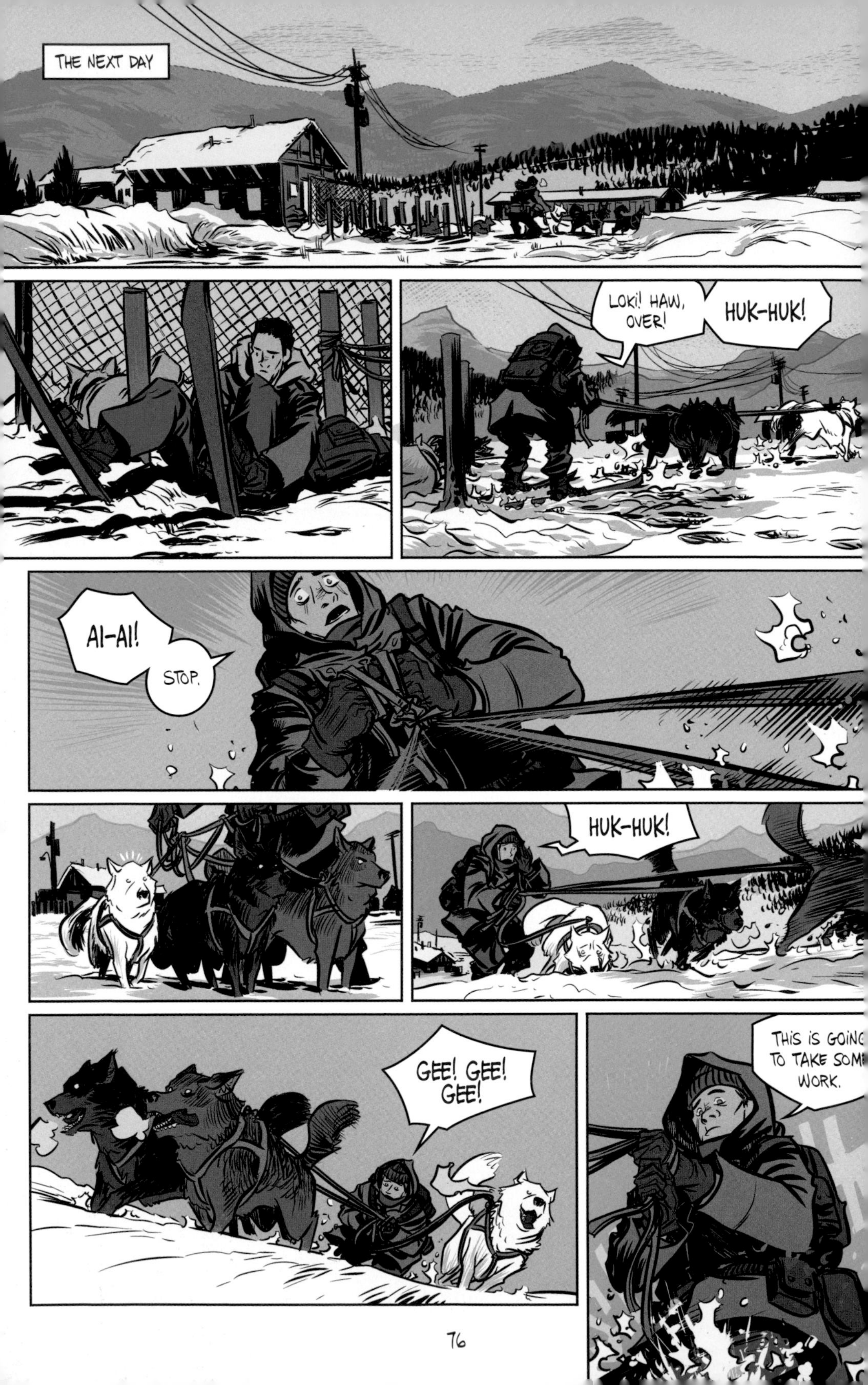
THE NEXT DAY
LOKI! HAW, OVER!
HUK-HUK!
AI-AI!
STOP.
HUK-HUK!
GEE! GEE! GEE!
THIS IS GOING TO TAKE SOME WORK.

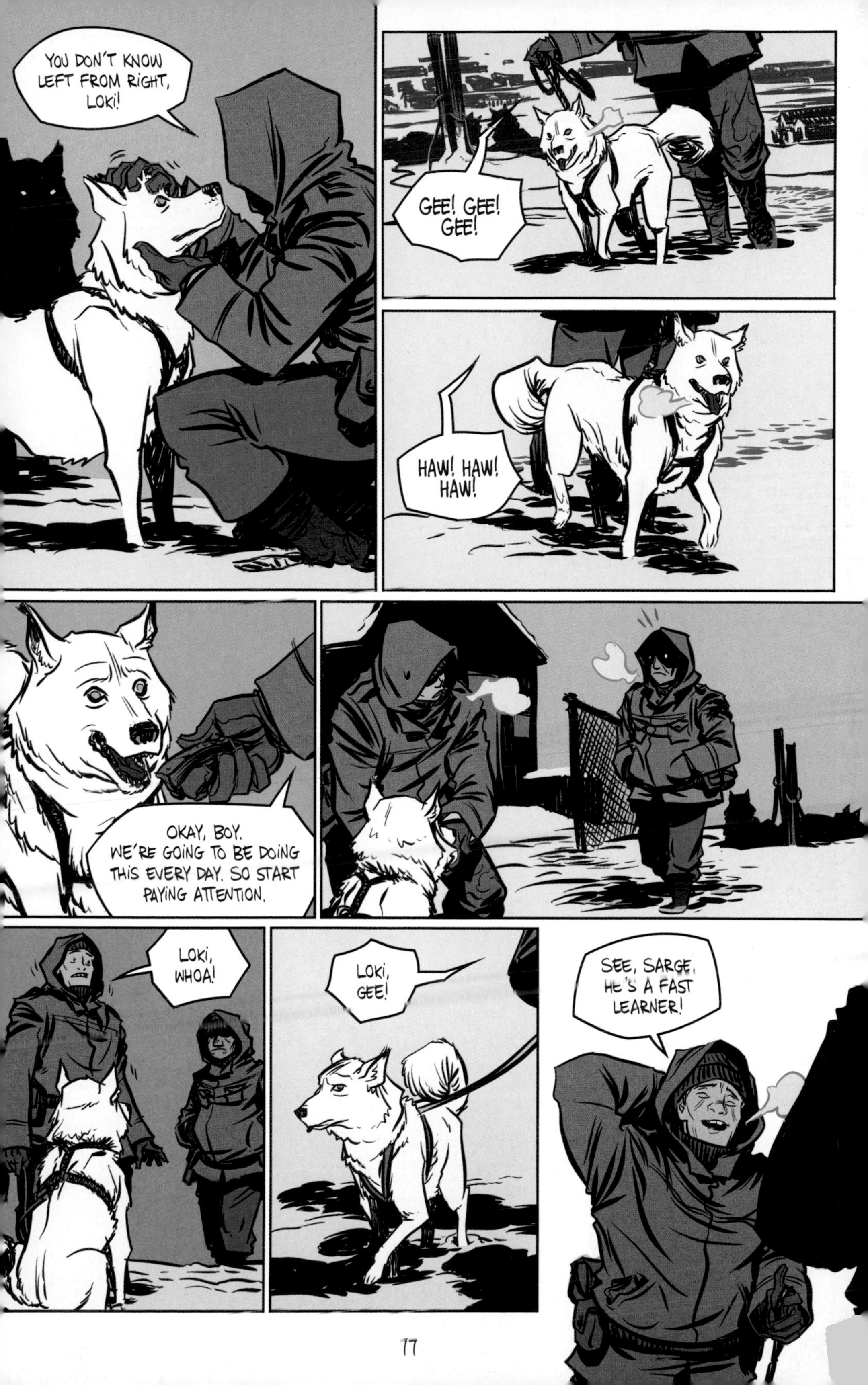
YOU DON'T KNOW LEFT FROM RIGHT, LOKI!
GEE! GEE! GEE!
HAW! HAW! HAW!
OKAY, BOY. WE'RE GOING TO BE DOING THIS EVERY DAY. SO START PAYING ATTENTION.
LOKI, WHOA!
LOKI, GEE!
SEE, SARGE, HE'S A FAST LEARNER!

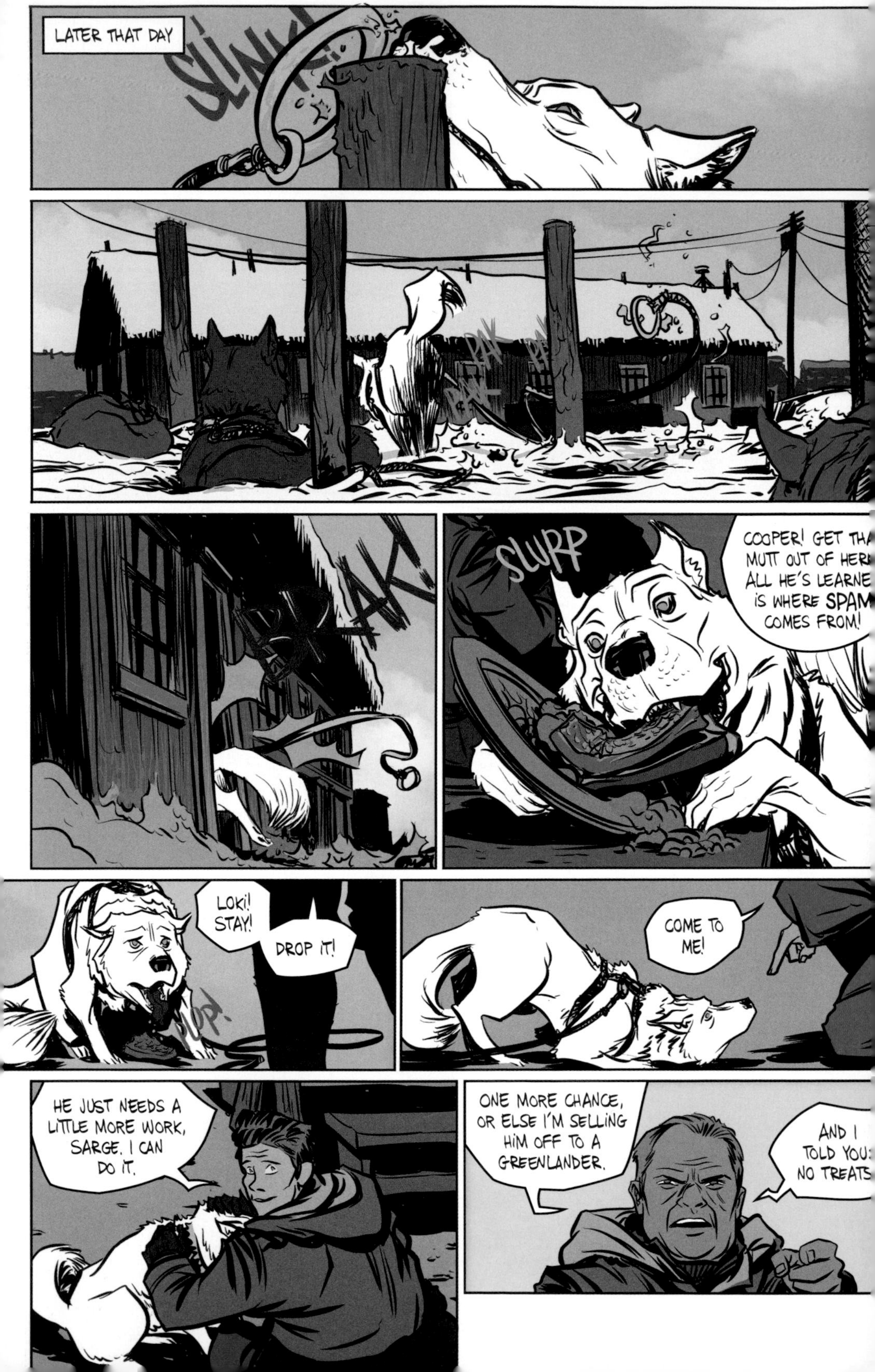
LATER THAT DAY
SLINK!
PAK PAK
BRAK!
SLURP
COOPER! GET THA MUTT OUT OF HER ALL HE'S LEARNE IS WHERE SPAM COMES FROM!
LOKI! STAY!
DROP IT!
PLOP!
COME TO ME!
HE JUST NEEDS A LITTLE MORE WORK, SARGE. I CAN DO IT.
ONE MORE CHANCE, OR ELSE I'M SELLING HIM OFF TO A GREENLANDER.
AND I TOLD YOU: NO TREATS

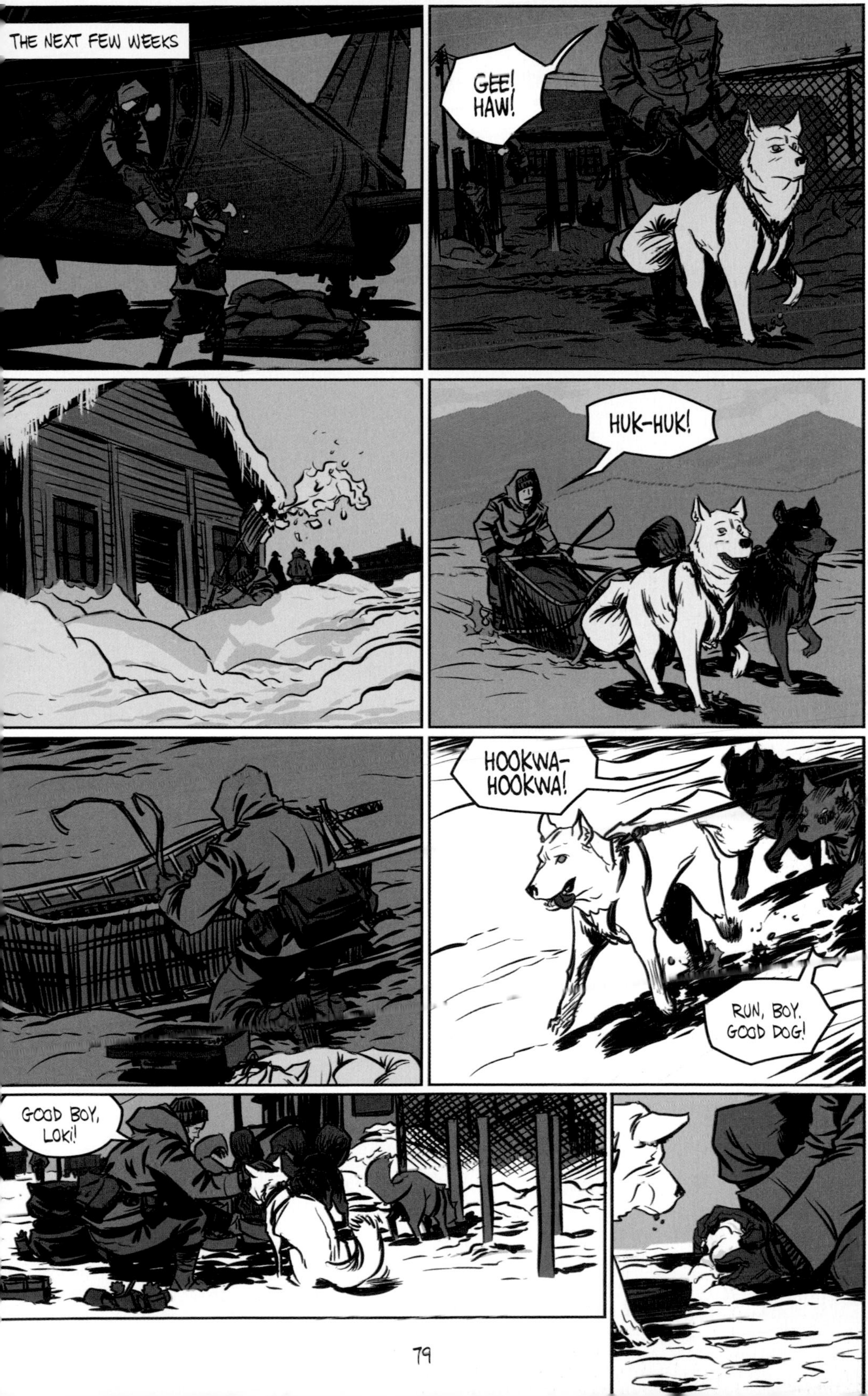
THE NEXT FEW WEEKS
GEE! HAW!
HUK-HUK!
HOOKWA-HOOKWA!
RUN, BOY. GOOD DOG!
GOOD BOY, LOKI!

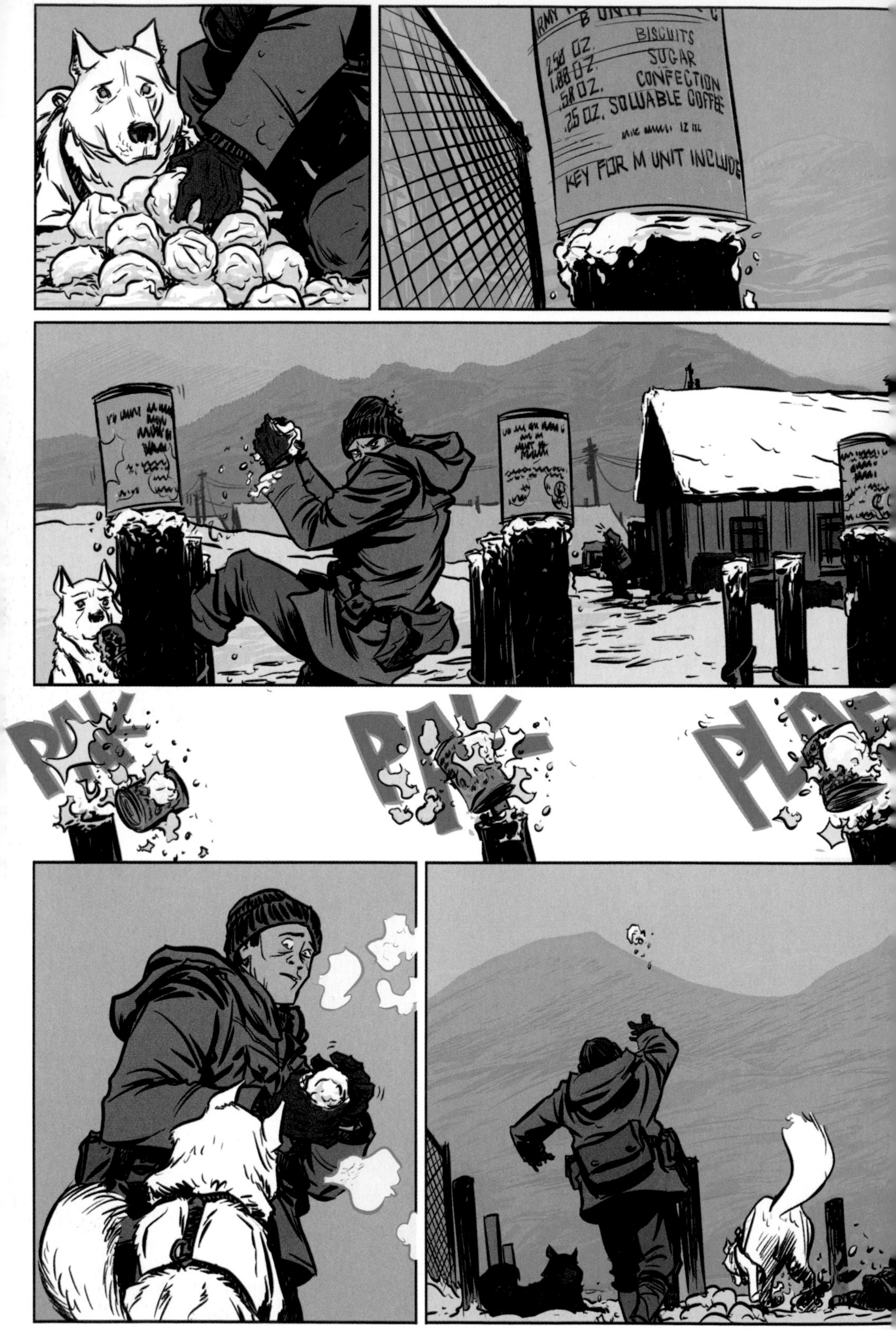
B UNIT
BISCUITS
SUGAR
CONFECTION
.25 OZ. SOLUABLE COFFEE
KEY FOR M UNIT INCLUDE
PAK
PAK

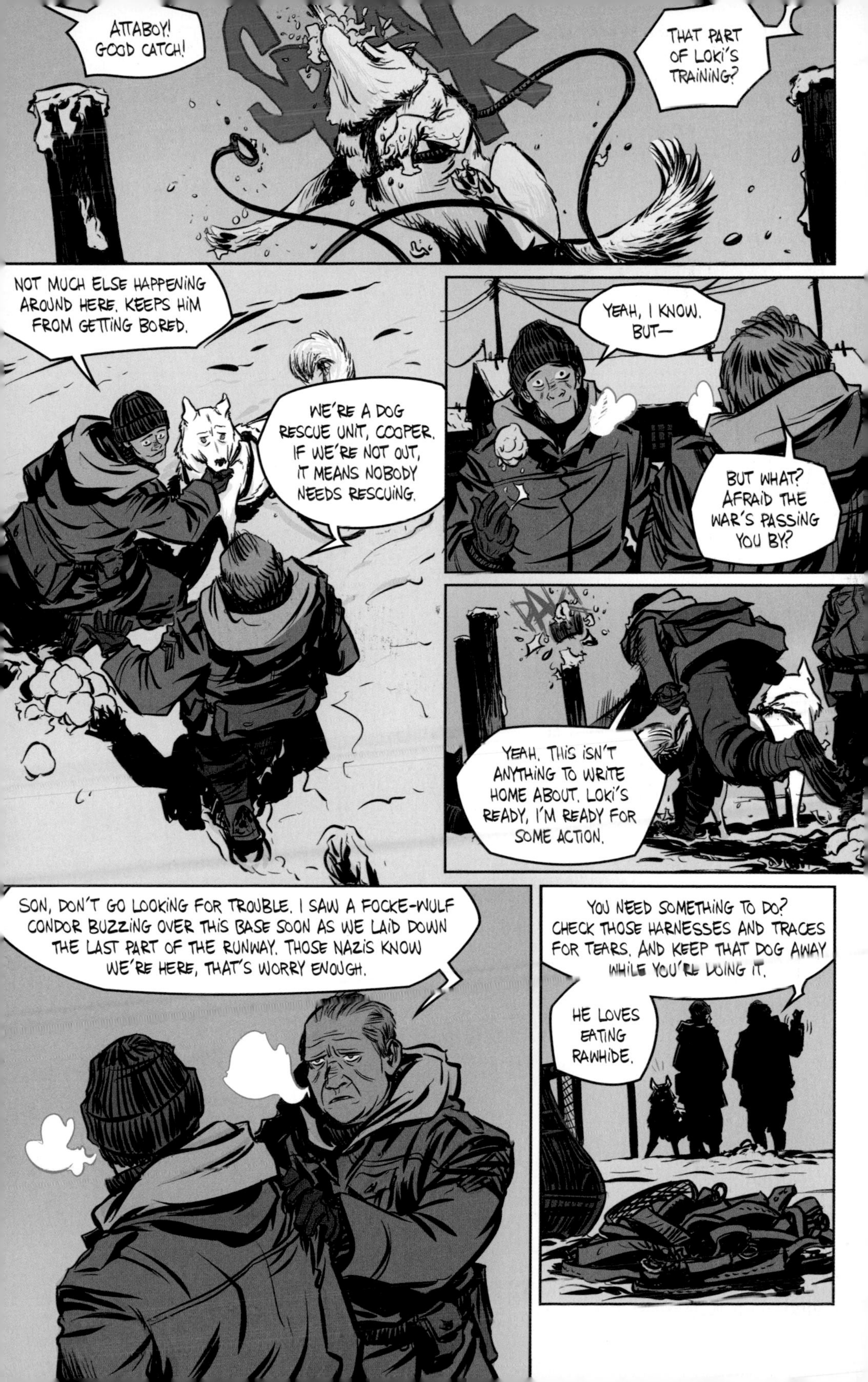
ATTABOY! GOOD CATCH!
THAT PART OF LOKI'S TRAINING?
NOT MUCH ELSE HAPPENING AROUND HERE. KEEPS HIM FROM GETTING BORED.
WE'RE A DOG RESCUE UNIT, COOPER. IF WE'RE NOT OUT, IT MEANS NOBODY NEEDS RESCUING.
YEAH, I KNOW. BUT—
BUT WHAT? AFRAID THE WAR'S PASSING YOU BY?
YEAH. THIS ISN'T ANYTHING TO WRITE HOME ABOUT. LOKI'S READY, I'M READY FOR SOME ACTION.
SON, DON'T GO LOOKING FOR TROUBLE. I SAW A FOCKE-WULF CONDOR BUZZING OVER THIS BASE SOON AS WE LAID DOWN THE LAST PART OF THE RUNWAY. THOSE NAZIS KNOW WE'RE HERE, THAT'S WORRY ENOUGH.
YOU NEED SOMETHING TO DO? CHECK THOSE HARNESSES AND TRACES FOR TEARS. AND KEEP THAT DOG AWAY WHILE YOU'RE DOING IT.
HE LOVES EATING RAWHIDE.

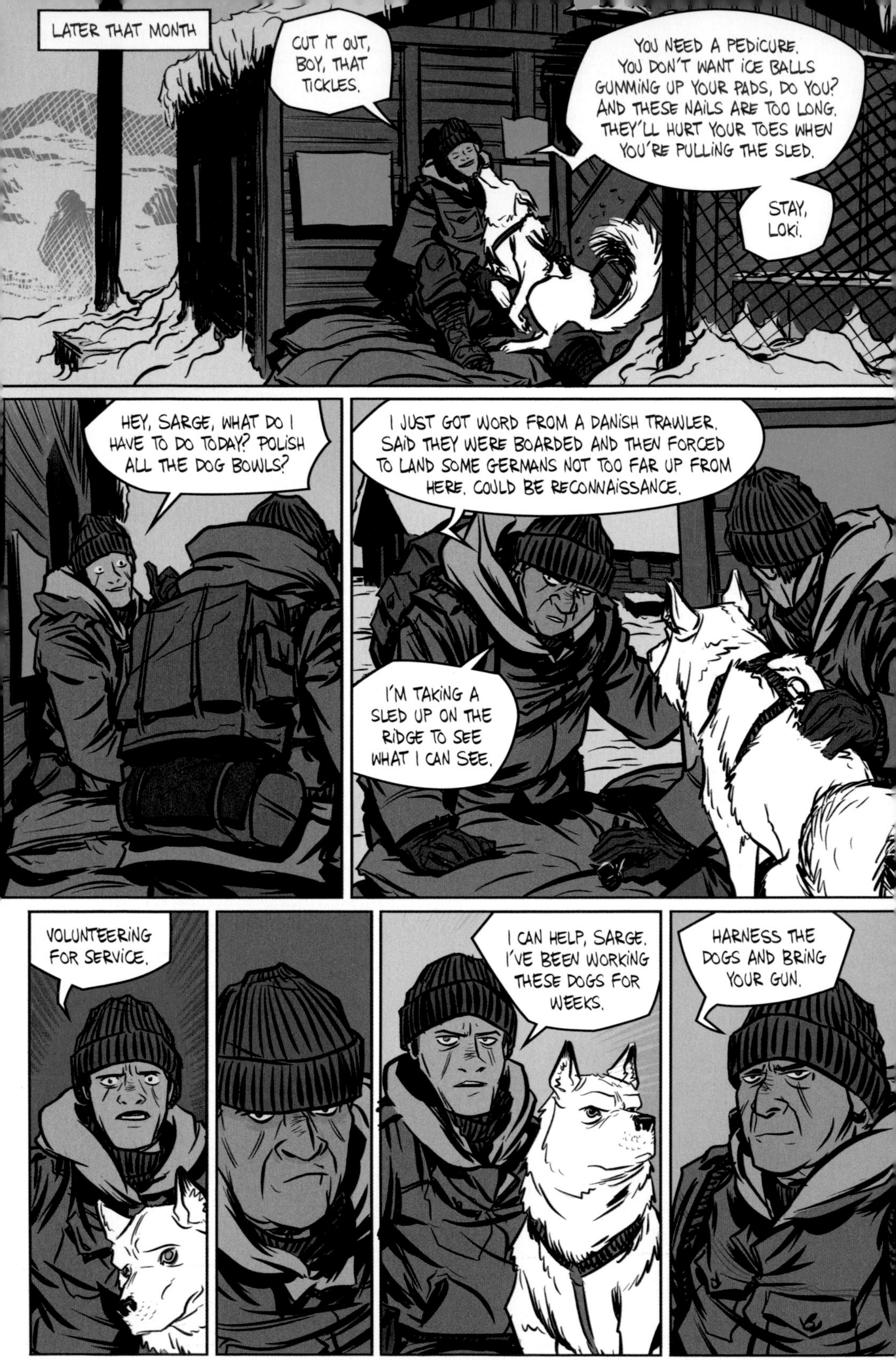
LATER THAT MONTH
CUT IT OUT, BOY, THAT TICKLES.
YOU NEED A PEDICURE. YOU DON'T WANT ICE BALLS GUMMING UP YOUR PADS, DO YOU? AND THESE NAILS ARE TOO LONG. THEY'LL HURT YOUR TOES WHEN YOU'RE PULLING THE SLED.
STAY, LOKI.
HEY, SARGE, WHAT DO I HAVE TO DO TODAY? POLISH ALL THE DOG BOWLS?
I JUST GOT WORD FROM A DANISH TRAWLER. SAID THEY WERE BOARDED AND THEN FORCED TO LAND SOME GERMANS NOT TOO FAR UP FROM HERE. COULD BE RECONNAISSANCE.
I'M TAKING A SLED UP ON THE RIDGE TO SEE WHAT I CAN SEE.
VOLUNTEERING FOR SERVICE.
I CAN HELP, SARGE. I'VE BEEN WORKING THESE DOGS FOR WEEKS.
HARNESS THE DOGS AND BRING YOUR GUN.

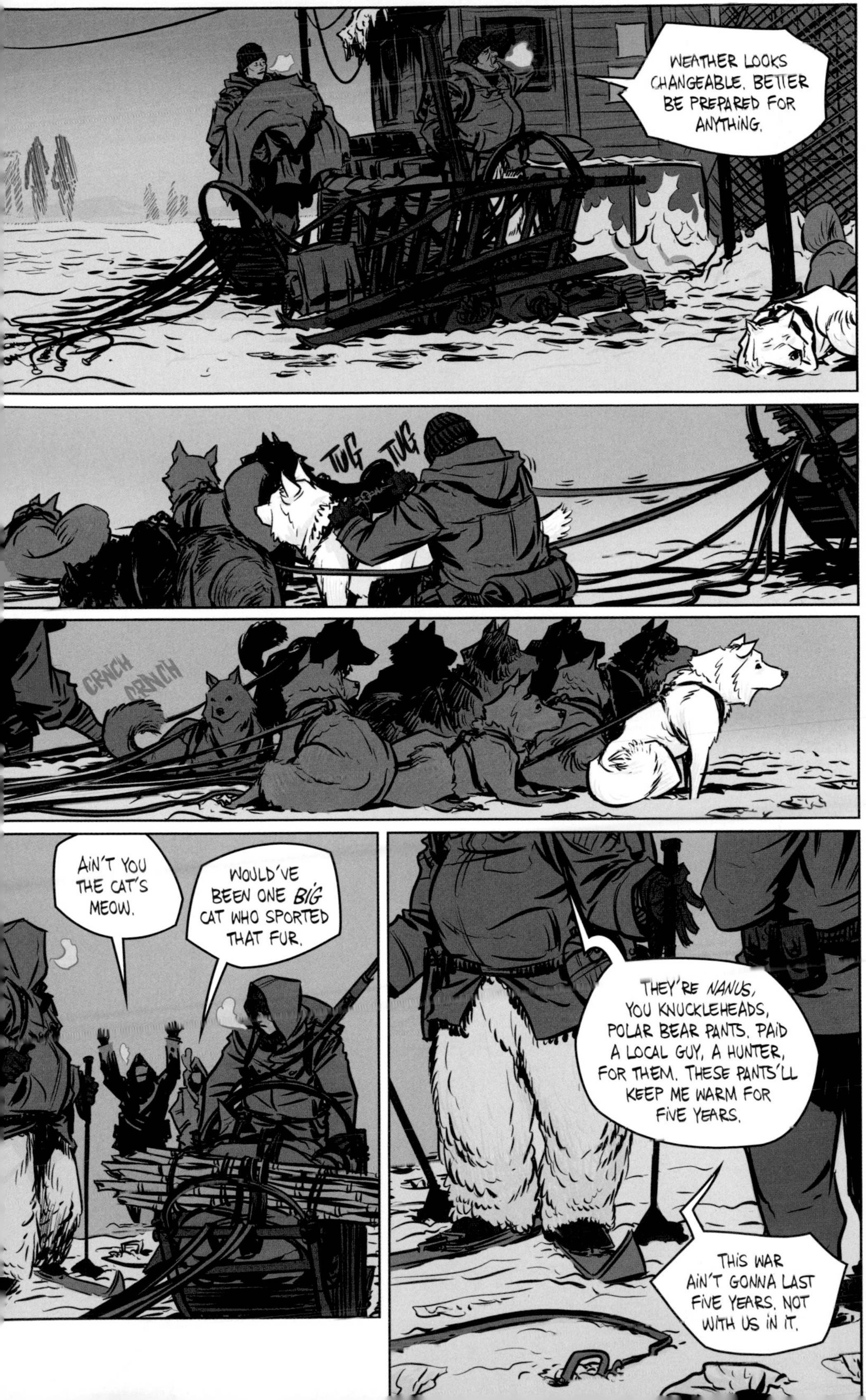
WEATHER LOOKS CHANGEABLE. BETTER BE PREPARED FOR ANYTHING.
TUG TUG
CRNCH CRNCH
AIN'T YOU THE CAT'S MEOW.
WOULD'VE BEEN ONE BIG CAT WHO SPORTED THAT FUR.
THEY'RE NANUS, YOU KNUCKLEHEADS, POLAR BEAR PANTS. PAID A LOCAL GUY, A HUNTER, FOR THEM. THESE PANTS'LL KEEP ME WARM FOR FIVE YEARS.
THIS WAR AIN'T GONNA LAST FIVE YEARS. NOT WITH US IN IT.

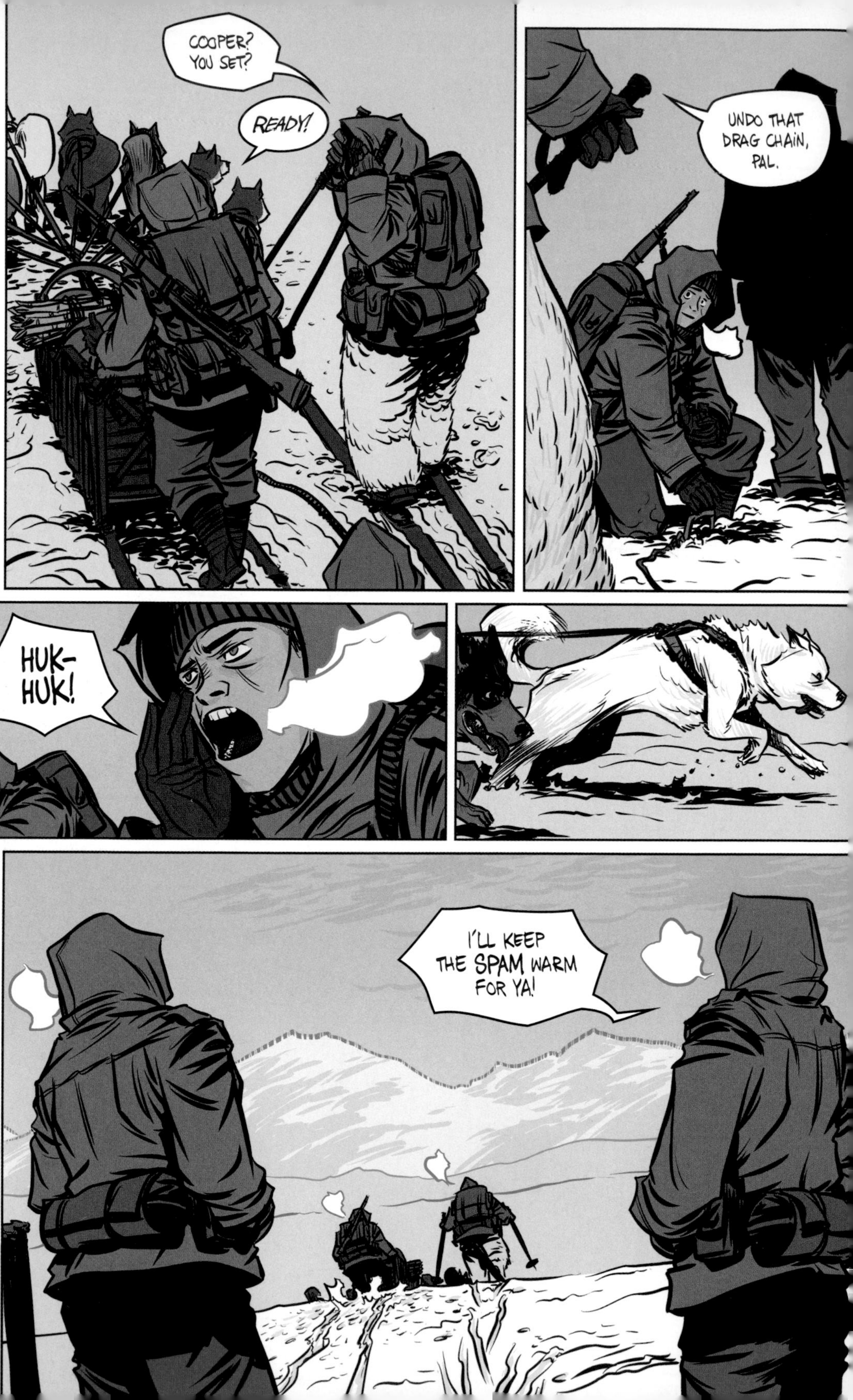
COOPER? YOU SET?
READY!
UNDO THAT DRAG CHAIN, PAL.
HUK-HUK!
I'LL KEEP THE SPAM WARM FOR YA!

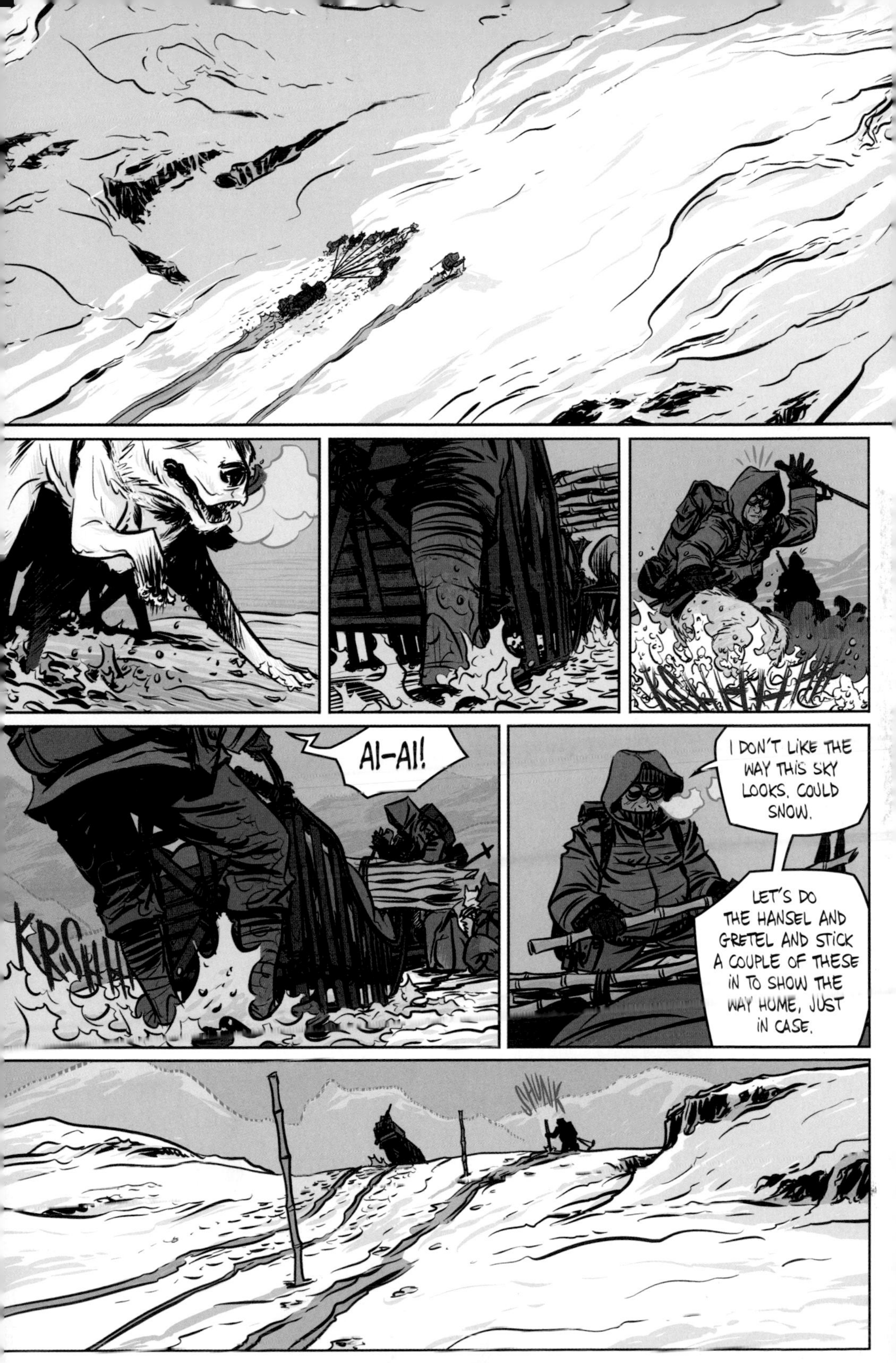
AI-AI!
KRSHHH
I DON'T LIKE THE WAY THIS SKY LOOKS. COULD SNOW.
LET'S DO THE HANSEL AND GRETEL AND STICK A COUPLE OF THESE IN TO SHOW THE WAY HOME, JUST IN CASE.
SHUNK

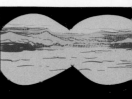

HUK-HUK!

WHOA!

GRRRR

GROWL

LOKI! *Ai-Ai!*
GET OVER,
BAD DOG.

BUT, SARGE,
THAT WASN'T LOKI,
IT WAS . . .

VWRRRR

QUIET!
WHAT'S THAT?

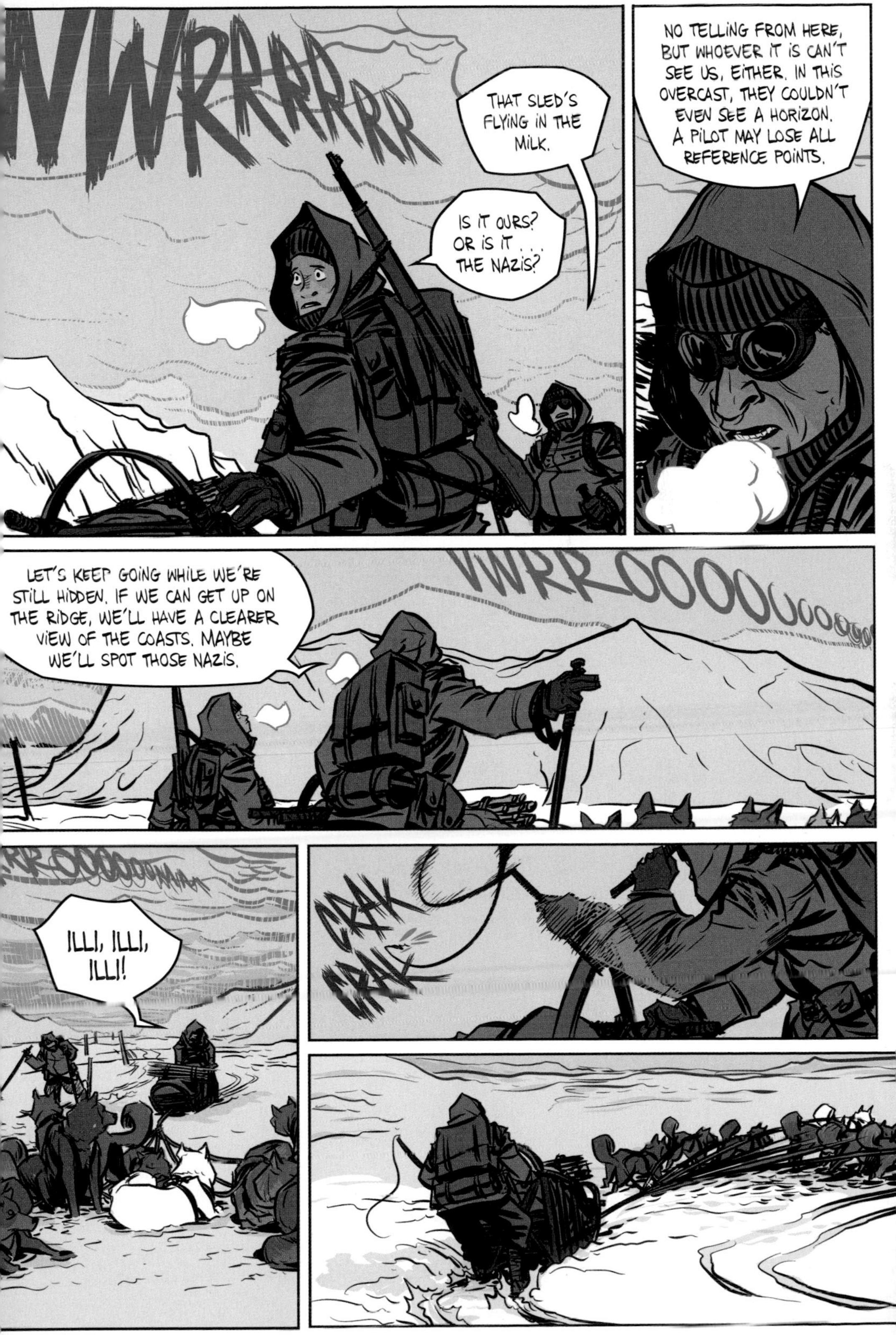
VWRRRRRRR
THAT SLED'S FLYING IN THE MILK.
IS IT OURS? OR IS IT . . . THE NAZIS?
NO TELLING FROM HERE, BUT WHOEVER IT IS CAN'T SEE US, EITHER. IN THIS OVERCAST, THEY COULDN'T EVEN SEE A HORIZON. A PILOT MAY LOSE ALL REFERENCE POINTS.
VWRROOOOOOOO
LET'S KEEP GOING WHILE WE'RE STILL HIDDEN. IF WE CAN GET UP ON THE RIDGE, WE'LL HAVE A CLEARER VIEW OF THE COASTS. MAYBE WE'LL SPOT THOSE NAZIS.
ILLI, ILLI, ILLI!
CRAK
CRAK

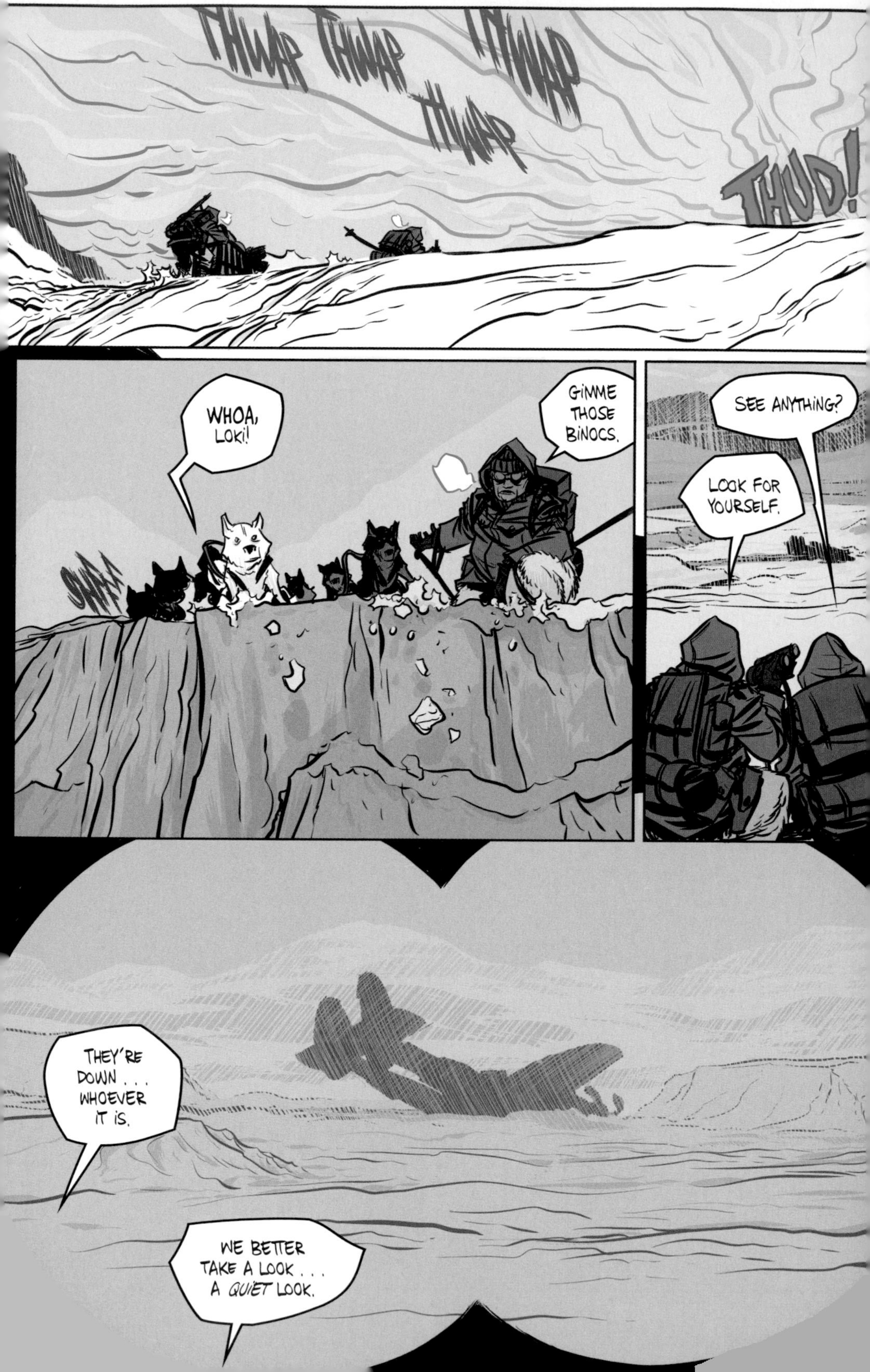
THWAP THWAP THWAP
THWAP
THUD!
WHOA, LOKI!
GIMME THOSE BINOCS.
SEE ANYTHING?
LOOK FOR YOURSELF.
THEY'RE DOWN . . . WHOEVER IT IS.
WE BETTER TAKE A LOOK . . . A *QUIET* LOOK.

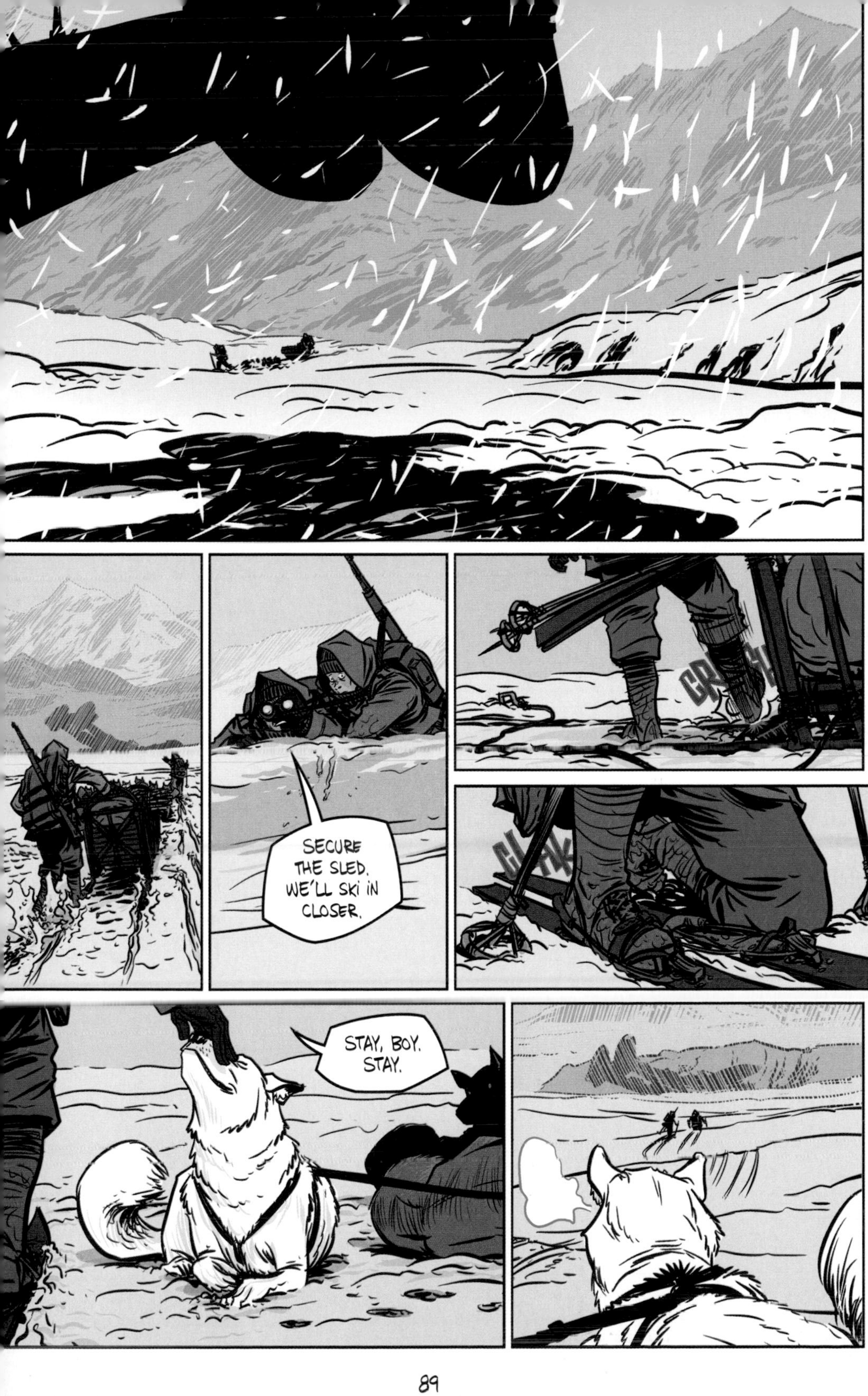
SECURE THE SLED. WE'LL SKI IN CLOSER.
STAY, BOY. STAY.

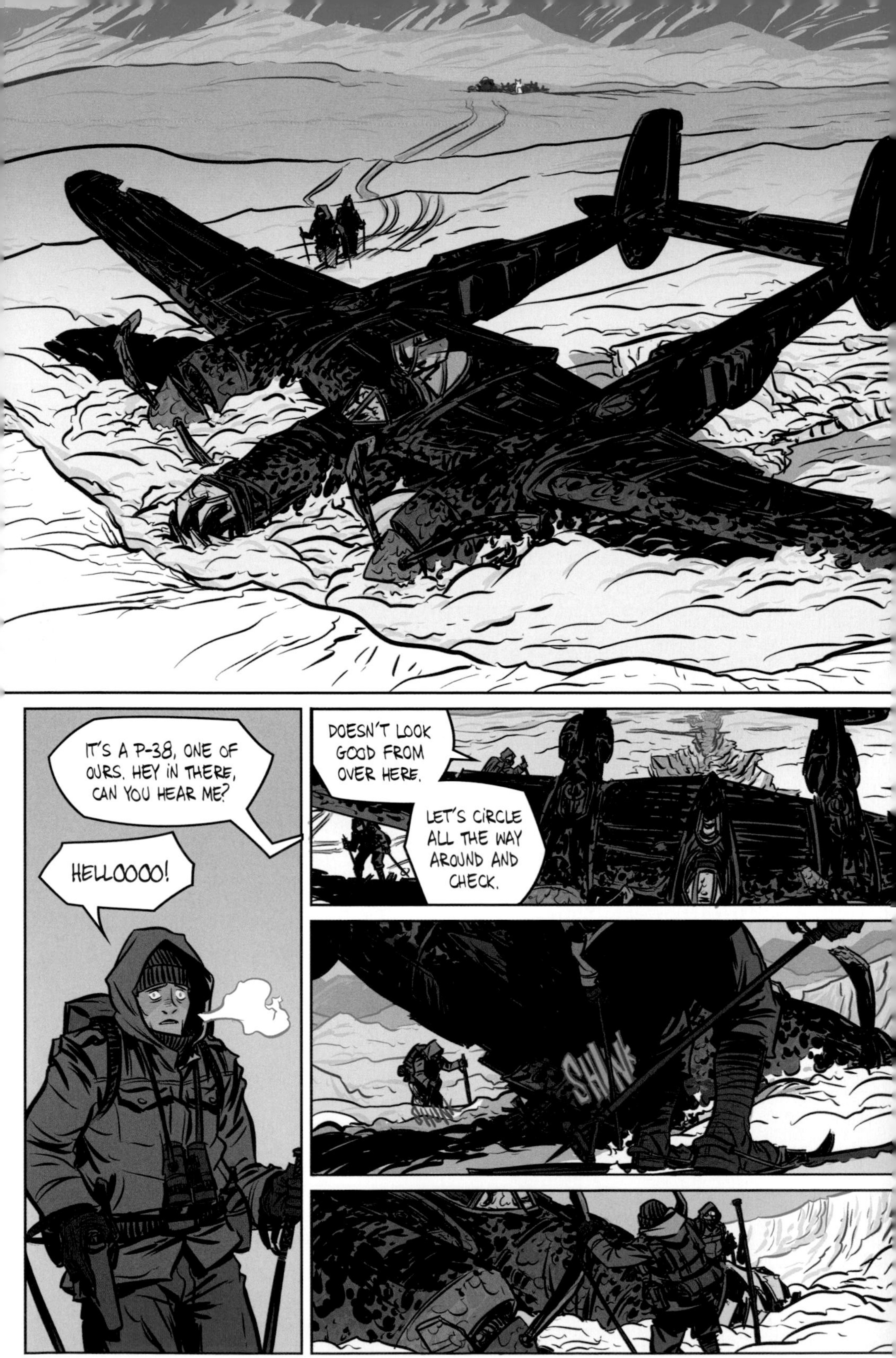
IT'S A P-38, ONE OF OURS. HEY IN THERE, CAN YOU HEAR ME?
HELLOOOO!
DOESN'T LOOK GOOD FROM OVER HERE.
LET'S CIRCLE ALL THE WAY AROUND AND CHECK.

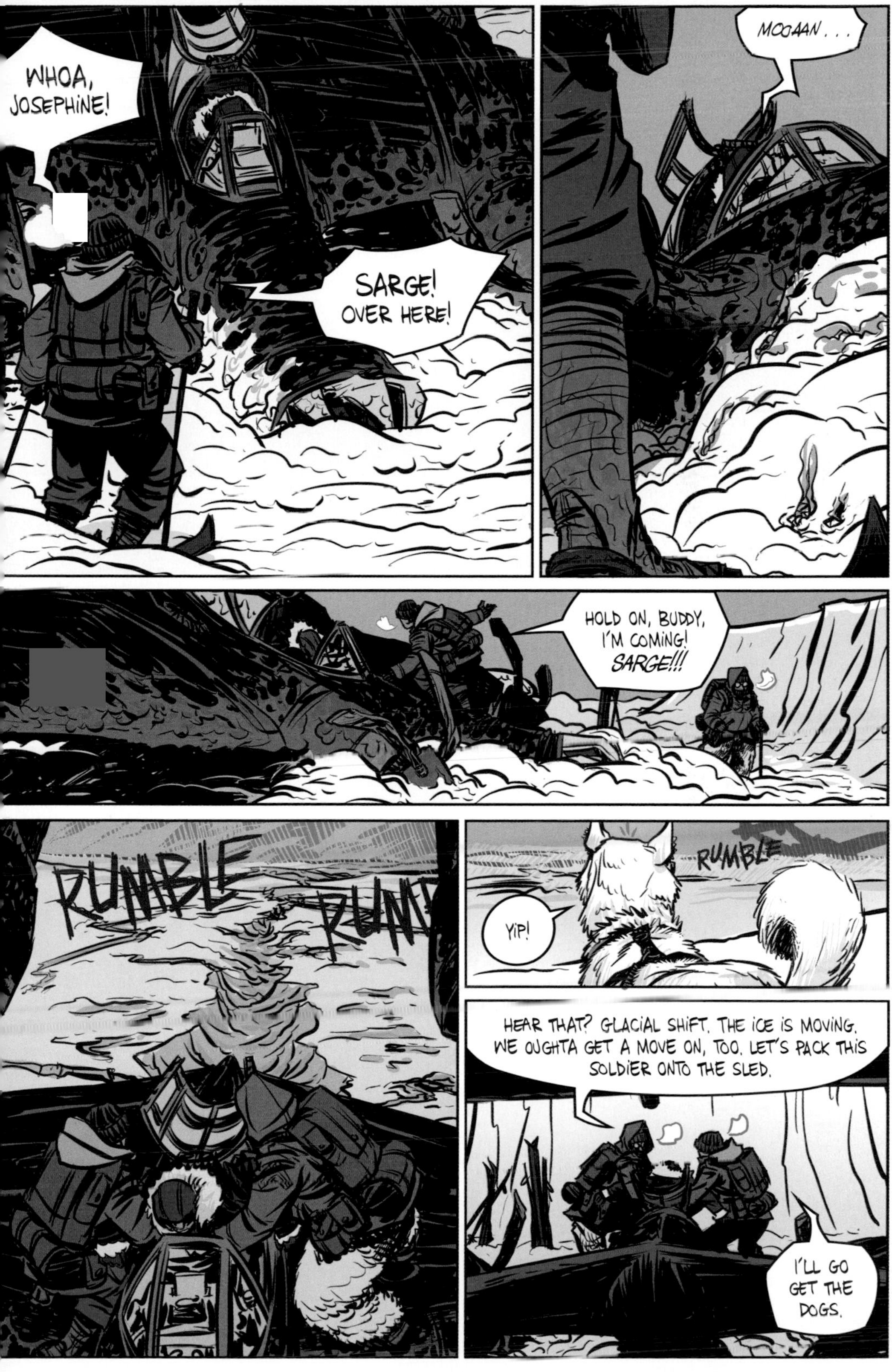
WHOA, JOSEPHINE!
MOOAAN . . .
SARGE! OVER HERE!
HOLD ON, BUDDY, I'M COMING! SARGE!!!
RUMBLE
RUMBLE
RUM
YIP!
HEAR THAT? GLACIAL SHIFT. THE ICE IS MOVING. WE OUGHTA GET A MOVE ON, TOO. LET'S PACK THIS SOLDIER ONTO THE SLED.
I'LL GO GET THE DOGS.

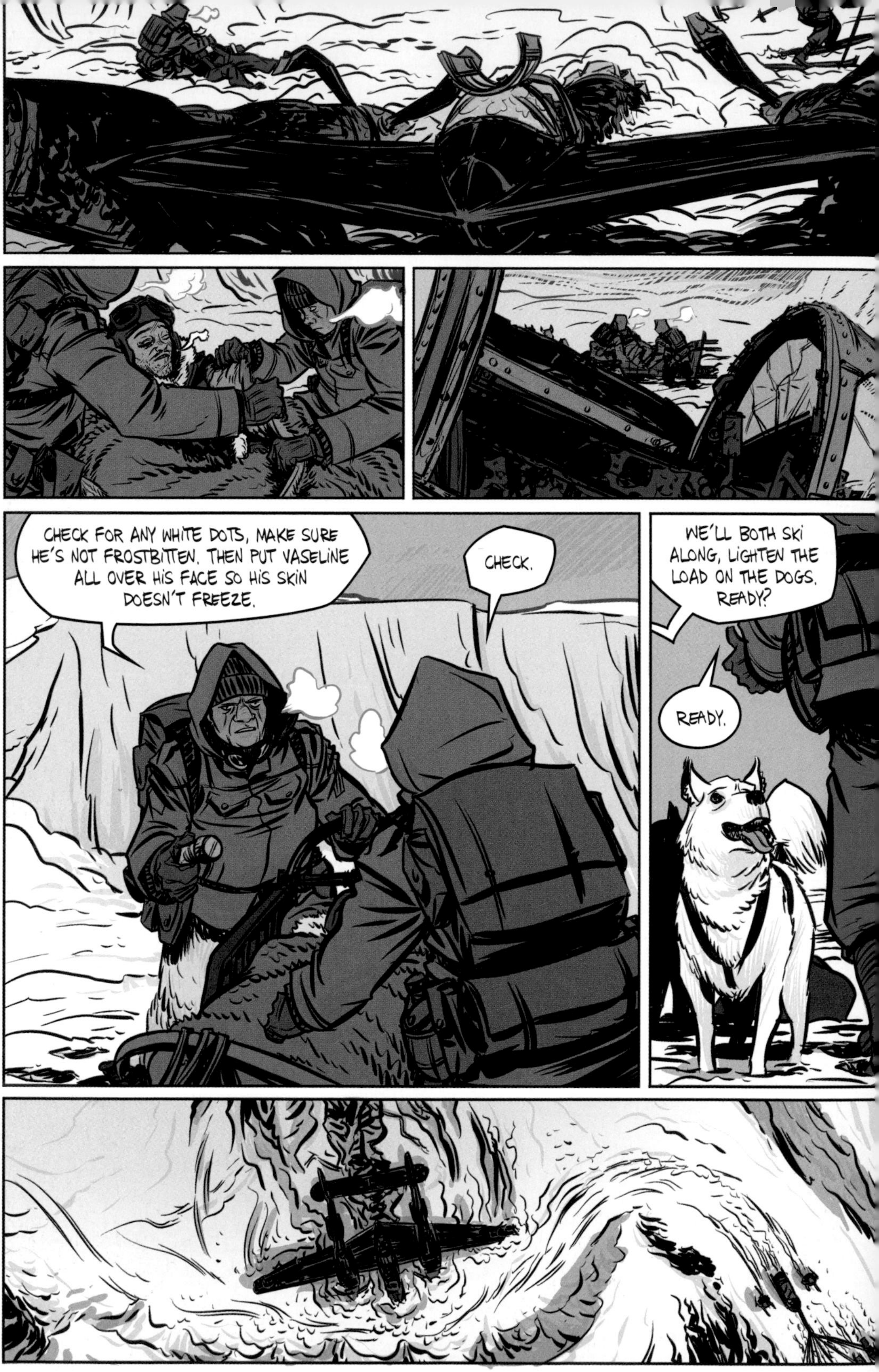
CHECK FOR ANY WHITE DOTS, MAKE SURE HE'S NOT FROSTBITTEN. THEN PUT VASELINE ALL OVER HIS FACE SO HIS SKIN DOESN'T FREEZE.
CHECK.
WE'LL BOTH SKI ALONG, LIGHTEN THE LOAD ON THE DOGS. READY?
READY.

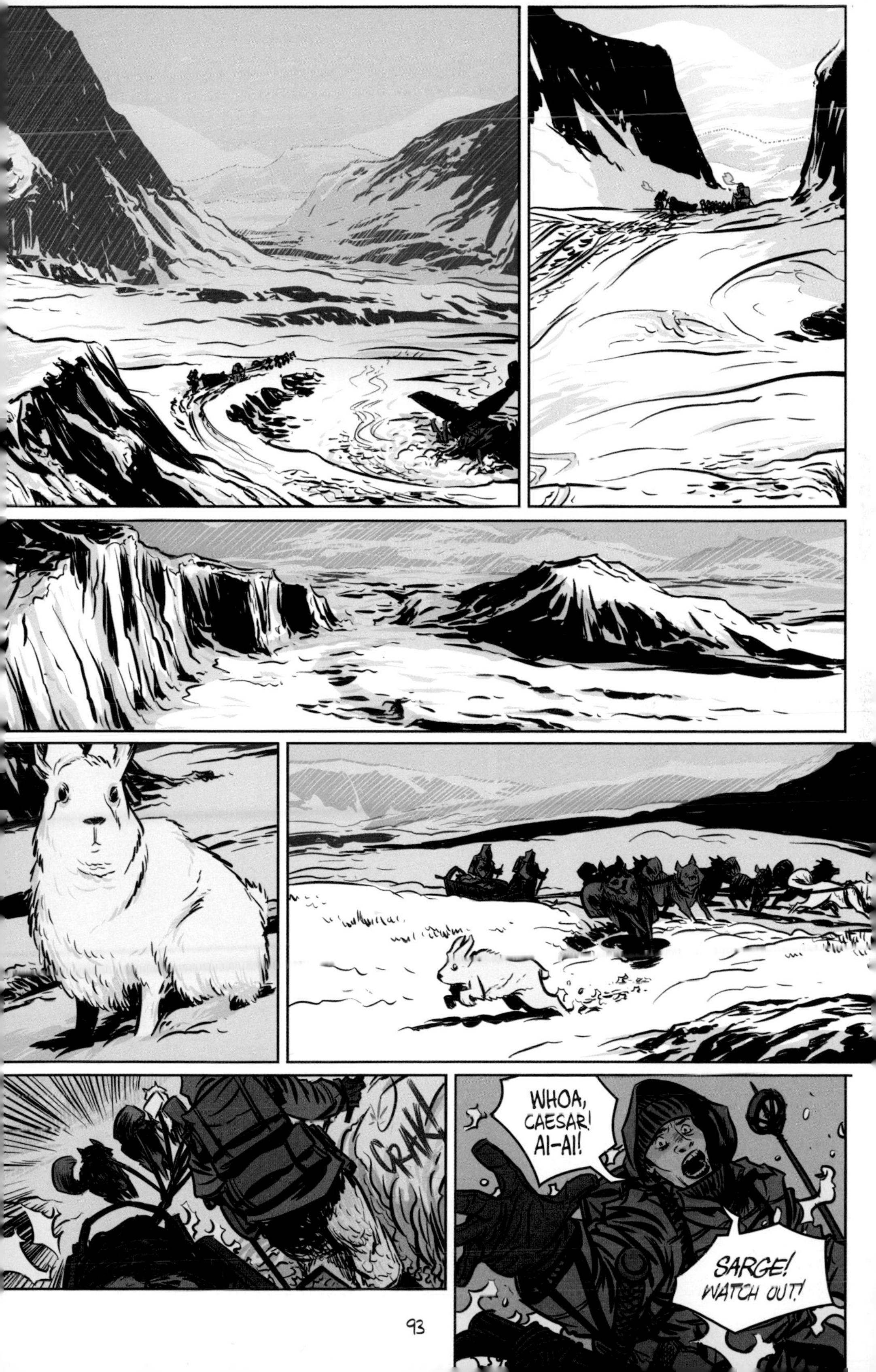
CRAK
WHOA, CAESAR! AI-AI!
SARGE! WATCH OUT!

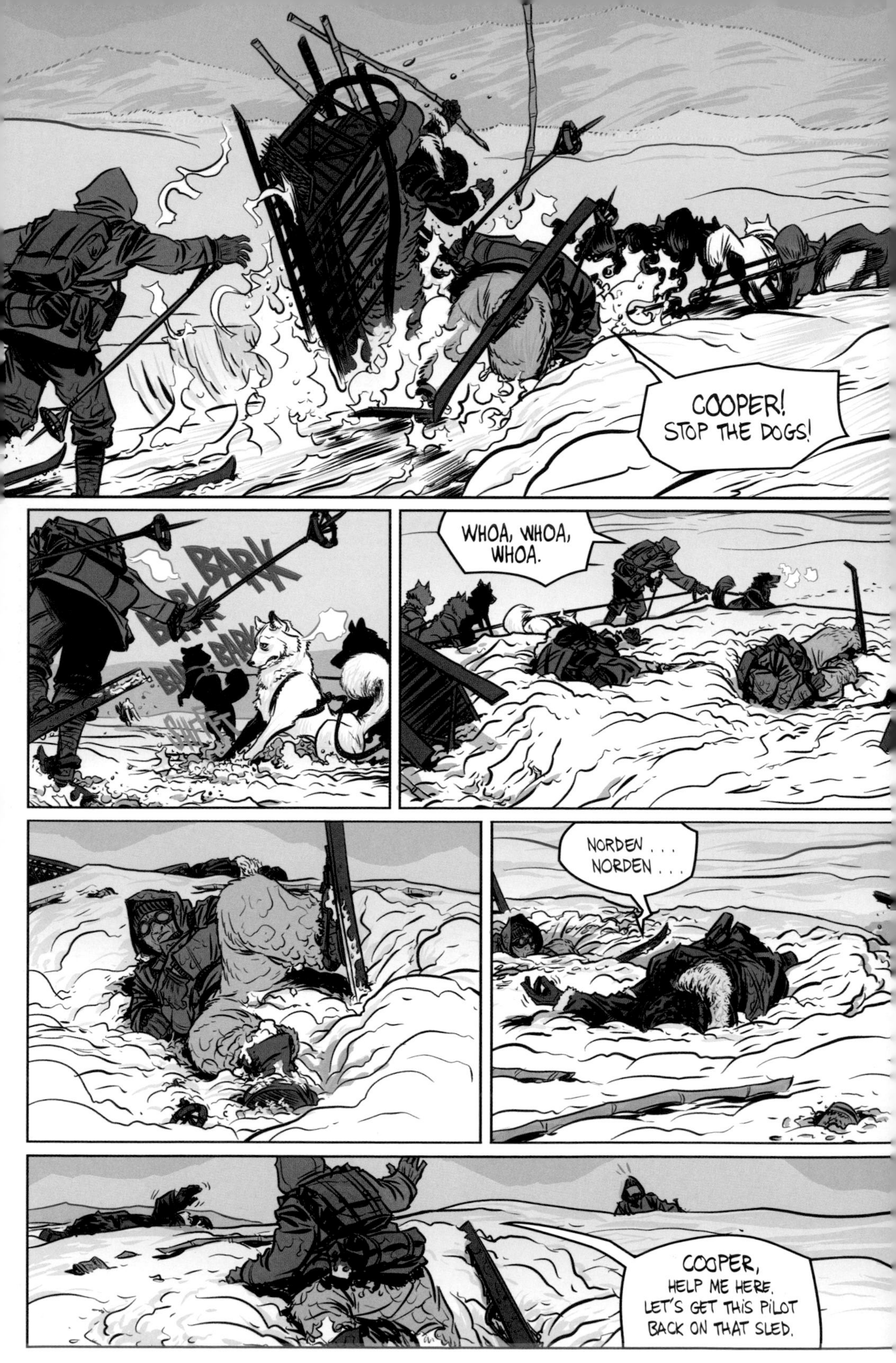
COOPER! STOP THE DOGS!
BARK
BARK
BARK
SHFFT
WHOA, WHOA, WHOA.
NORDEN . . . NORDEN . . .
COOPER, HELP ME HERE. LET'S GET THIS PILOT BACK ON THAT SLED.

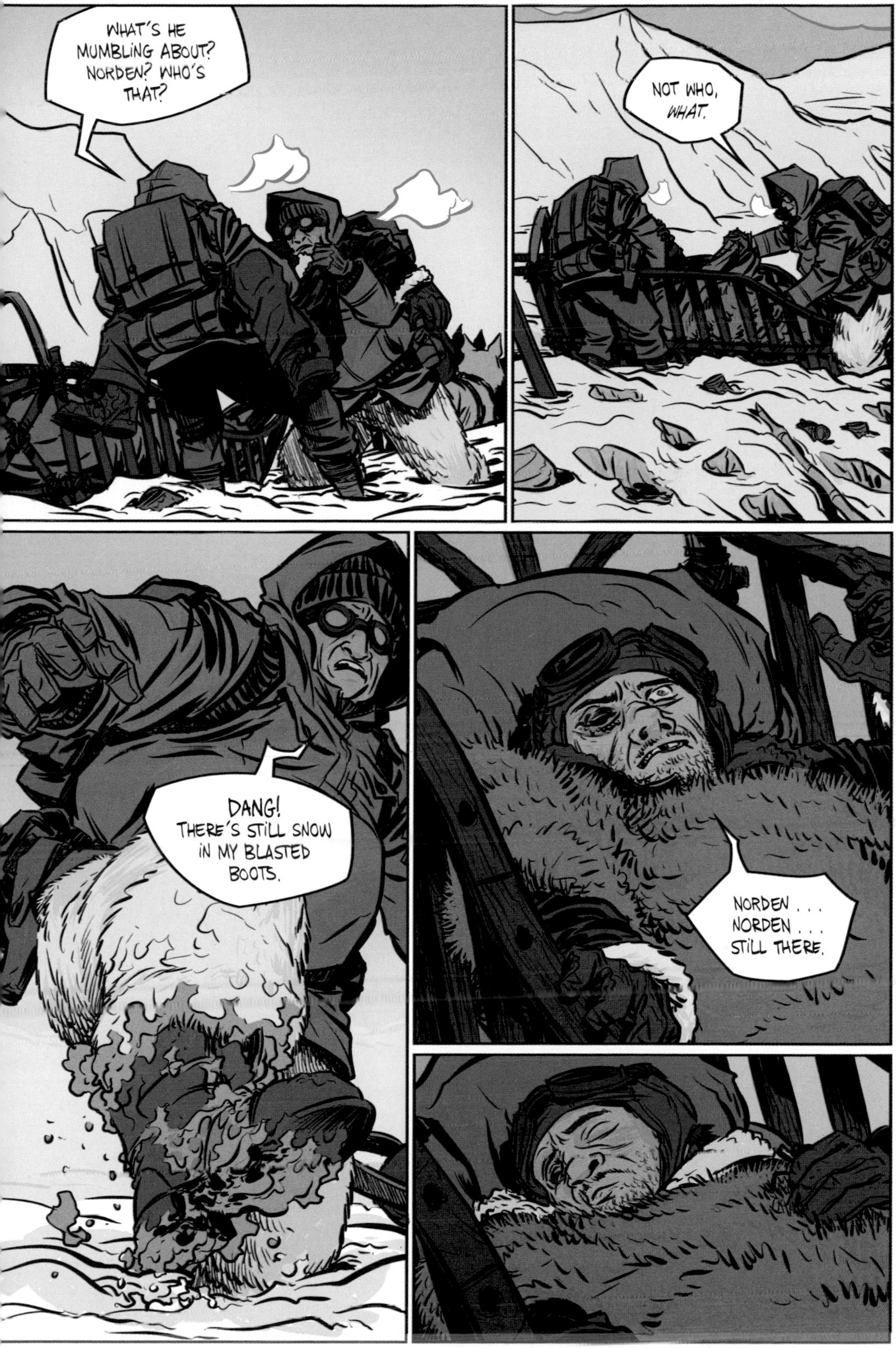
WHAT'S HE MUMBLING ABOUT? NORDEN? WHO'S THAT?
NOT WHO, *WHAT.*
DANG! THERE'S STILL SNOW IN MY BLASTED BOOTS.
NORDEN . . . NORDEN . . . STILL THERE.

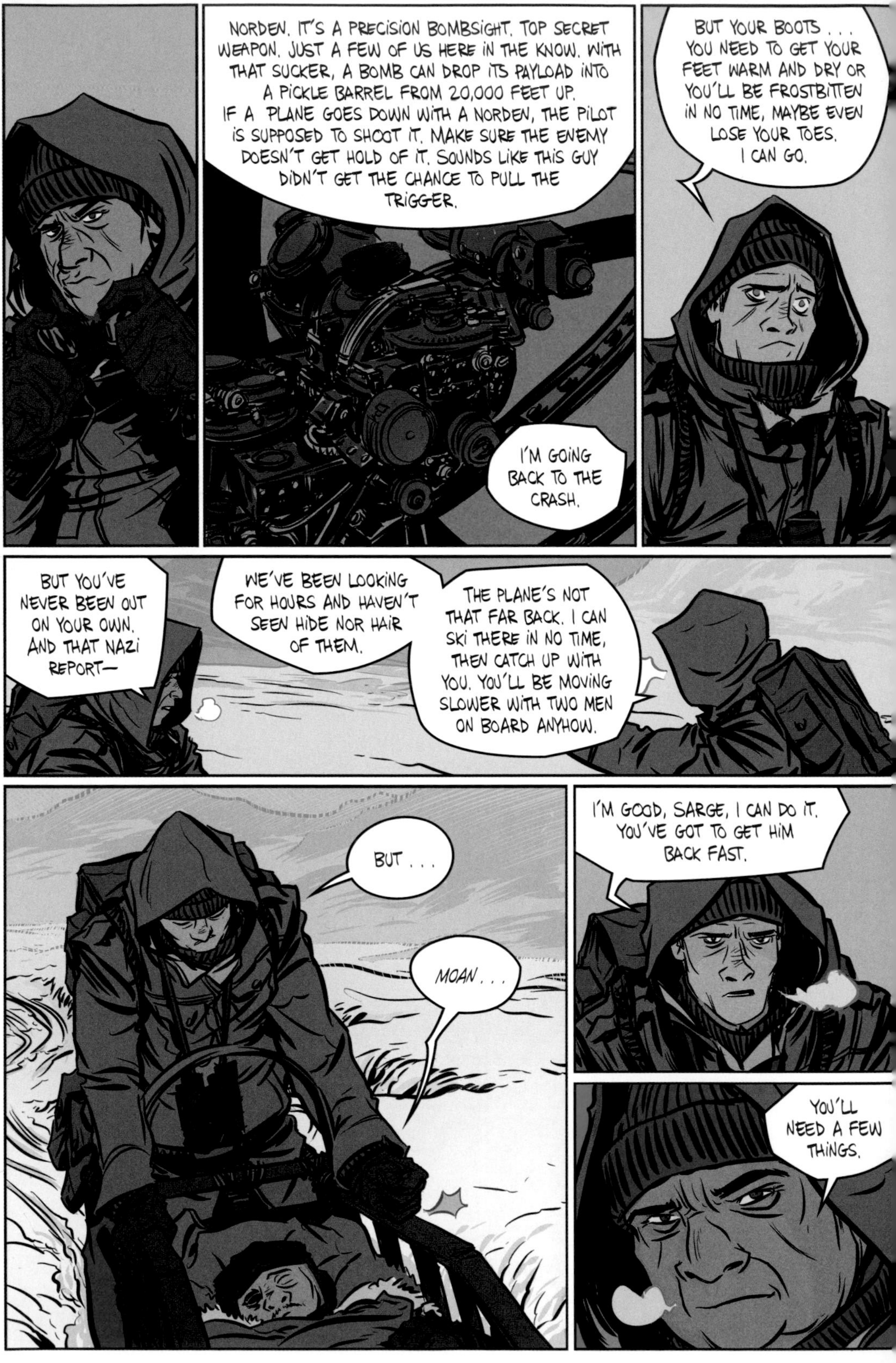
NORDEN. IT'S A PRECISION BOMBSIGHT. TOP SECRET WEAPON. JUST A FEW OF US HERE IN THE KNOW. WITH THAT SUCKER, A BOMB CAN DROP ITS PAYLOAD INTO A PICKLE BARREL FROM 20,000 FEET UP. IF A PLANE GOES DOWN WITH A NORDEN, THE PILOT IS SUPPOSED TO SHOOT IT. MAKE SURE THE ENEMY DOESN'T GET HOLD OF IT. SOUNDS LIKE THIS GUY DIDN'T GET THE CHANCE TO PULL THE TRIGGER.
I'M GOING BACK TO THE CRASH.
BUT YOUR BOOTS . . . YOU NEED TO GET YOUR FEET WARM AND DRY OR YOU'LL BE FROSTBITTEN IN NO TIME, MAYBE EVEN LOSE YOUR TOES. I CAN GO.
BUT YOU'VE NEVER BEEN OUT ON YOUR OWN. AND THAT NAZI REPORT—
WE'VE BEEN LOOKING FOR HOURS AND HAVEN'T SEEN HIDE NOR HAIR OF THEM.
THE PLANE'S NOT THAT FAR BACK. I CAN SKI THERE IN NO TIME, THEN CATCH UP WITH YOU. YOU'LL BE MOVING SLOWER WITH TWO MEN ON BOARD ANYHOW.
BUT . . .
MOAN . . .
I'M GOOD, SARGE, I CAN DO IT. YOU'VE GOT TO GET HIM BACK FAST.
YOU'LL NEED A FEW THINGS.

KEEP YOUR WEAPON OUT SO IT STAYS FROZEN, OTHERWISE MOISTURE CONDENSES, AND WHEN YOU PULL IT OUT, IT JAMS WITH ICE. KNOW HOW TO BUILD A SNOW WALL IF YOU NEED TO?

I'M FROM MAINE, REMEMBER? I SNOW-CAMPED AS A BOY.

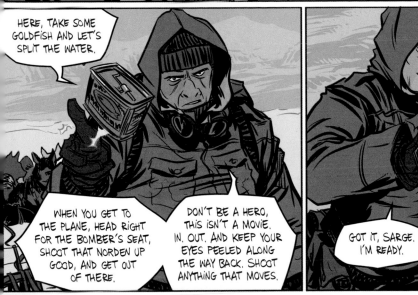

HERE, TAKE SOME GOLDFISH AND LET'S SPLIT THE WATER.

WHEN YOU GET TO THE PLANE, HEAD RIGHT FOR THE BOMBER'S SEAT, SHOOT THAT NORDEN UP GOOD, AND GET OUT OF THERE.

DON'T BE A HERO, THIS ISN'T A MOVIE. IN. OUT. AND KEEP YOUR EYES PEELED ALONG THE WAY BACK. SHOOT ANYTHING THAT MOVES.

GOT IT, SARGE. I'M READY.

TAKE THIS, TOO. THEY SAY IT BRINGS LUCK, MAKES YOU STRONG LIKE *NANOQ*.

I EXPECT YOU TO BRING IT BACK, SOLDIER!

SURE THING, SARGE.

NOW GET GOING . . . AND HURRY.

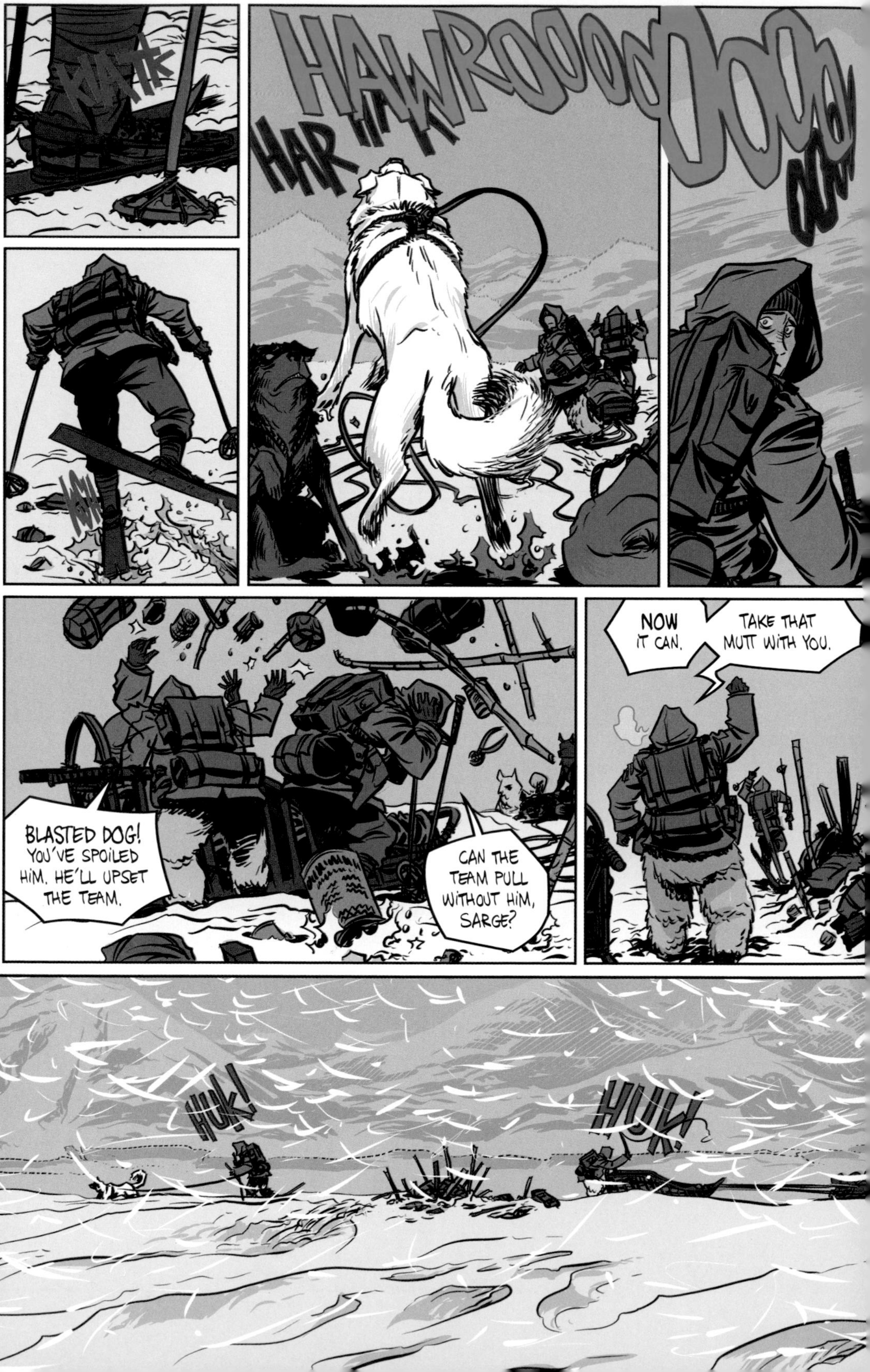

KLAKK
HAWROOOOOOOOOOOOOO
HAR HAR HAR
BLASTED DOG! YOU'VE SPOILED HIM. HE'LL UPSET THE TEAM.
CAN THE TEAM PULL WITHOUT HIM, SARGE?
NOW IT CAN.
TAKE THAT MUTT WITH YOU.
HUK!
HUK!

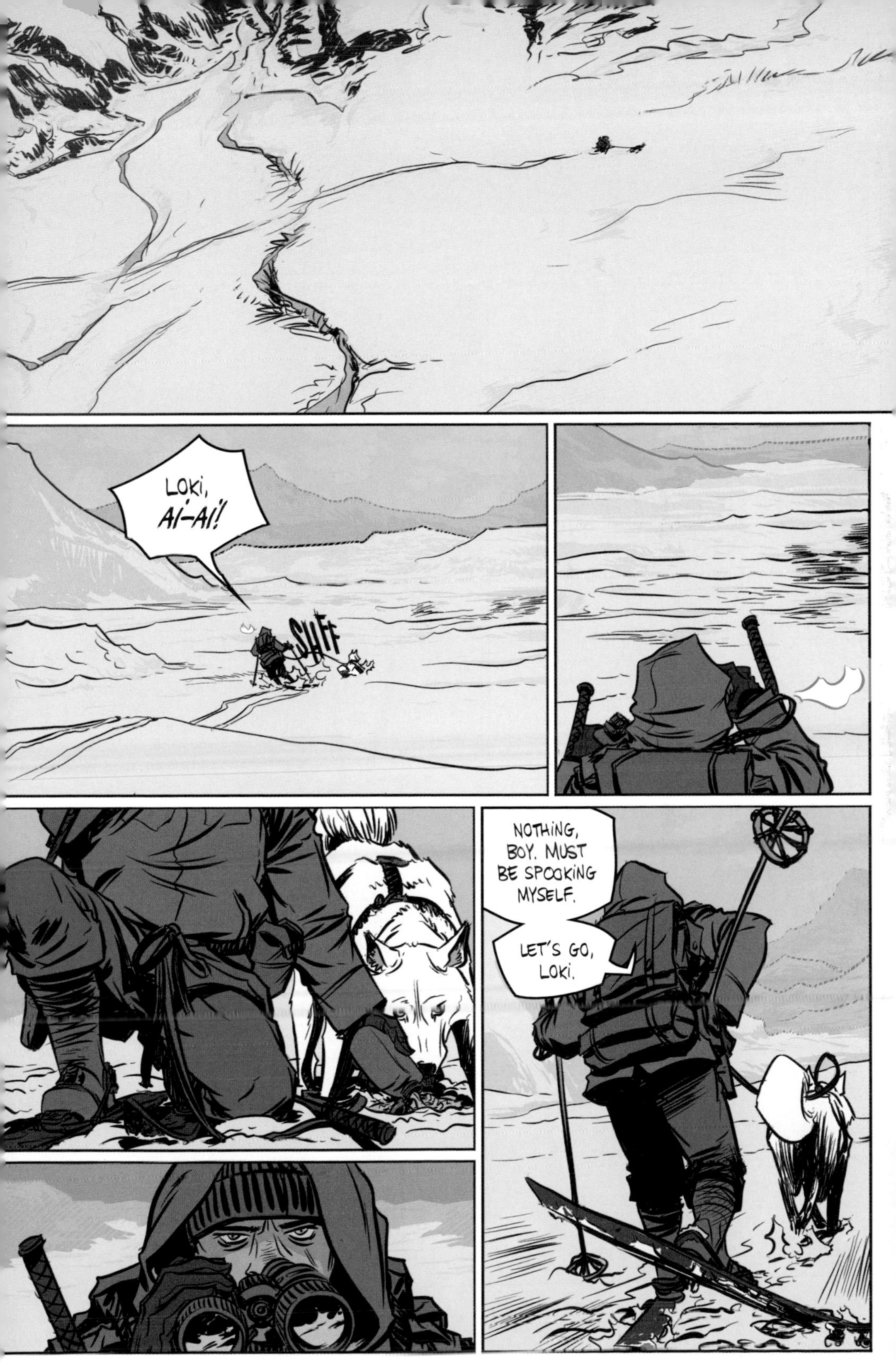
LOKI, AI-AI!
SHFF
NOTHING, BOY. MUST BE SPOOKING MYSELF.
LET'S GO, LOKI.

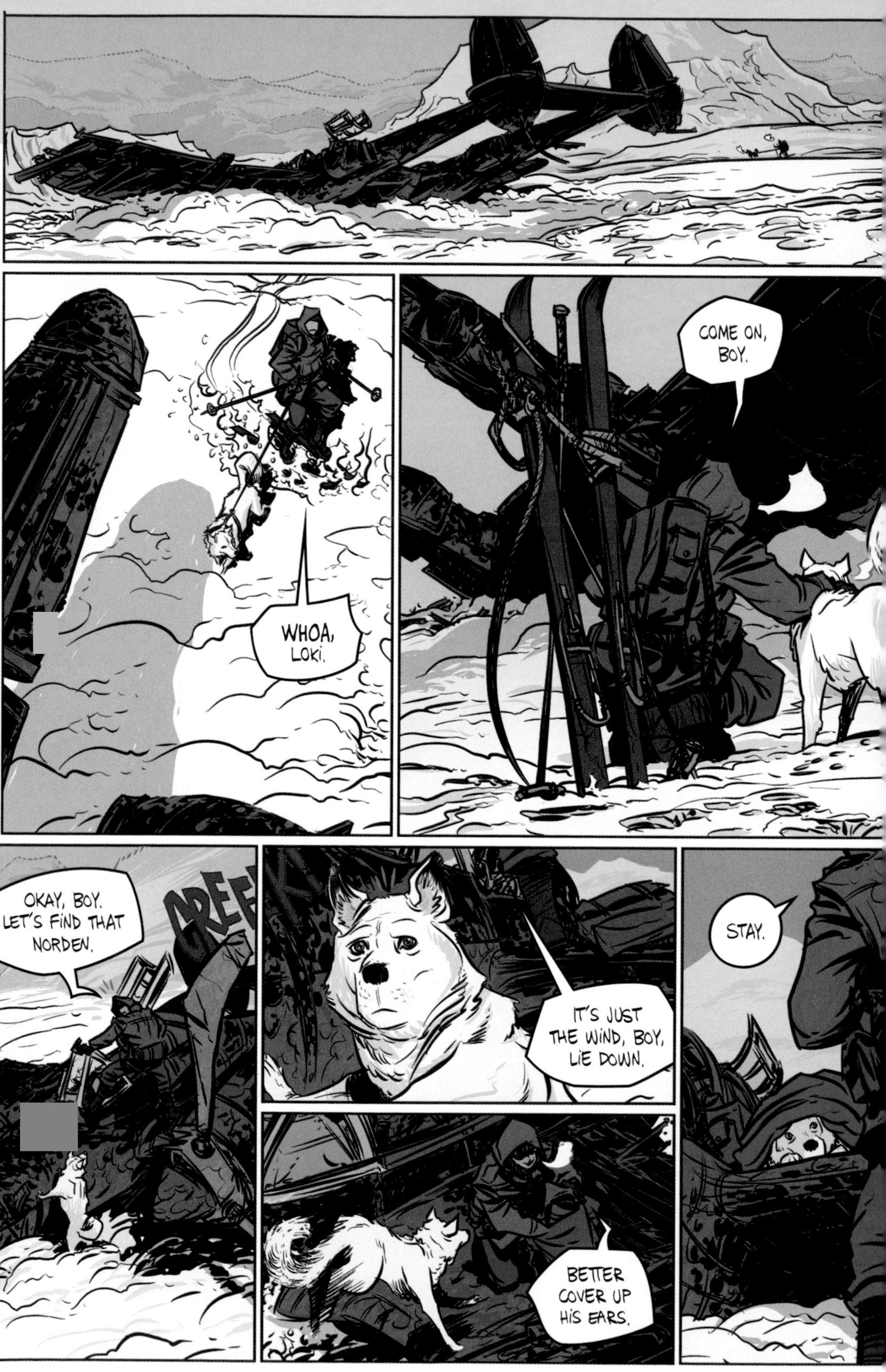
WHOA, LOKI.
COME ON, BOY.
OKAY, BOY. LET'S FIND THAT NORDEN.
IT'S JUST THE WIND, BOY, LIE DOWN.
BETTER COVER UP HIS EARS.
STAY.

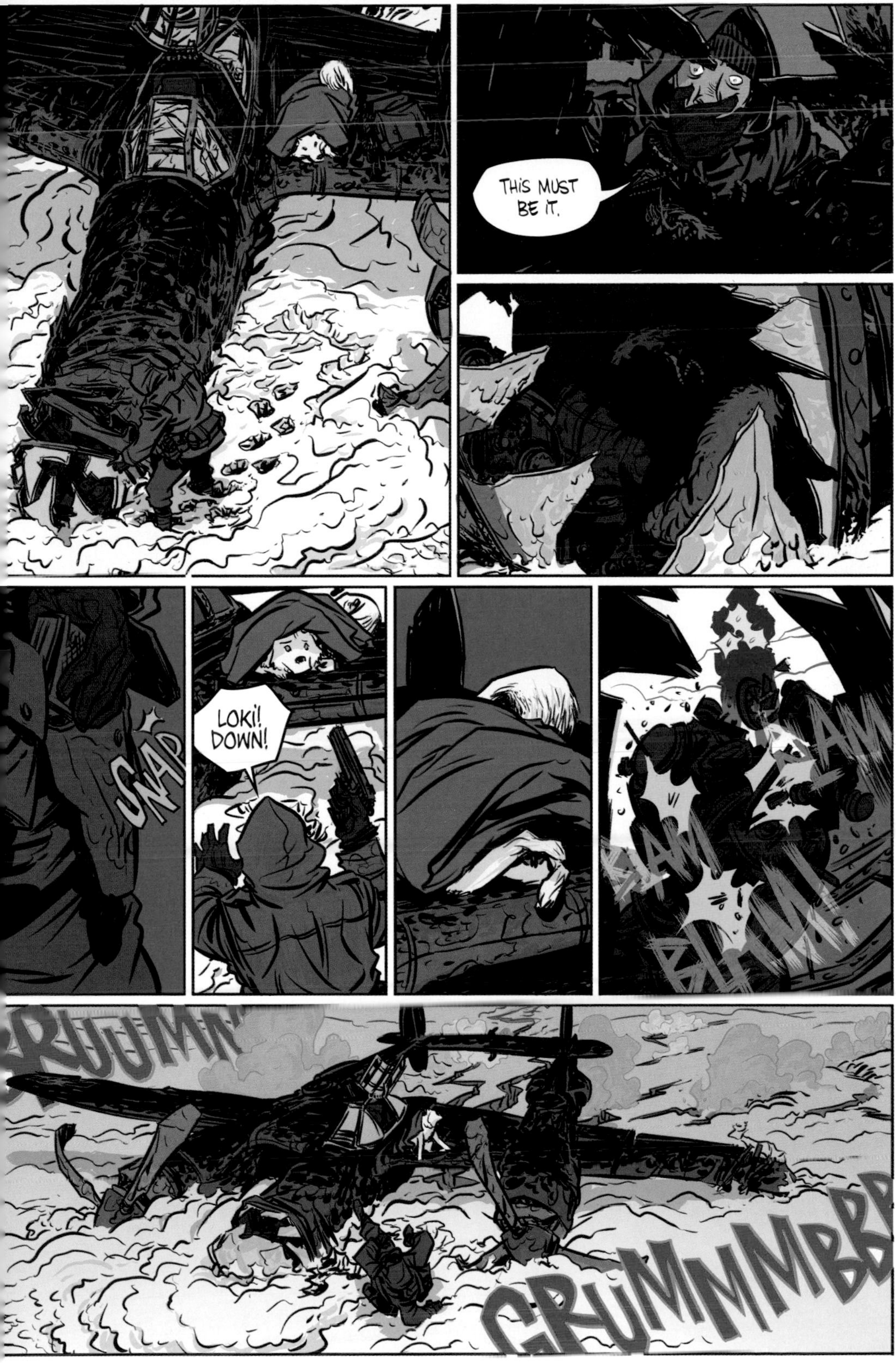
THIS MUST BE IT.
SNAP
LOKI! DOWN!
BLAM
BLAM
BLAM
GRUUMM
GRUMMMBB

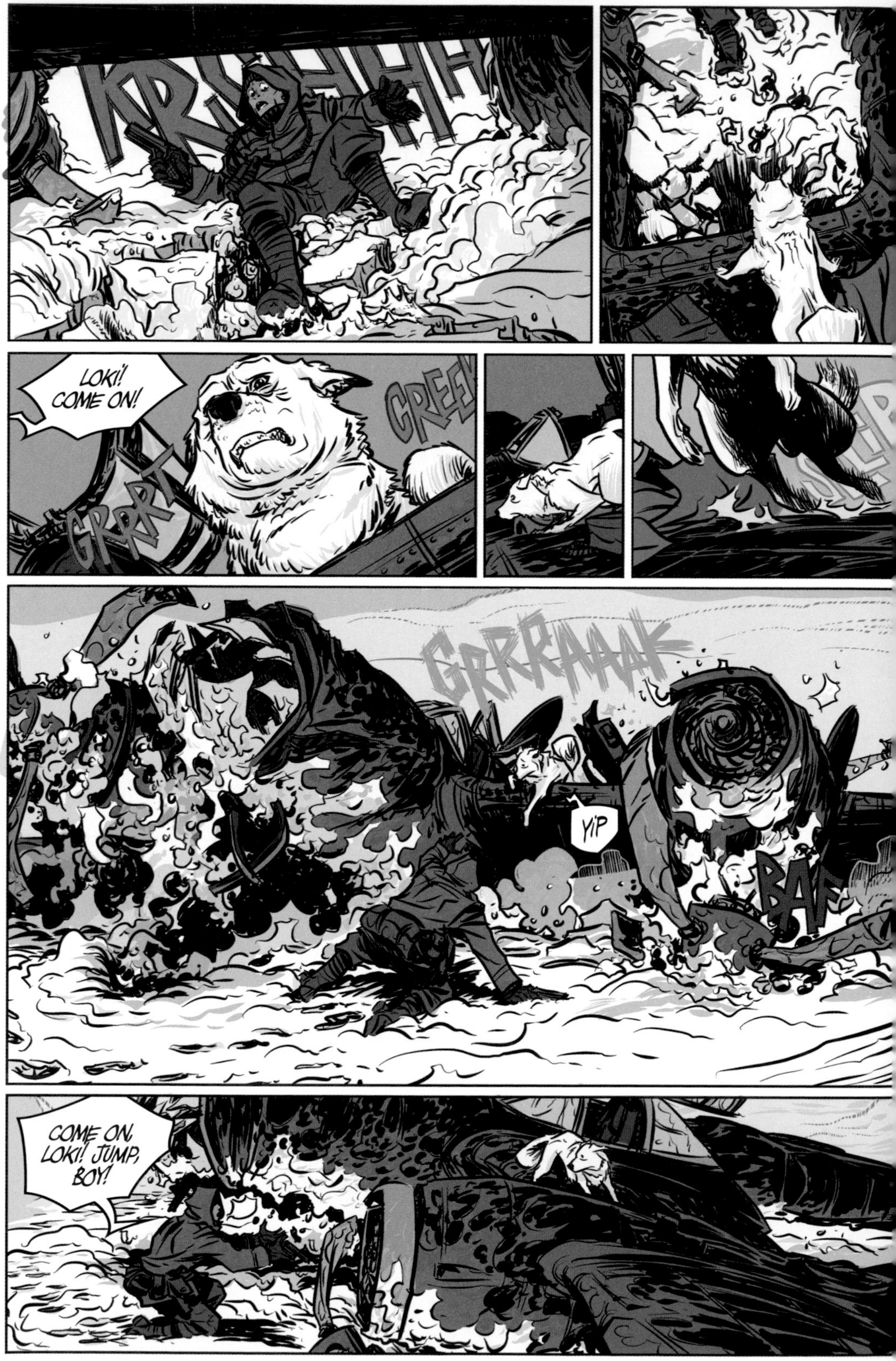
KRSHHH
LOKI! COME ON!
CREEK
GRRRT
GRRRAAAK
YIP
BAF
COME ON, LOKI! JUMP, BOY!

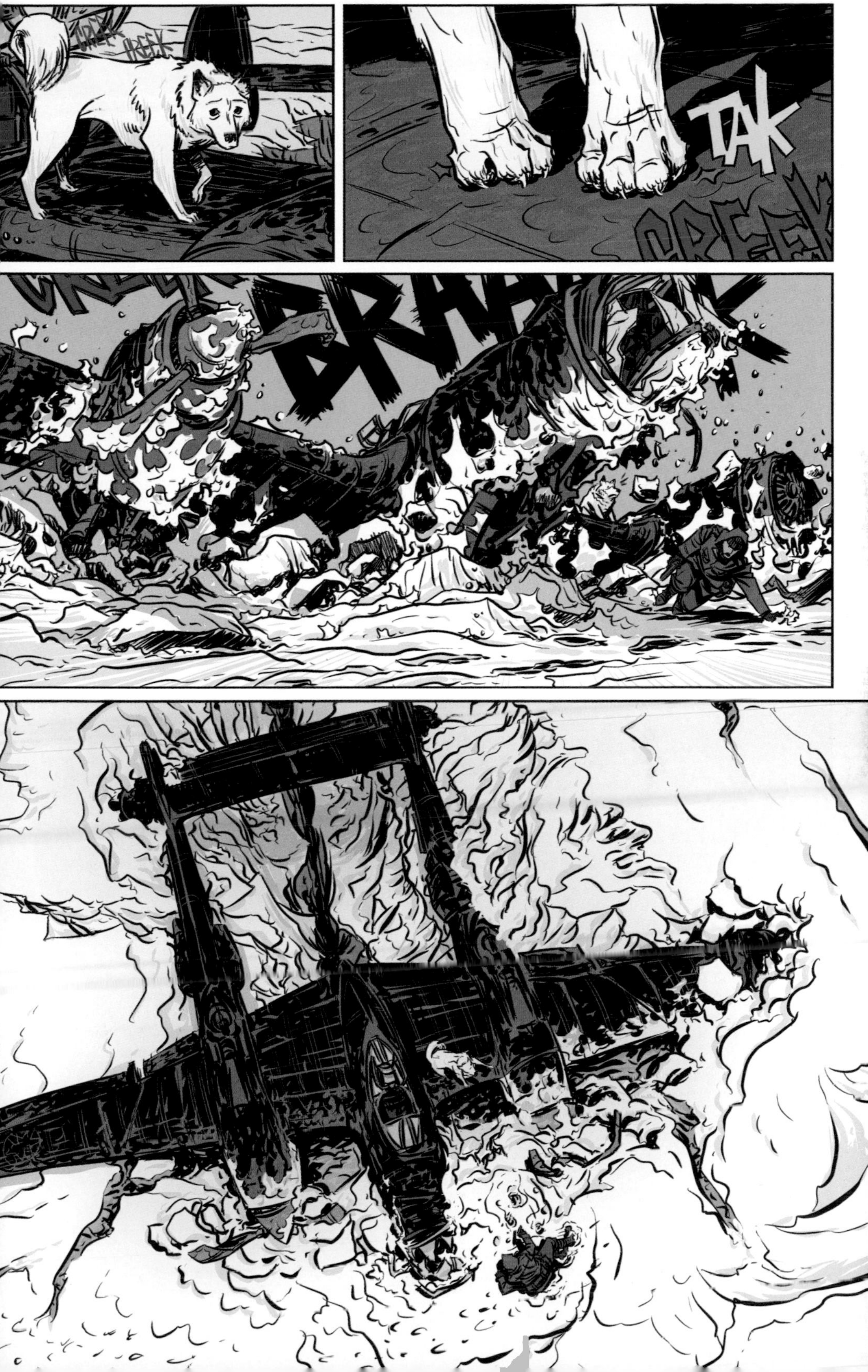
CREEK CREEK
TAK

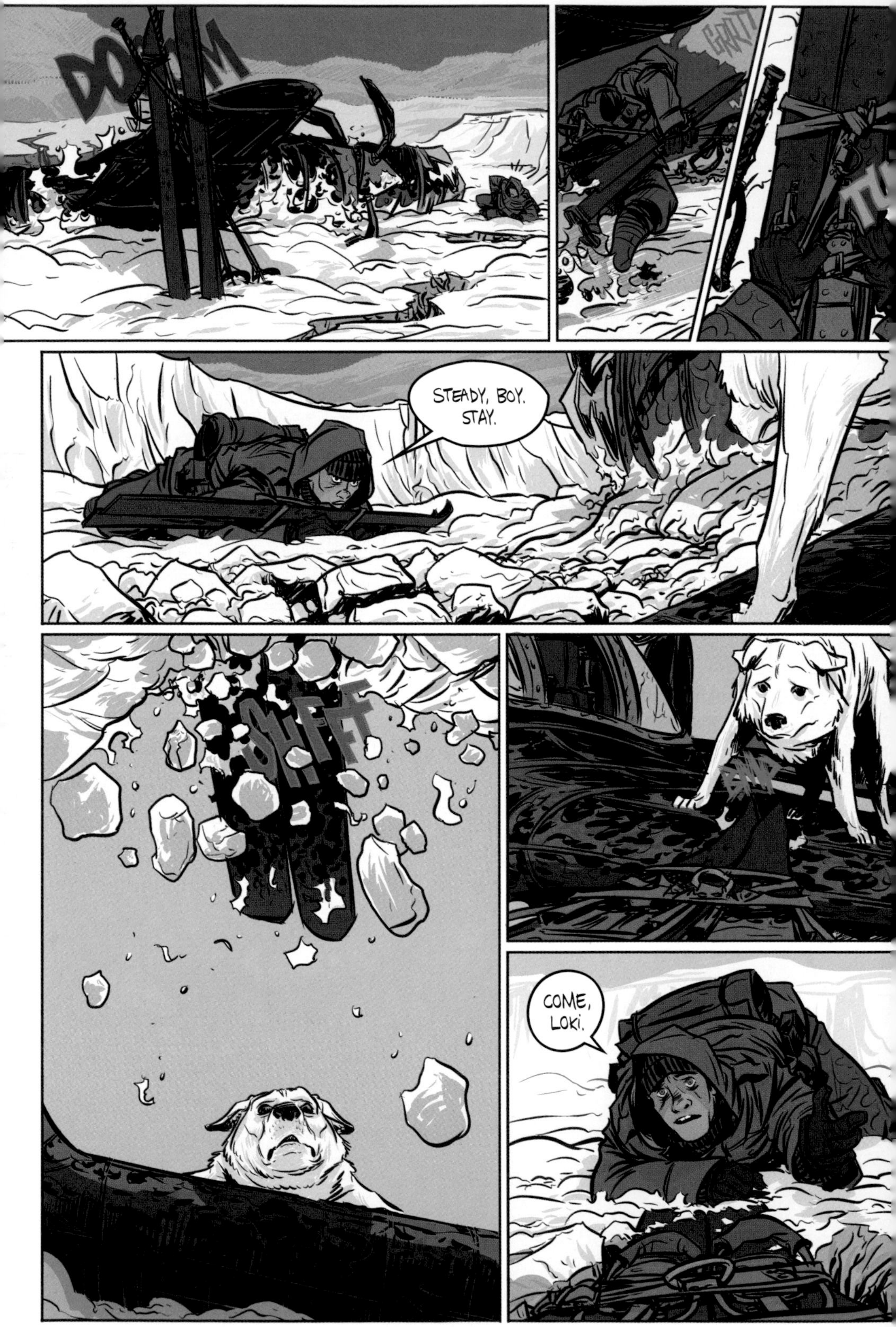
GRRT!
STEADY, BOY.
STAY.
SHFF
COME,
LOKi.

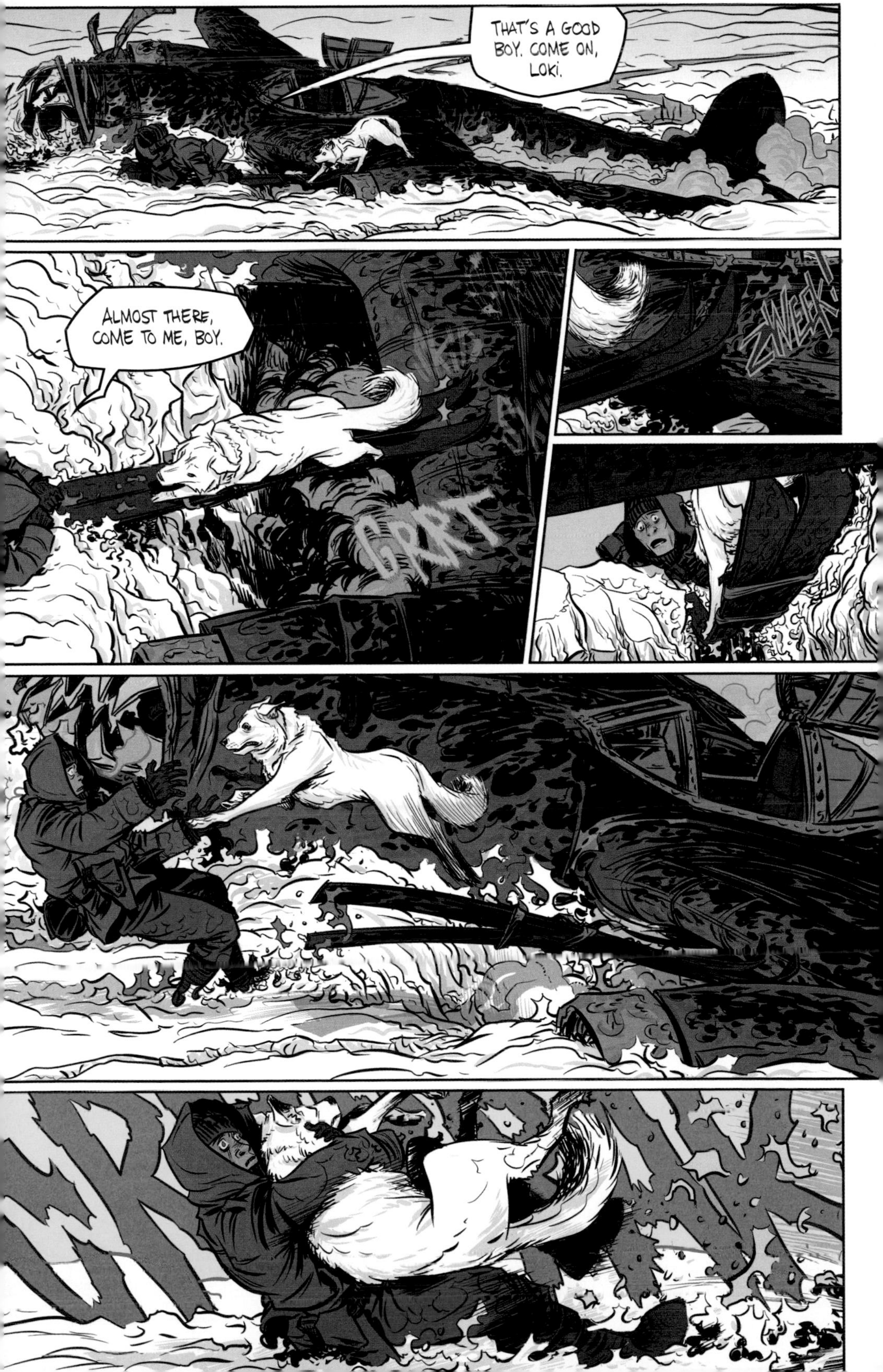
THAT'S A GOOD BOY. COME ON, LOKI.
ALMOST THERE, COME TO ME, BOY.
GRRT
ZWEEK!

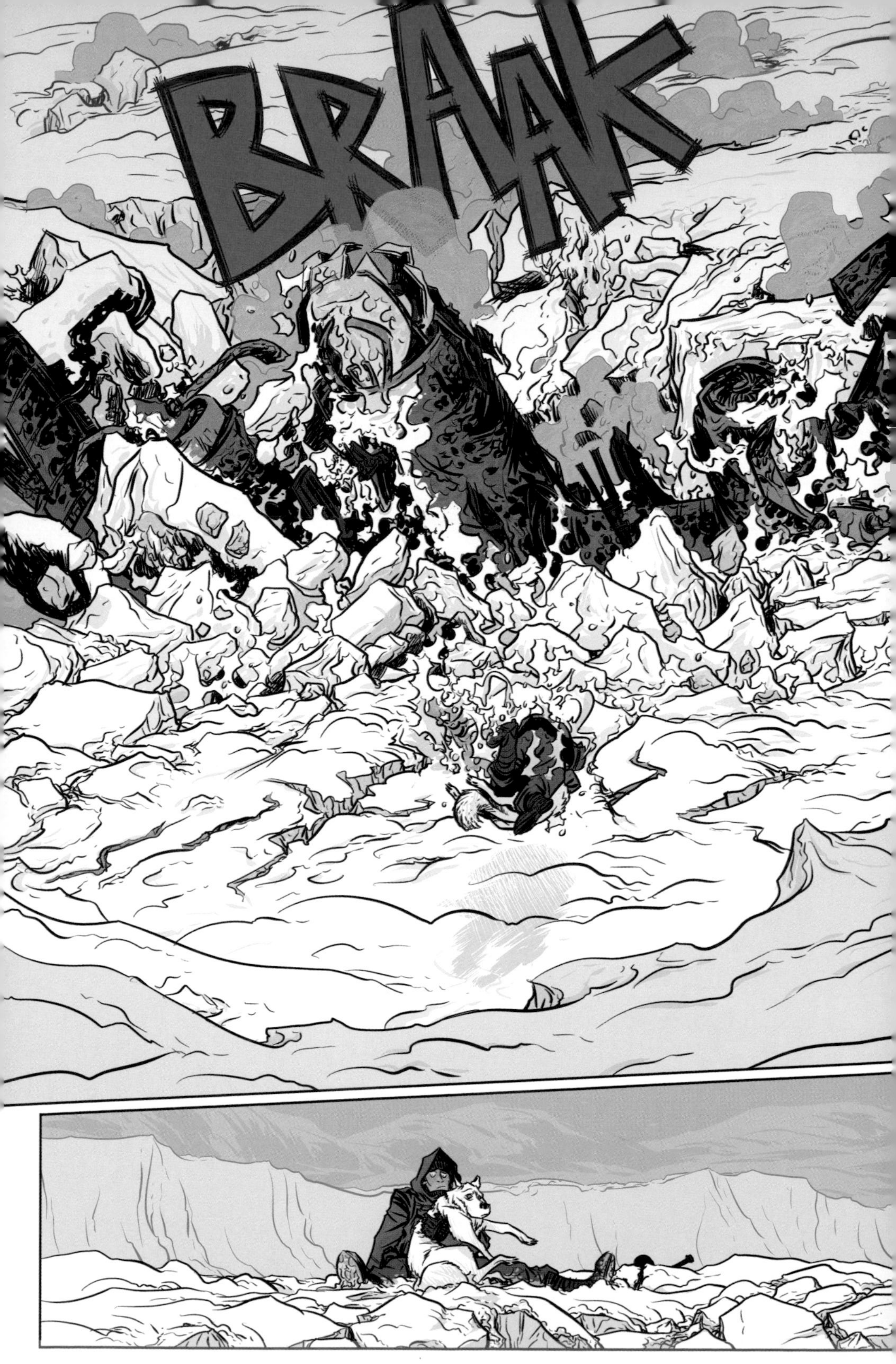
BRAAK

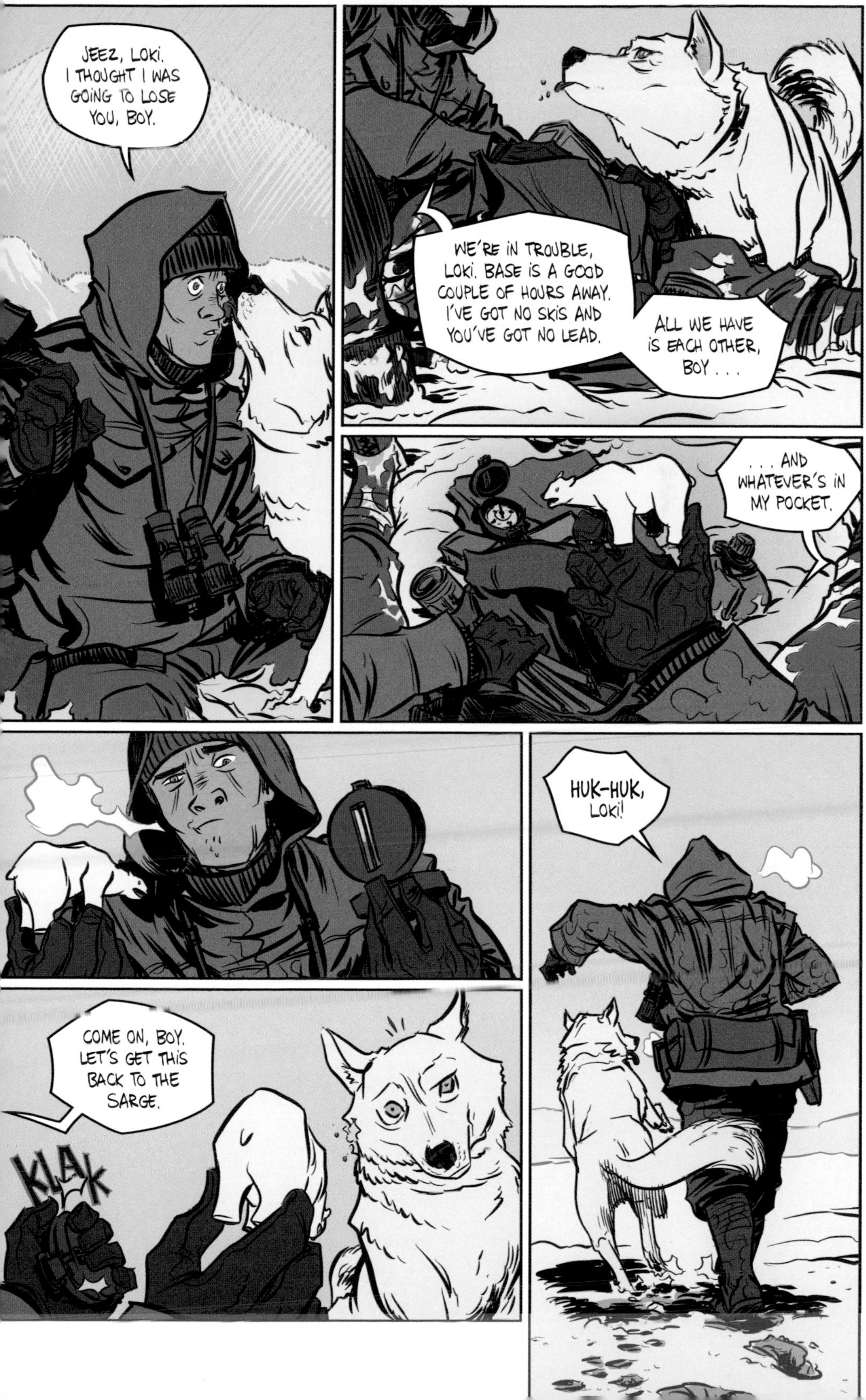
JEEZ, LOKi. I THOUGHT I WAS GOING TO LOSE YOU, BOY.
WE'RE iN TROUBLE, LOKi. BASE iS A GOOD COUPLE OF HOURS AWAY. I'VE GOT NO SKiS AND YOU'VE GOT NO LEAD.
ALL WE HAVE iS EACH OTHER, BOY . . .
. . . AND WHATEVER'S iN MY POCKET.
HUK-HUK, LOKi!
COME ON, BOY. LET'S GET THiS BACK TO THE SARGE.
KLAK

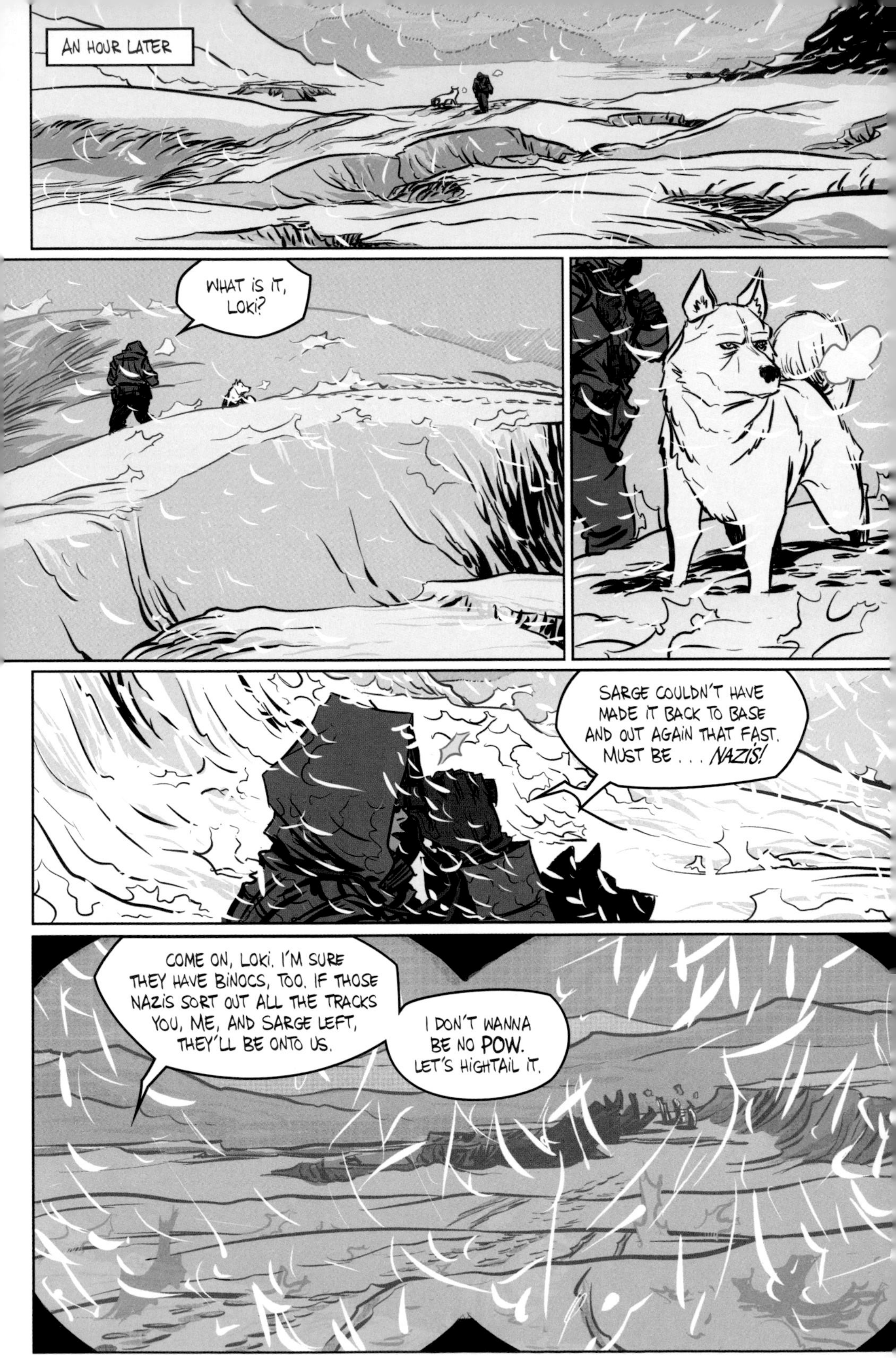
AN HOUR LATER
WHAT IS IT, LOKI?
SARGE COULDN'T HAVE MADE IT BACK TO BASE AND OUT AGAIN THAT FAST. MUST BE . . . NAZIS!
COME ON, LOKI. I'M SURE THEY HAVE BINOCS, TOO. IF THOSE NAZIS SORT OUT ALL THE TRACKS YOU, ME, AND SARGE LEFT, THEY'LL BE ONTO US.
I DON'T WANNA BE NO POW. LET'S HIGHTAIL IT.

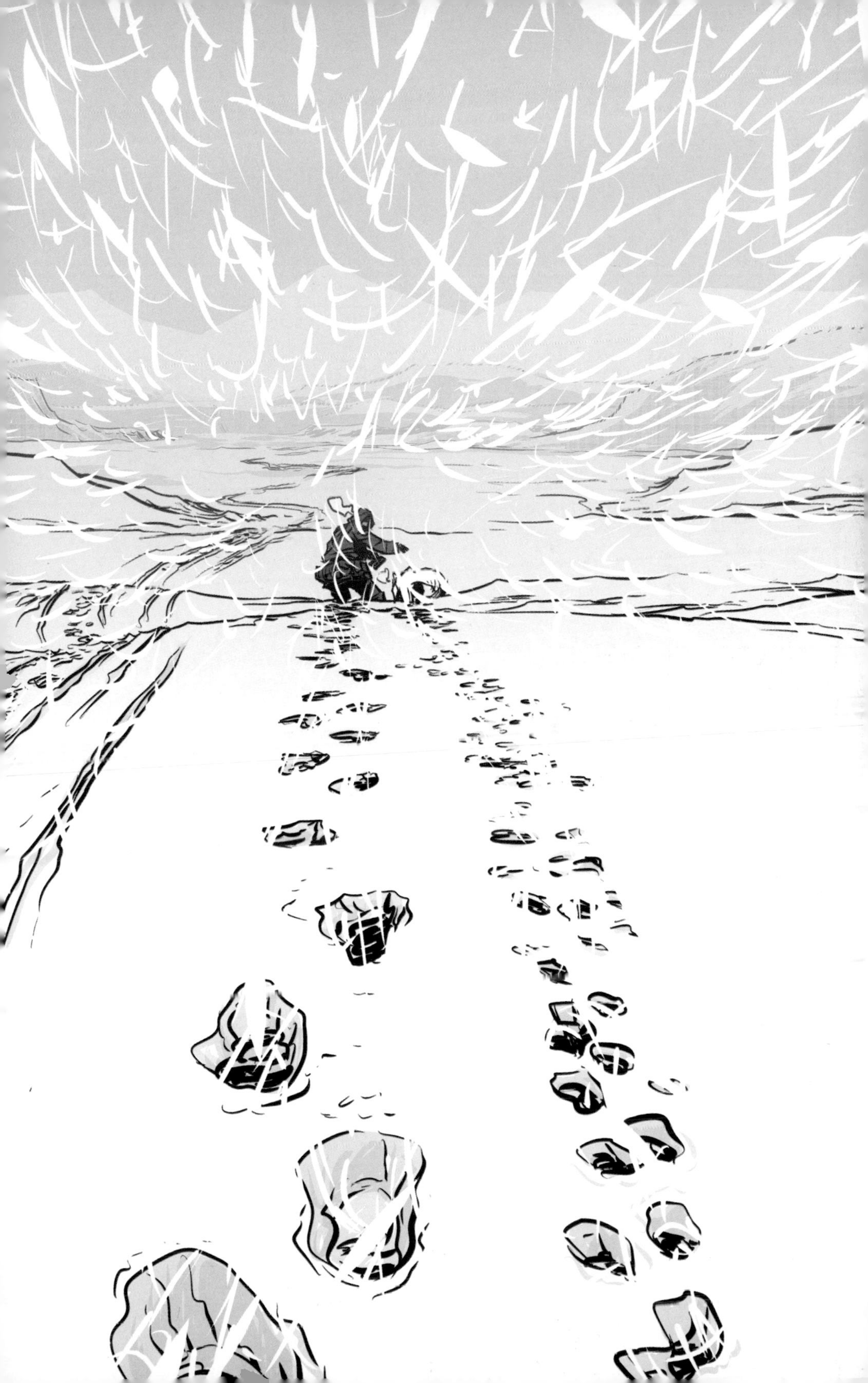

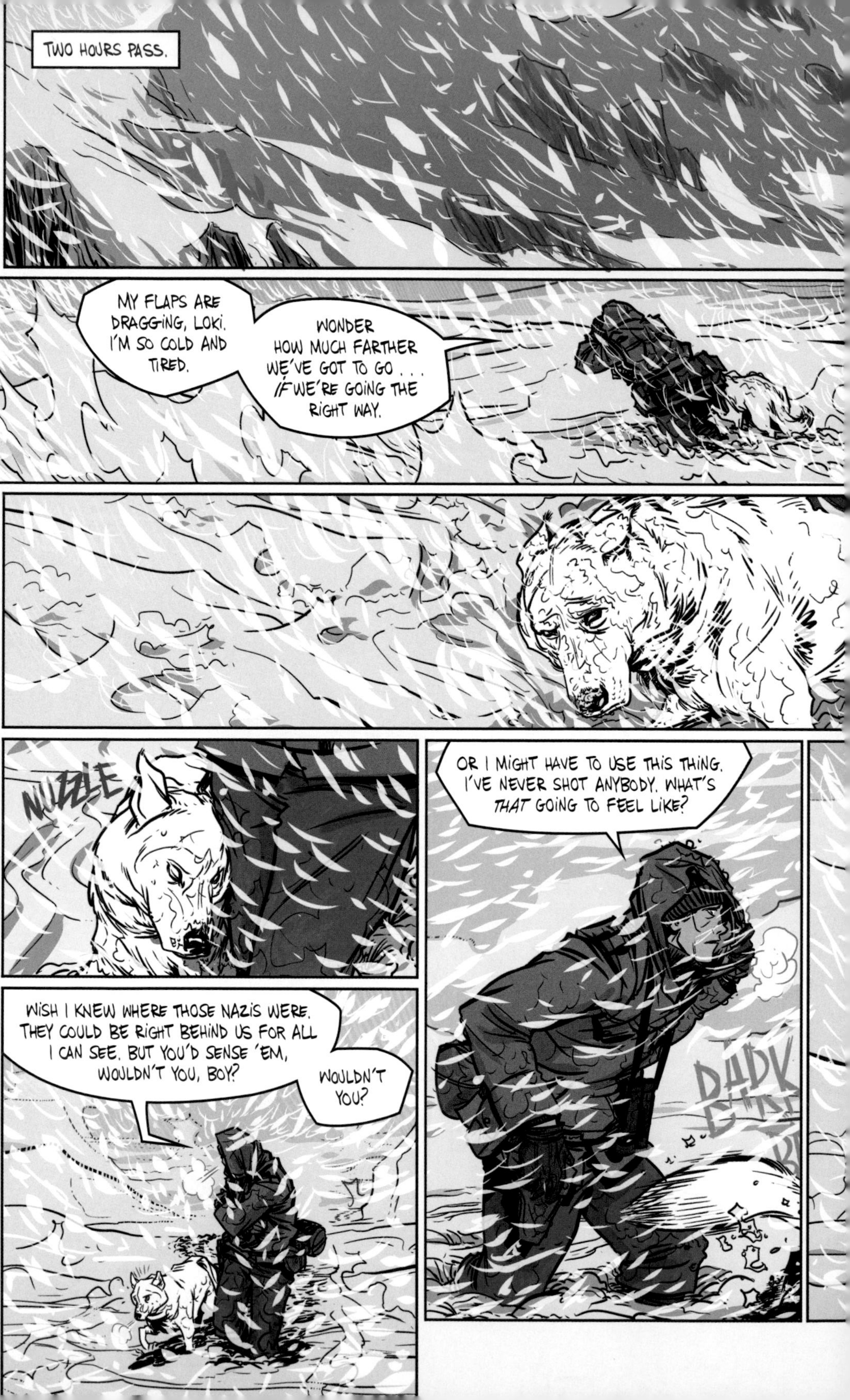
TWO HOURS PASS.
MY FLAPS ARE DRAGGING, LOKI. I'M SO COLD AND TIRED.
WONDER HOW MUCH FARTHER WE'VE GOT TO GO . . . *IF* WE'RE GOING THE RIGHT WAY.
NUZZLE
OR I MIGHT HAVE TO USE THIS THING. I'VE NEVER SHOT ANYBODY. WHAT'S *THAT* GOING TO FEEL LIKE?
WISH I KNEW WHERE THOSE NAZIS WERE. THEY COULD BE RIGHT BEHIND US FOR ALL I CAN SEE. BUT YOU'D SENSE 'EM, WOULDN'T YOU, BOY?
WOULDN'T YOU?

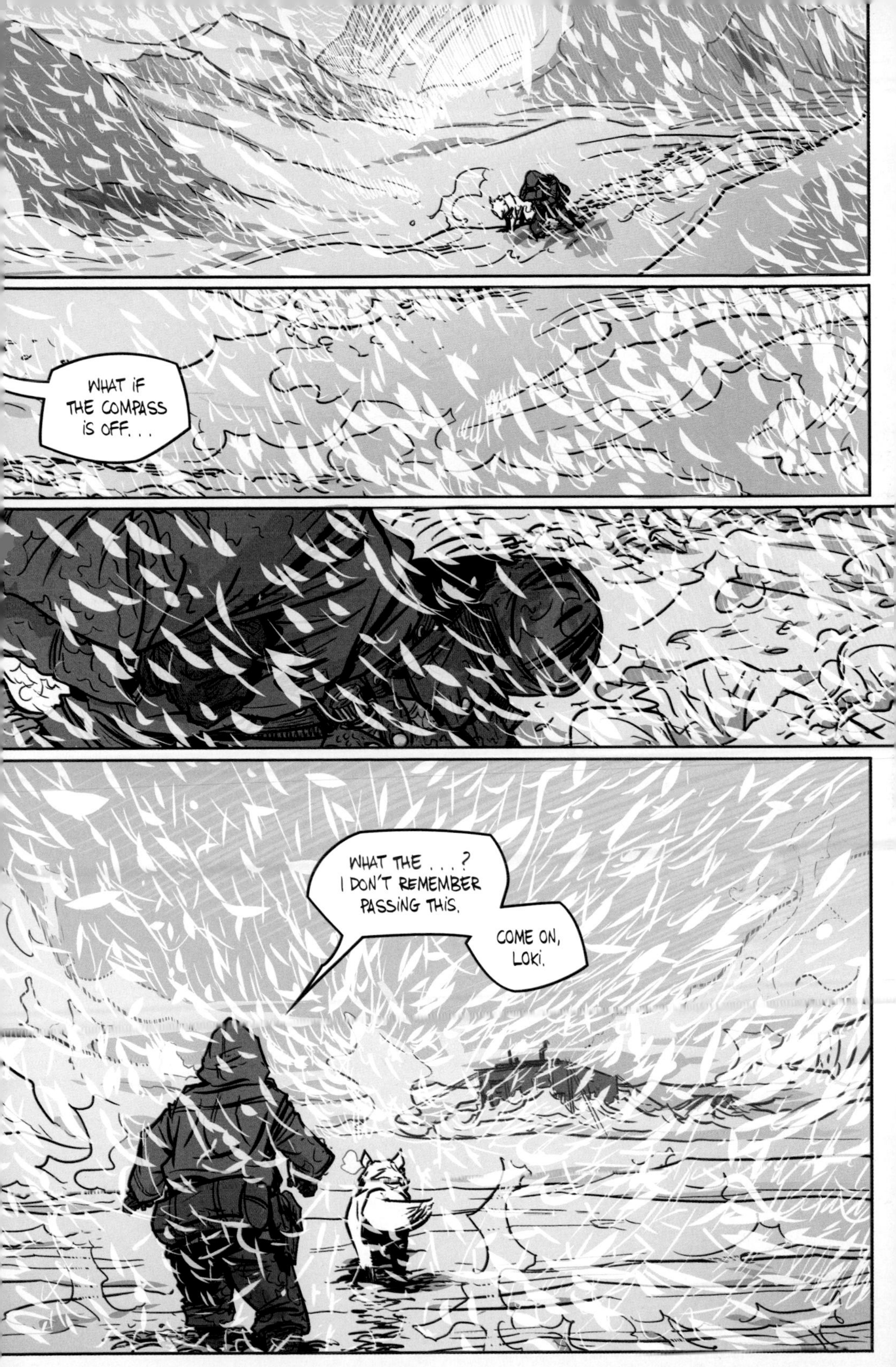
WHAT IF THE COMPASS IS OFF. . .
WHAT THE . . . ? I DON'T REMEMBER PASSING THIS.
COME ON, LOKI.

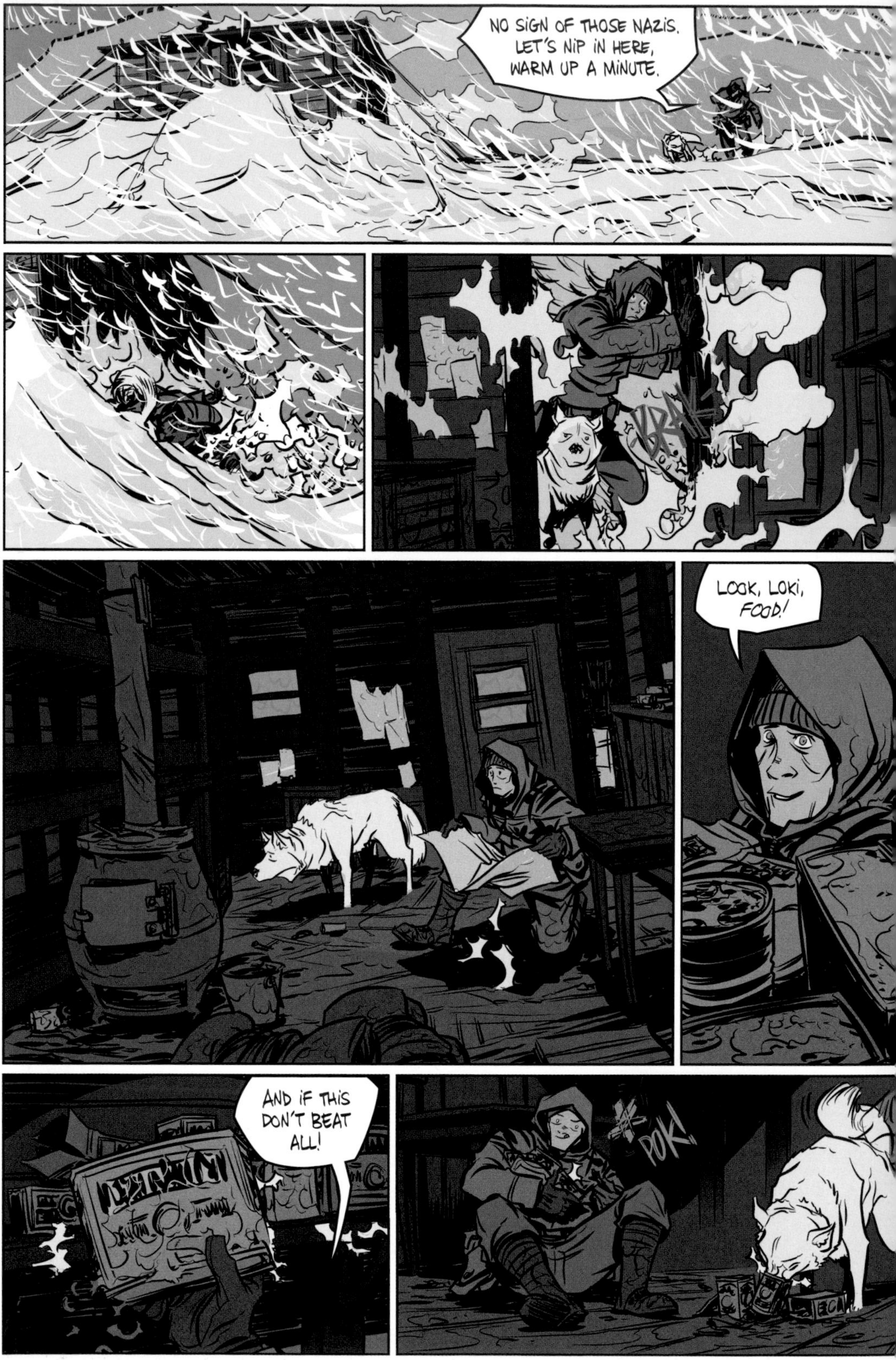
NO SIGN OF THOSE NAZIS. LET'S NIP IN HERE, WARM UP A MINUTE.
LOOK, LOKI, FOOD!
AND IF THIS DON'T BEAT ALL!
POK!

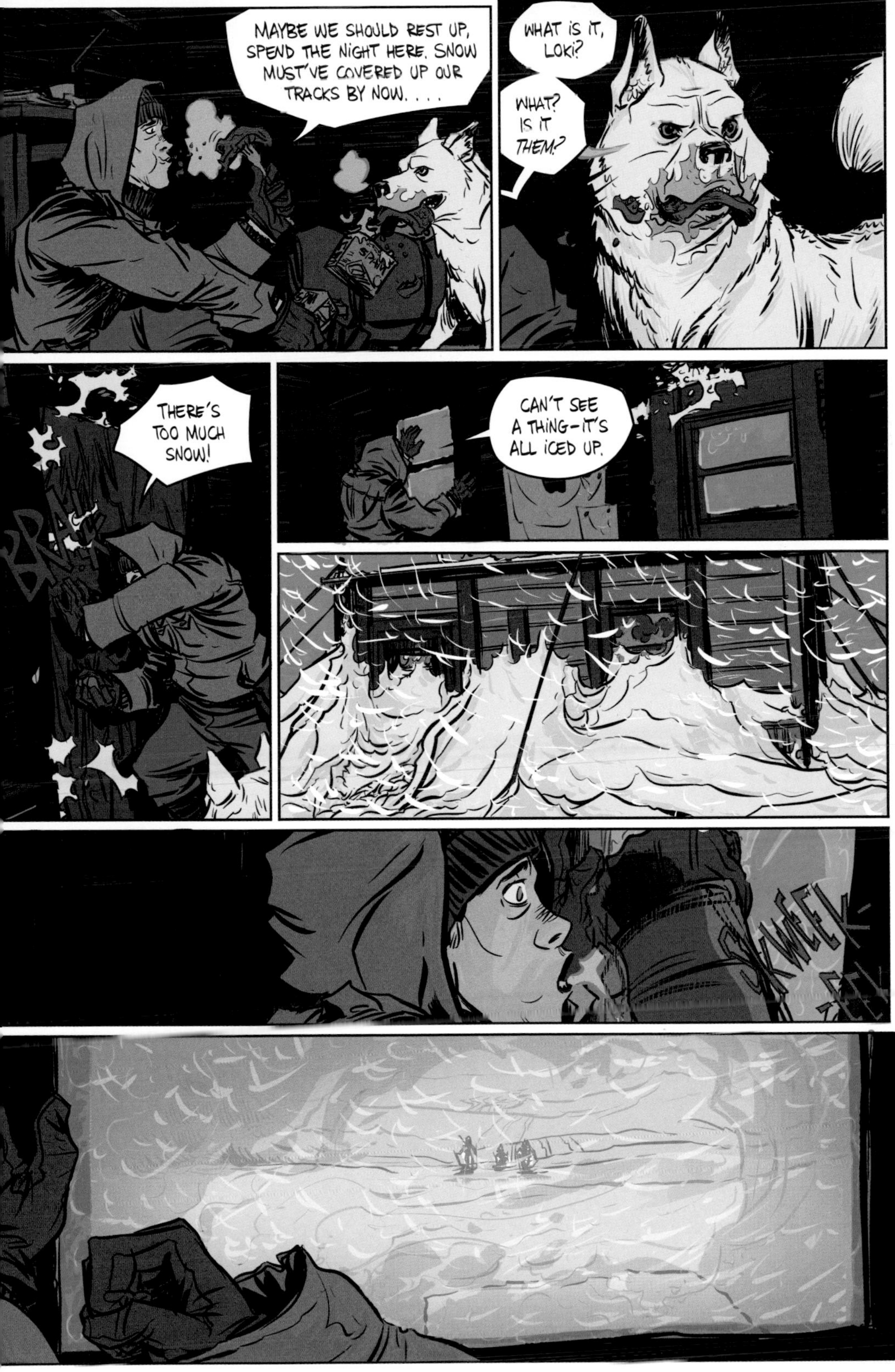
MAYBE WE SHOULD REST UP, SPEND THE NIGHT HERE. SNOW MUST'VE COVERED UP OUR TRACKS BY NOW. . . .
WHAT IS IT, LOKI?
WHAT? IS IT *THEM?*
THERE'S TOO MUCH SNOW!
CAN'T SEE A THING—IT'S ALL ICED UP.

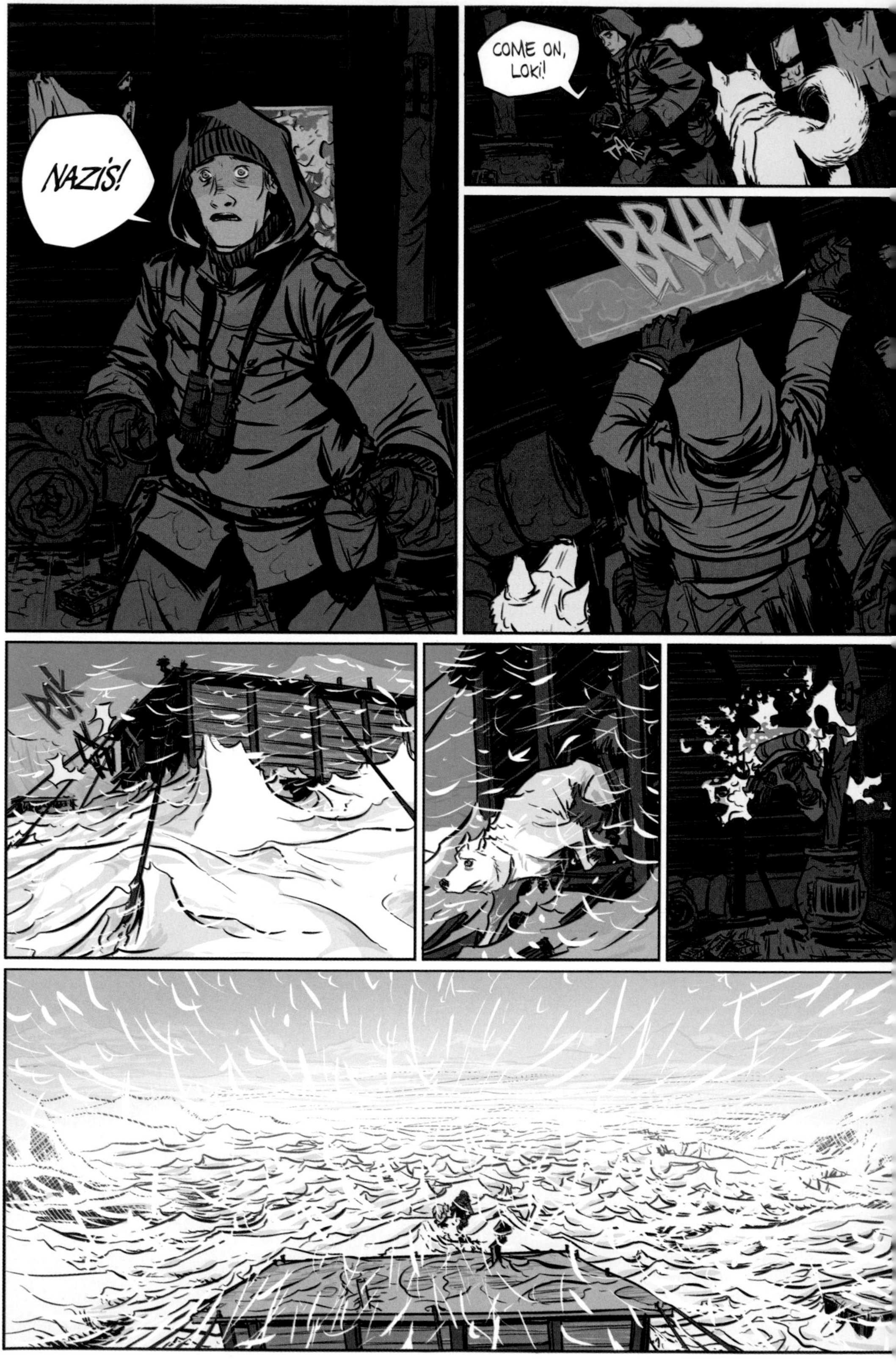
NAZIS!
COME ON, LOKI!
BRAK

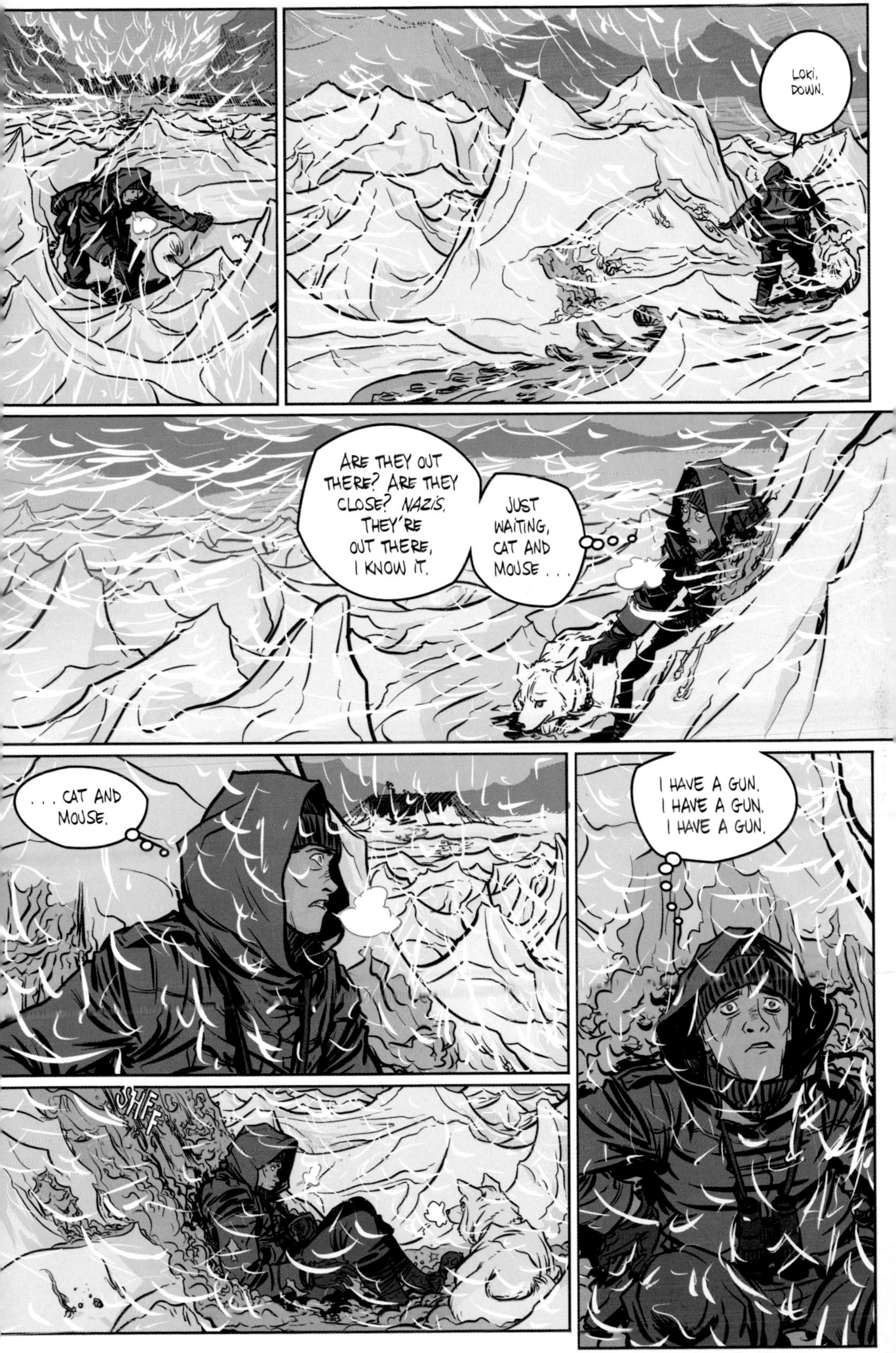
LOKI, DOWN.
ARE THEY OUT THERE? ARE THEY CLOSE? NAZIS, THEY'RE OUT THERE, I KNOW IT.
JUST WAITING, CAT AND MOUSE . . .
. . . CAT AND MOUSE.
I HAVE A GUN. I HAVE A GUN. I HAVE A GUN.
SHFF

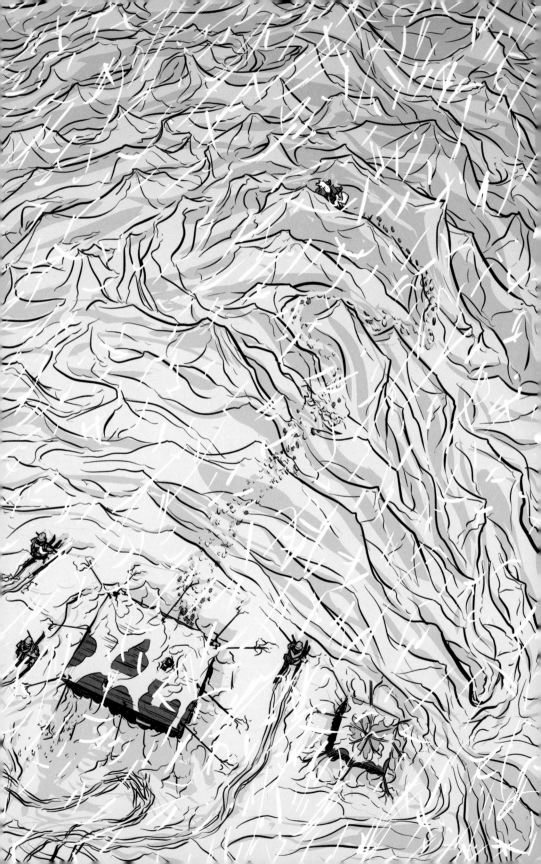

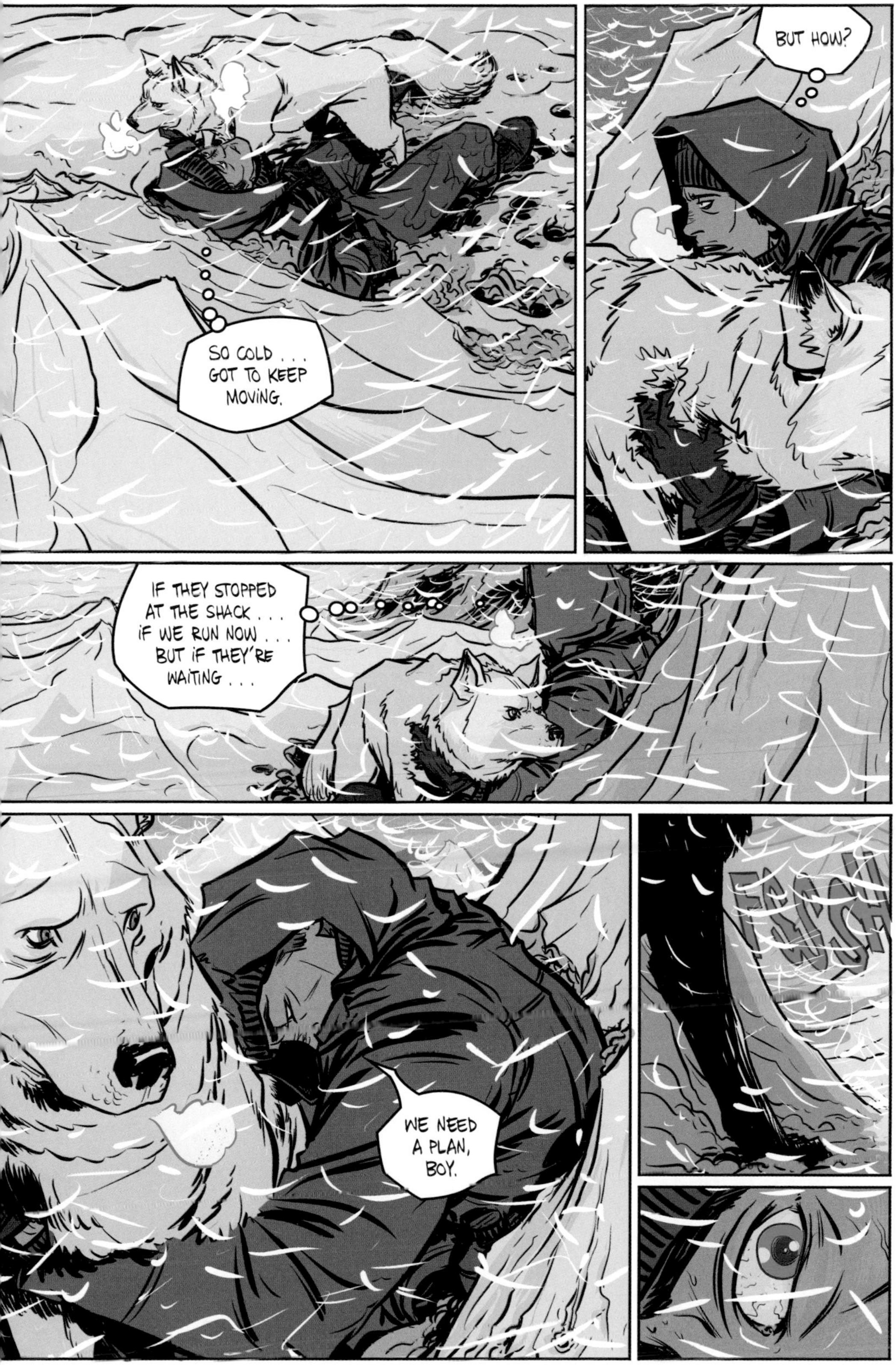
SO COLD . . . GOT TO KEEP MOVING.
BUT HOW?
IF THEY STOPPED AT THE SHACK . . . IF WE RUN NOW . . . BUT IF THEY'RE WAITING . . .
WE NEED A PLAN, BOY.
FSSSH

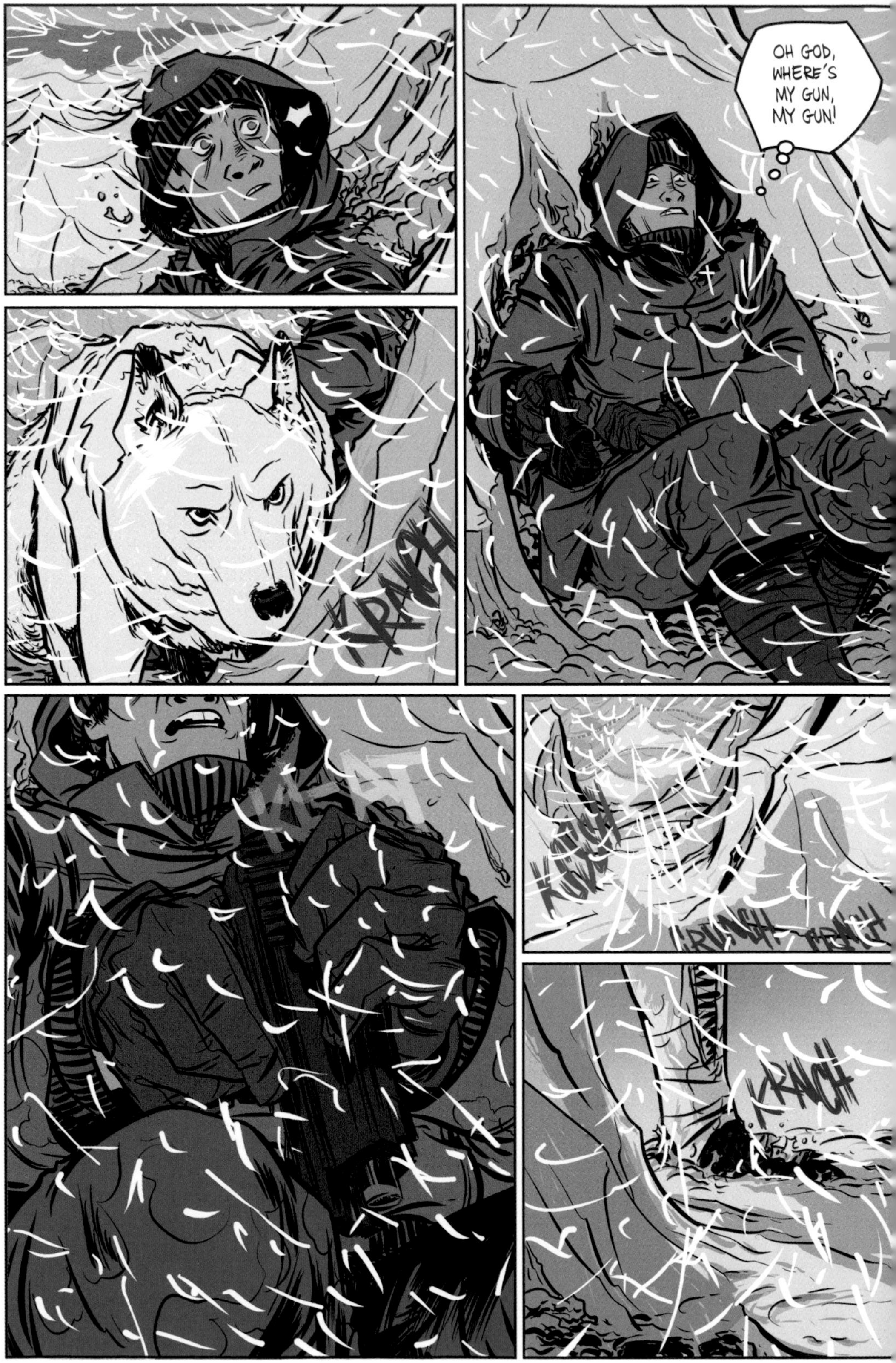
OH GOD, WHERE'S MY GUN, MY GUN!
KRANCH
KRANCH

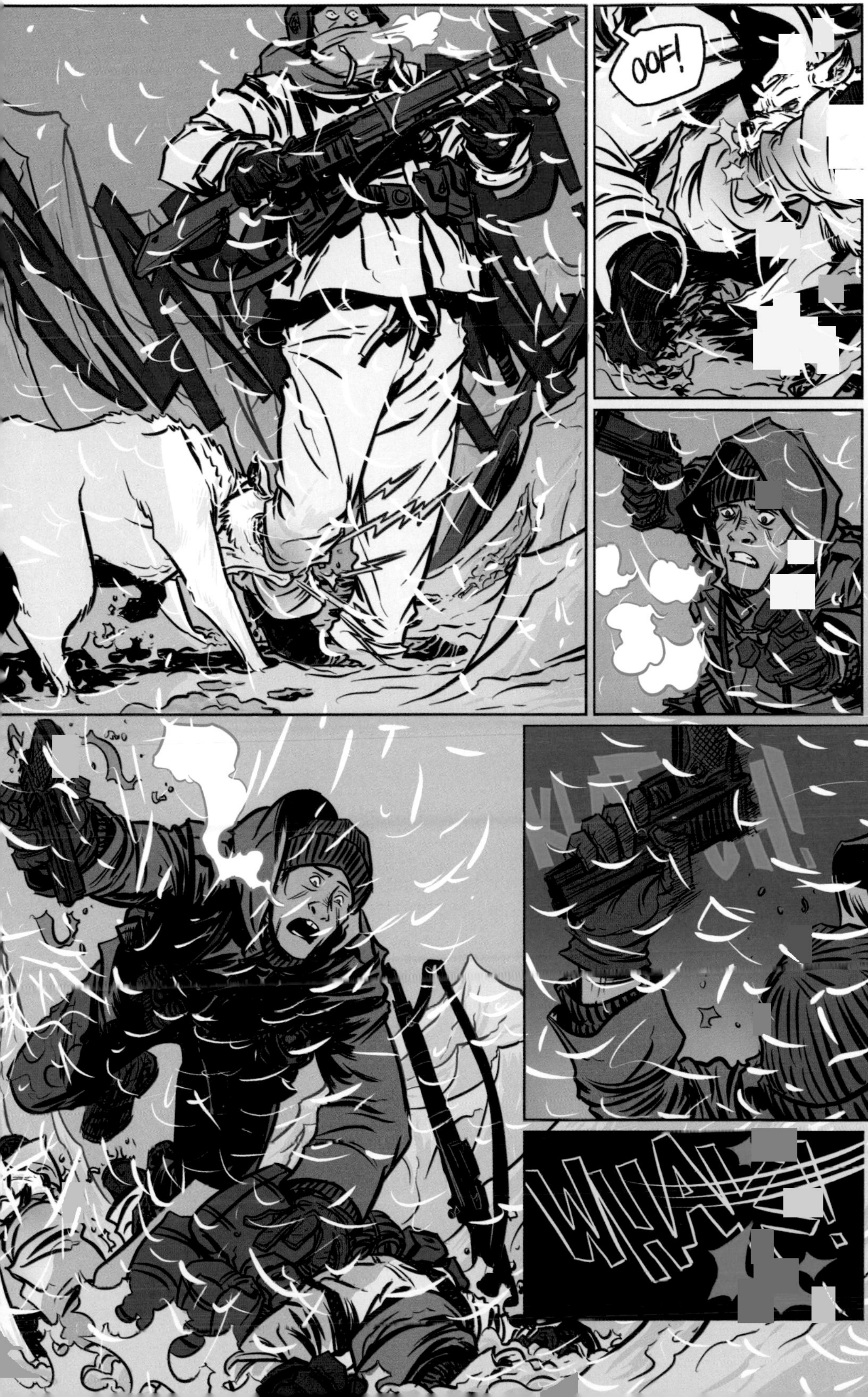
OOF!

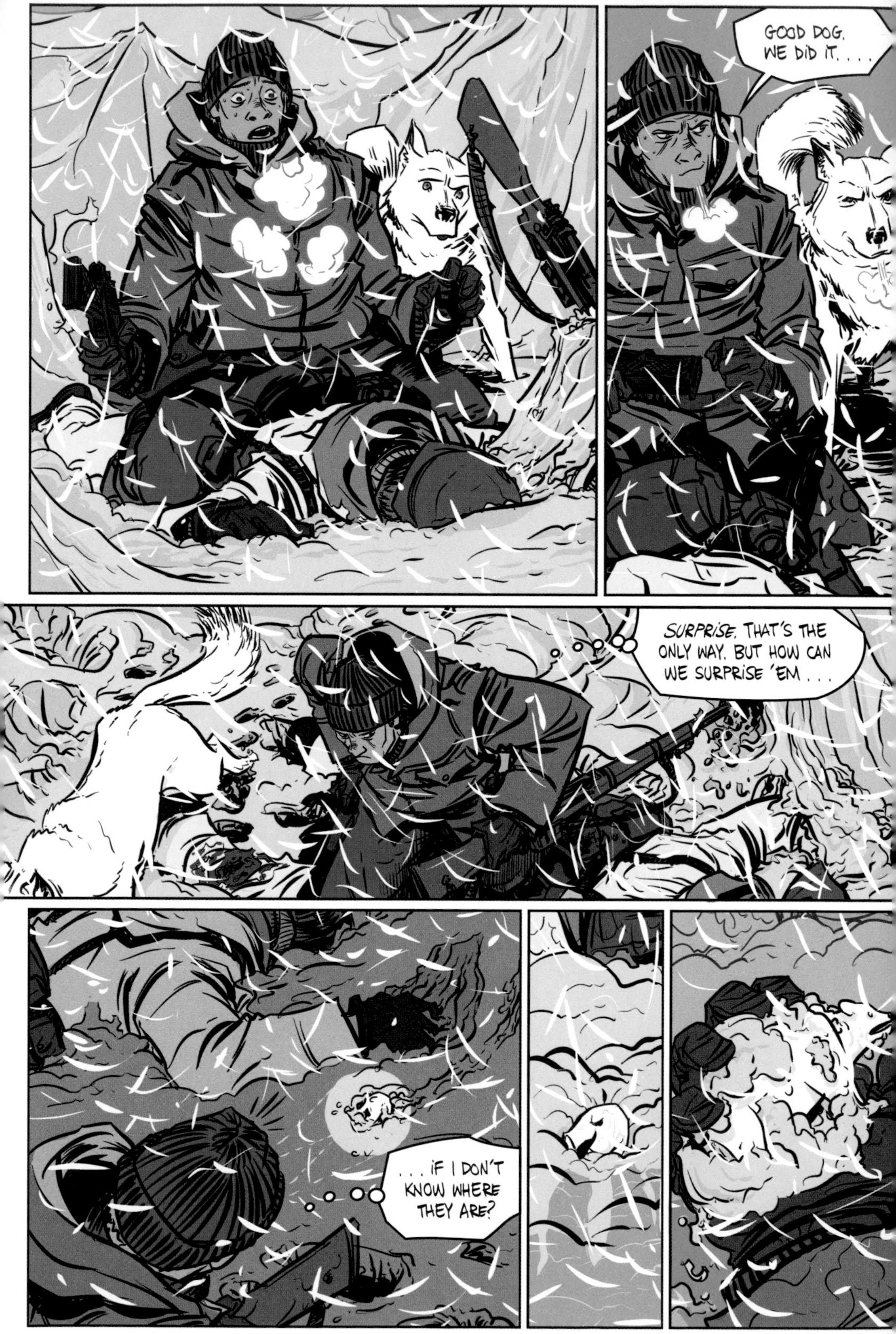
GOOD DOG. WE DID IT. . . .
SURPRISE. THAT'S THE ONLY WAY. BUT HOW CAN WE SURPRISE 'EM . . .
. . . IF I DON'T KNOW WHERE THEY ARE?

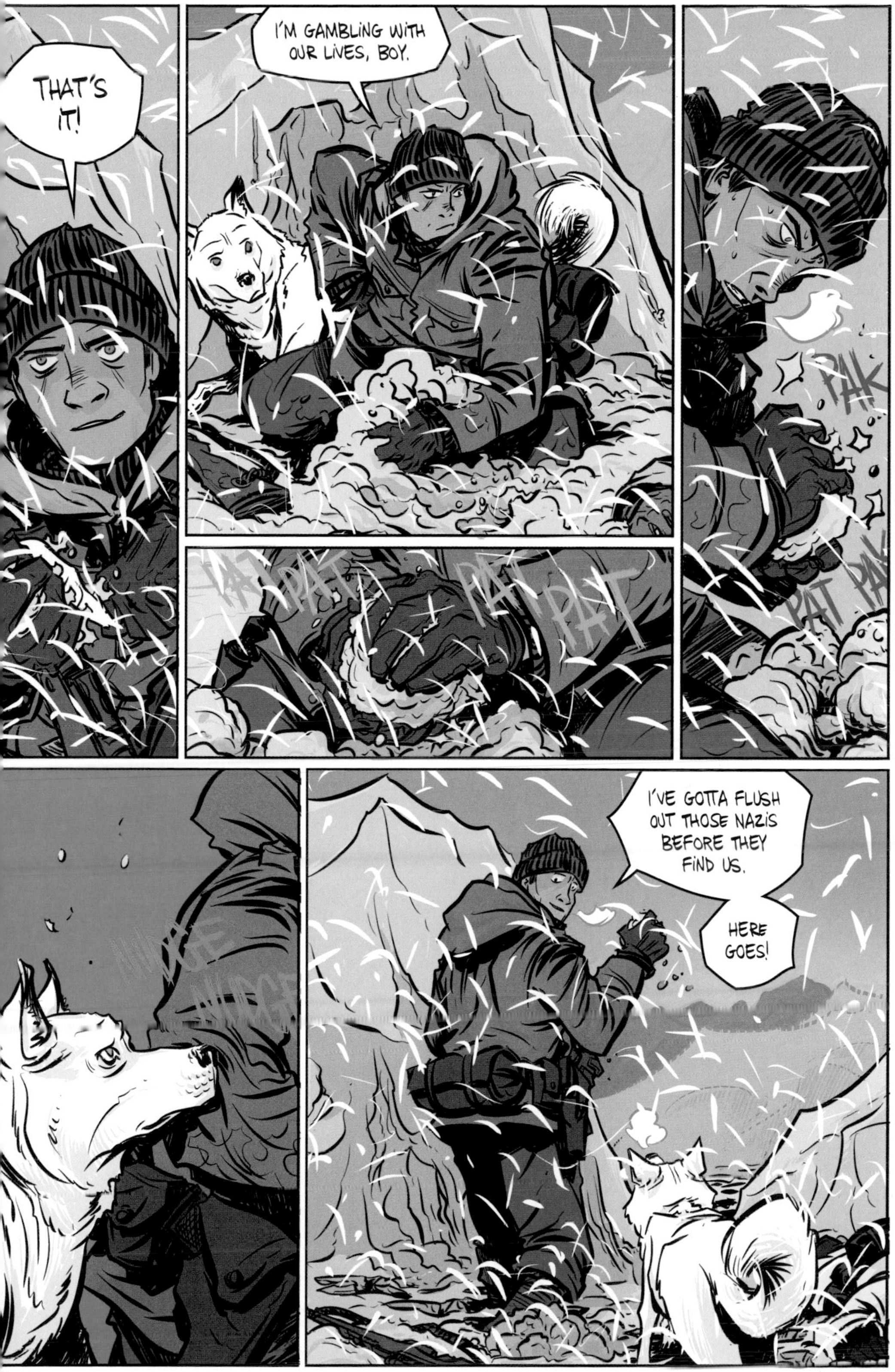
THAT'S IT!
I'M GAMBLING WITH OUR LIVES, BOY.
PAK
PAT PAT
PAT PAT
PAT
I'VE GOTTA FLUSH OUT THOSE NAZIS BEFORE THEY FIND US.
HERE GOES!

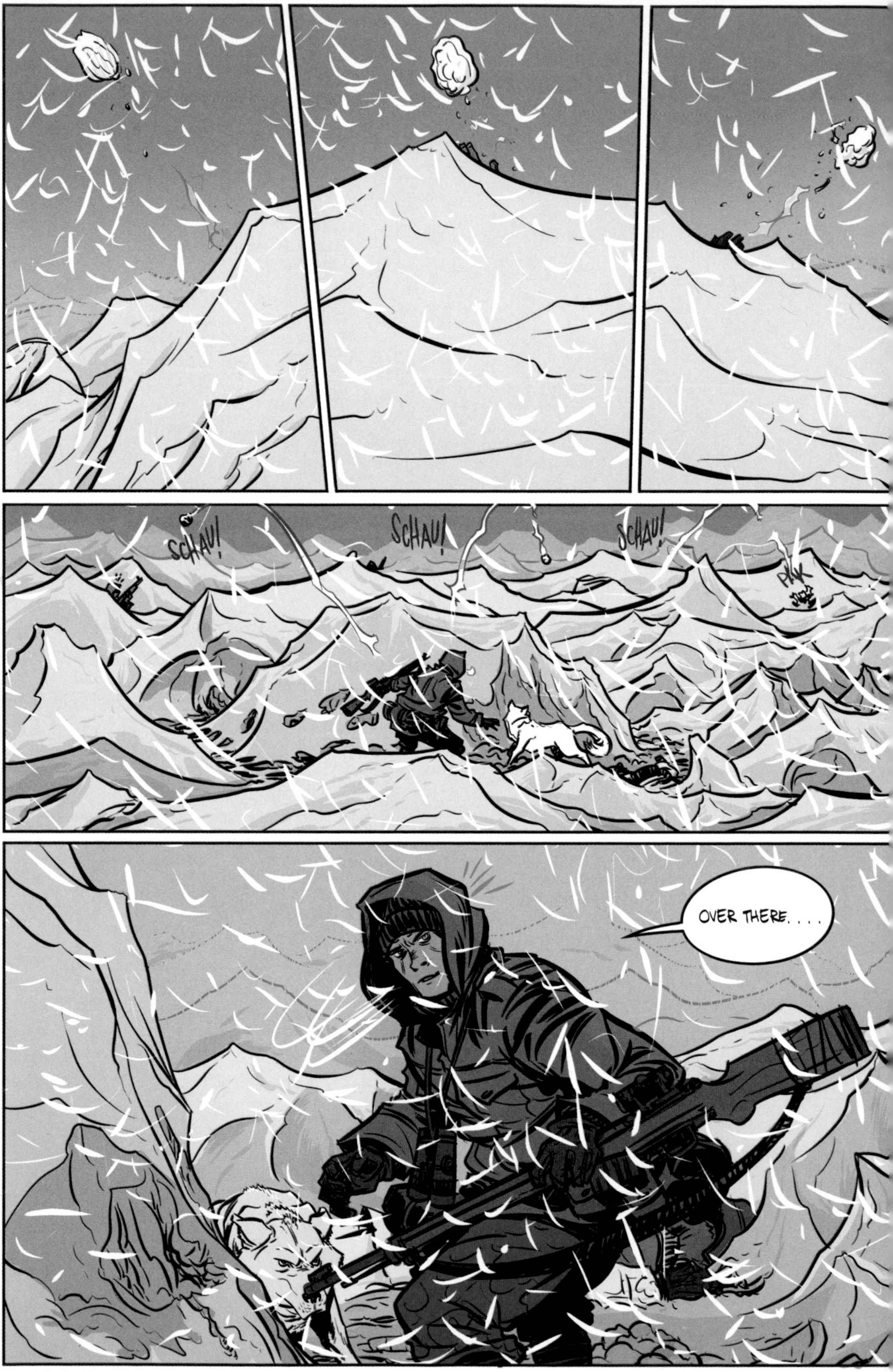
SCHAU!
SCHAU!
SCHAU!
OVER THERE. . . .

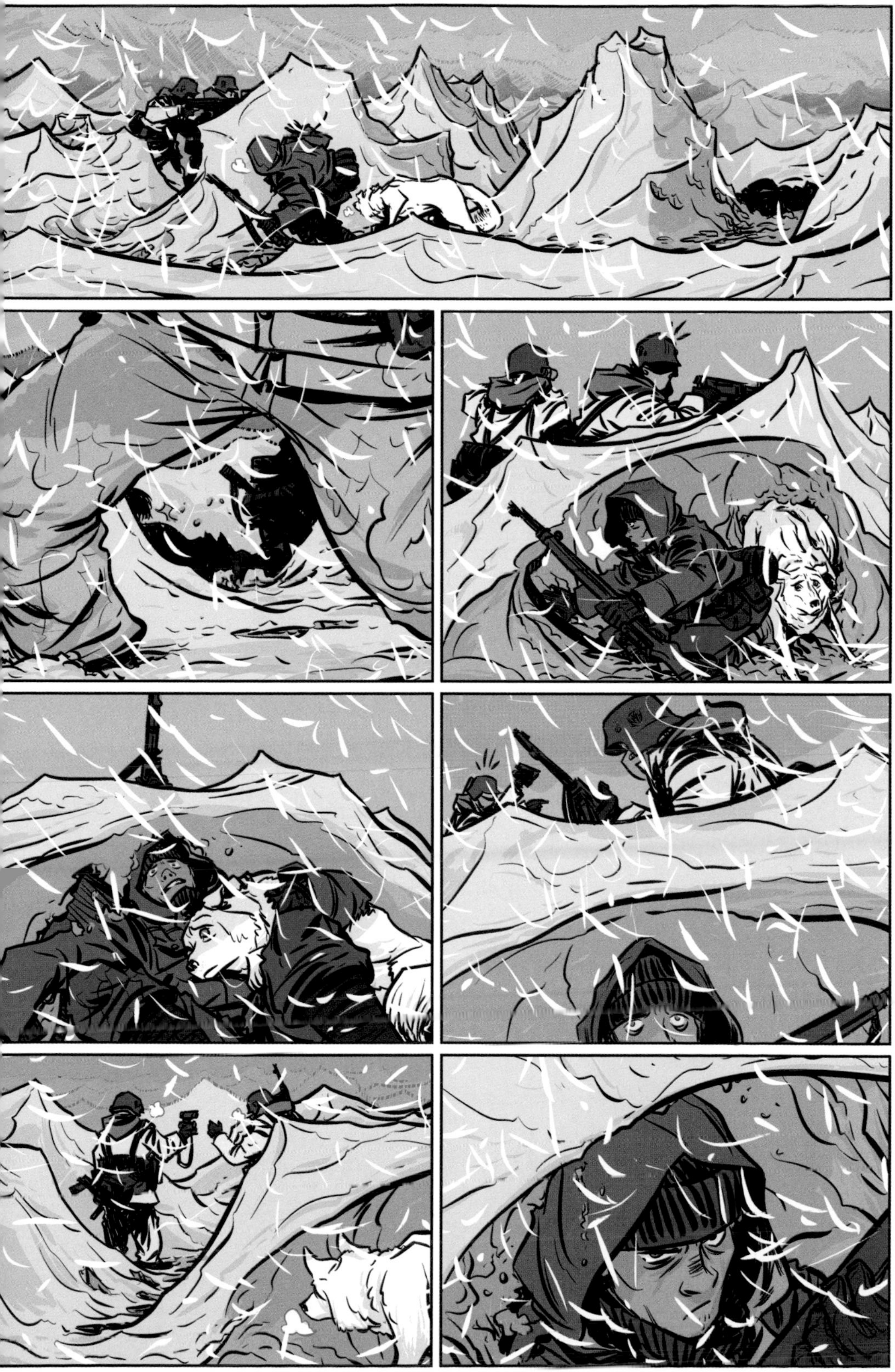

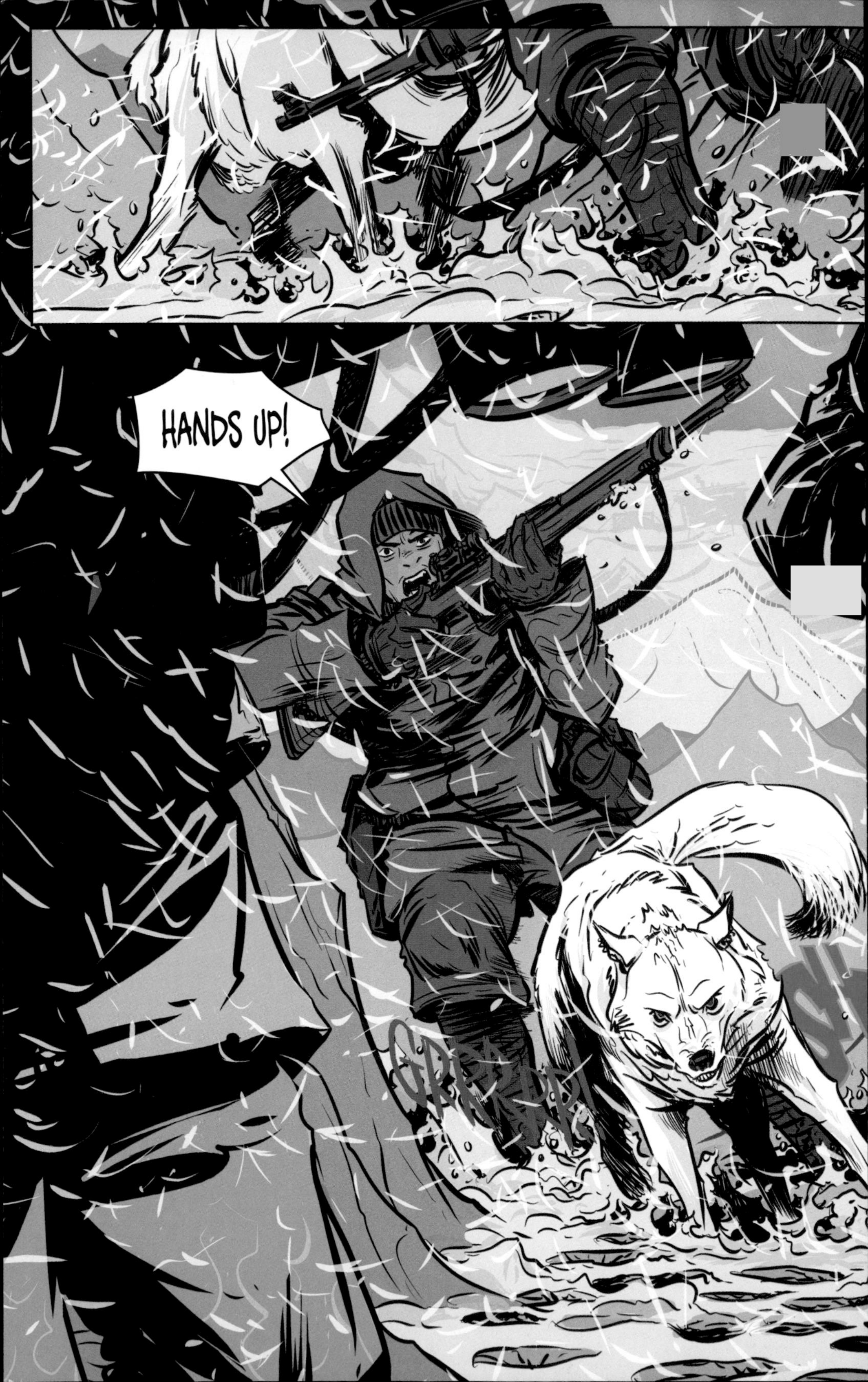
HANDS UP!
GRRRR!

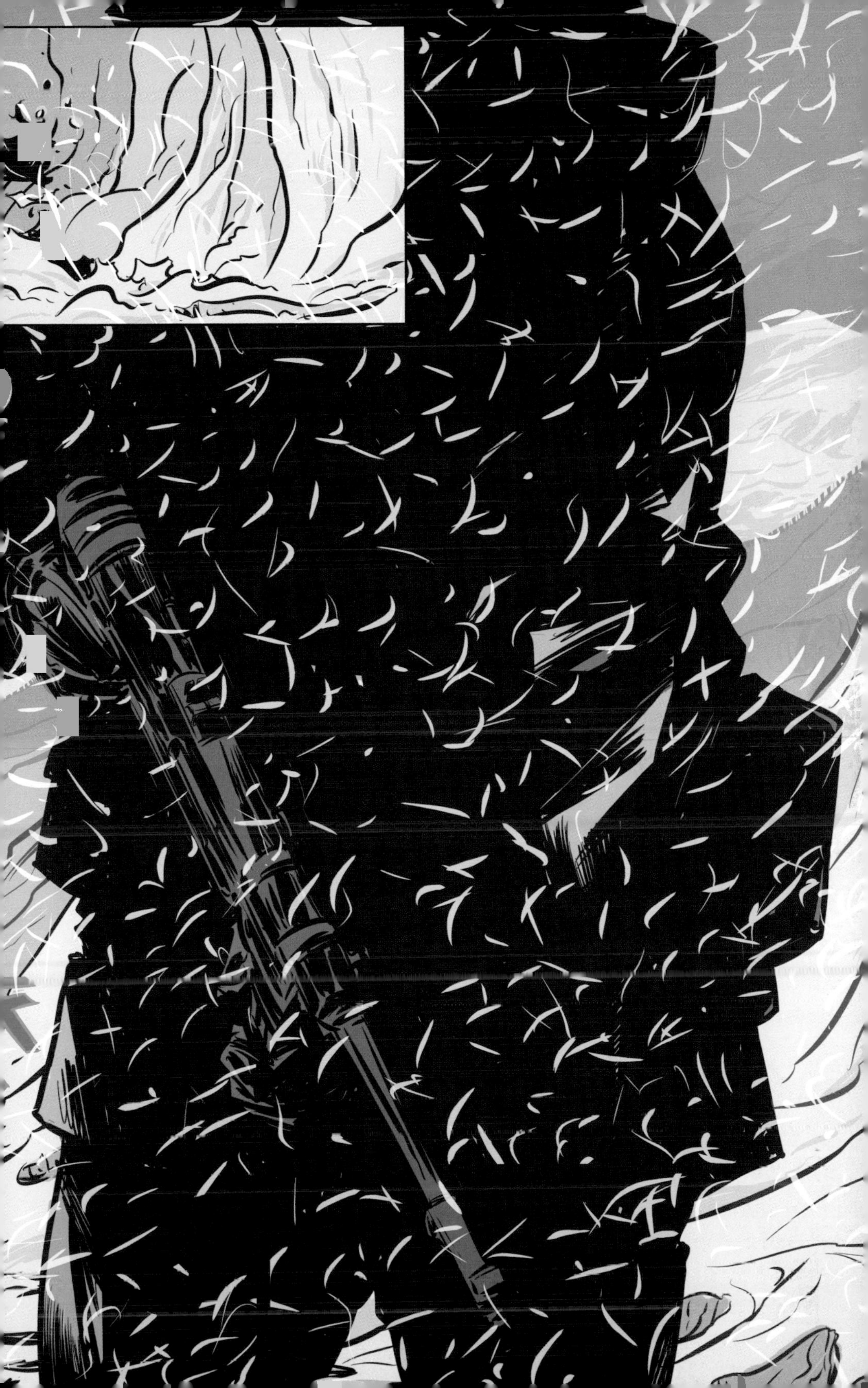

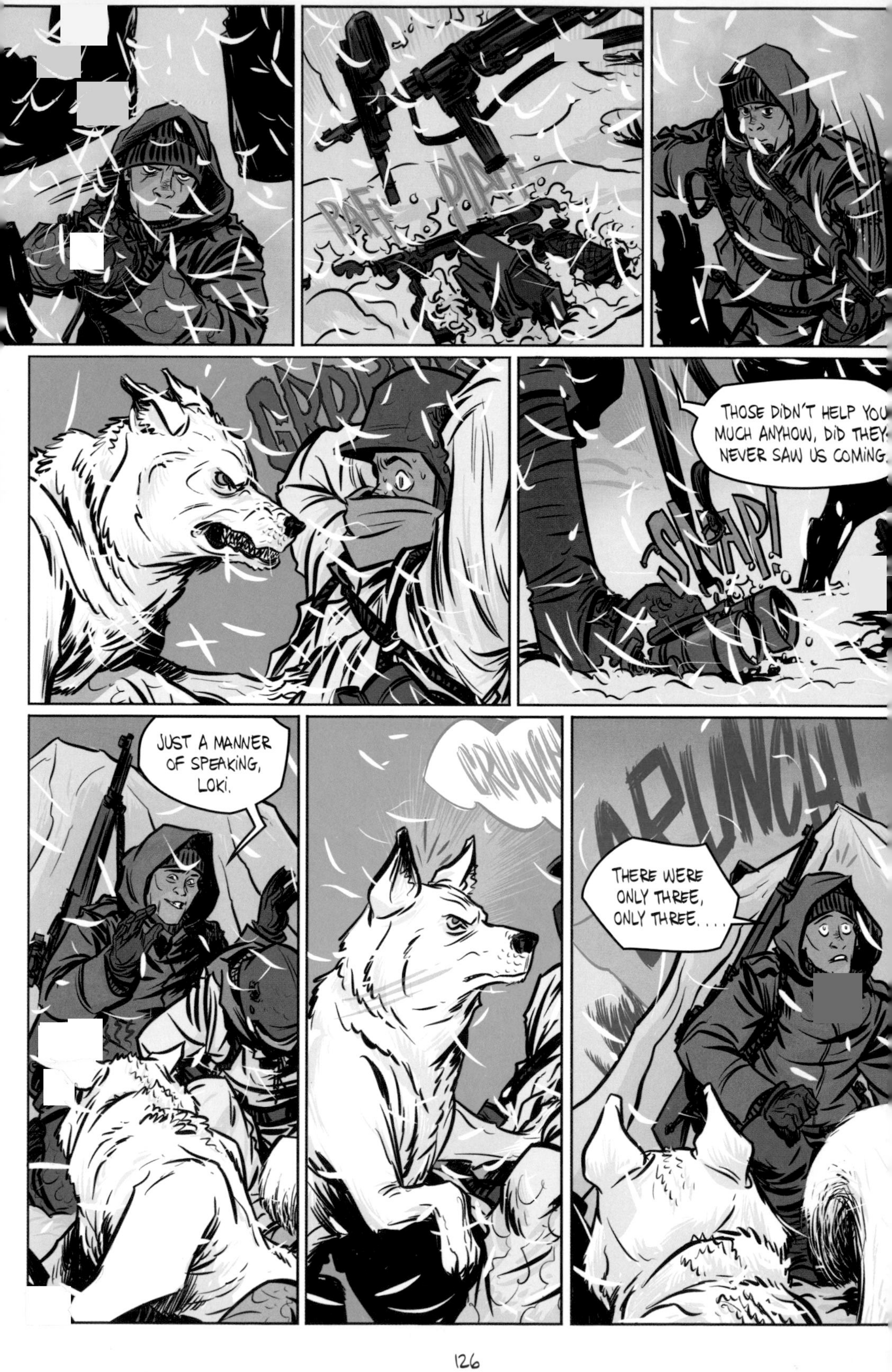
PAFF
PAFF
GRRR
THOSE DIDN'T HELP YOU MUCH ANYHOW, DID THEY? NEVER SAW US COMING.
SNAP!
JUST A MANNER OF SPEAKING, LOKI.
CRUNCH
CRUNCH!
THERE WERE ONLY THREE, ONLY THREE. . . .

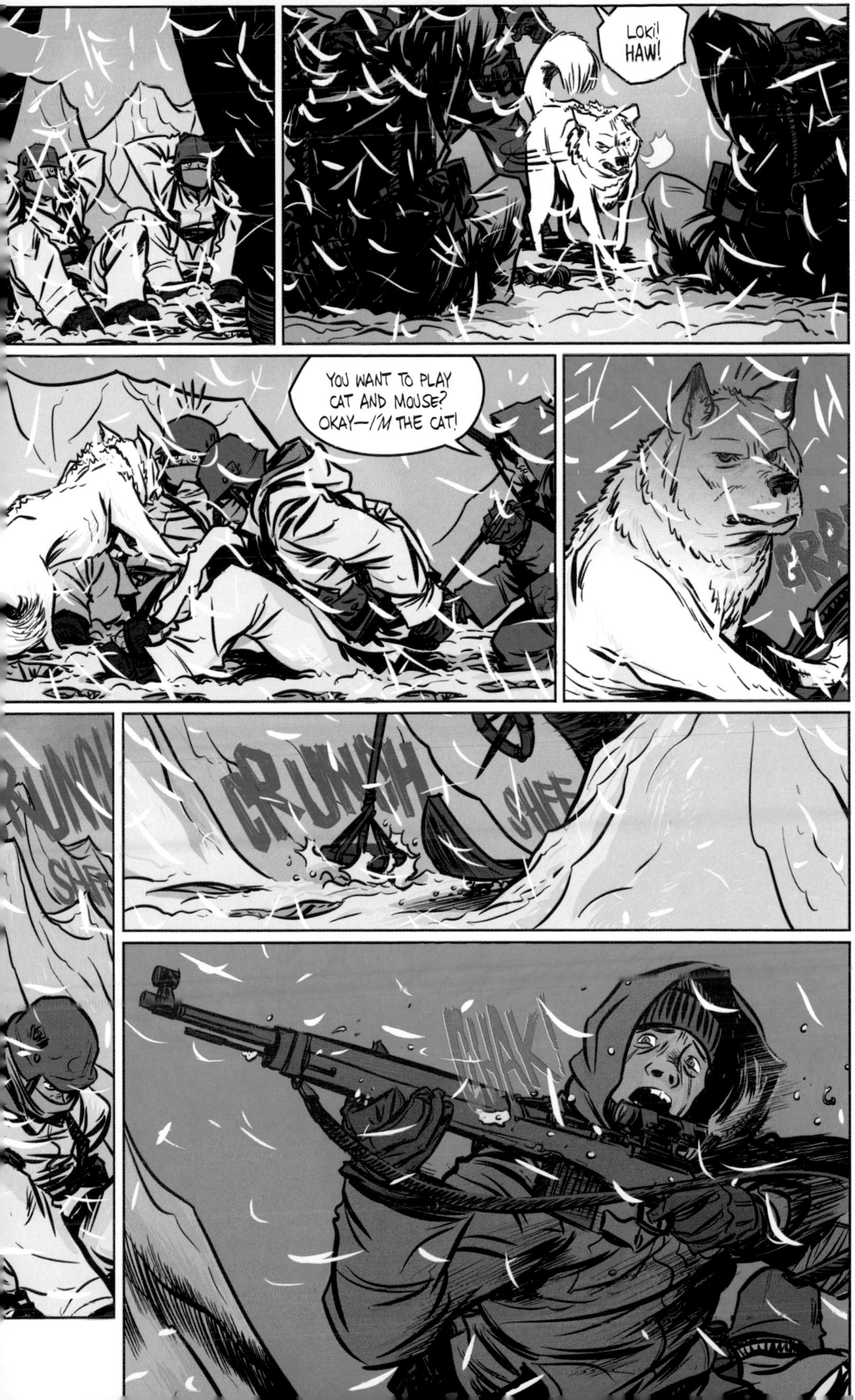
LOKI! HAW!
YOU WANT TO PLAY CAT AND MOUSE? OKAY—I'M THE CAT!
GRR
CRUNCH
SHFF
CRUNCH
SHFF
WHAK!

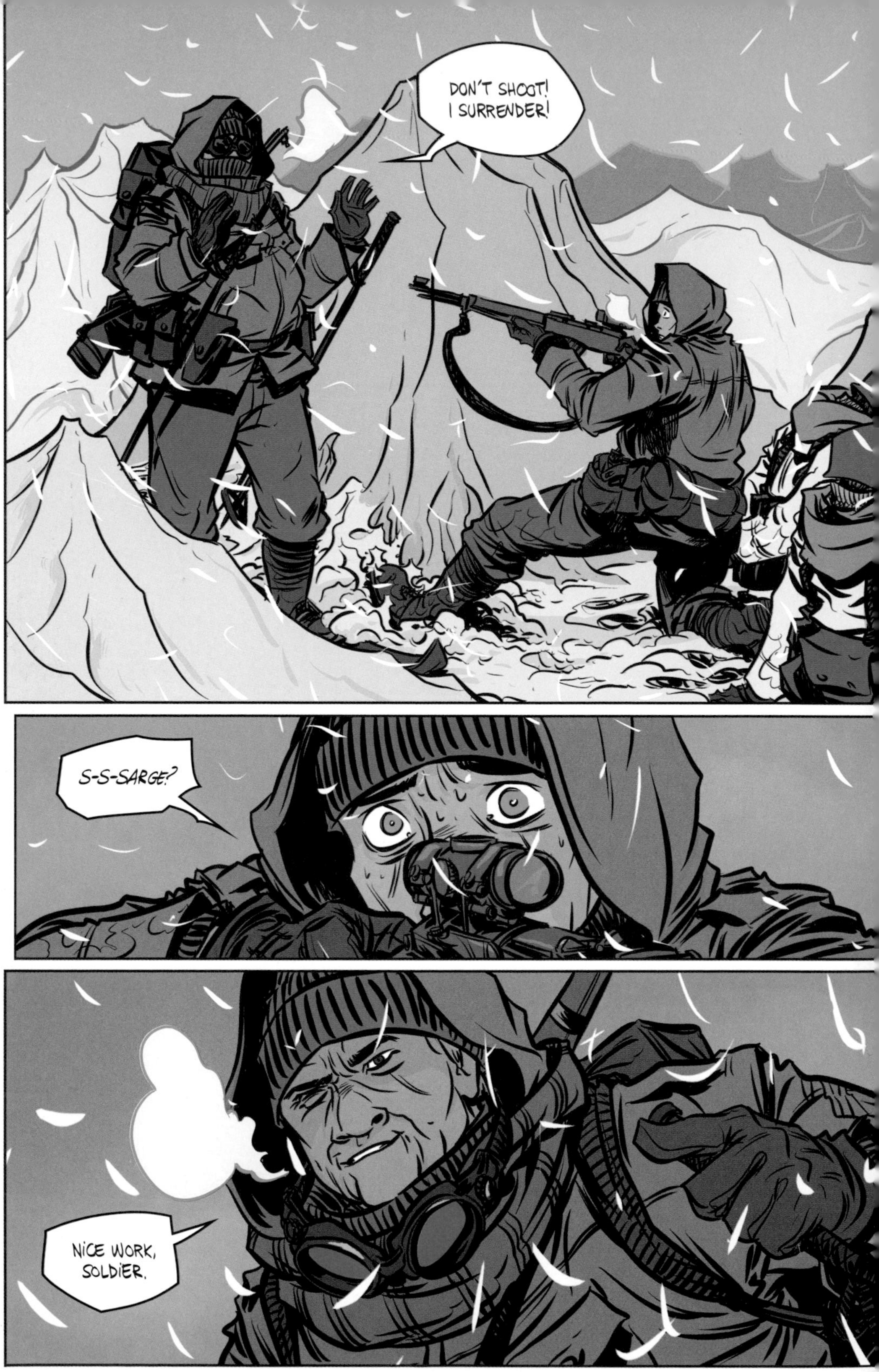
DON'T SHOOT! I SURRENDER!
S-S-SARGE?
NICE WORK, SOLDIER.

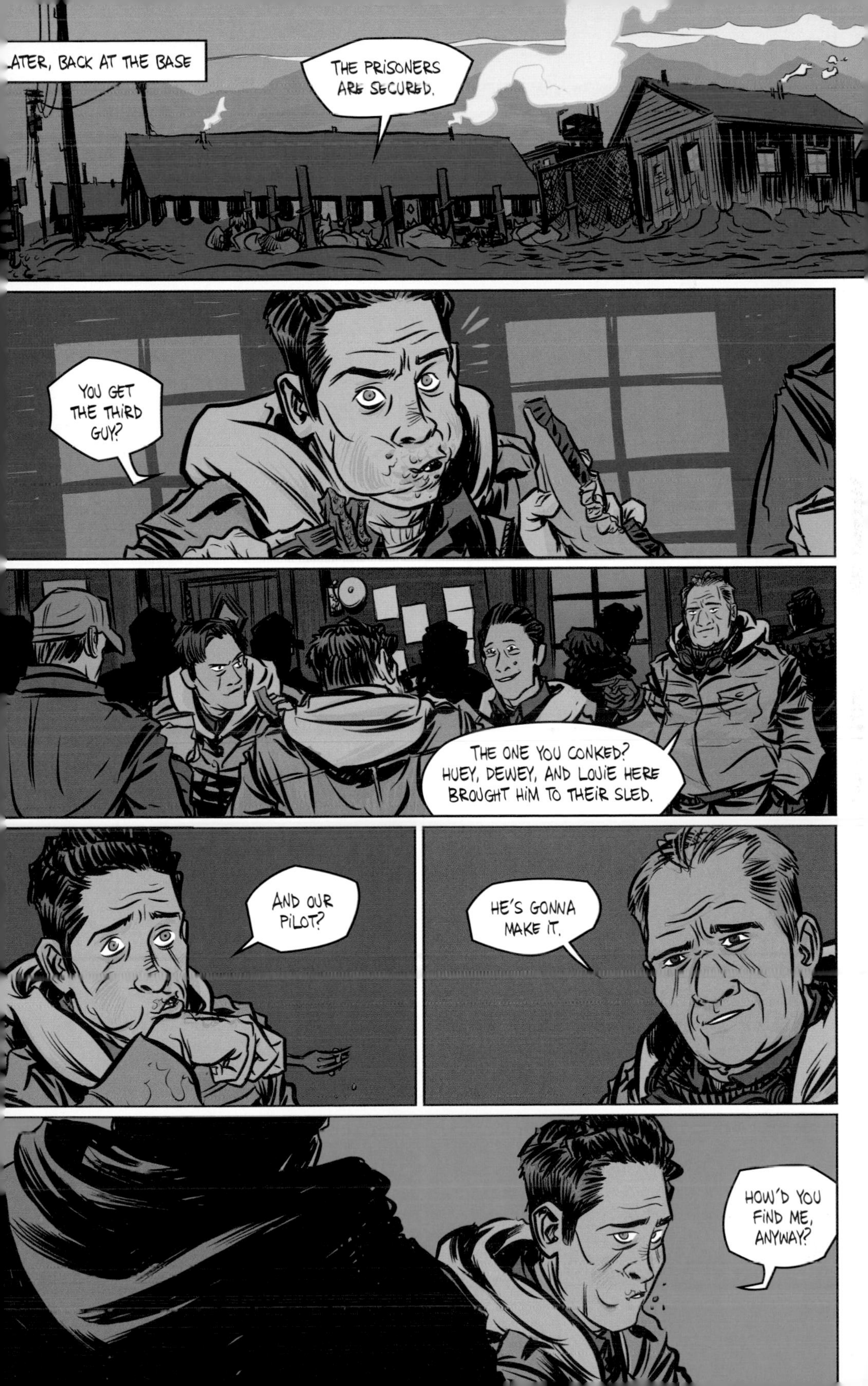
LATER, BACK AT THE BASE
THE PRISONERS ARE SECURED.
YOU GET THE THIRD GUY?
THE ONE YOU CONKED? HUEY, DEWEY, AND LOUIE HERE BROUGHT HIM TO THEIR SLED.
AND OUR PILOT?
HE'S GONNA MAKE IT.
HOW'D YOU FIND ME, ANYWAY?

WHEN YOU DIDN'T CATCH UP WITH ME, I KNEW THERE WAS TROUBLE.... ME AND THE BOYS SKIED BACK TO THE PLANE—

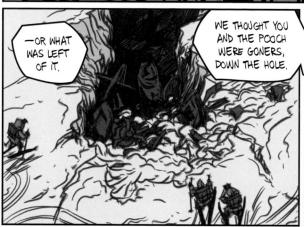

—OR WHAT WAS LEFT OF IT.

WE THOUGHT YOU AND THE POOCH WERE GONERS, DOWN THE HOLE.

BUT THEN SARGE SPOTTED FOOTPRINTS . . .

. . . PAWPRINTS . . .

. . . AND SKI TRACKS . . .

CUT TO THE CHASE!

THE NAZIS WERE ON YOUR TAIL, SO WE GOT ON THEIRS.

THANKS, FELLAS. I WAS LOOKING FOR A RIDE HOME. I OWE YOU.

130

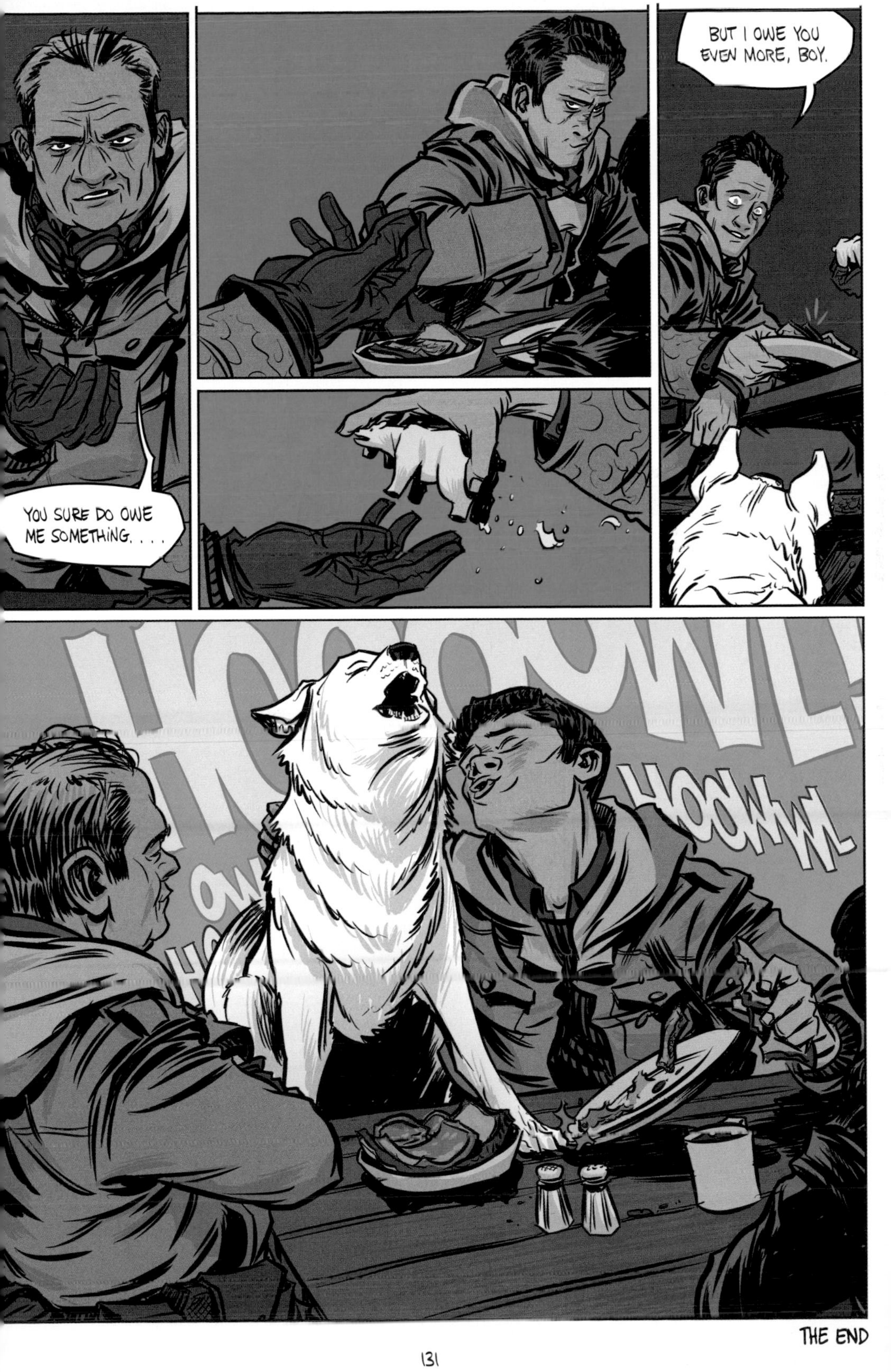
YOU SURE DO OWE ME SOMETHING. . . .
BUT I OWE YOU EVEN MORE, BOY.

THE END

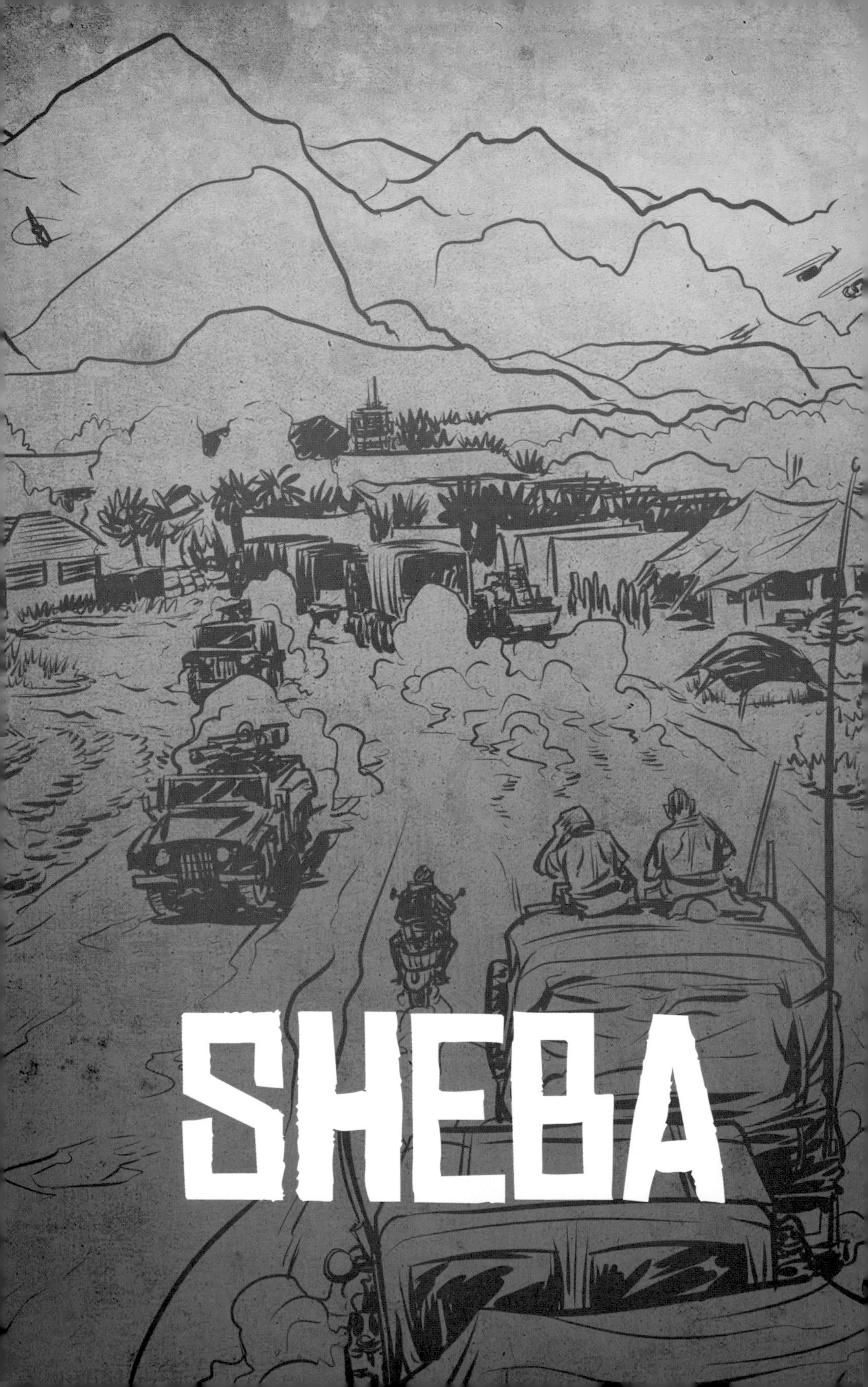
SHEBA

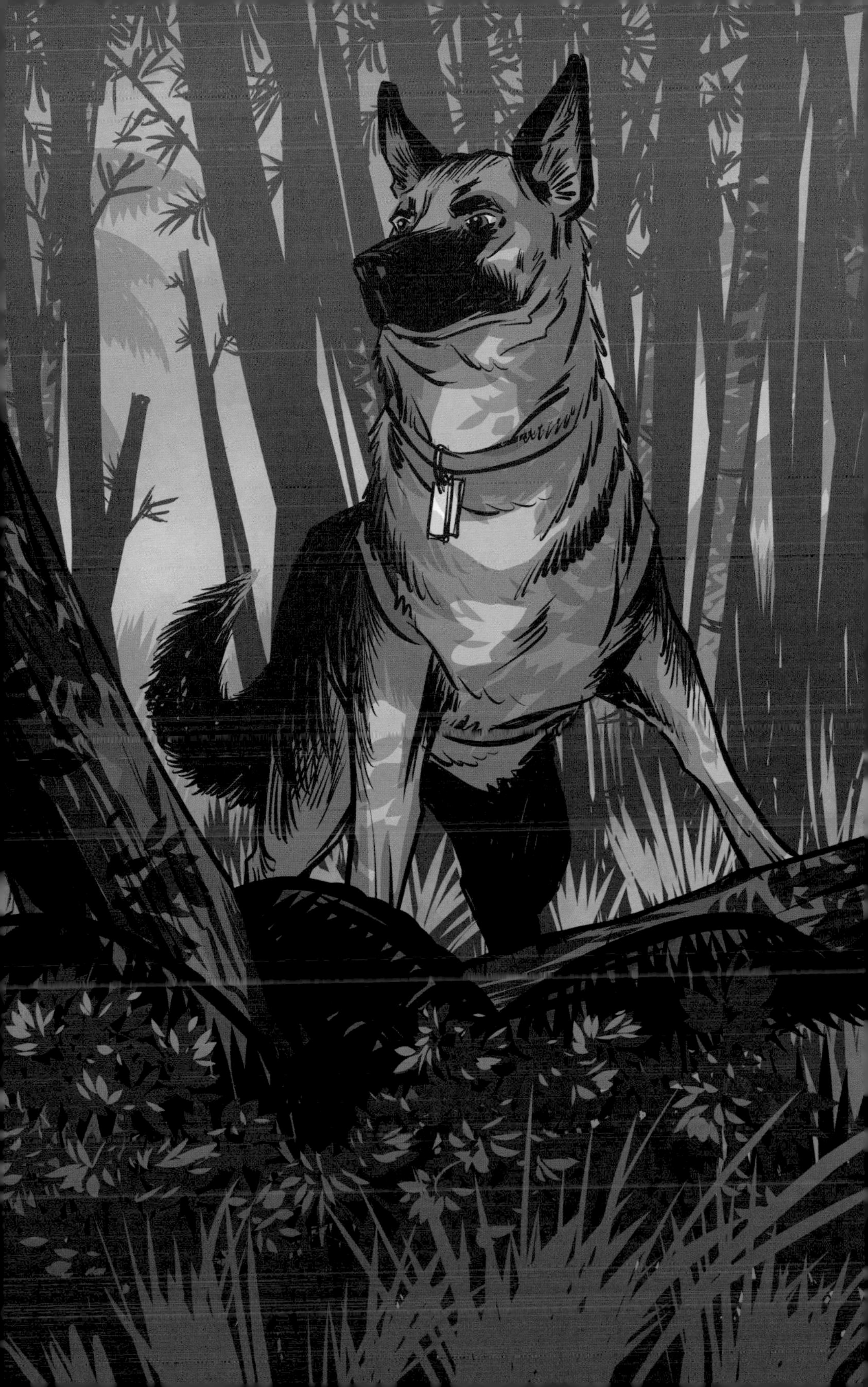

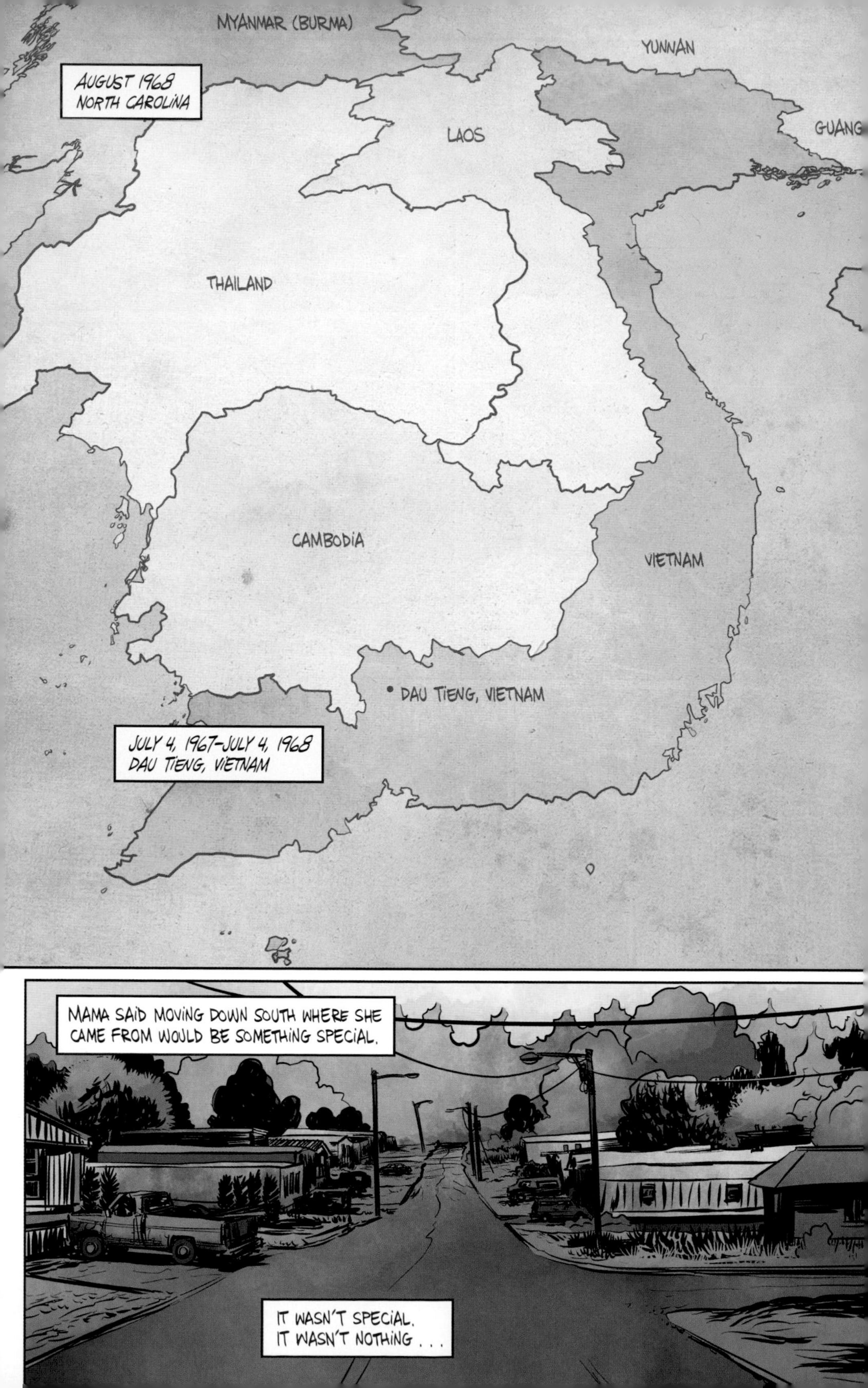
AUGUST 1968
NORTH CAROLINA
MYANMAR (BURMA)
YUNNAN
GUANG
LAOS
THAILAND
CAMBODIA
VIETNAM
DAU TIENG, VIETNAM
JULY 4, 1967–JULY 4, 1968
DAU TIENG, VIETNAM
MAMA SAID MOVING DOWN SOUTH WHERE SHE CAME FROM WOULD BE SOMETHING SPECIAL.
IT WASN'T SPECIAL.
IT WASN'T NOTHING . . .

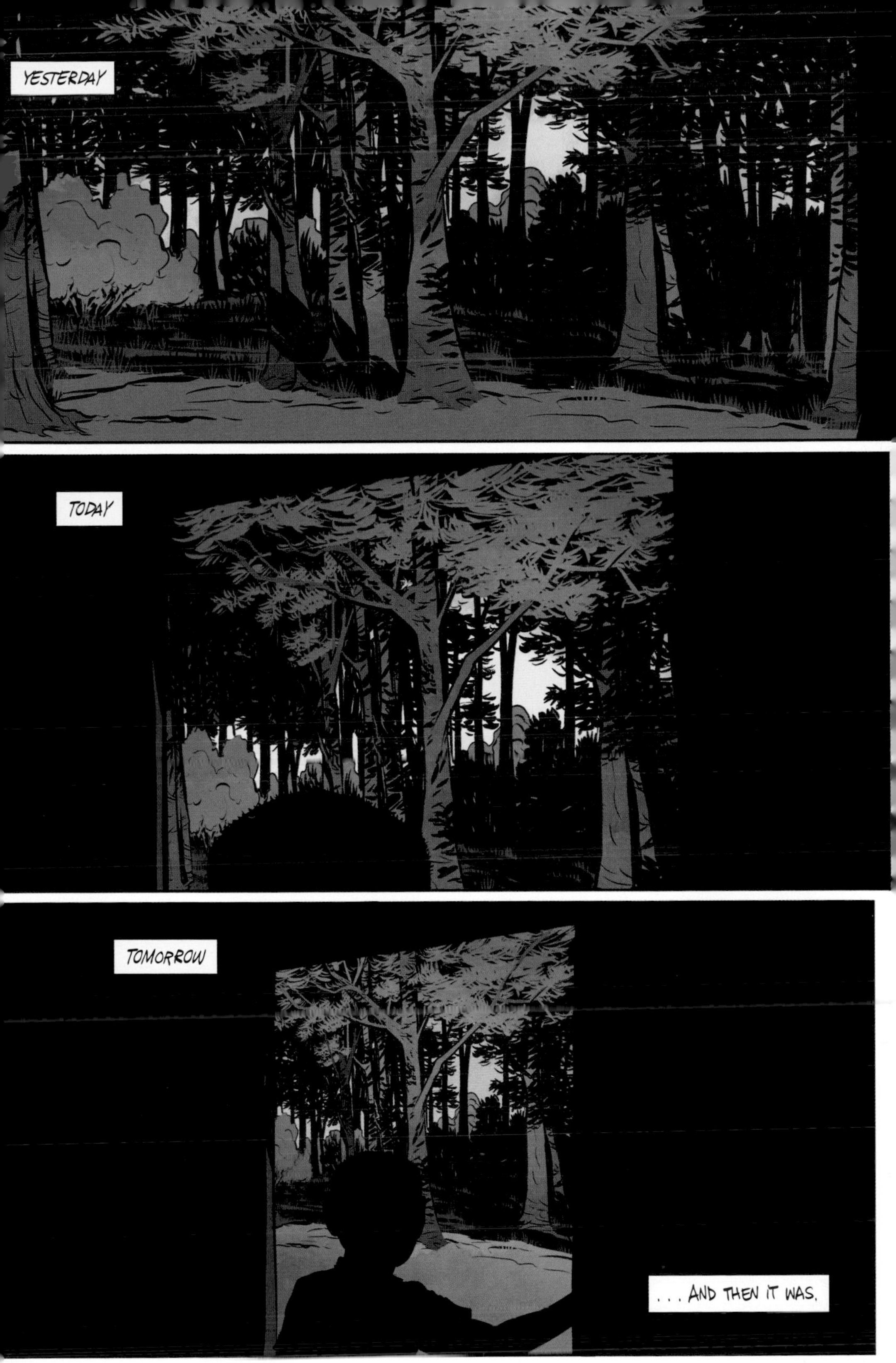
YESTERDAY
TODAY
TOMORROW
. . . AND THEN IT WAS.

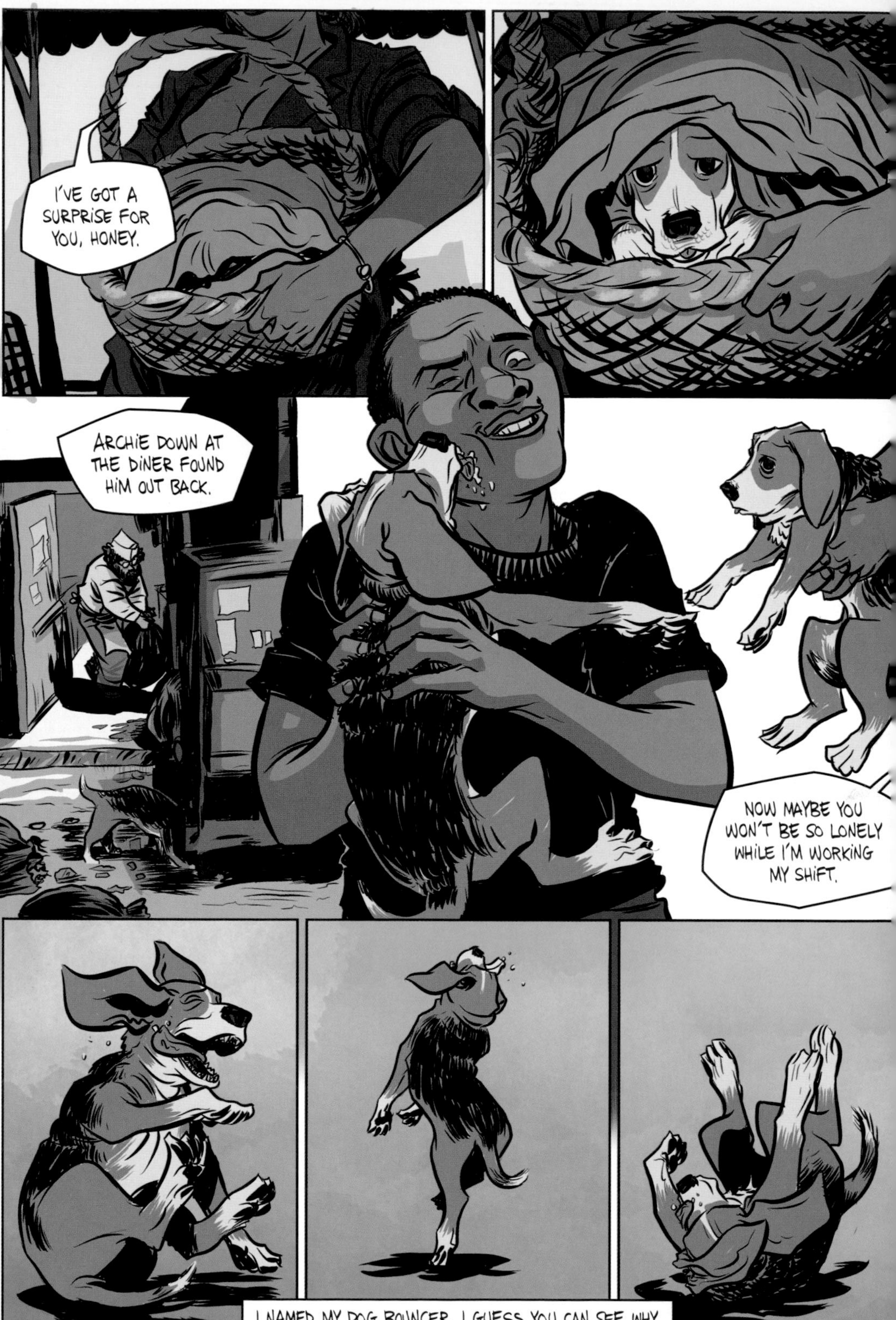
I'VE GOT A SURPRISE FOR YOU, HONEY.
ARCHIE DOWN AT THE DINER FOUND HIM OUT BACK.
NOW MAYBE YOU WON'T BE SO LONELY WHILE I'M WORKING MY SHIFT.
I NAMED MY DOG BOUNCER. I GUESS YOU CAN SEE WHY.

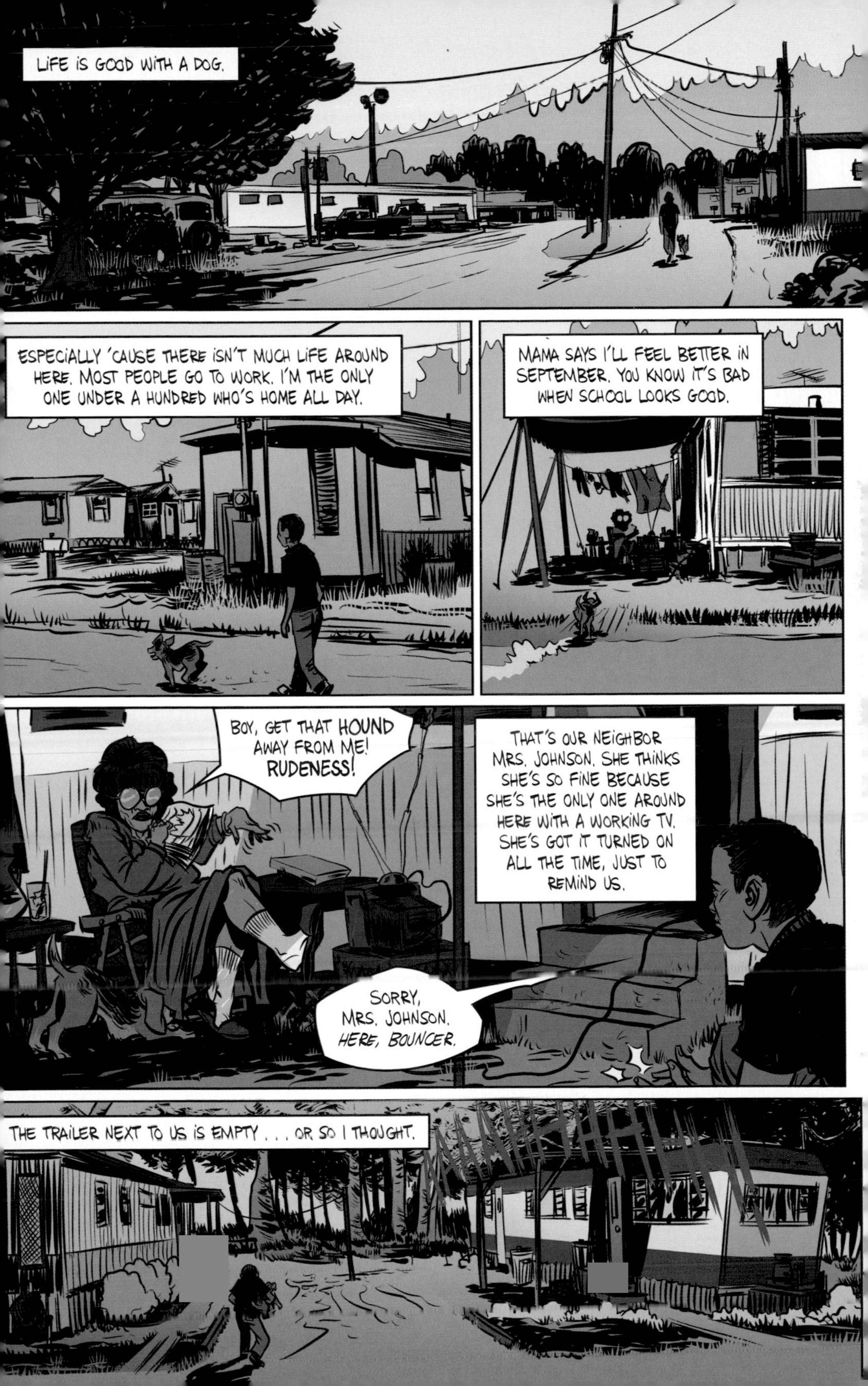
LIFE IS GOOD WITH A DOG.
ESPECIALLY 'CAUSE THERE ISN'T MUCH LIFE AROUND HERE. MOST PEOPLE GO TO WORK. I'M THE ONLY ONE UNDER A HUNDRED WHO'S HOME ALL DAY.
MAMA SAYS I'LL FEEL BETTER IN SEPTEMBER. YOU KNOW IT'S BAD WHEN SCHOOL LOOKS GOOD.
BOY, GET THAT HOUND AWAY FROM ME! RUDENESS!
THAT'S OUR NEIGHBOR MRS. JOHNSON. SHE THINKS SHE'S SO FINE BECAUSE SHE'S THE ONLY ONE AROUND HERE WITH A WORKING TV. SHE'S GOT IT TURNED ON ALL THE TIME, JUST TO REMIND US.
SORRY, MRS. JOHNSON. HERE, BOUNCER.
THE TRAILER NEXT TO US IS EMPTY . . . OR SO I THOUGHT.

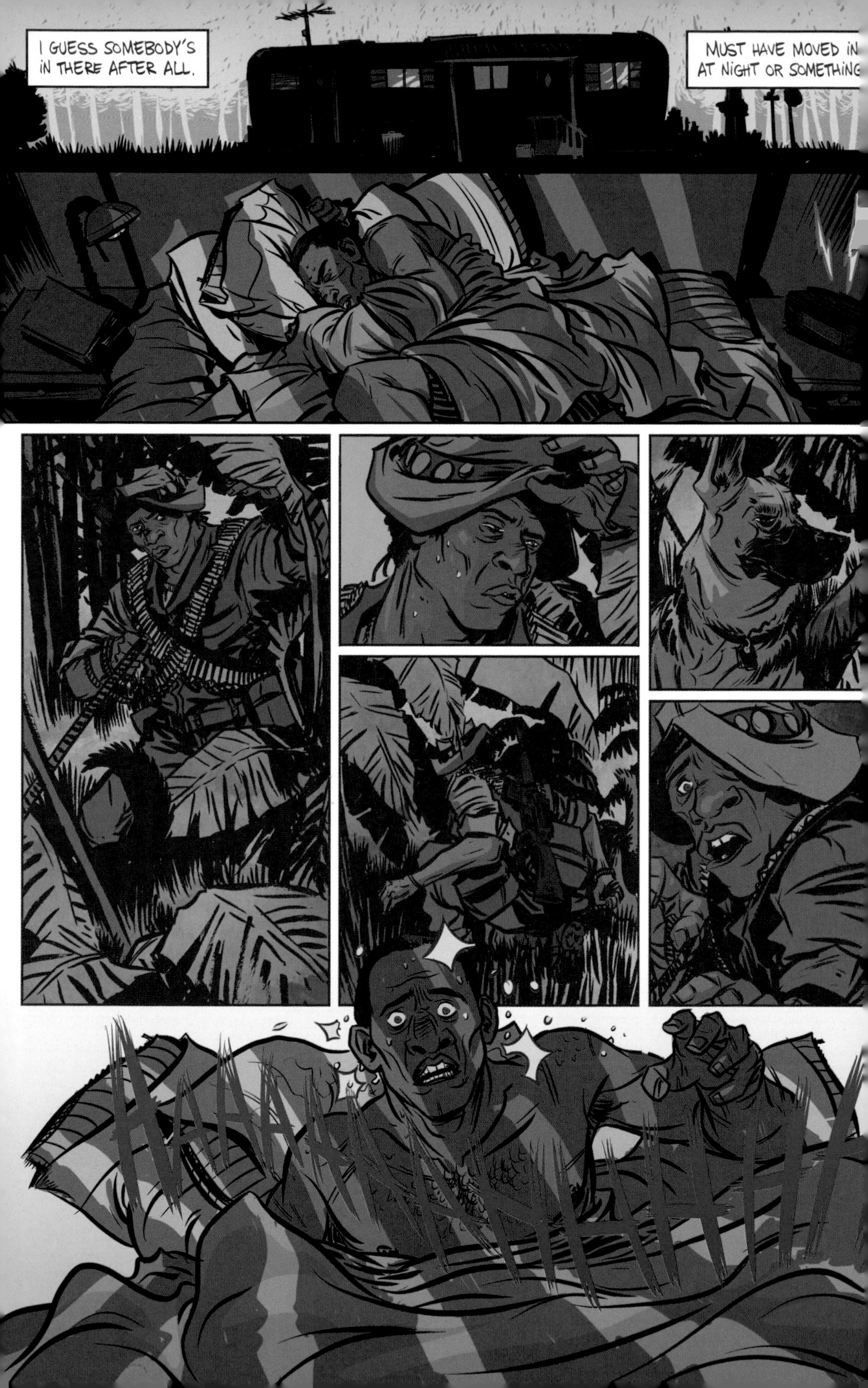
I GUESS SOMEBODY'S IN THERE AFTER ALL.
MUST HAVE MOVED IN AT NIGHT OR SOMETHING

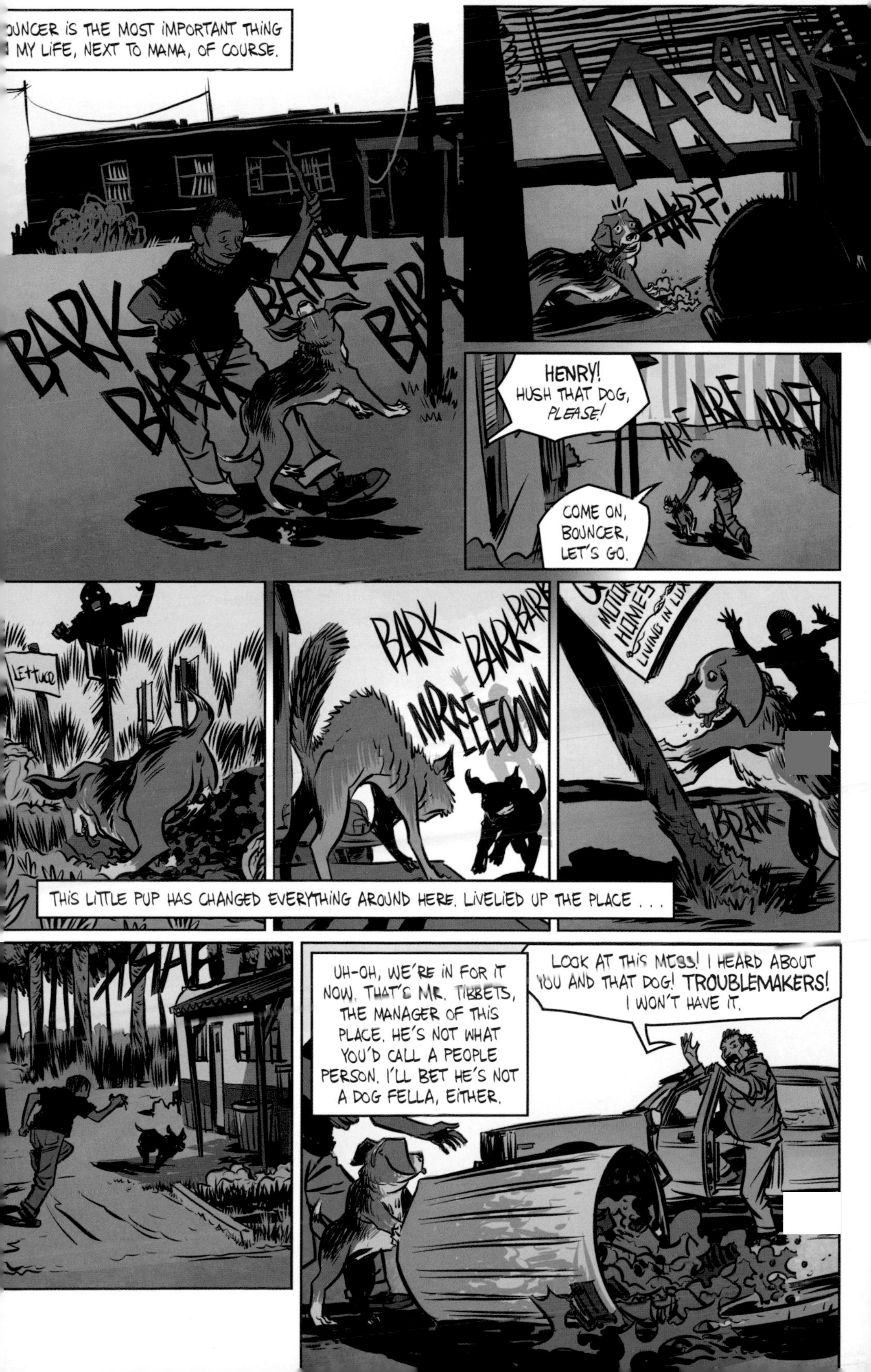
OUNCER IS THE MOST IMPORTANT THING
MY LIFE, NEXT TO MAMA, OF COURSE.
BARK
BARK
BARK
BARK
BARK
KA-SHAK
ARF!
HENRY! HUSH THAT DOG, PLEASE!
ARF ARF ARF
COME ON, BOUNCER, LET'S GO.
Lettuce
BARK
BARK BARK
MOTOR HOMES
BRAK
THIS LITTLE PUP HAS CHANGED EVERYTHING AROUND HERE. LIVELIED UP THE PLACE . . .
UH-OH, WE'RE IN FOR IT NOW. THAT'S MR. TIBBETS, THE MANAGER OF THIS PLACE. HE'S NOT WHAT YOU'D CALL A PEOPLE PERSON. I'LL BET HE'S NOT A DOG FELLA, EITHER.
LOOK AT THIS MESS! I HEARD ABOUT YOU AND THAT DOG! TROUBLEMAKERS! I WON'T HAVE IT.

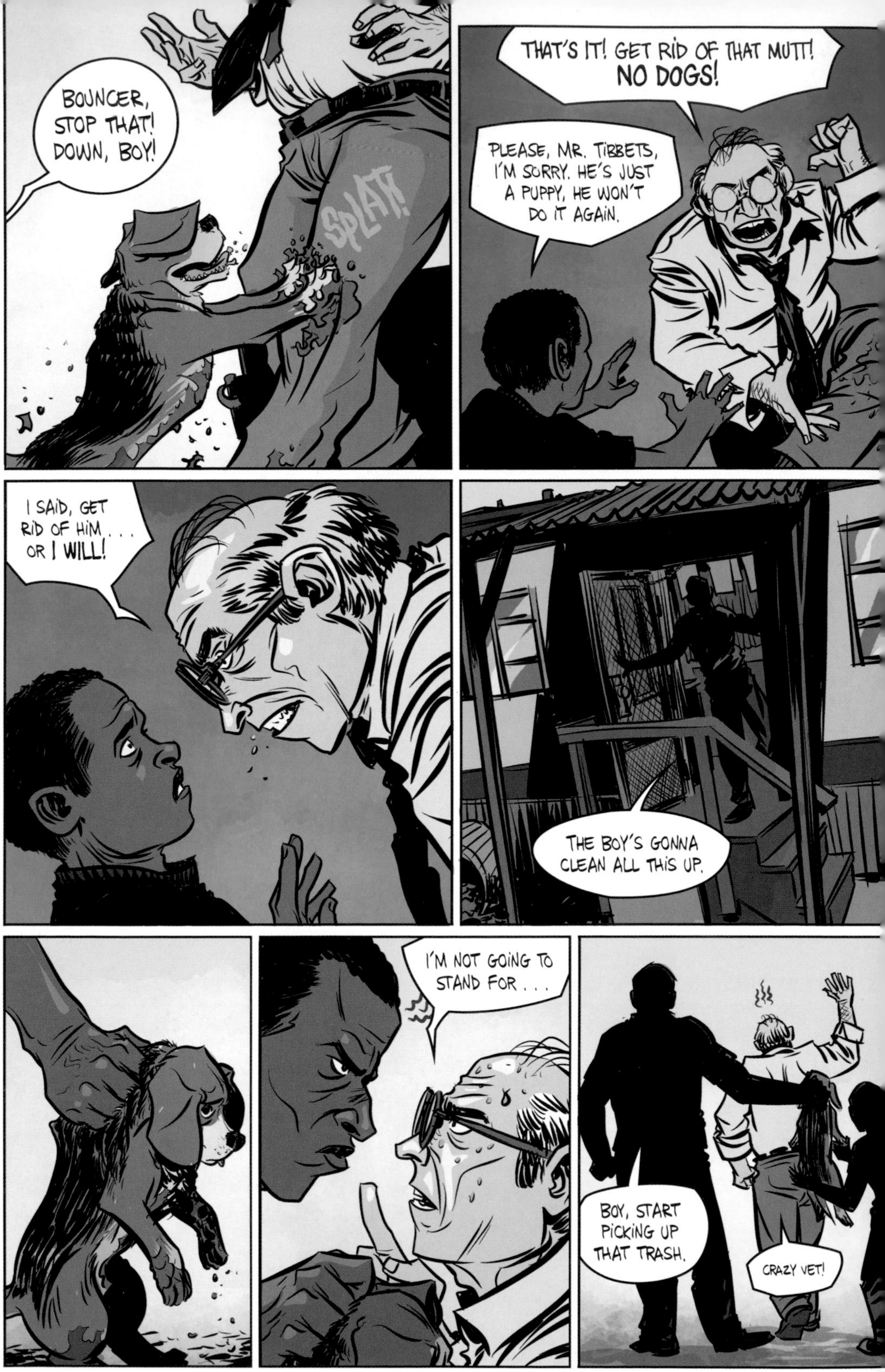
BOUNCER, STOP THAT! DOWN, BOY!
SPLAT!
THAT'S IT! GET RID OF THAT MUTT! NO DOGS!
PLEASE, MR. TIBBETS, I'M SORRY. HE'S JUST A PUPPY, HE WON'T DO IT AGAIN.
I SAID, GET RID OF HIM . . . OR I WILL!
THE BOY'S GONNA CLEAN ALL THIS UP.
I'M NOT GOING TO STAND FOR . . .
BOY, START PICKING UP THAT TRASH.
CRAZY VET!

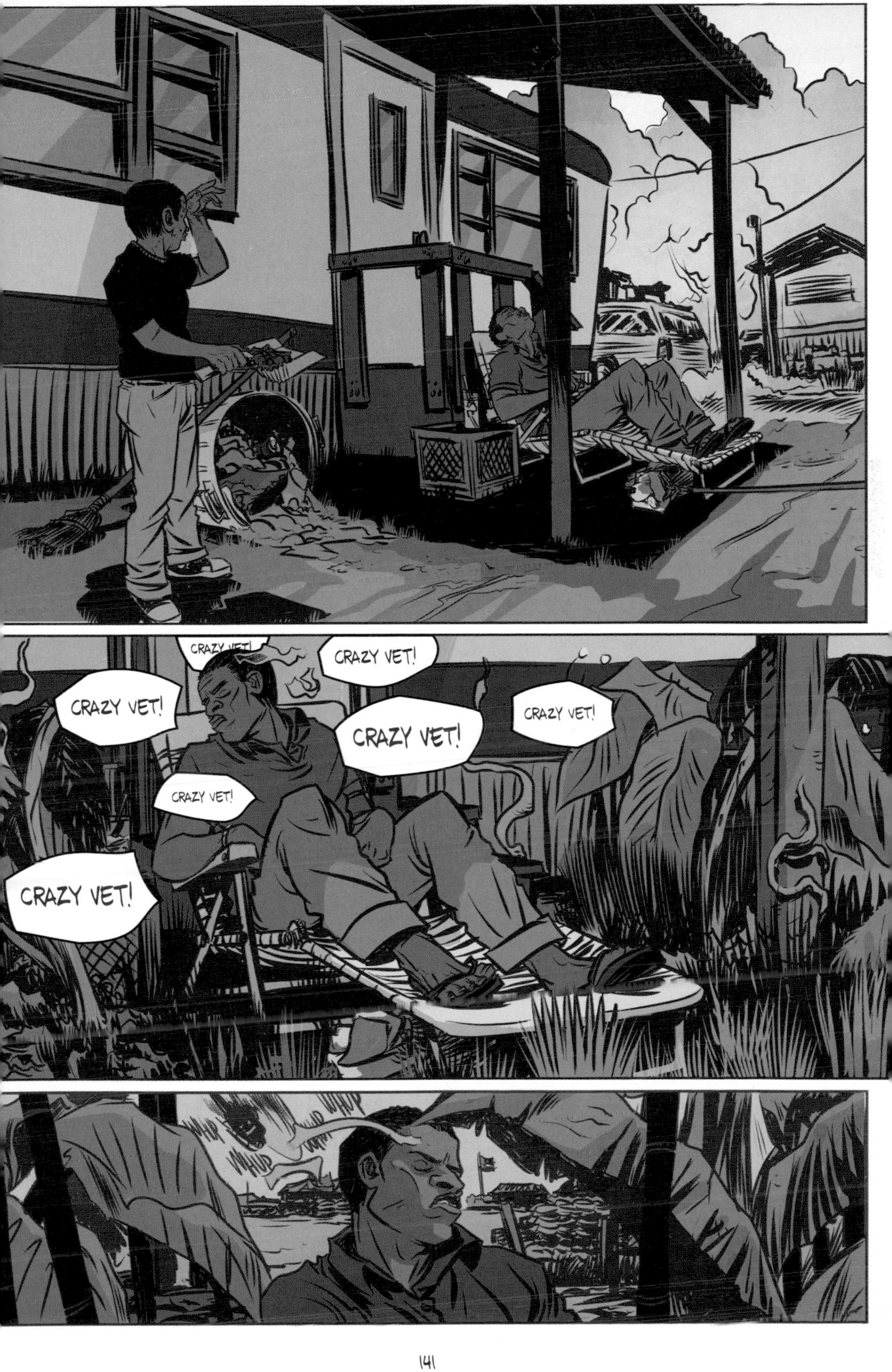
CRAZY VET!
CRAZY VET!
CRAZY VET!
CRAZY VET!
CRAZY VET!
CRAZY VET!
CRAZY VET!
WHUP
WHUP
WHUP

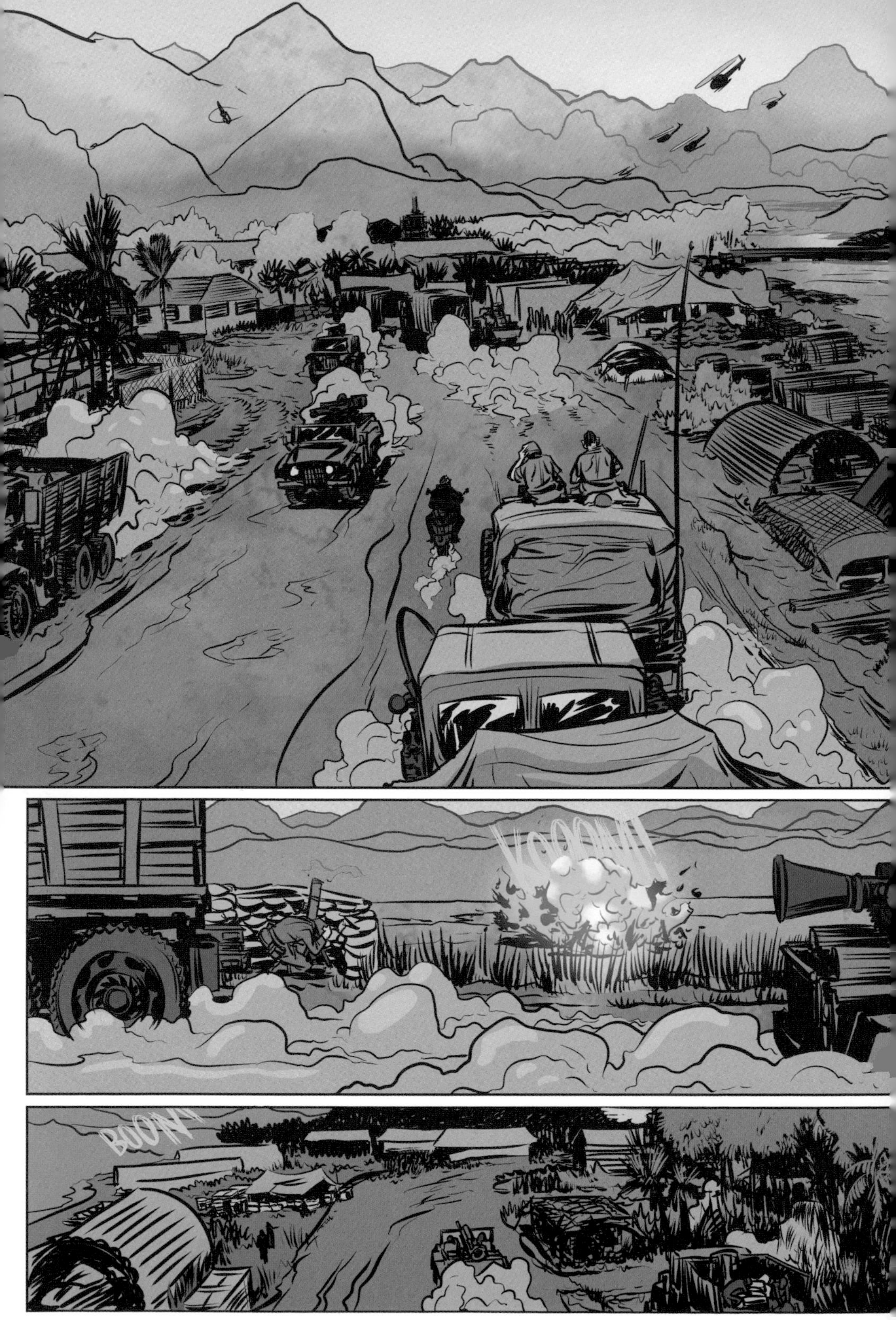
KOOOM!!
BOOM!!

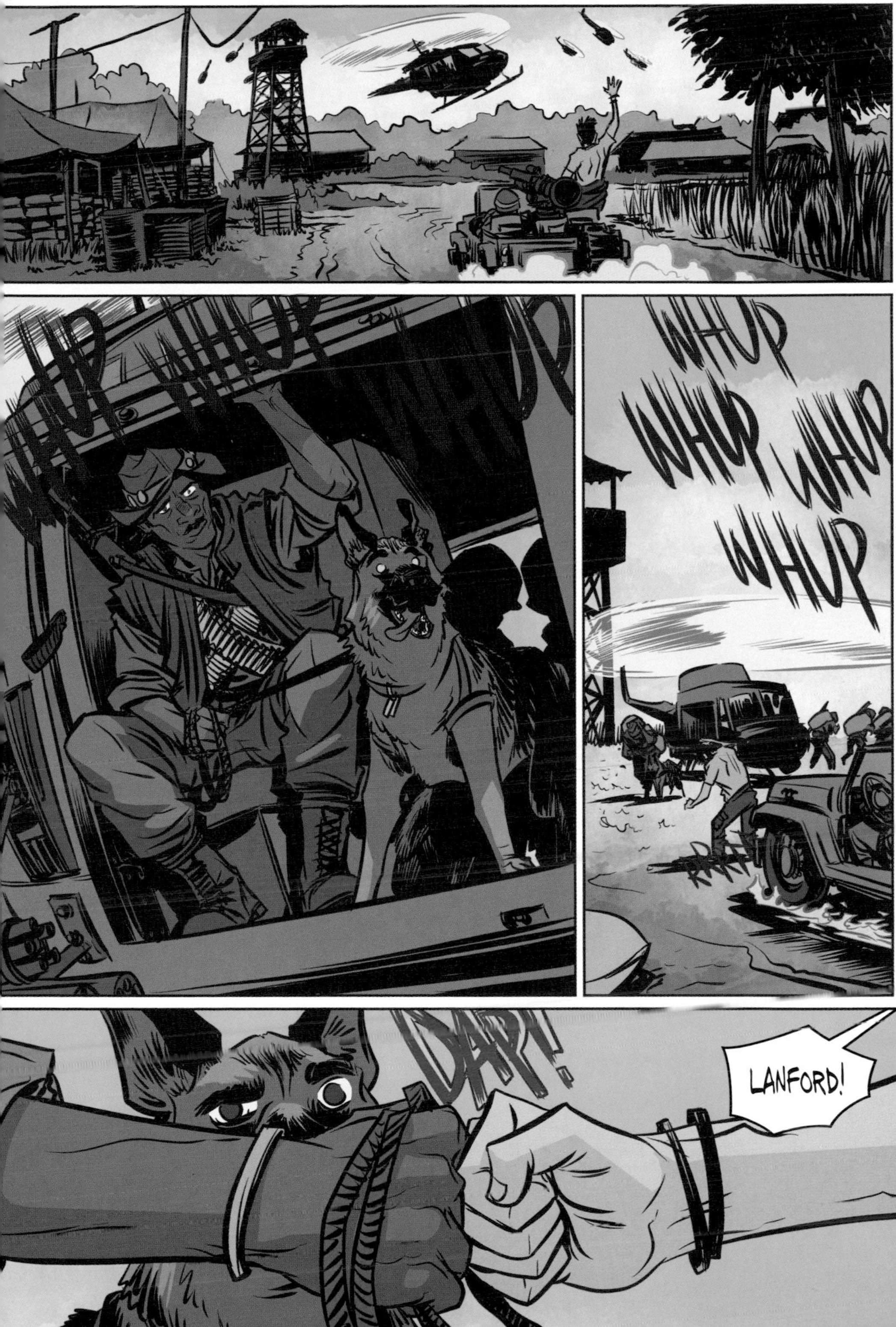
WHUP
WHUP
WHUP
WHUP
DAP!
LANFORD!

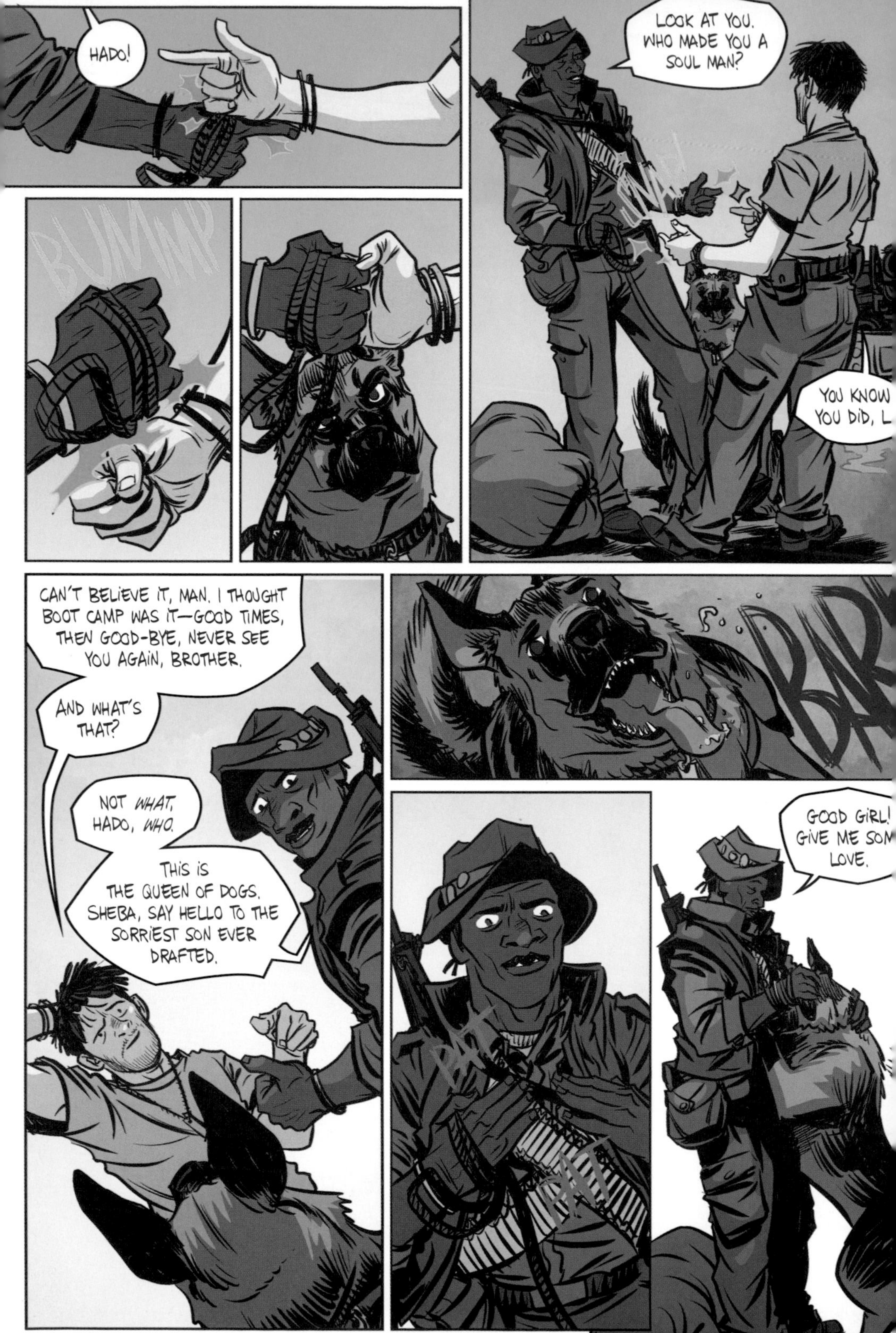
HADO!
LOOK AT YOU. WHO MADE YOU A SOUL MAN?
BUMMP
YOU KNOW YOU DID, L
CAN'T BELIEVE IT, MAN. I THOUGHT BOOT CAMP WAS IT—GOOD TIMES, THEN GOOD-BYE, NEVER SEE YOU AGAIN, BROTHER.
AND WHAT'S THAT?
NOT *WHAT*, HADO, *WHO*.
THIS IS THE QUEEN OF DOGS. SHEBA, SAY HELLO TO THE SORRIEST SON EVER DRAFTED.
GOOD GIRL! GIVE ME SOM
LOVE.

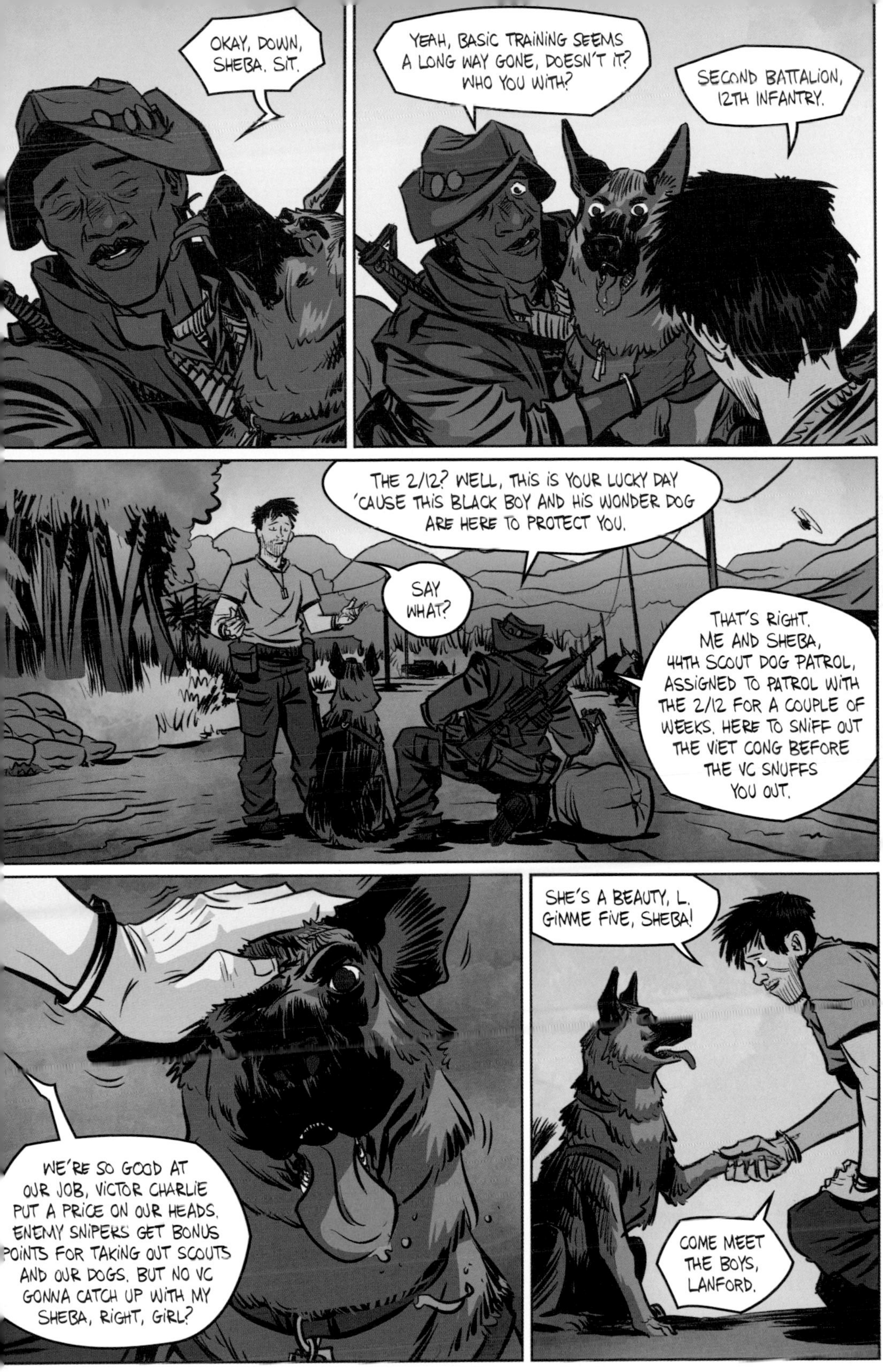
OKAY, DOWN, SHEBA. SIT.
YEAH, BASIC TRAINING SEEMS A LONG WAY GONE, DOESN'T IT? WHO YOU WITH?
SECOND BATTALION, 12TH INFANTRY.
THE 2/12? WELL, THIS IS YOUR LUCKY DAY 'CAUSE THIS BLACK BOY AND HIS WONDER DOG ARE HERE TO PROTECT YOU.
SAY WHAT?
THAT'S RIGHT. ME AND SHEBA, 44TH SCOUT DOG PATROL, ASSIGNED TO PATROL WITH THE 2/12 FOR A COUPLE OF WEEKS. HERE TO SNIFF OUT THE VIET CONG BEFORE THE VC SNUFFS YOU OUT.
WE'RE SO GOOD AT OUR JOB, VICTOR CHARLIE PUT A PRICE ON OUR HEADS. ENEMY SNIPERS GET BONUS POINTS FOR TAKING OUT SCOUTS AND OUR DOGS. BUT NO VC GONNA CATCH UP WITH MY SHEBA, RIGHT, GIRL?
SHE'S A BEAUTY, L. GIMME FIVE, SHEBA!
COME MEET THE BOYS, LANFORD.

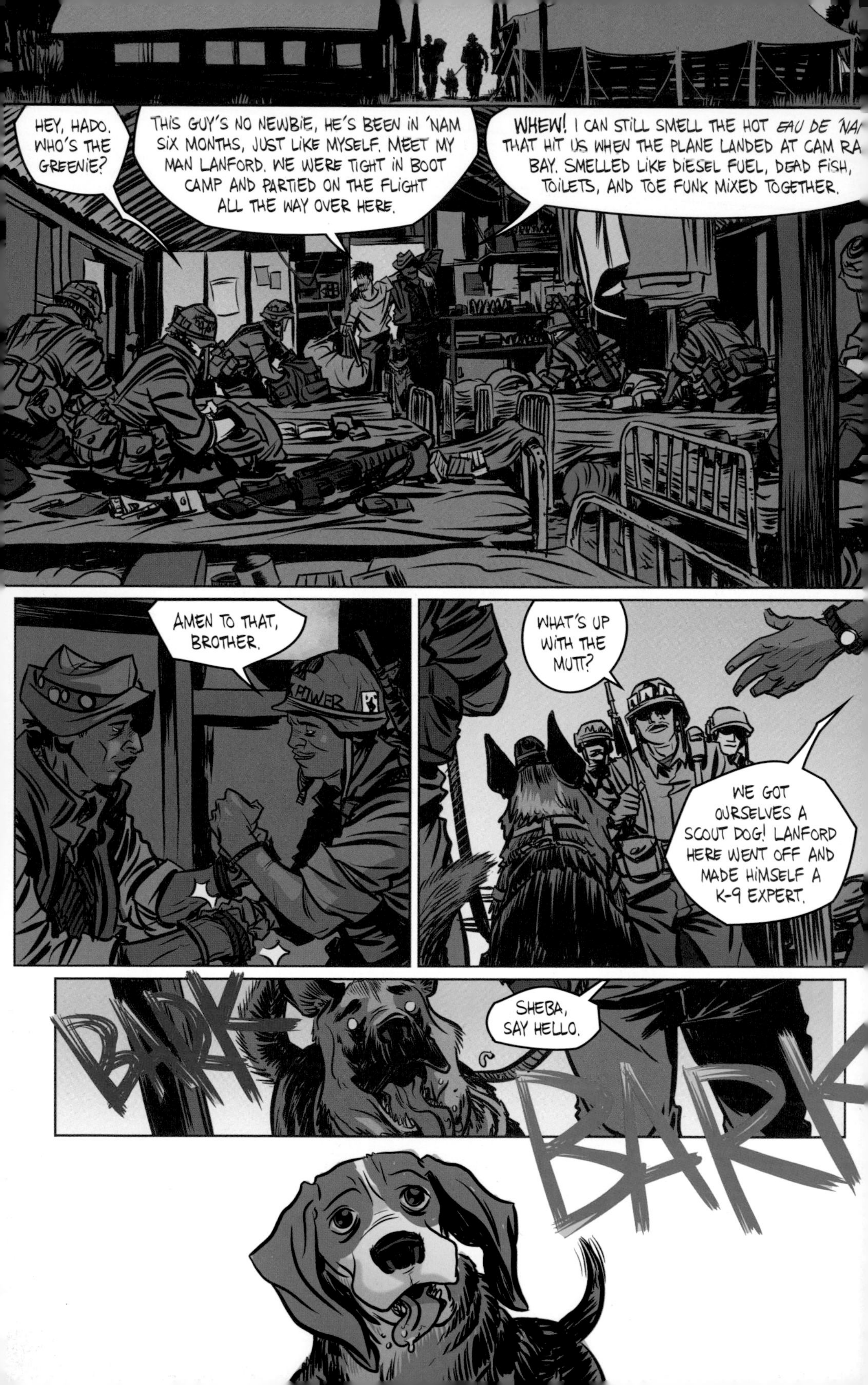
HEY, HADO. WHO'S THE GREENIE?
THIS GUY'S NO NEWBIE, HE'S BEEN IN 'NAM SIX MONTHS, JUST LIKE MYSELF. MEET MY MAN LANFORD. WE WERE TIGHT IN BOOT CAMP AND PARTIED ON THE FLIGHT ALL THE WAY OVER HERE.
WHEW! I CAN STILL SMELL THE HOT *EAU DE 'NA* THAT HIT US WHEN THE PLANE LANDED AT CAM RA BAY. SMELLED LIKE DIESEL FUEL, DEAD FISH, TOILETS, AND TOE FUNK MIXED TOGETHER.
AMEN TO THAT, BROTHER.
WHAT'S UP WITH THE MUTT?
WE GOT OURSELVES A SCOUT DOG! LANFORD HERE WENT OFF AND MADE HIMSELF A K-9 EXPERT.
SHEBA, SAY HELLO.
BARK
BARK

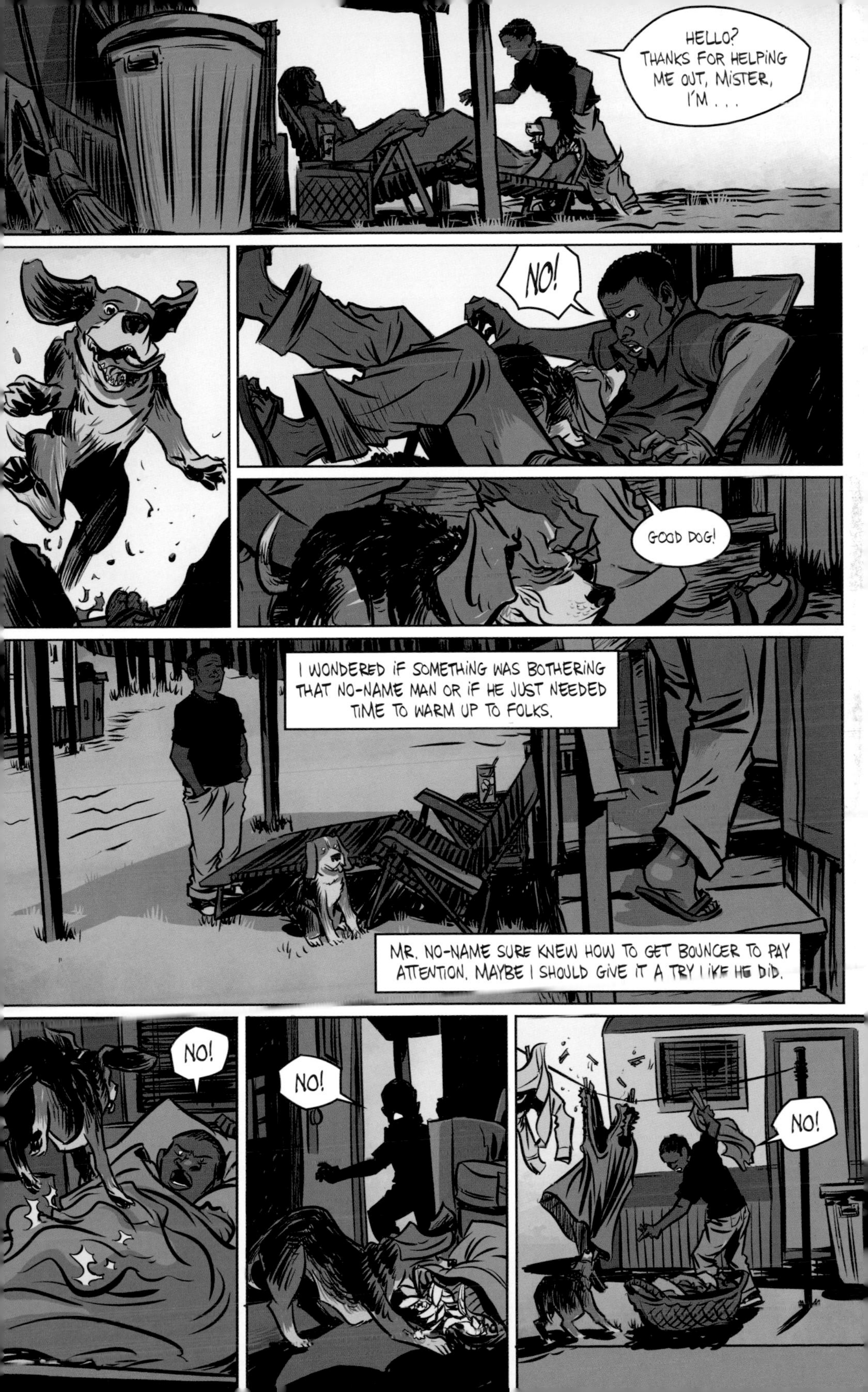
HELLO? THANKS FOR HELPING ME OUT, MISTER, I'M . . .
NO!
GOOD DOG!
I WONDERED IF SOMETHING WAS BOTHERING THAT NO-NAME MAN OR IF HE JUST NEEDED TIME TO WARM UP TO FOLKS.
MR. NO-NAME SURE KNEW HOW TO GET BOUNCER TO PAY ATTENTION. MAYBE I SHOULD GIVE IT A TRY LIKE HE DID.
NO!
NO!
NO!

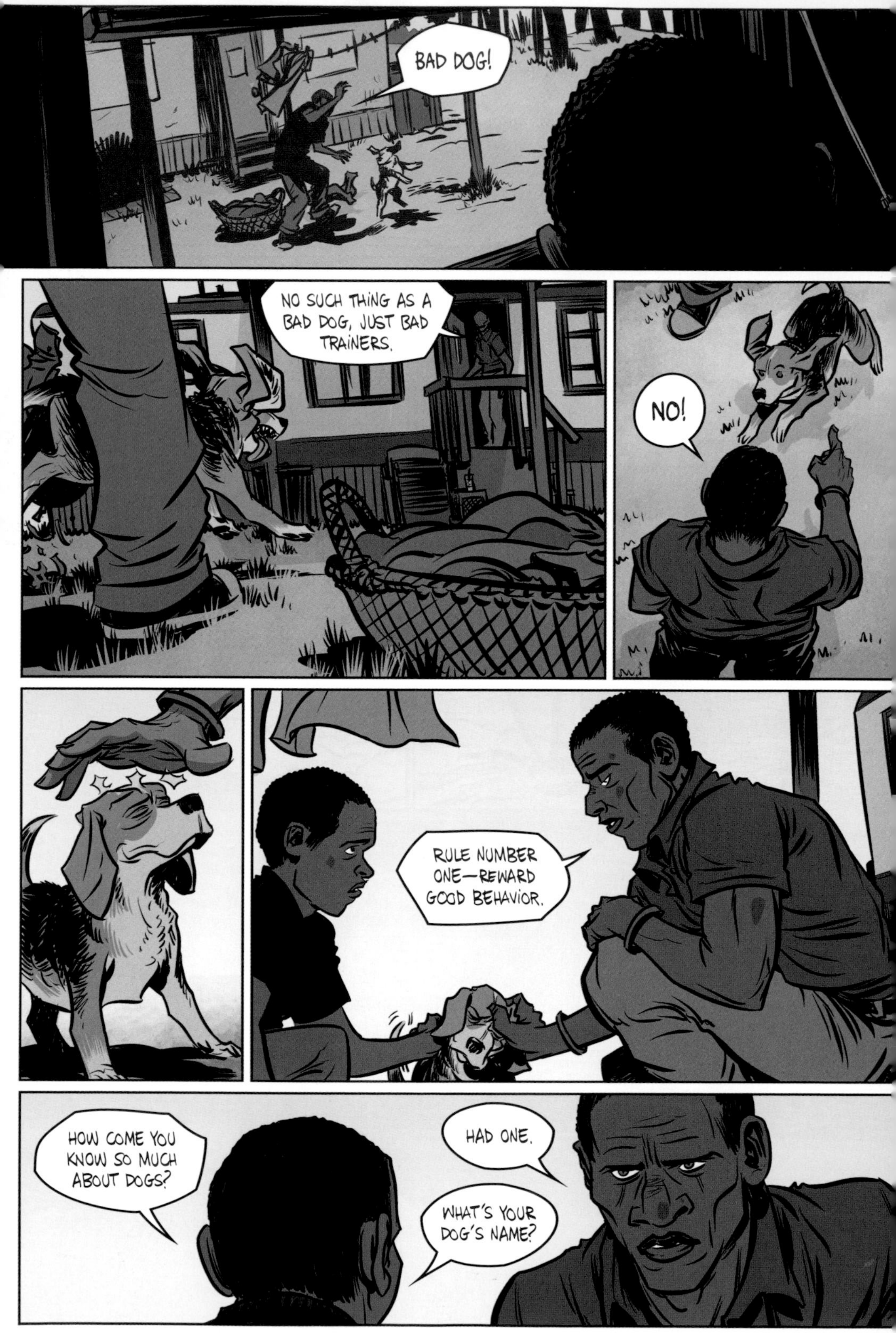
BAD DOG!
NO SUCH THING AS A BAD DOG, JUST BAD TRAINERS.
NO!
RULE NUMBER ONE—REWARD GOOD BEHAVIOR.
HOW COME YOU KNOW SO MUCH ABOUT DOGS?
HAD ONE.
WHAT'S YOUR DOG'S NAME?

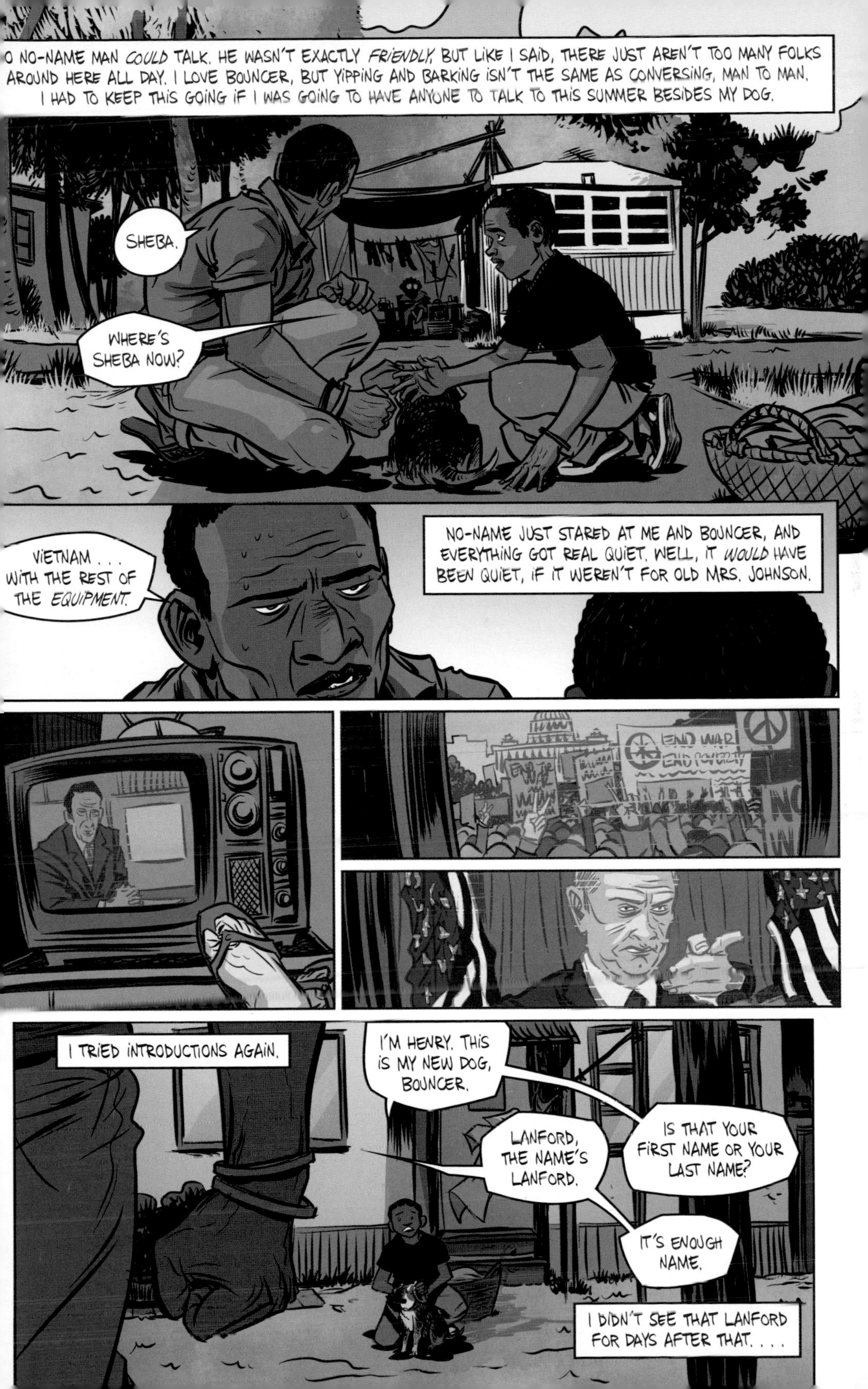
O NO-NAME MAN *COULD* TALK. HE WASN'T EXACTLY *FRIENDLY*, BUT LIKE I SAID, THERE JUST AREN'T TOO MANY FOLKS AROUND HERE ALL DAY. I LOVE BOUNCER, BUT YIPPING AND BARKING ISN'T THE SAME AS CONVERSING, MAN TO MAN. I HAD TO KEEP THIS GOING IF I WAS GOING TO HAVE ANYONE TO TALK TO THIS SUMMER BESIDES MY DOG.
SHEBA.
WHERE'S SHEBA NOW?
VIETNAM . . . WITH THE REST OF THE *EQUIPMENT*.
NO-NAME JUST STARED AT ME AND BOUNCER, AND EVERYTHING GOT REAL QUIET. WELL, IT *WOULD* HAVE BEEN QUIET, IF IT WEREN'T FOR OLD MRS. JOHNSON.
END WAR
I TRIED INTRODUCTIONS AGAIN.
I'M HENRY. THIS IS MY NEW DOG, BOUNCER.
LANFORD, THE NAME'S LANFORD.
IS THAT YOUR FIRST NAME OR YOUR LAST NAME?
IT'S ENOUGH NAME.
I DIDN'T SEE THAT LANFORD FOR DAYS AFTER THAT. . . .

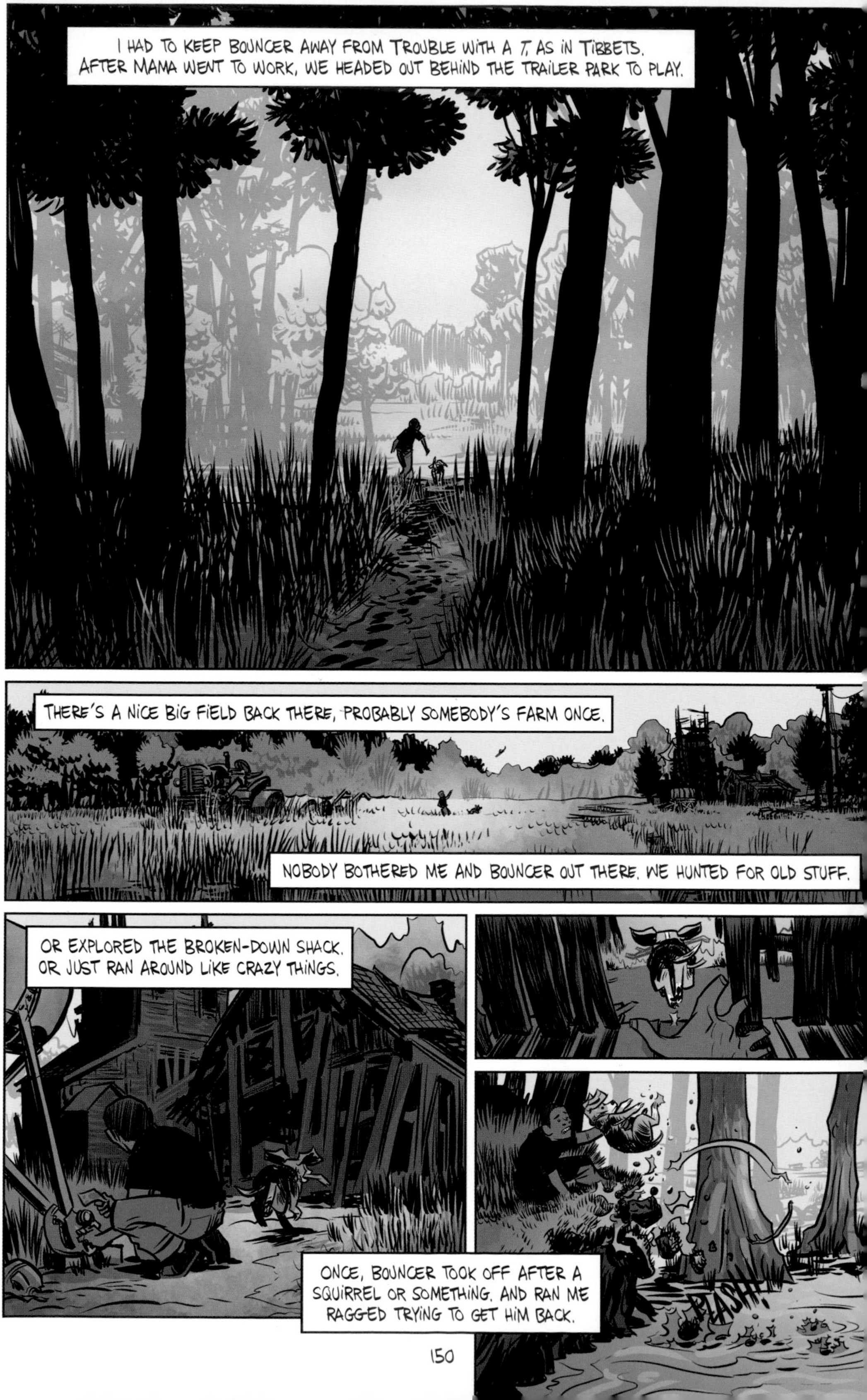
I HAD TO KEEP BOUNCER AWAY FROM TROUBLE WITH A T, AS IN TIBBETS. AFTER MAMA WENT TO WORK, WE HEADED OUT BEHIND THE TRAILER PARK TO PLAY.
THERE'S A NICE BIG FIELD BACK THERE, PROBABLY SOMEBODY'S FARM ONCE.
NOBODY BOTHERED ME AND BOUNCER OUT THERE. WE HUNTED FOR OLD STUFF.
OR EXPLORED THE BROKEN-DOWN SHACK. OR JUST RAN AROUND LIKE CRAZY THINGS.
ONCE, BOUNCER TOOK OFF AFTER A SQUIRREL OR SOMETHING, AND RAN ME RAGGED TRYING TO GET HIM BACK.

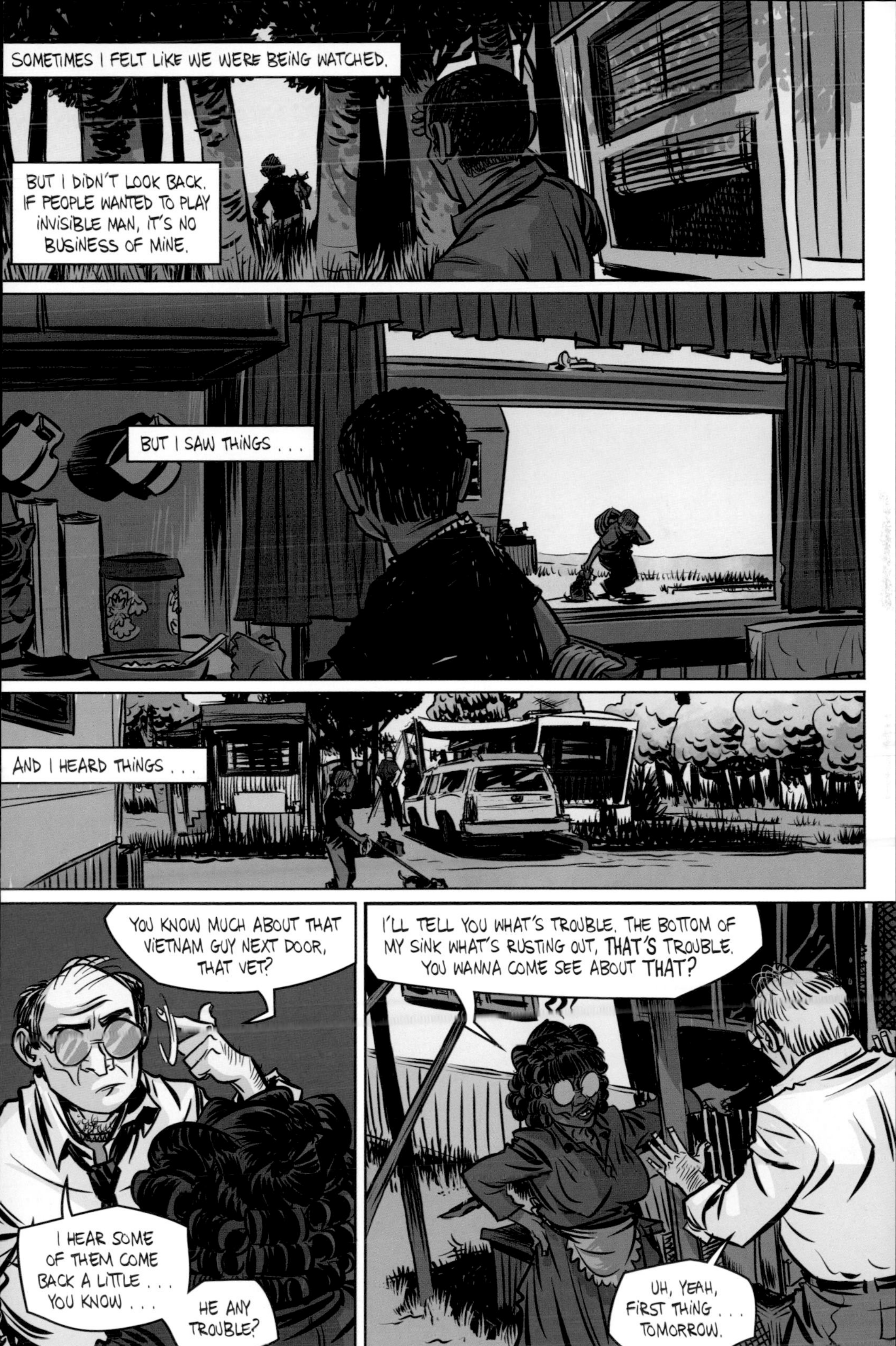
SOMETIMES I FELT LIKE WE WERE BEING WATCHED.
BUT I DIDN'T LOOK BACK. IF PEOPLE WANTED TO PLAY INVISIBLE MAN, IT'S NO BUSINESS OF MINE.
BUT I SAW THINGS . . .
AND I HEARD THINGS . . .
YOU KNOW MUCH ABOUT THAT VIETNAM GUY NEXT DOOR, THAT VET?
I HEAR SOME OF THEM COME BACK A LITTLE . . . YOU KNOW . . .
HE ANY TROUBLE?
I'LL TELL YOU WHAT'S TROUBLE. THE BOTTOM OF MY SINK WHAT'S RUSTING OUT, THAT'S TROUBLE. YOU WANNA COME SEE ABOUT THAT?
UH, YEAH, FIRST THING . . . TOMORROW.

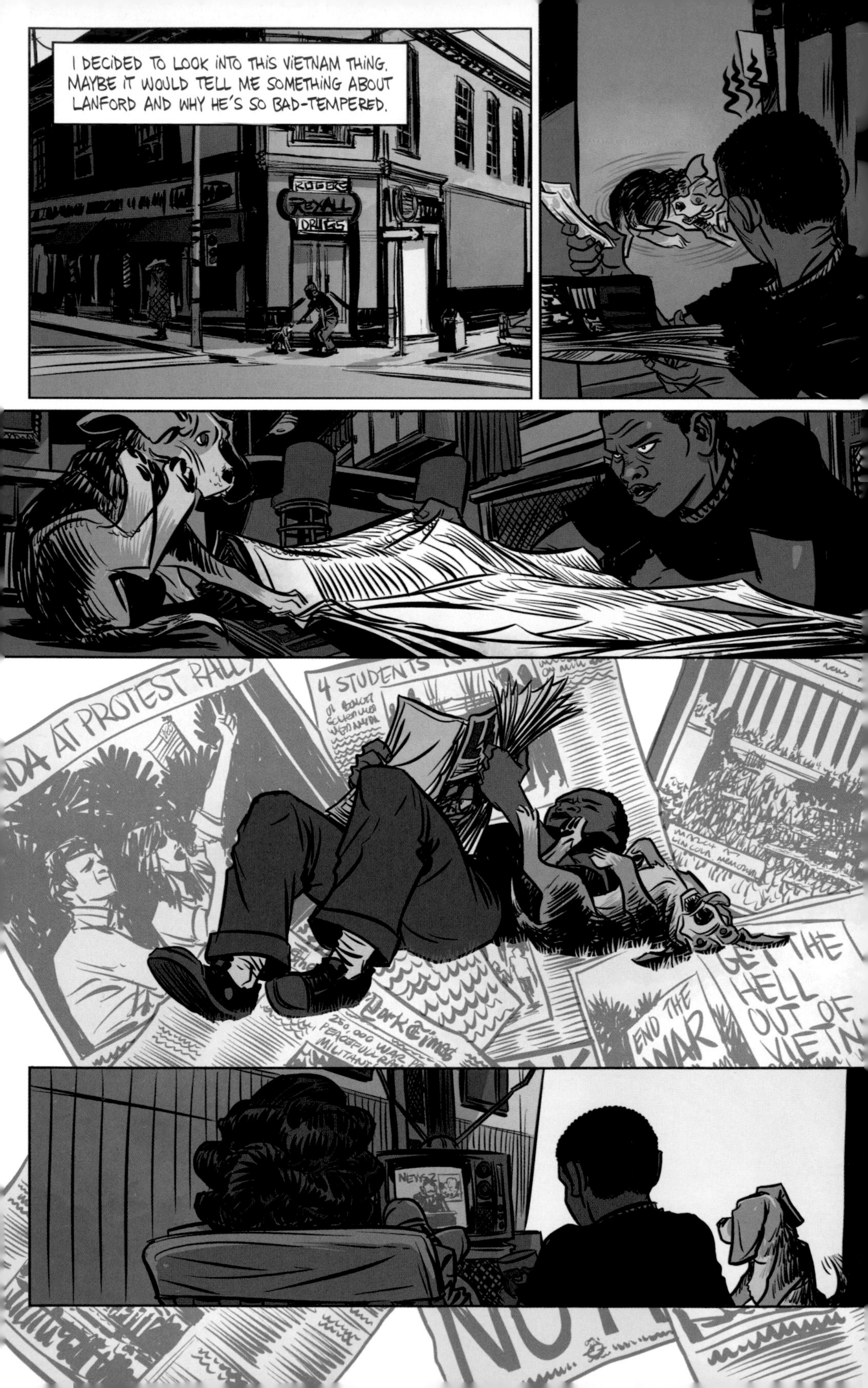
I DECIDED TO LOOK INTO THIS VIETNAM THING. MAYBE IT WOULD TELL ME SOMETHING ABOUT LANFORD AND WHY HE'S SO BAD-TEMPERED.
ROGERS
REXALL
DRUGS
4 STUDENTS
END THE WAR
GET THE HELL OUT OF

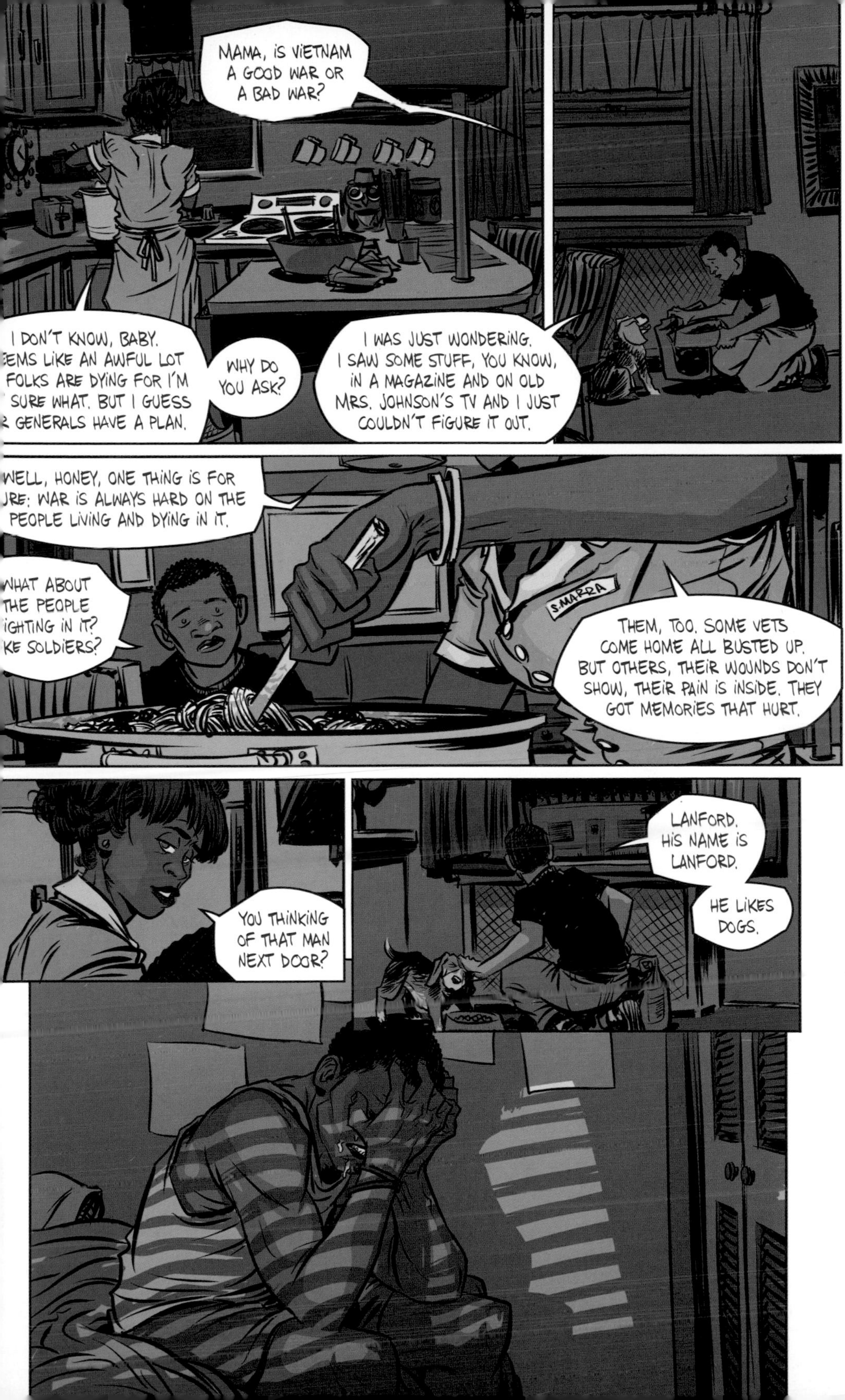
MAMA, IS VIETNAM A GOOD WAR OR A BAD WAR?
I DON'T KNOW, BABY. EEMS LIKE AN AWFUL LOT FOLKS ARE DYING FOR I'M SURE WHAT. BUT I GUESS GENERALS HAVE A PLAN.
WHY DO YOU ASK?
I WAS JUST WONDERING. I SAW SOME STUFF, YOU KNOW, IN A MAGAZINE AND ON OLD MRS. JOHNSON'S TV AND I JUST COULDN'T FIGURE IT OUT.
WELL, HONEY, ONE THING IS FOR RE: WAR IS ALWAYS HARD ON THE PEOPLE LIVING AND DYING IN IT.
WHAT ABOUT THE PEOPLE IGHTING IN IT? KE SOLDIERS?
S.MARRA
THEM, TOO. SOME VETS COME HOME ALL BUSTED UP. BUT OTHERS, THEIR WOUNDS DON'T SHOW, THEIR PAIN IS INSIDE. THEY GOT MEMORIES THAT HURT.
YOU THINKING OF THAT MAN NEXT DOOR?
LANFORD. HIS NAME IS LANFORD.
HE LIKES DOGS.

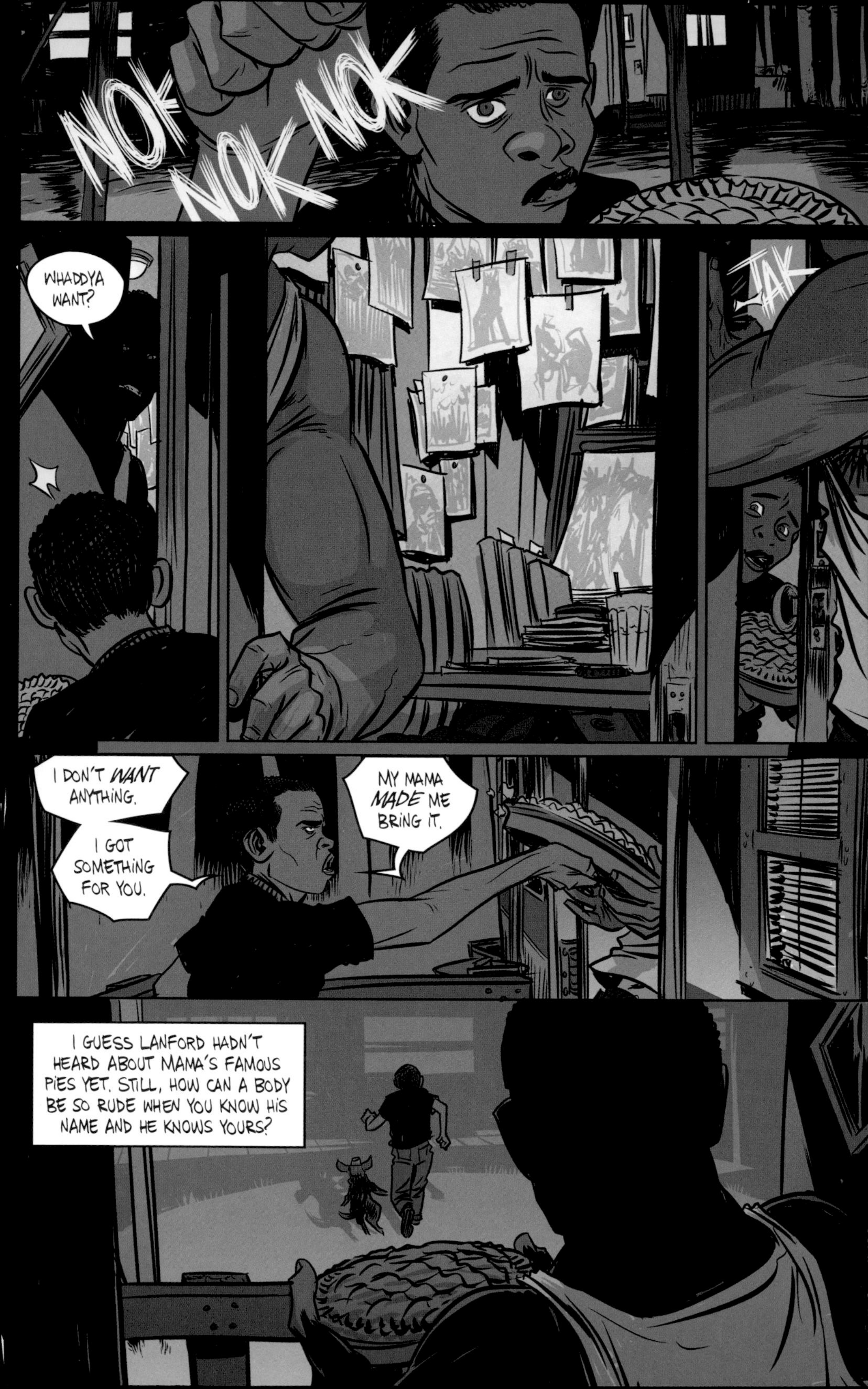
NOK NOK NOK
WHADDYA WANT?
TAK
I DON'T WANT ANYTHING.
I GOT SOMETHING FOR YOU.
MY MAMA MADE ME BRING IT.
I GUESS LANFORD HADN'T HEARD ABOUT MAMA'S FAMOUS PIES YET. STILL, HOW CAN A BODY BE SO RUDE WHEN YOU KNOW HIS NAME AND HE KNOWS YOURS?

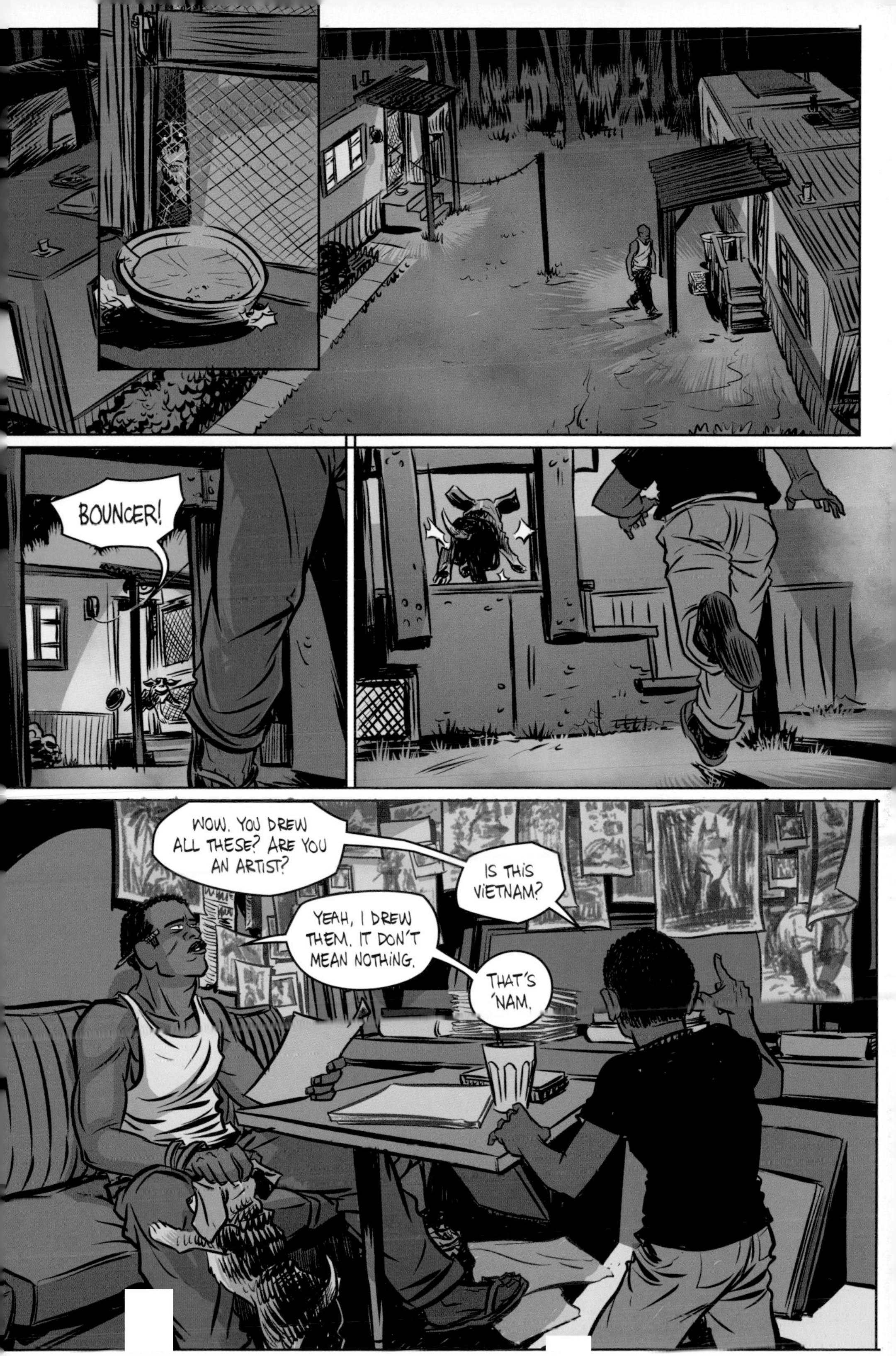
BOUNCER!
WOW. YOU DREW ALL THESE? ARE YOU AN ARTIST?
IS THIS VIETNAM?
YEAH, I DREW THEM. IT DON'T MEAN NOTHING.
THAT'S 'NAM.

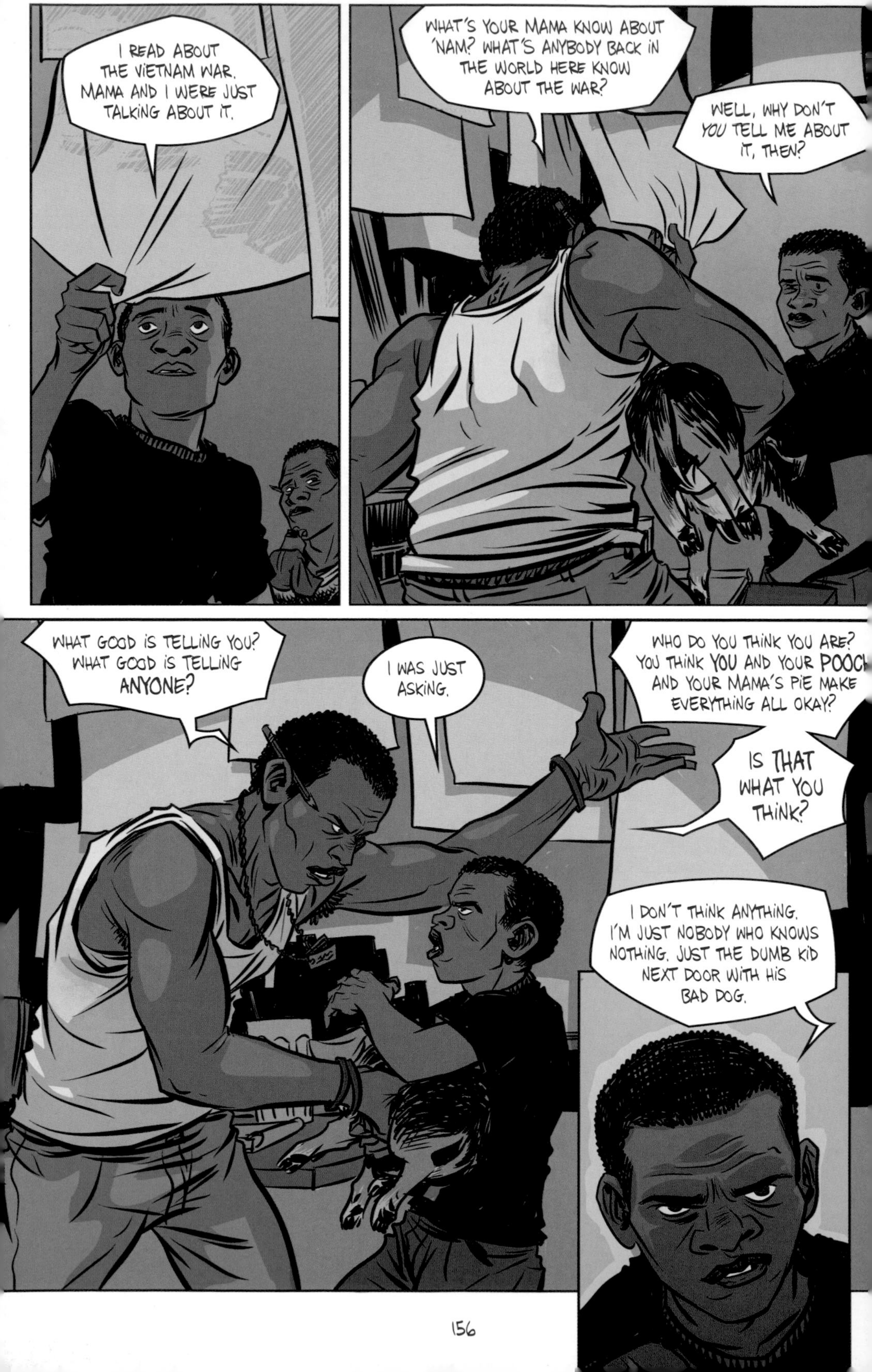
I READ ABOUT THE VIETNAM WAR. MAMA AND I WERE JUST TALKING ABOUT IT.
WHAT'S YOUR MAMA KNOW ABOUT 'NAM? WHAT'S ANYBODY BACK IN THE WORLD HERE KNOW ABOUT THE WAR?
WELL, WHY DON'T *YOU* TELL ME ABOUT IT, THEN?
WHAT GOOD IS TELLING YOU? WHAT GOOD IS TELLING **ANYONE**?
I WAS JUST ASKING.
WHO DO YOU THINK YOU ARE? YOU THINK **YOU** AND YOUR **POOCH** AND YOUR MAMA'S PIE MAKE EVERYTHING ALL OKAY?
IS **THAT** WHAT YOU THINK?
I DON'T THINK ANYTHING. I'M JUST NOBODY WHO KNOWS NOTHING. JUST THE DUMB KID NEXT DOOR WITH HIS BAD DOG.

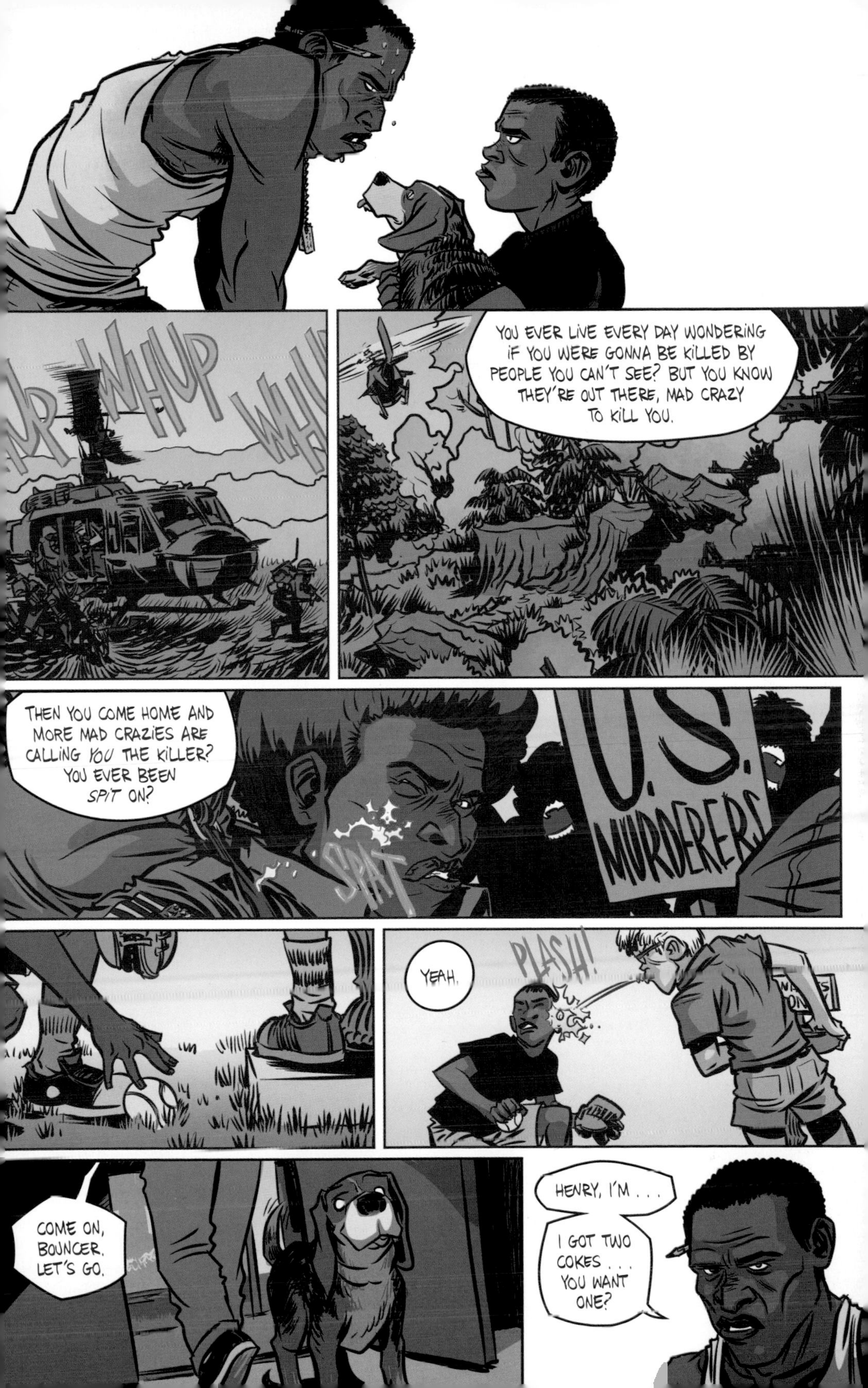
WHUP WHUP
WHUP
YOU EVER LIVE EVERY DAY WONDERING IF YOU WERE GONNA BE KILLED BY PEOPLE YOU CAN'T SEE? BUT YOU KNOW THEY'RE OUT THERE, MAD CRAZY TO KILL YOU.
THEN YOU COME HOME AND MORE MAD CRAZIES ARE CALLING *YOU* THE KILLER? YOU EVER BEEN *SPIT* ON?
U.S. MURDERERS
SPAT
YEAH.
PLASH!
COME ON, BOUNCER. LET'S GO.
HENRY, I'M . . .
I GOT TWO COKES . . . YOU WANT ONE?

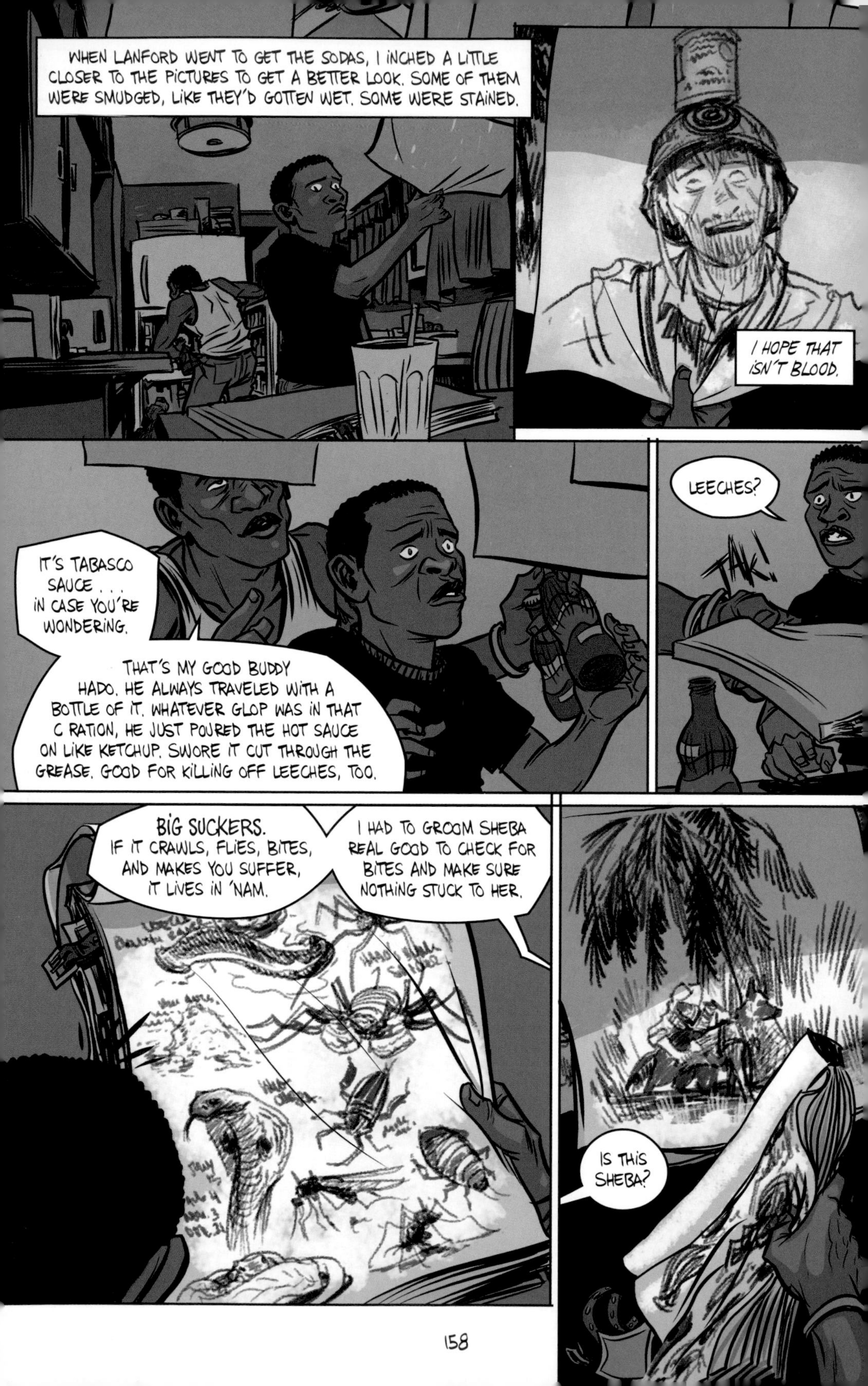
WHEN LANFORD WENT TO GET THE SODAS, I INCHED A LITTLE CLOSER TO THE PICTURES TO GET A BETTER LOOK. SOME OF THEM WERE SMUDGED, LIKE THEY'D GOTTEN WET. SOME WERE STAINED.
I HOPE THAT ISN'T BLOOD.
IT'S TABASCO SAUCE . . . IN CASE YOU'RE WONDERING.
THAT'S MY GOOD BUDDY HADO. HE ALWAYS TRAVELED WITH A BOTTLE OF IT. WHATEVER GLOP WAS IN THAT C RATION, HE JUST POURED THE HOT SAUCE ON LIKE KETCHUP. SWORE IT CUT THROUGH THE GREASE. GOOD FOR KILLING OFF LEECHES, TOO.
LEECHES?
TAK!
BIG SUCKERS. IF IT CRAWLS, FLIES, BITES, AND MAKES YOU SUFFER, IT LIVES IN 'NAM.
I HAD TO GROOM SHEBA REAL GOOD TO CHECK FOR BITES AND MAKE SURE NOTHING STUCK TO HER.
IS THIS SHEBA?

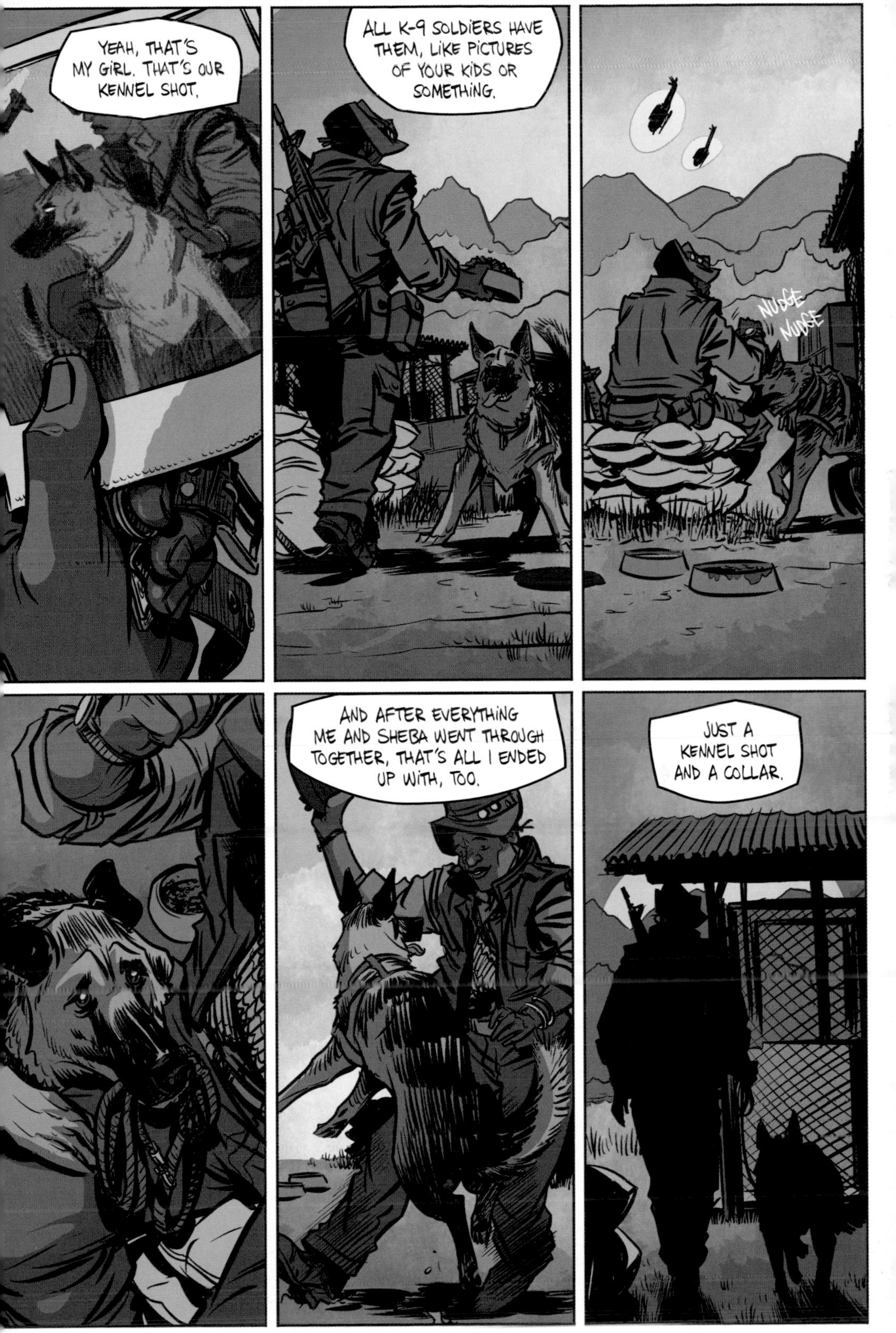
YEAH, THAT'S MY GIRL. THAT'S OUR KENNEL SHOT.
ALL K-9 SOLDIERS HAVE THEM, LIKE PICTURES OF YOUR KIDS OR SOMETHING.
NUDGE NUDGE
AND AFTER EVERYTHING ME AND SHEBA WENT THROUGH TOGETHER, THAT'S ALL I ENDED UP WITH, TOO.
JUST A KENNEL SHOT AND A COLLAR.

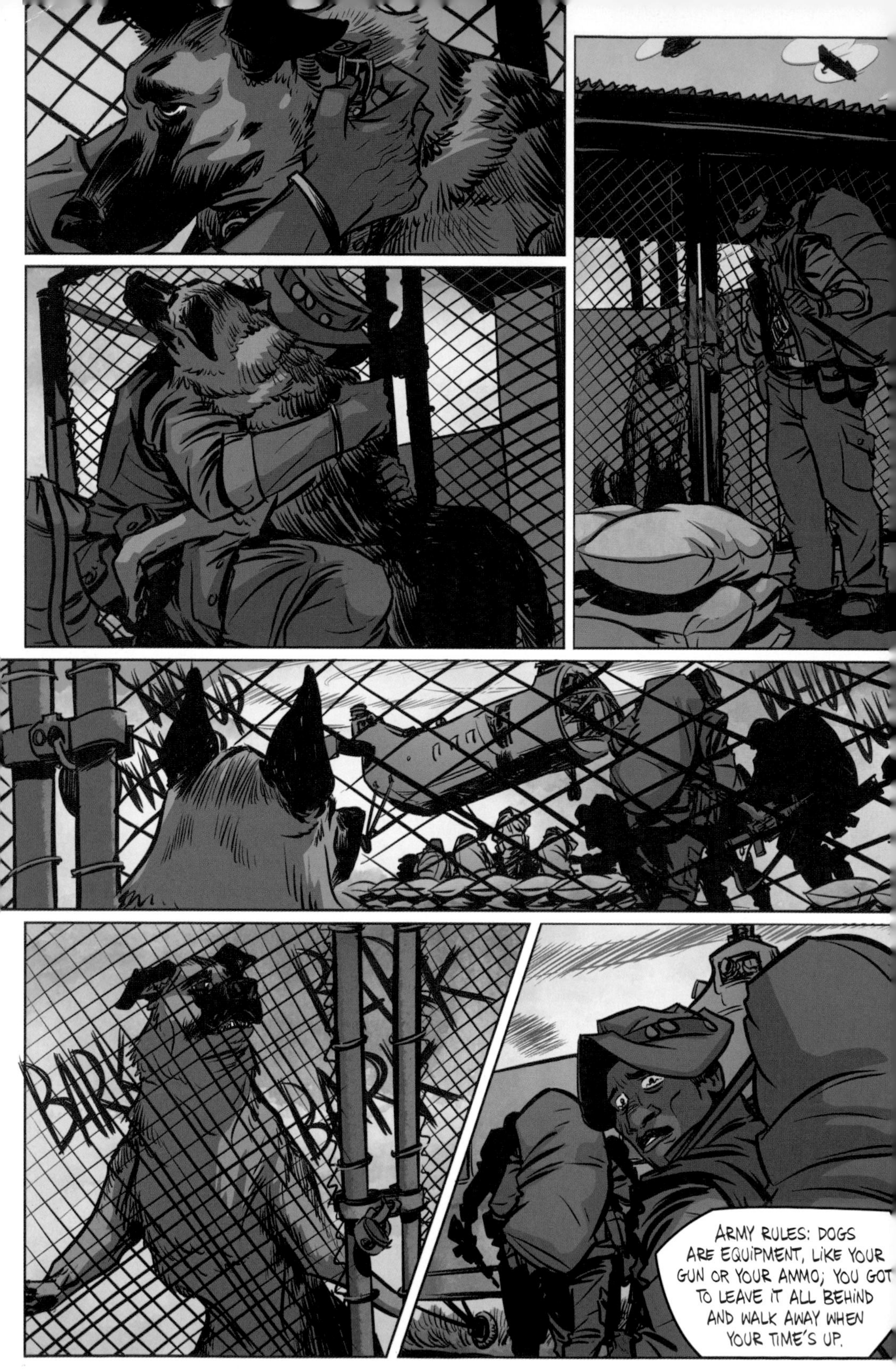
WHUP
WHUP
WHUP
BARK
BARK
BARK
ARMY RULES: DOGS ARE EQUIPMENT, LIKE YOUR GUN OR YOUR AMMO; YOU GOT TO LEAVE IT ALL BEHIND AND WALK AWAY WHEN YOUR TIME'S UP.

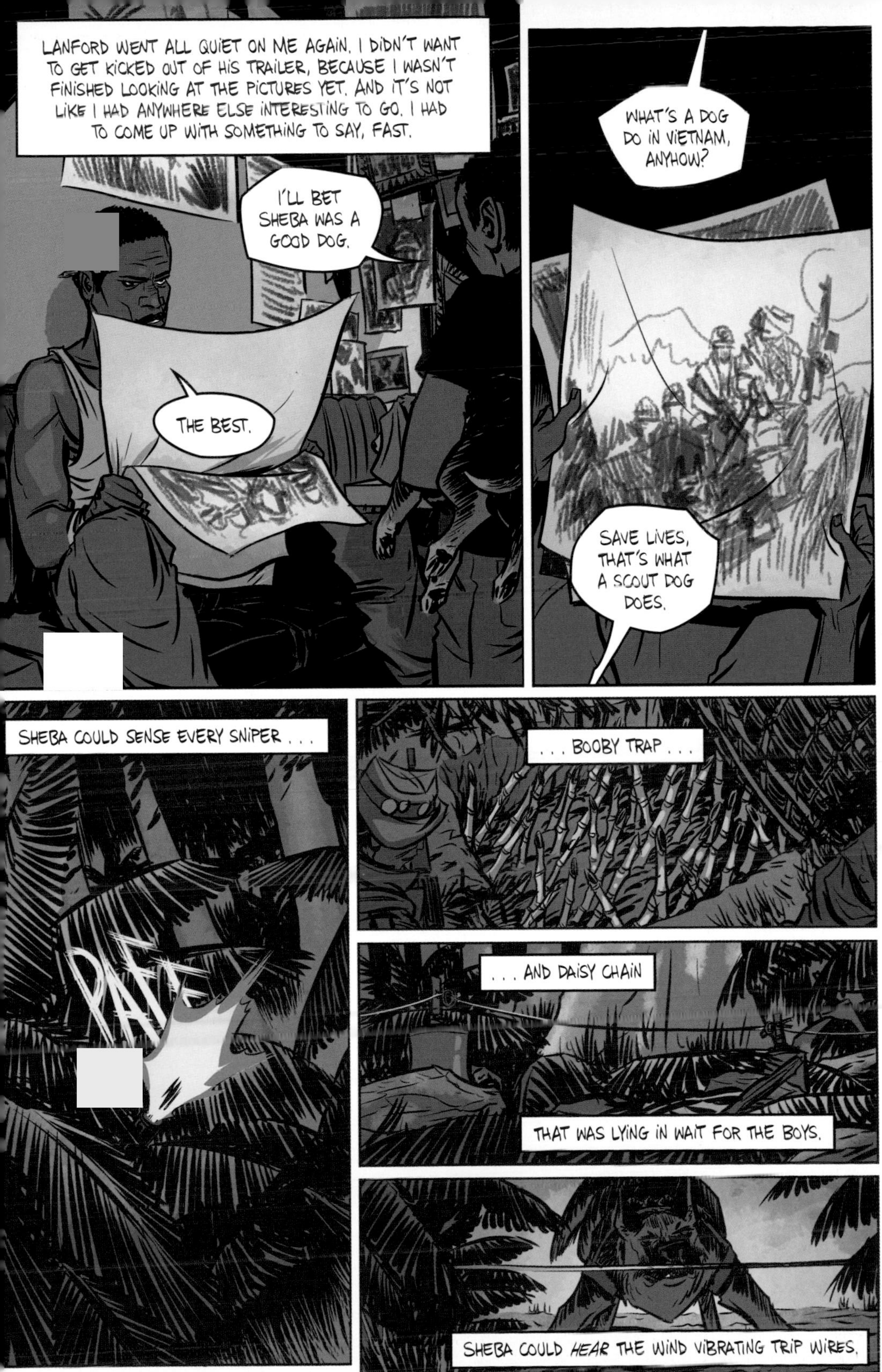
LANFORD WENT ALL QUIET ON ME AGAIN. I DIDN'T WANT TO GET KICKED OUT OF HIS TRAILER, BECAUSE I WASN'T FINISHED LOOKING AT THE PICTURES YET. AND IT'S NOT LIKE I HAD ANYWHERE ELSE INTERESTING TO GO. I HAD TO COME UP WITH SOMETHING TO SAY, FAST.
I'LL BET SHEBA WAS A GOOD DOG.
THE BEST.
WHAT'S A DOG DO IN VIETNAM, ANYHOW?
SAVE LIVES, THAT'S WHAT A SCOUT DOG DOES.
SHEBA COULD SENSE EVERY SNIPER . . .
. . . BOOBY TRAP . . .
. . . AND DAISY CHAIN
THAT WAS LYING IN WAIT FOR THE BOYS.
SHEBA COULD *HEAR* THE WIND VIBRATING TRIP WIRES.

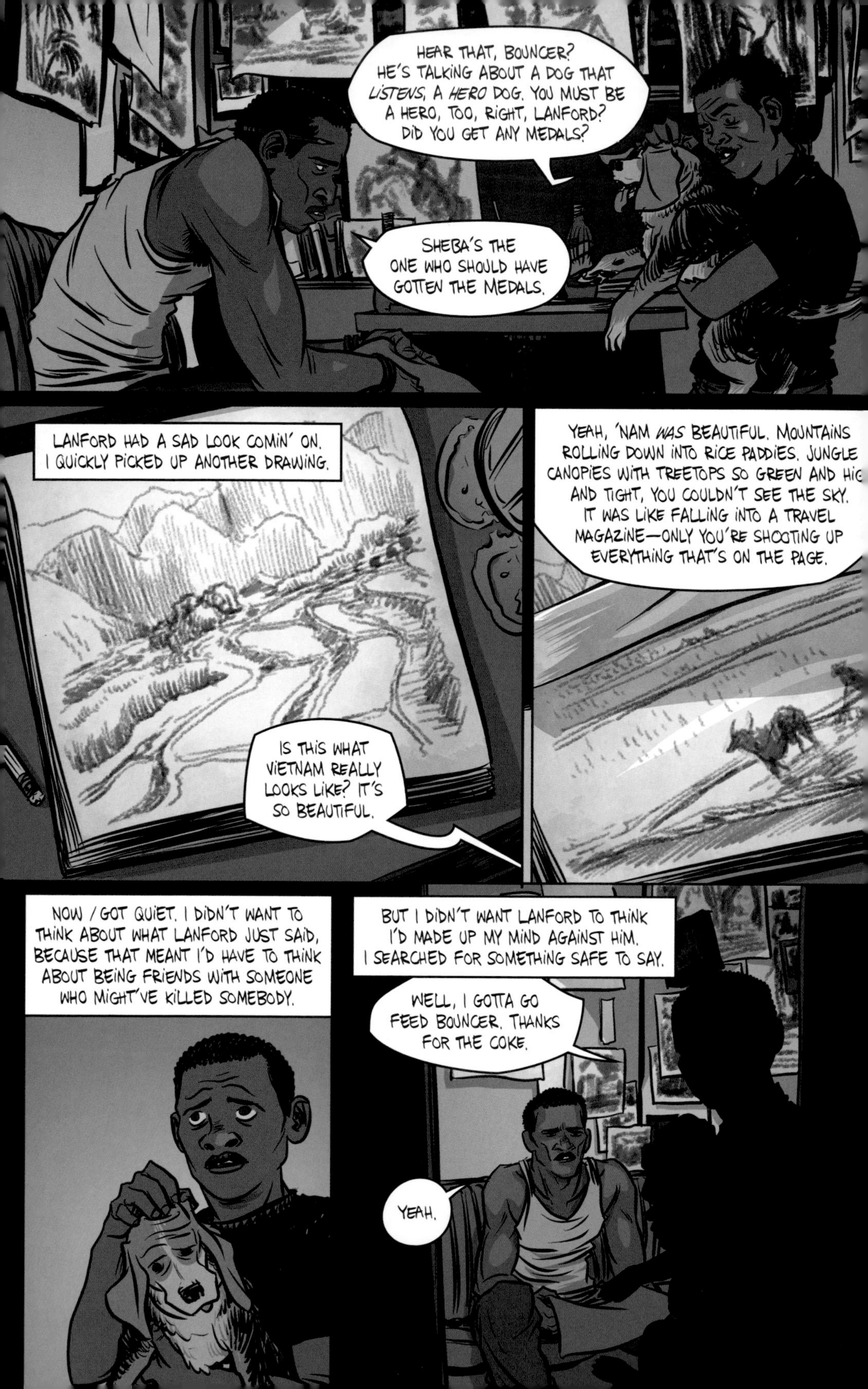
HEAR THAT, BOUNCER? HE'S TALKING ABOUT A DOG THAT *LISTENS*, A *HERO* DOG. YOU MUST BE A HERO, TOO, RIGHT, LANFORD? DID YOU GET ANY MEDALS?
SHEBA'S THE ONE WHO SHOULD HAVE GOTTEN THE MEDALS.
LANFORD HAD A SAD LOOK COMIN' ON. I QUICKLY PICKED UP ANOTHER DRAWING.
IS THIS WHAT VIETNAM REALLY LOOKS LIKE? IT'S SO BEAUTIFUL.
YEAH, 'NAM *WAS* BEAUTIFUL. MOUNTAINS ROLLING DOWN INTO RICE PADDIES. JUNGLE CANOPIES WITH TREETOPS SO GREEN AND HIG AND TIGHT, YOU COULDN'T SEE THE SKY. IT WAS LIKE FALLING INTO A TRAVEL MAGAZINE—ONLY YOU'RE SHOOTING UP EVERYTHING THAT'S ON THE PAGE.
NOW *I* GOT QUIET. I DIDN'T WANT TO THINK ABOUT WHAT LANFORD JUST SAID, BECAUSE THAT MEANT I'D HAVE TO THINK ABOUT BEING FRIENDS WITH SOMEONE WHO MIGHT'VE KILLED SOMEBODY.
BUT I DIDN'T WANT LANFORD TO THINK I'D MADE UP MY MIND AGAINST HIM. I SEARCHED FOR SOMETHING SAFE TO SAY.
WELL, I GOTTA GO FEED BOUNCER. THANKS FOR THE COKE.
YEAH.

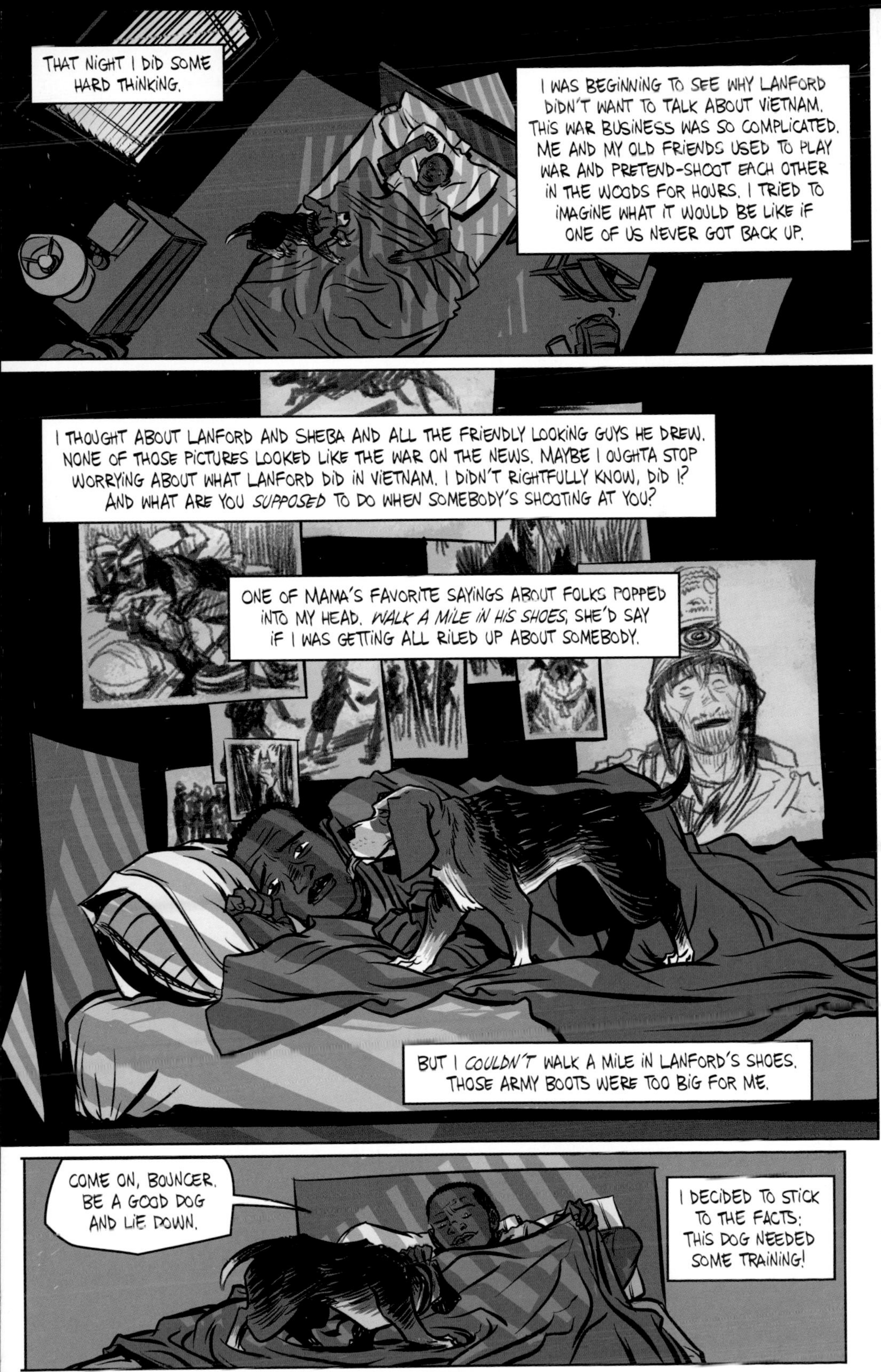
THAT NIGHT I DID SOME HARD THINKING.
I WAS BEGINNING TO SEE WHY LANFORD DIDN'T WANT TO TALK ABOUT VIETNAM. THIS WAR BUSINESS WAS SO COMPLICATED. ME AND MY OLD FRIENDS USED TO PLAY WAR AND PRETEND-SHOOT EACH OTHER IN THE WOODS FOR HOURS. I TRIED TO IMAGINE WHAT IT WOULD BE LIKE IF ONE OF US NEVER GOT BACK UP.
I THOUGHT ABOUT LANFORD AND SHEBA AND ALL THE FRIENDLY LOOKING GUYS HE DREW. NONE OF THOSE PICTURES LOOKED LIKE THE WAR ON THE NEWS. MAYBE I OUGHTA STOP WORRYING ABOUT WHAT LANFORD DID IN VIETNAM. I DIDN'T RIGHTFULLY KNOW, DID I? AND WHAT ARE YOU *SUPPOSED* TO DO WHEN SOMEBODY'S SHOOTING AT YOU?
ONE OF MAMA'S FAVORITE SAYINGS ABOUT FOLKS POPPED INTO MY HEAD. *WALK A MILE IN HIS SHOES,* SHE'D SAY IF I WAS GETTING ALL RILED UP ABOUT SOMEBODY.
BUT I *COULDN'T* WALK A MILE IN LANFORD'S SHOES. THOSE ARMY BOOTS WERE TOO BIG FOR ME.
COME ON, BOUNCER. BE A GOOD DOG AND LIE DOWN.
I DECIDED TO STICK TO THE FACTS: THIS DOG NEEDED SOME TRAINING!

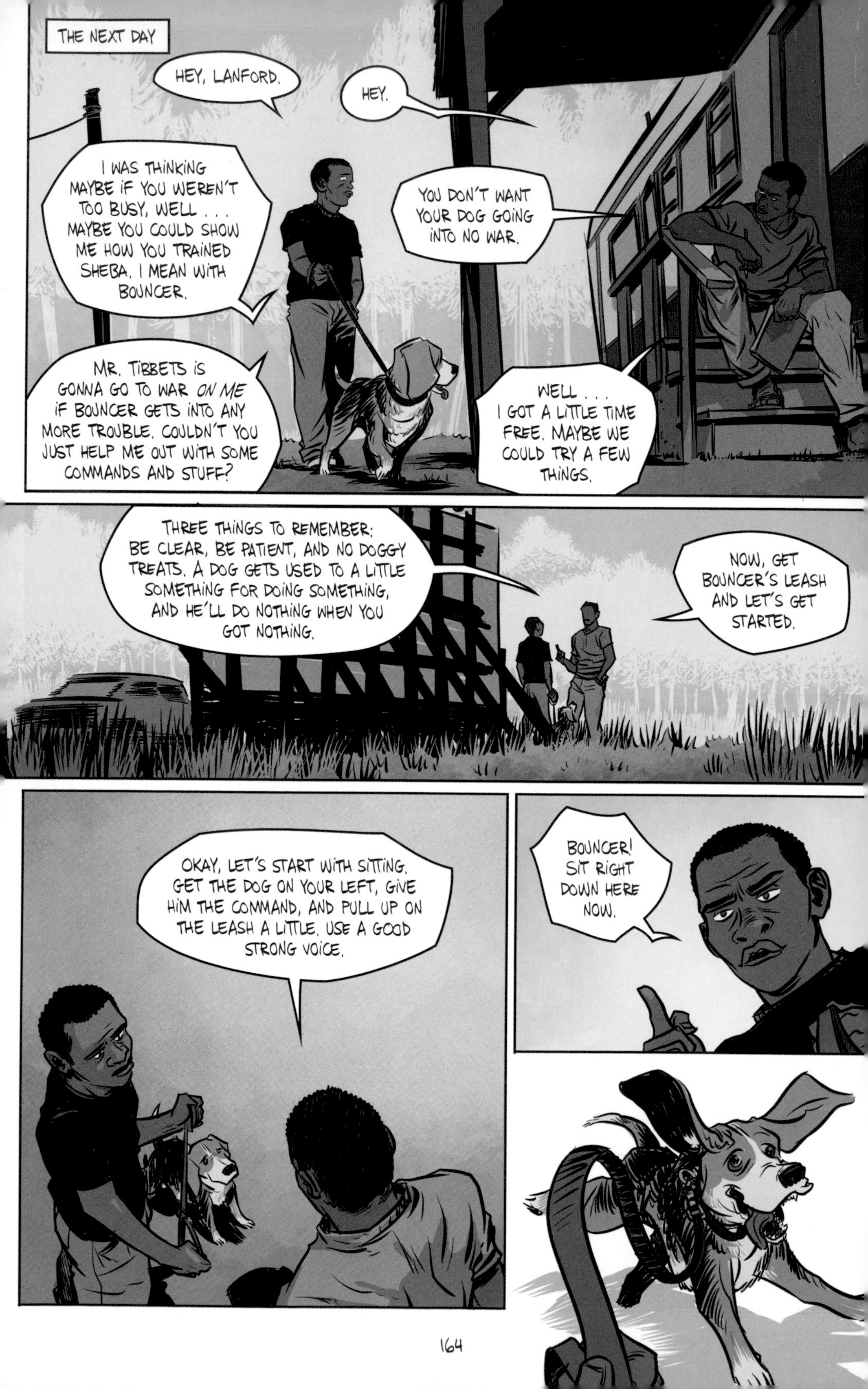
THE NEXT DAY
HEY, LANFORD.
HEY.
I WAS THINKING MAYBE IF YOU WEREN'T TOO BUSY, WELL . . . MAYBE YOU COULD SHOW ME HOW YOU TRAINED SHEBA. I MEAN WITH BOUNCER.
YOU DON'T WANT YOUR DOG GOING INTO NO WAR.
MR. TIBBETS IS GONNA GO TO WAR *ON ME* IF BOUNCER GETS INTO ANY MORE TROUBLE. COULDN'T YOU JUST HELP ME OUT WITH SOME COMMANDS AND STUFF?
WELL . . . I GOT A LITTLE TIME FREE. MAYBE WE COULD TRY A FEW THINGS.
THREE THINGS TO REMEMBER: BE CLEAR, BE PATIENT, AND NO DOGGY TREATS. A DOG GETS USED TO A LITTLE SOMETHING FOR DOING SOMETHING, AND HE'LL DO NOTHING WHEN YOU GOT NOTHING.
NOW, GET BOUNCER'S LEASH AND LET'S GET STARTED.
OKAY, LET'S START WITH SITTING. GET THE DOG ON YOUR LEFT, GIVE HIM THE COMMAND, AND PULL UP ON THE LEASH A LITTLE. USE A GOOD STRONG VOICE.
BOUNCER! SIT RIGHT DOWN HERE NOW.

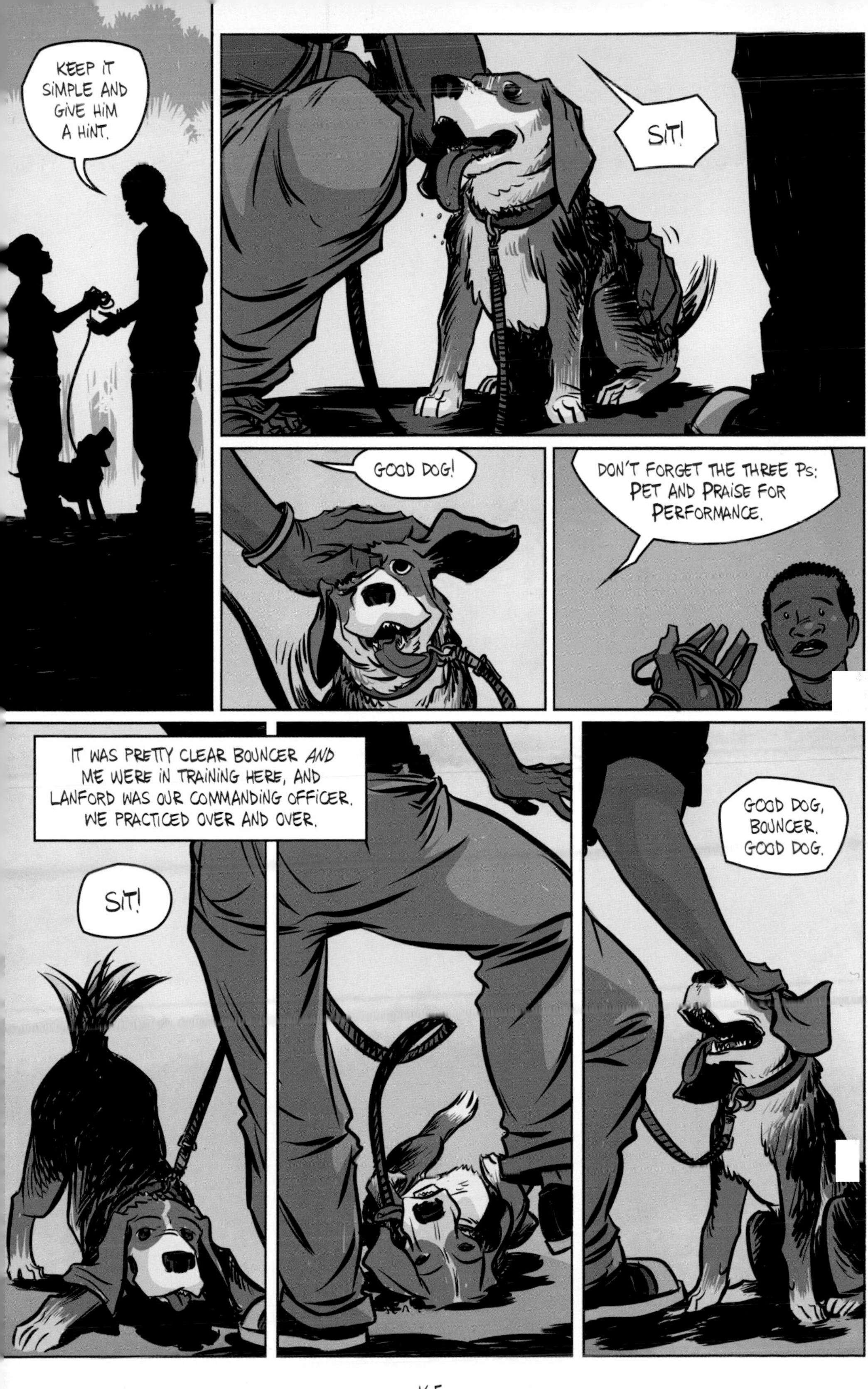
KEEP IT SIMPLE AND GIVE HIM A HINT.
SIT!
GOOD DOG!
DON'T FORGET THE THREE Ps: PET AND PRAISE FOR PERFORMANCE.
IT WAS PRETTY CLEAR BOUNCER *AND* ME WERE IN TRAINING HERE, AND LANFORD WAS OUR COMMANDING OFFICER. WE PRACTICED OVER AND OVER.
SIT!
GOOD DOG, BOUNCER. GOOD DOG.

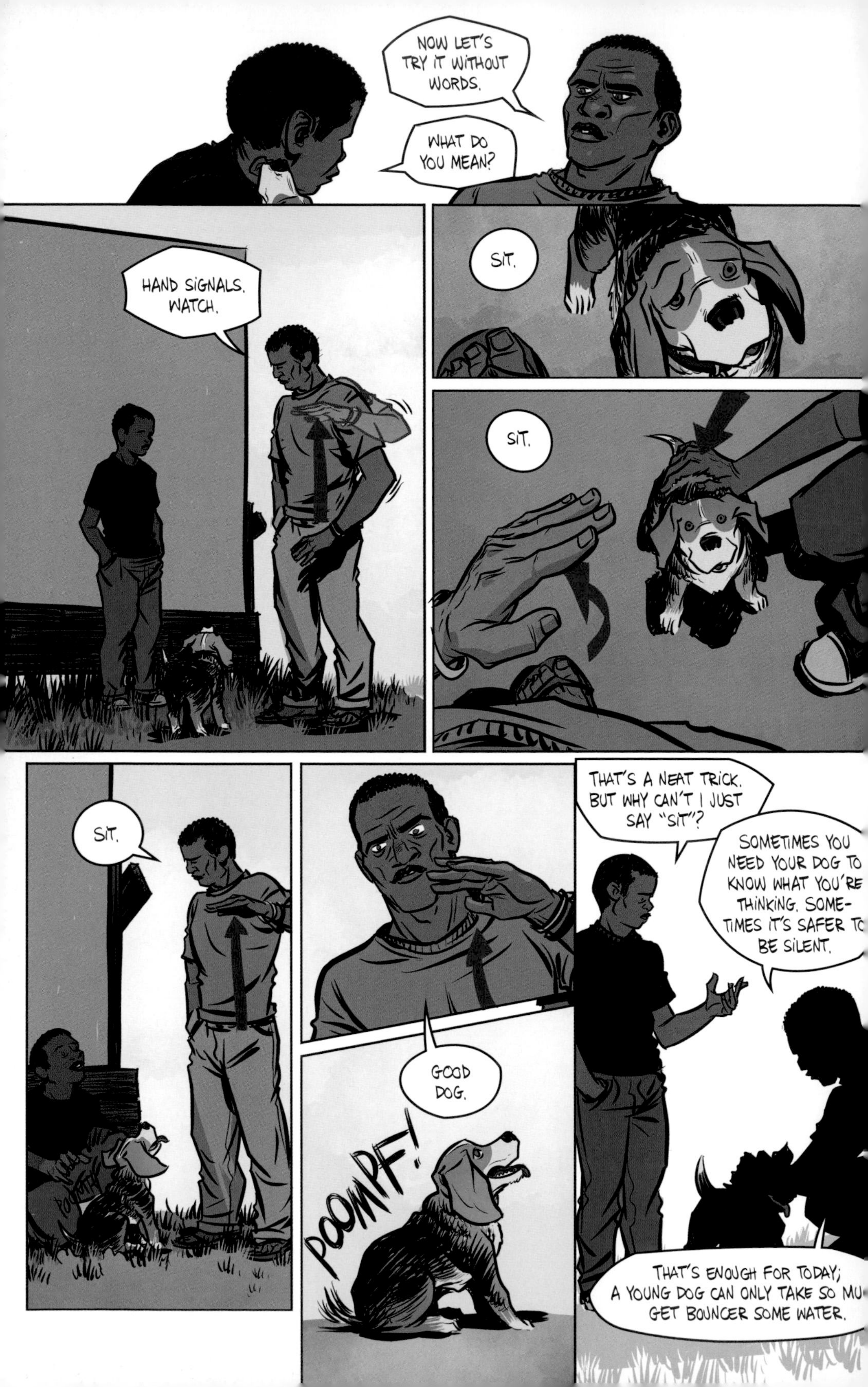
NOW LET'S TRY IT WITHOUT WORDS.
WHAT DO YOU MEAN?
HAND SIGNALS. WATCH.
SIT.
SIT.
SIT.
GOOD DOG.
POOMPF!
THAT'S A NEAT TRICK. BUT WHY CAN'T I JUST SAY "SIT"?
SOMETIMES YOU NEED YOUR DOG TO KNOW WHAT YOU'RE THINKING. SOMETIMES IT'S SAFER TO BE SILENT.
THAT'S ENOUGH FOR TODAY; A YOUNG DOG CAN ONLY TAKE SO MU
GET BOUNCER SOME WATER.

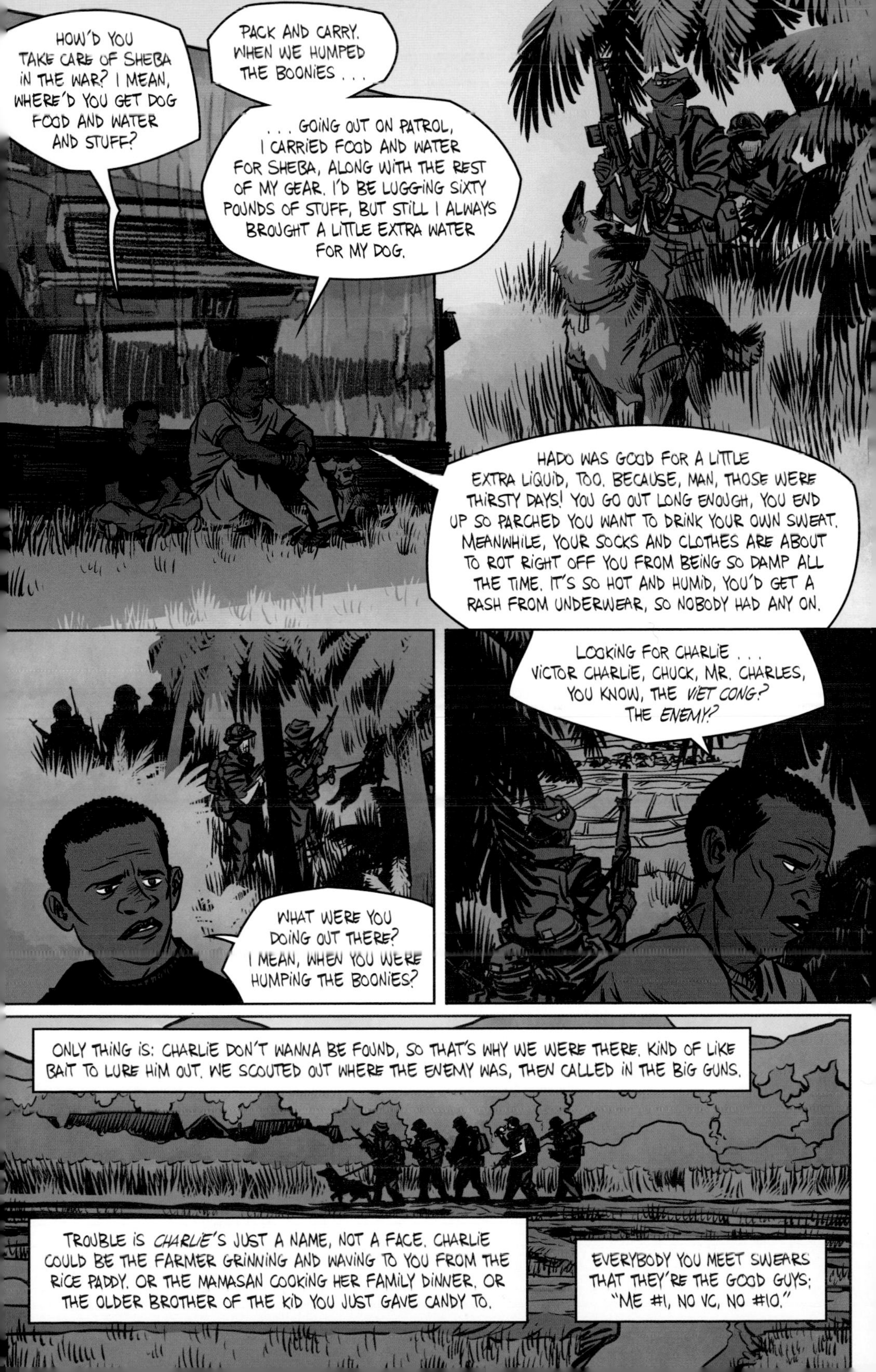
HOW'D YOU TAKE CARE OF SHEBA IN THE WAR? I MEAN, WHERE'D YOU GET DOG FOOD AND WATER AND STUFF?
PACK AND CARRY. WHEN WE HUMPED THE BOONIES . . .
. . . GOING OUT ON PATROL, I CARRIED FOOD AND WATER FOR SHEBA, ALONG WITH THE REST OF MY GEAR. I'D BE LUGGING SIXTY POUNDS OF STUFF, BUT STILL I ALWAYS BROUGHT A LITTLE EXTRA WATER FOR MY DOG.
HADO WAS GOOD FOR A LITTLE EXTRA LIQUID, TOO. BECAUSE, MAN, THOSE WERE THIRSTY DAYS! YOU GO OUT LONG ENOUGH, YOU END UP SO PARCHED YOU WANT TO DRINK YOUR OWN SWEAT. MEANWHILE, YOUR SOCKS AND CLOTHES ARE ABOUT TO ROT RIGHT OFF YOU FROM BEING SO DAMP ALL THE TIME. IT'S SO HOT AND HUMID, YOU'D GET A RASH FROM UNDERWEAR, SO NOBODY HAD ANY ON.
WHAT WERE YOU DOING OUT THERE? I MEAN, WHEN YOU WERE HUMPING THE BOONIES?
LOOKING FOR CHARLIE . . . VICTOR CHARLIE, CHUCK, MR. CHARLES, YOU KNOW, THE *VIET CONG*? THE *ENEMY*?
ONLY THING IS: CHARLIE DON'T WANNA BE FOUND, SO THAT'S WHY WE WERE THERE. KIND OF LIKE BAIT TO LURE HIM OUT. WE SCOUTED OUT WHERE THE ENEMY WAS, THEN CALLED IN THE BIG GUNS.
TROUBLE IS *CHARLIE*'S JUST A NAME, NOT A FACE. CHARLIE COULD BE THE FARMER GRINNING AND WAVING TO YOU FROM THE RICE PADDY. OR THE MAMASAN COOKING HER FAMILY DINNER. OR THE OLDER BROTHER OF THE KID YOU JUST GAVE CANDY TO.
EVERYBODY YOU MEET SWEARS THAT THEY'RE THE GOOD GUYS: "ME #1, NO VC, NO #10."

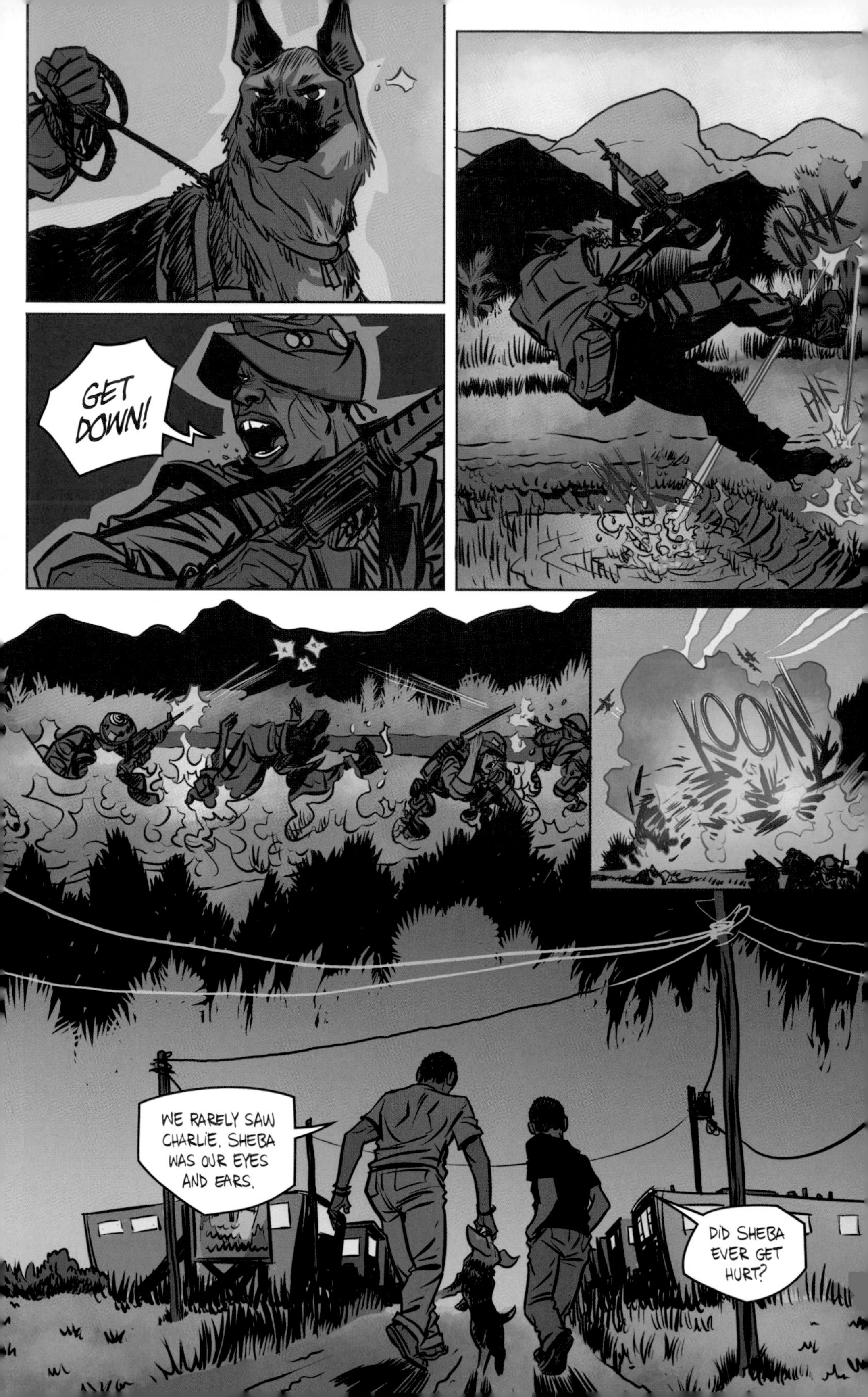
GET DOWN!
CRAK
PAF
KOOOM
WE RARELY SAW CHARLIE. SHEBA WAS OUR EYES AND EARS.
DID SHEBA EVER GET HURT?

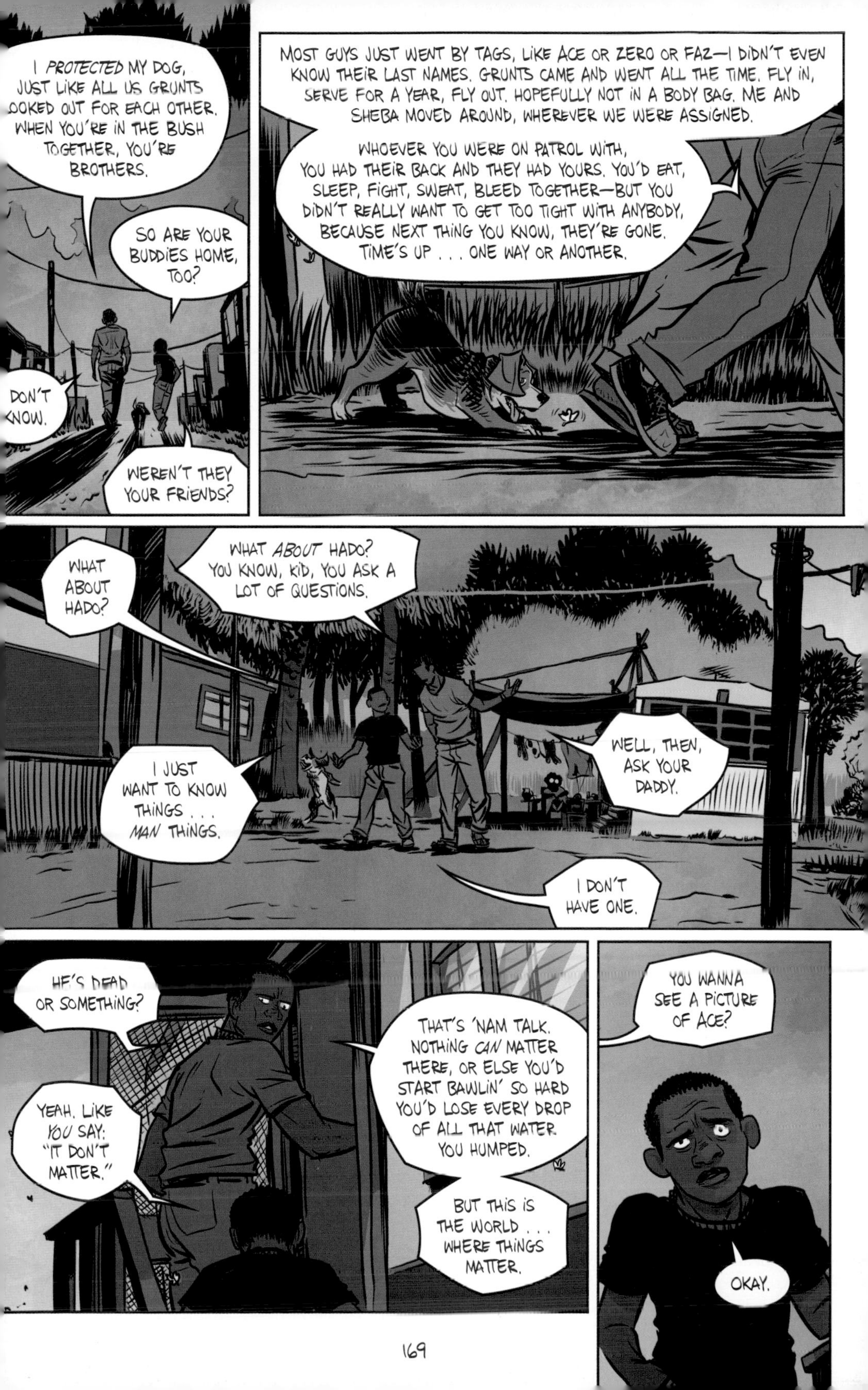

I *PROTECTED* MY DOG, JUST LIKE ALL US GRUNTS LOOKED OUT FOR EACH OTHER. WHEN YOU'RE IN THE BUSH TOGETHER, YOU'RE BROTHERS.
SO ARE YOUR BUDDIES HOME, TOO?
DON'T KNOW.
WEREN'T THEY YOUR FRIENDS?
MOST GUYS JUST WENT BY TAGS, LIKE ACE OR ZERO OR FAZ—I DIDN'T EVEN KNOW THEIR LAST NAMES. GRUNTS CAME AND WENT ALL THE TIME. FLY IN, SERVE FOR A YEAR, FLY OUT. HOPEFULLY NOT IN A BODY BAG. ME AND SHEBA MOVED AROUND, WHEREVER WE WERE ASSIGNED.
WHOEVER YOU WERE ON PATROL WITH, YOU HAD THEIR BACK AND THEY HAD YOURS. YOU'D EAT, SLEEP, FIGHT, SWEAT, BLEED TOGETHER—BUT YOU DIDN'T REALLY WANT TO GET TOO TIGHT WITH ANYBODY, BECAUSE NEXT THING YOU KNOW, THEY'RE GONE. TIME'S UP . . . ONE WAY OR ANOTHER.
WHAT ABOUT HADO?
WHAT *ABOUT* HADO? YOU KNOW, KID, YOU ASK A LOT OF QUESTIONS.
I JUST WANT TO KNOW THINGS . . . *MAN* THINGS.
WELL, THEN, ASK YOUR DADDY.
I DON'T HAVE ONE.
HE'S DEAD OR SOMETHING?
YEAH. LIKE *YOU* SAY: "IT DON'T MATTER."
THAT'S 'NAM TALK. NOTHING *CAN* MATTER THERE, OR ELSE YOU'D START BAWLIN' SO HARD YOU'D LOSE EVERY DROP OF ALL THAT WATER YOU HUMPED.
BUT THIS IS THE WORLD . . . WHERE THINGS MATTER.
YOU WANNA SEE A PICTURE OF ACE?
OKAY.

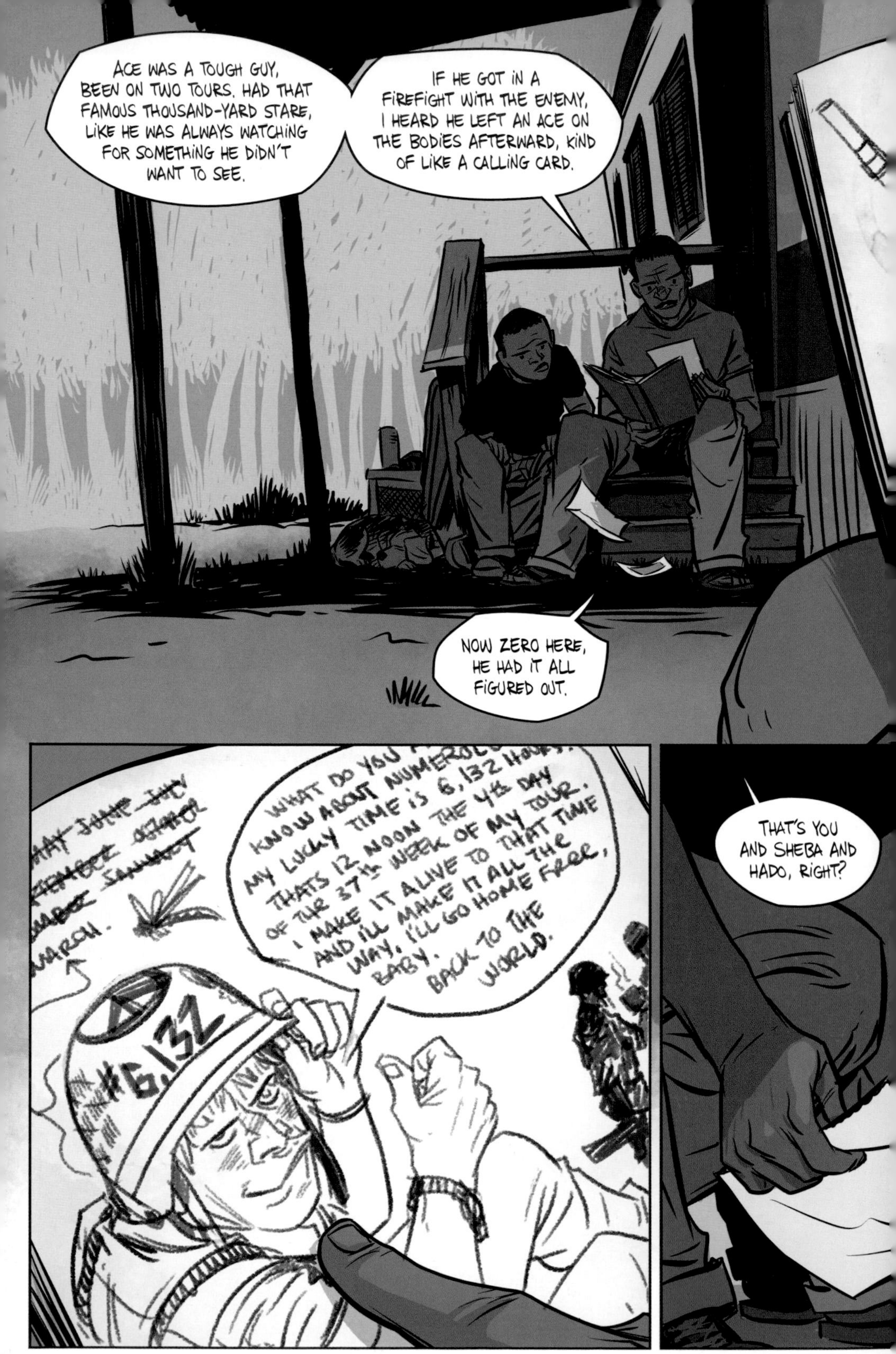
ACE WAS A TOUGH GUY, BEEN ON TWO TOURS. HAD THAT FAMOUS THOUSAND-YARD STARE, LIKE HE WAS ALWAYS WATCHING FOR SOMETHING HE DIDN'T WANT TO SEE.
IF HE GOT IN A FIREFIGHT WITH THE ENEMY, I HEARD HE LEFT AN ACE ON THE BODIES AFTERWARD, KIND OF LIKE A CALLING CARD.
NOW ZERO HERE, HE HAD IT ALL FIGURED OUT.
MARCH.
WHAT DO YOU
KNOW ABOUT NUMEROL
MY LUCKY TIME IS 6,132
THATS 12 NOON THE 4th DAY
OF THE 37th WEEK OF MY TOUR.
I MAKE IT ALIVE TO THAT TIME
AND ILL MAKE IT ALL THE WAY. I'LL GO HOME FREE,
BABY. BACK TO THE WORLD.
#6,132
THAT'S YOU AND SHEBA AND HADO, RIGHT?

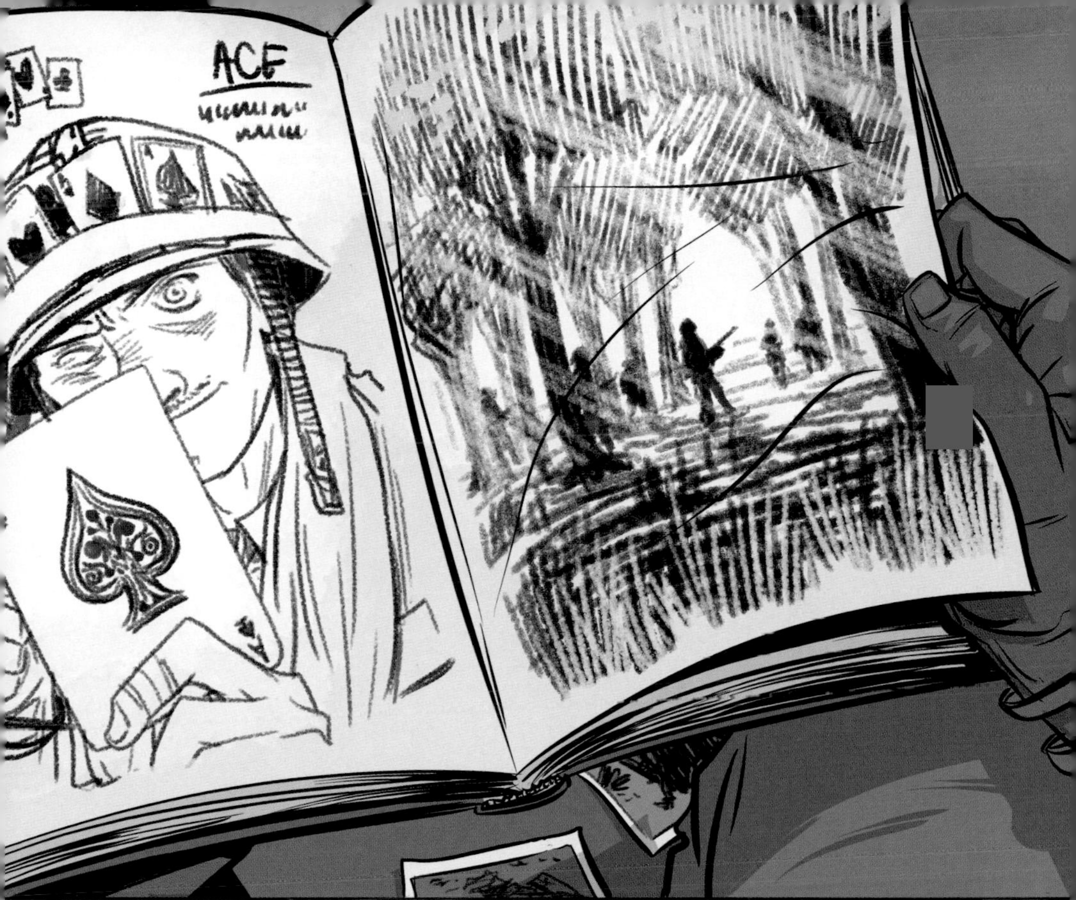
ACE

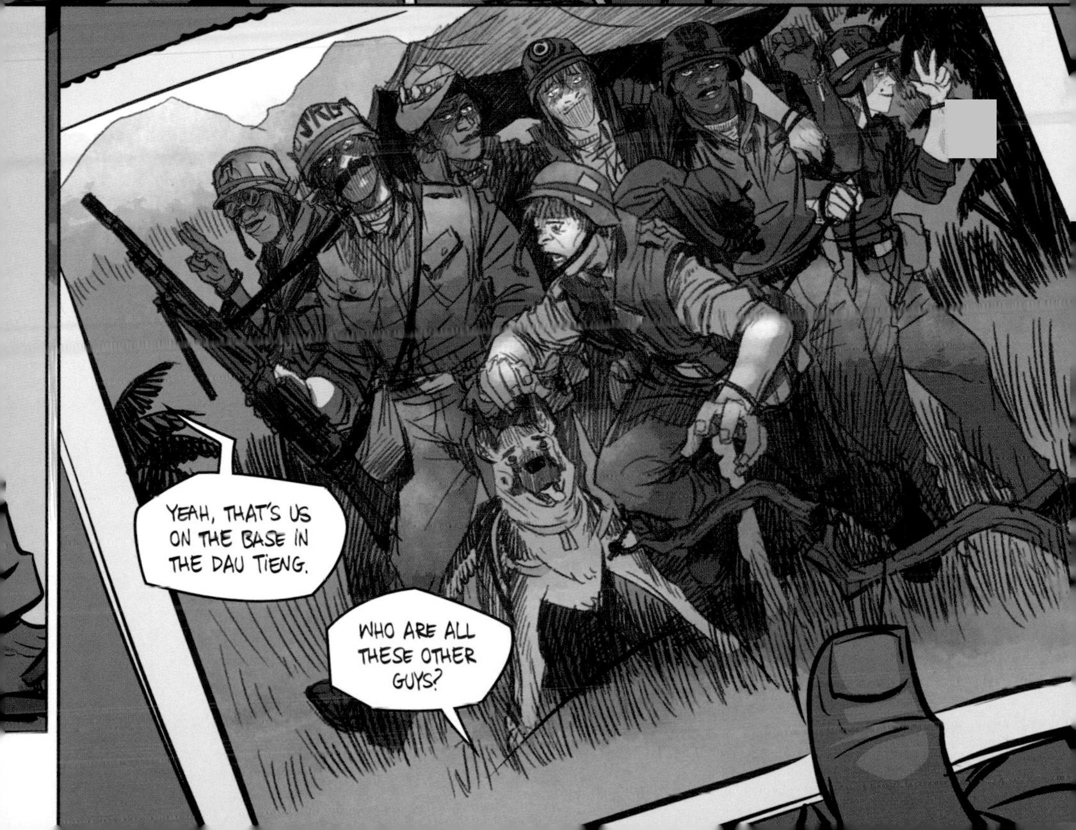
YEAH, THAT'S US ON THE BASE IN THE DAU TIENG.
WHO ARE ALL THESE OTHER GUYS?

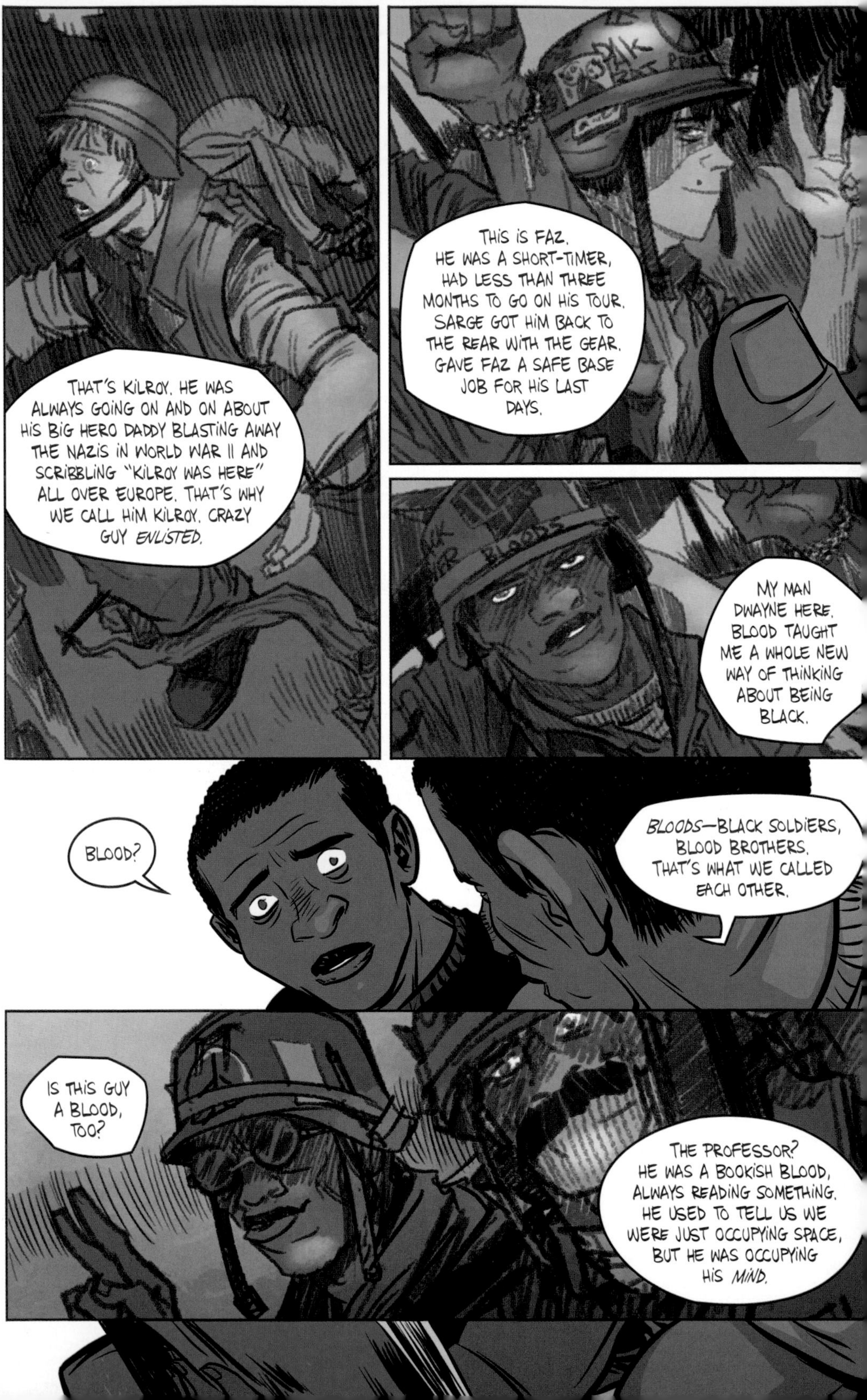
THAT'S KILROY. HE WAS ALWAYS GOING ON AND ON ABOUT HIS BIG HERO DADDY BLASTING AWAY THE NAZIS IN WORLD WAR II AND SCRIBBLING "KILROY WAS HERE" ALL OVER EUROPE. THAT'S WHY WE CALL HIM KILROY. CRAZY GUY *ENLISTED*.
THIS IS FAZ. HE WAS A SHORT-TIMER, HAD LESS THAN THREE MONTHS TO GO ON HIS TOUR. SARGE GOT HIM BACK TO THE REAR WITH THE GEAR. GAVE FAZ A SAFE BASE JOB FOR HIS LAST DAYS.
MY MAN DWAYNE HERE. BLOOD TAUGHT ME A WHOLE NEW WAY OF THINKING ABOUT BEING BLACK.
BLOOD?
BLOODS—BLACK SOLDIERS, BLOOD BROTHERS. THAT'S WHAT WE CALLED EACH OTHER.
IS THIS GUY A BLOOD, TOO?
THE PROFESSOR? HE WAS A BOOKISH BLOOD, ALWAYS READING SOMETHING. HE USED TO TELL US WE WERE JUST OCCUPYING SPACE, BUT HE WAS OCCUPYING HIS *MIND*.

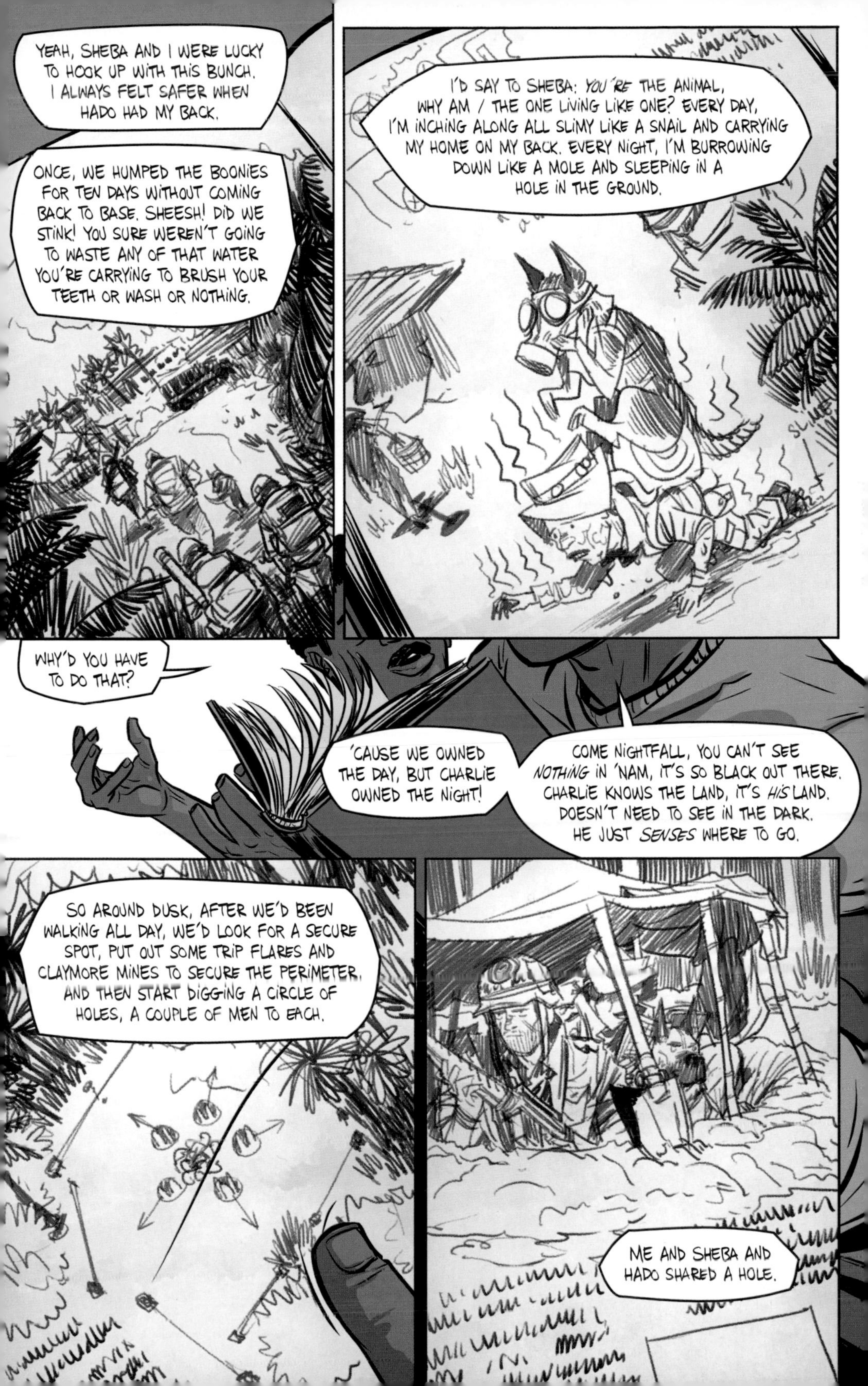
YEAH, SHEBA AND I WERE LUCKY TO HOOK UP WITH THIS BUNCH. I ALWAYS FELT SAFER WHEN HADO HAD MY BACK.
ONCE, WE HUMPED THE BOONIES FOR TEN DAYS WITHOUT COMING BACK TO BASE. SHEESH! DID WE STINK! YOU SURE WEREN'T GOING TO WASTE ANY OF THAT WATER YOU'RE CARRYING TO BRUSH YOUR TEETH OR WASH OR NOTHING.
I'D SAY TO SHEBA: *YOU'RE* THE ANIMAL, WHY AM *I* THE ONE LIVING LIKE ONE? EVERY DAY, I'M INCHING ALONG ALL SLIMY LIKE A SNAIL AND CARRYING MY HOME ON MY BACK. EVERY NIGHT, I'M BURROWING DOWN LIKE A MOLE AND SLEEPING IN A HOLE IN THE GROUND.
SLIME
WHY'D YOU HAVE TO DO THAT?
'CAUSE WE OWNED THE DAY, BUT CHARLIE OWNED THE NIGHT!
COME NIGHTFALL, YOU CAN'T SEE *NOTHING* IN 'NAM, IT'S SO BLACK OUT THERE. CHARLIE KNOWS THE LAND, IT'S *HIS* LAND. DOESN'T NEED TO SEE IN THE DARK. HE JUST *SENSES* WHERE TO GO.
SO AROUND DUSK, AFTER WE'D BEEN WALKING ALL DAY, WE'D LOOK FOR A SECURE SPOT, PUT OUT SOME TRIP FLARES AND CLAYMORE MINES TO SECURE THE PERIMETER. AND THEN START DIGGING A CIRCLE OF HOLES, A COUPLE OF MEN TO EACH.
ME AND SHEBA AND HADO SHARED A HOLE.

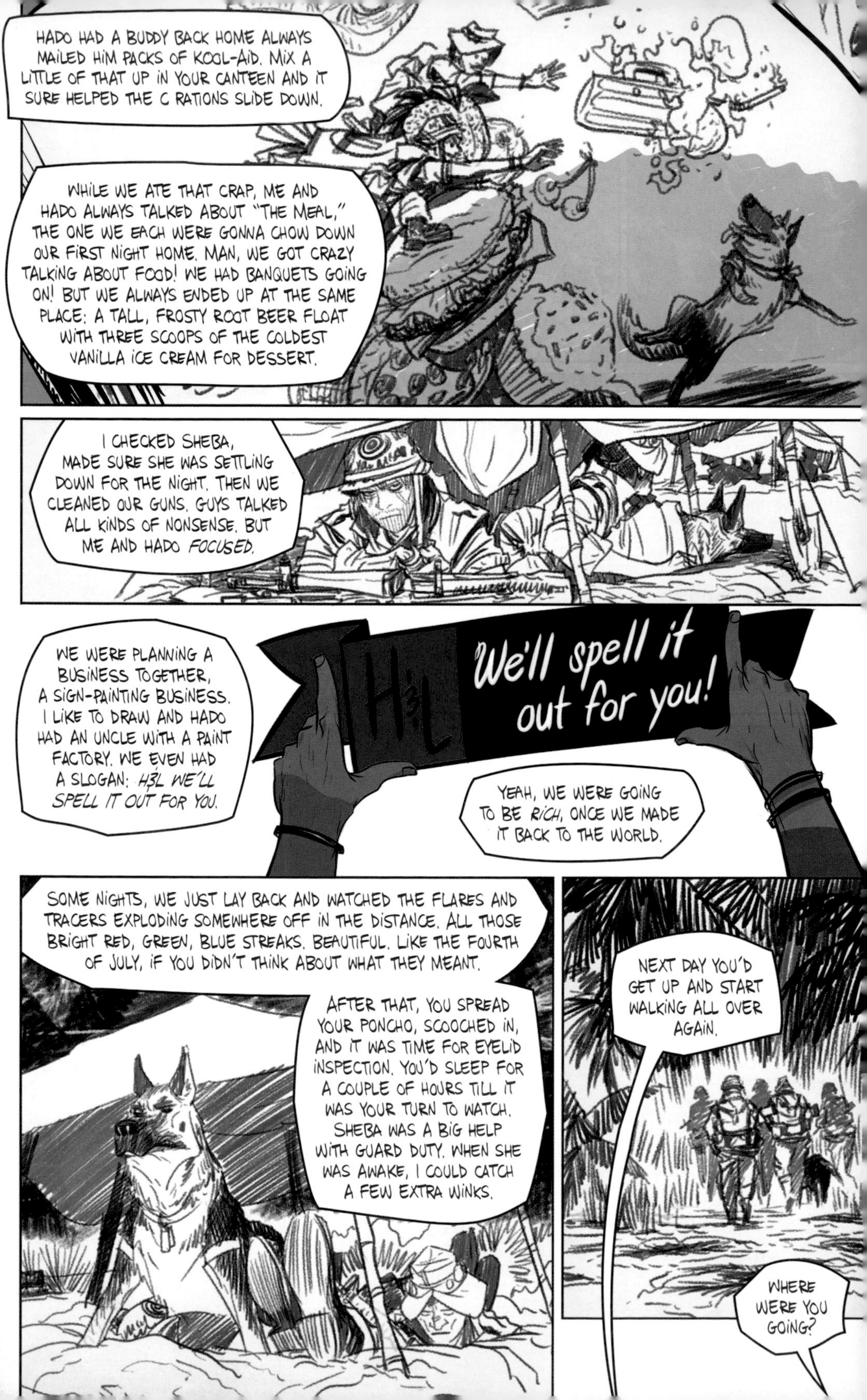
HADO HAD A BUDDY BACK HOME ALWAYS MAILED HIM PACKS OF KOOL-AID. MIX A LITTLE OF THAT UP IN YOUR CANTEEN AND IT SURE HELPED THE C RATIONS SLIDE DOWN.
WHILE WE ATE THAT CRAP, ME AND HADO ALWAYS TALKED ABOUT "THE MEAL," THE ONE WE EACH WERE GONNA CHOW DOWN OUR FIRST NIGHT HOME. MAN, WE GOT CRAZY TALKING ABOUT FOOD! WE HAD BANQUETS GOING ON! BUT WE ALWAYS ENDED UP AT THE SAME PLACE: A TALL, FROSTY ROOT BEER FLOAT WITH THREE SCOOPS OF THE COLDEST VANILLA ICE CREAM FOR DESSERT.
I CHECKED SHEBA, MADE SURE SHE WAS SETTLING DOWN FOR THE NIGHT. THEN WE CLEANED OUR GUNS. GUYS TALKED ALL KINDS OF NONSENSE. BUT ME AND HADO *FOCUSED*.
WE WERE PLANNING A BUSINESS TOGETHER, A SIGN-PAINTING BUSINESS. I LIKE TO DRAW AND HADO HAD AN UNCLE WITH A PAINT FACTORY. WE EVEN HAD A SLOGAN: *H3L WE'LL SPELL IT OUT FOR YOU.*
H3L
We'll spell it out for you!
YEAH, WE WERE GOING TO BE *RICH*, ONCE WE MADE IT BACK TO THE WORLD.
SOME NIGHTS, WE JUST LAY BACK AND WATCHED THE FLARES AND TRACERS EXPLODING SOMEWHERE OFF IN THE DISTANCE. ALL THOSE BRIGHT RED, GREEN, BLUE STREAKS. BEAUTIFUL. LIKE THE FOURTH OF JULY, IF YOU DIDN'T THINK ABOUT WHAT THEY MEANT.
AFTER THAT, YOU SPREAD YOUR PONCHO, SCOOCHED IN, AND IT WAS TIME FOR EYELID INSPECTION. YOU'D SLEEP FOR A COUPLE OF HOURS TILL IT WAS YOUR TURN TO WATCH. SHEBA WAS A BIG HELP WITH GUARD DUTY. WHEN SHE WAS AWAKE, I COULD CATCH A FEW EXTRA WINKS.
NEXT DAY YOU'D GET UP AND START WALKING ALL OVER AGAIN.
WHERE WERE YOU GOING?

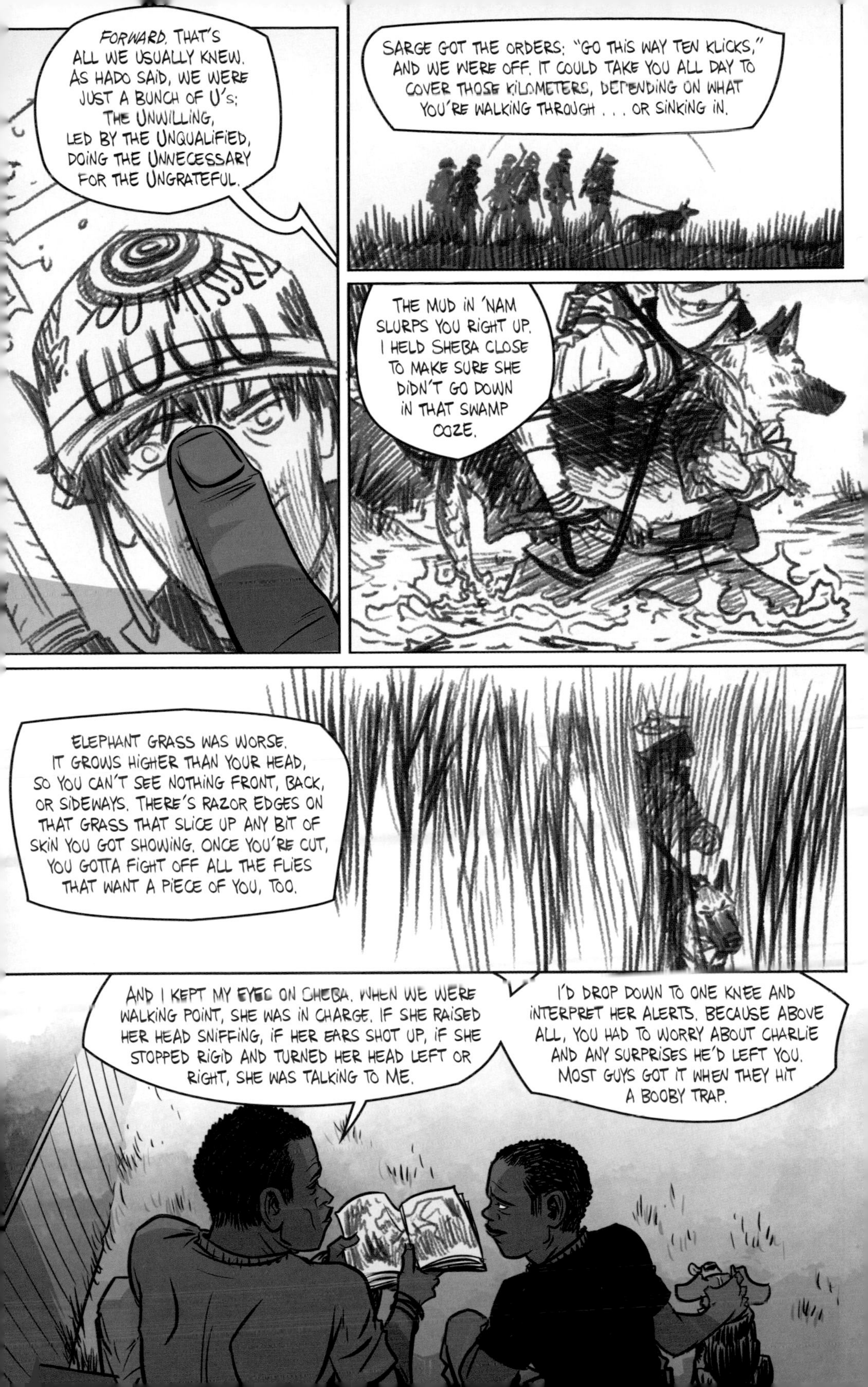
FORWARD. THAT'S ALL WE USUALLY KNEW. AS HADO SAID, WE WERE JUST A BUNCH OF U'S: THE UNWILLING, LED BY THE UNQUALIFIED, DOING THE UNNECESSARY FOR THE UNGRATEFUL.
YOU MISSED
SARGE GOT THE ORDERS: "GO THIS WAY TEN KLICKS," AND WE WERE OFF. IT COULD TAKE YOU ALL DAY TO COVER THOSE KILOMETERS, DEPENDING ON WHAT YOU'RE WALKING THROUGH . . . OR SINKING IN.
THE MUD IN 'NAM SLURPS YOU RIGHT UP. I HELD SHEBA CLOSE TO MAKE SURE SHE DIDN'T GO DOWN IN THAT SWAMP OOZE.
ELEPHANT GRASS WAS WORSE. IT GROWS HIGHER THAN YOUR HEAD, SO YOU CAN'T SEE NOTHING FRONT, BACK, OR SIDEWAYS. THERE'S RAZOR EDGES ON THAT GRASS THAT SLICE UP ANY BIT OF SKIN YOU GOT SHOWING. ONCE YOU'RE CUT, YOU GOTTA FIGHT OFF ALL THE FLIES THAT WANT A PIECE OF YOU, TOO.
AND I KEPT MY EYES ON SHEBA. WHEN WE WERE WALKING POINT, SHE WAS IN CHARGE. IF SHE RAISED HER HEAD SNIFFING, IF HER EARS SHOT UP, IF SHE STOPPED RIGID AND TURNED HER HEAD LEFT OR RIGHT, SHE WAS TALKING TO ME.
I'D DROP DOWN TO ONE KNEE AND INTERPRET HER ALERTS. BECAUSE ABOVE ALL, YOU HAD TO WORRY ABOUT CHARLIE AND ANY SURPRISES HE'D LEFT YOU. MOST GUYS GOT IT WHEN THEY HIT A BOOBY TRAP.

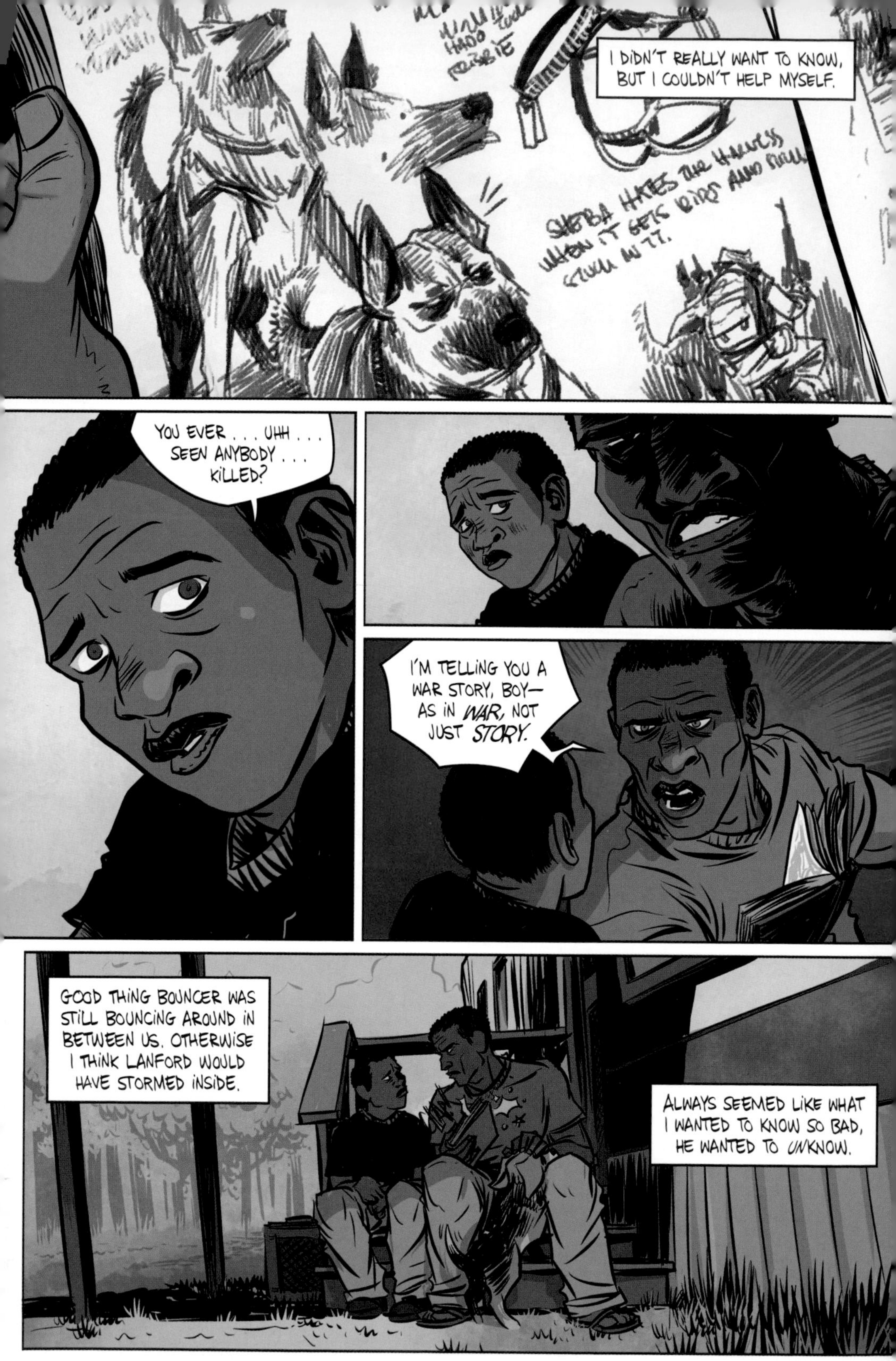
I DIDN'T REALLY WANT TO KNOW, BUT I COULDN'T HELP MYSELF.
YOU EVER . . . UHH . . . SEEN ANYBODY . . . KILLED?
I'M TELLING YOU A WAR STORY, BOY— AS IN *WAR*, NOT JUST *STORY*.
GOOD THING BOUNCER WAS STILL BOUNCING AROUND IN BETWEEN US. OTHERWISE I THINK LANFORD WOULD HAVE STORMED INSIDE.
ALWAYS SEEMED LIKE WHAT I WANTED TO KNOW SO BAD, HE WANTED TO *UN*KNOW.

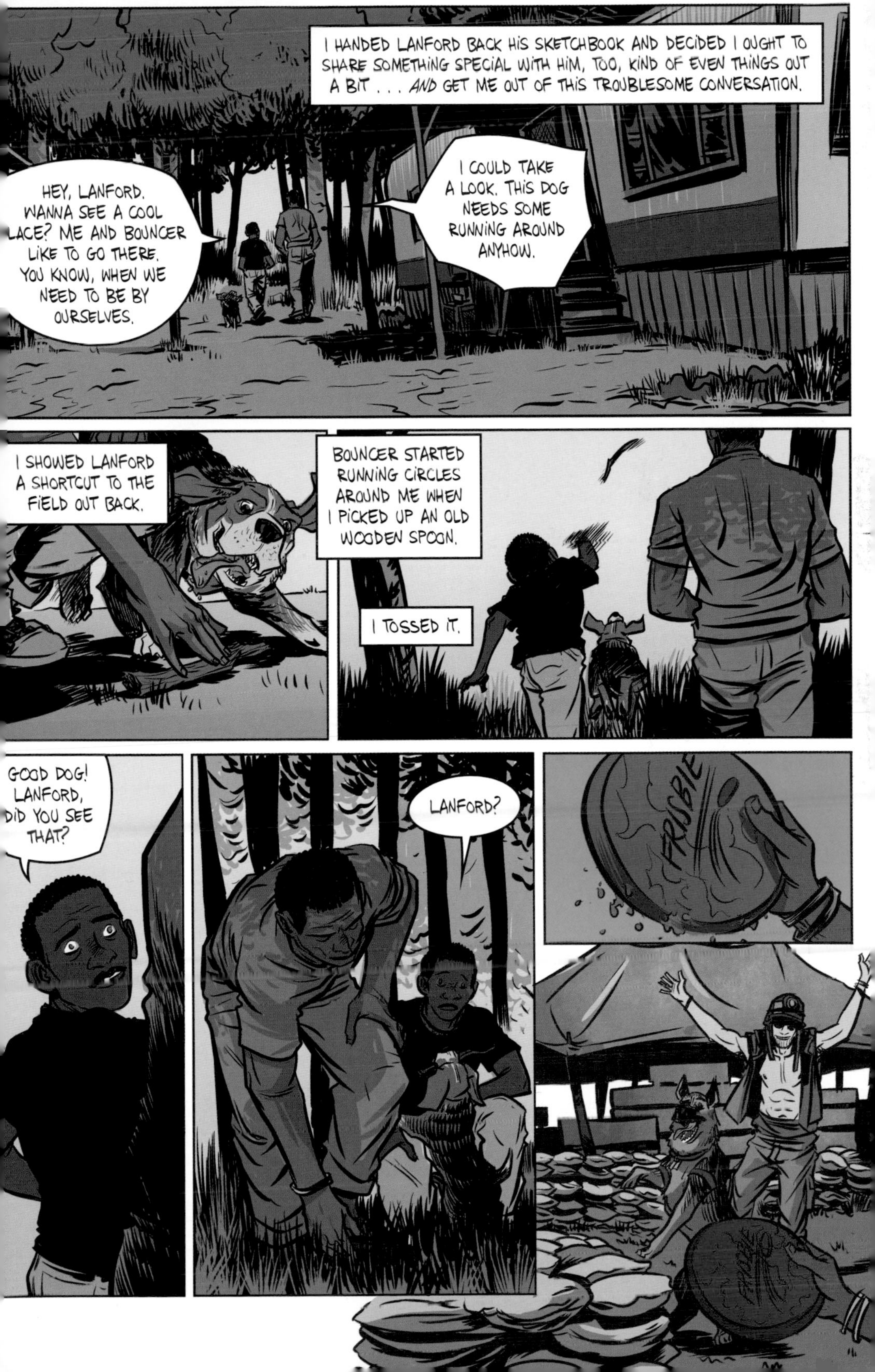

I HANDED LANFORD BACK HIS SKETCHBOOK AND DECIDED I OUGHT TO SHARE SOMETHING SPECIAL WITH HIM, TOO, KIND OF EVEN THINGS OUT A BIT . . . *AND* GET ME OUT OF THIS TROUBLESOME CONVERSATION.
HEY, LANFORD. WANNA SEE A COOL LACE? ME AND BOUNCER LIKE TO GO THERE. YOU KNOW, WHEN WE NEED TO BE BY OURSELVES.
I COULD TAKE A LOOK. THIS DOG NEEDS SOME RUNNING AROUND ANYHOW.
I SHOWED LANFORD A SHORTCUT TO THE FIELD OUT BACK.
BOUNCER STARTED RUNNING CIRCLES AROUND ME WHEN I PICKED UP AN OLD WOODEN SPOON.
I TOSSED IT.
GOOD DOG! LANFORD, DID YOU SEE THAT?
LANFORD?
FRISBIE

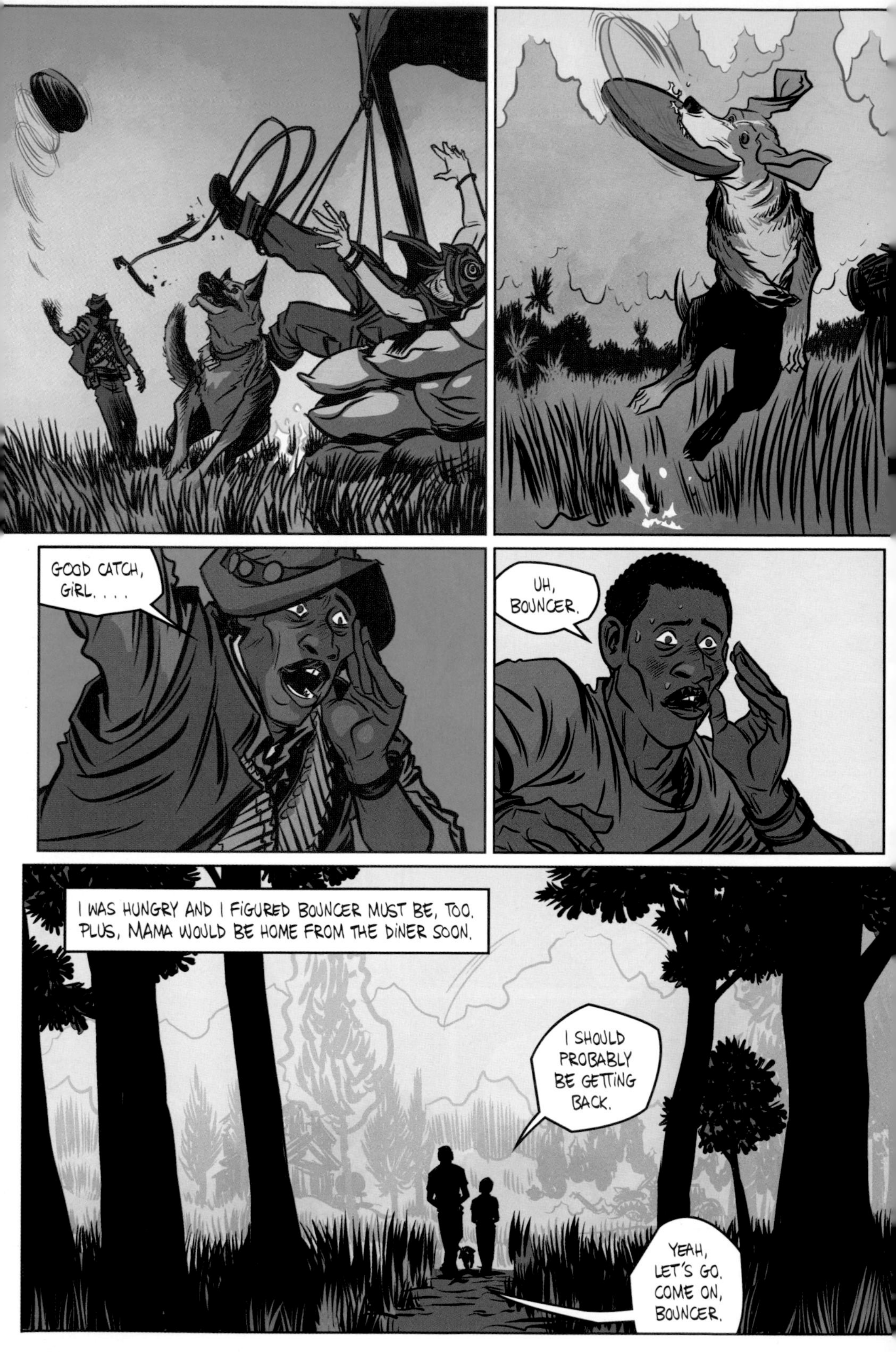
GOOD CATCH, GIRL. . . .
UH, BOUNCER.
I WAS HUNGRY AND I FIGURED BOUNCER MUST BE, TOO. PLUS, MAMA WOULD BE HOME FROM THE DINER SOON.
I SHOULD PROBABLY BE GETTING BACK.
YEAH, LET'S GO. COME ON, BOUNCER.

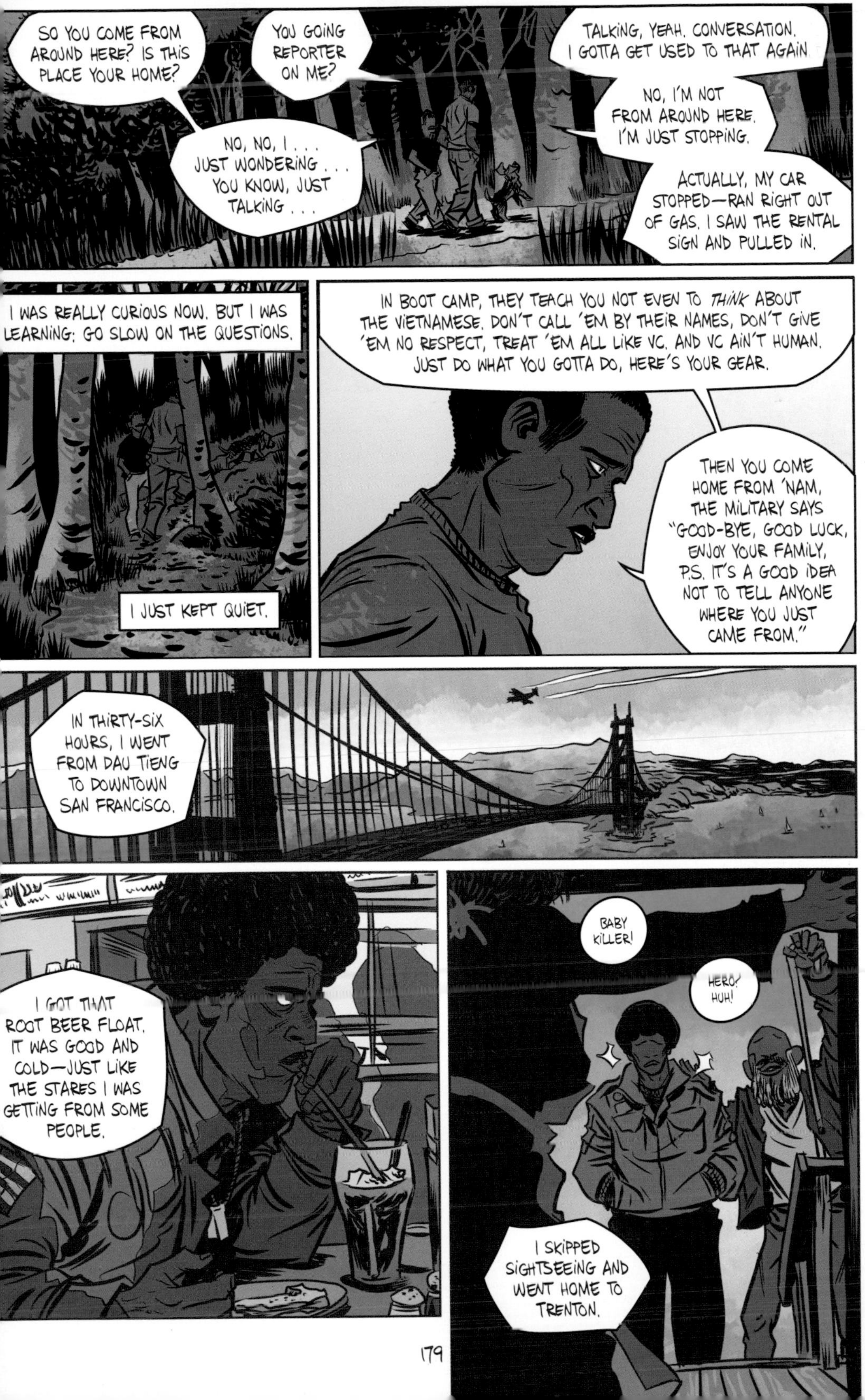
SO YOU COME FROM AROUND HERE? IS THIS PLACE YOUR HOME?
YOU GOING REPORTER ON ME?
NO, NO, I . . . JUST WONDERING . . . YOU KNOW, JUST TALKING . . .
TALKING, YEAH. CONVERSATION. I GOTTA GET USED TO THAT AGAIN.
NO, I'M NOT FROM AROUND HERE. I'M JUST STOPPING.
ACTUALLY, MY CAR STOPPED—RAN RIGHT OUT OF GAS. I SAW THE RENTAL SIGN AND PULLED IN.
I WAS REALLY CURIOUS NOW. BUT I WAS LEARNING: GO SLOW ON THE QUESTIONS.
I JUST KEPT QUIET.
IN BOOT CAMP, THEY TEACH YOU NOT EVEN TO *THINK* ABOUT THE VIETNAMESE. DON'T CALL 'EM BY THEIR NAMES, DON'T GIVE 'EM NO RESPECT, TREAT 'EM ALL LIKE VC. AND VC AIN'T HUMAN. JUST DO WHAT YOU GOTTA DO, HERE'S YOUR GEAR.
THEN YOU COME HOME FROM 'NAM, THE MILITARY SAYS "GOOD-BYE, GOOD LUCK, ENJOY YOUR FAMILY, P.S. IT'S A GOOD IDEA NOT TO TELL ANYONE WHERE YOU JUST CAME FROM."
IN THIRTY-SIX HOURS, I WENT FROM DAU TIENG TO DOWNTOWN SAN FRANCISCO.
I GOT THAT ROOT BEER FLOAT. IT WAS GOOD AND COLD—JUST LIKE THE STARES I WAS GETTING FROM SOME PEOPLE.
BABY KILLER!
HERO? HUH!
I SKIPPED SIGHTSEEING AND WENT HOME TO TRENTON.

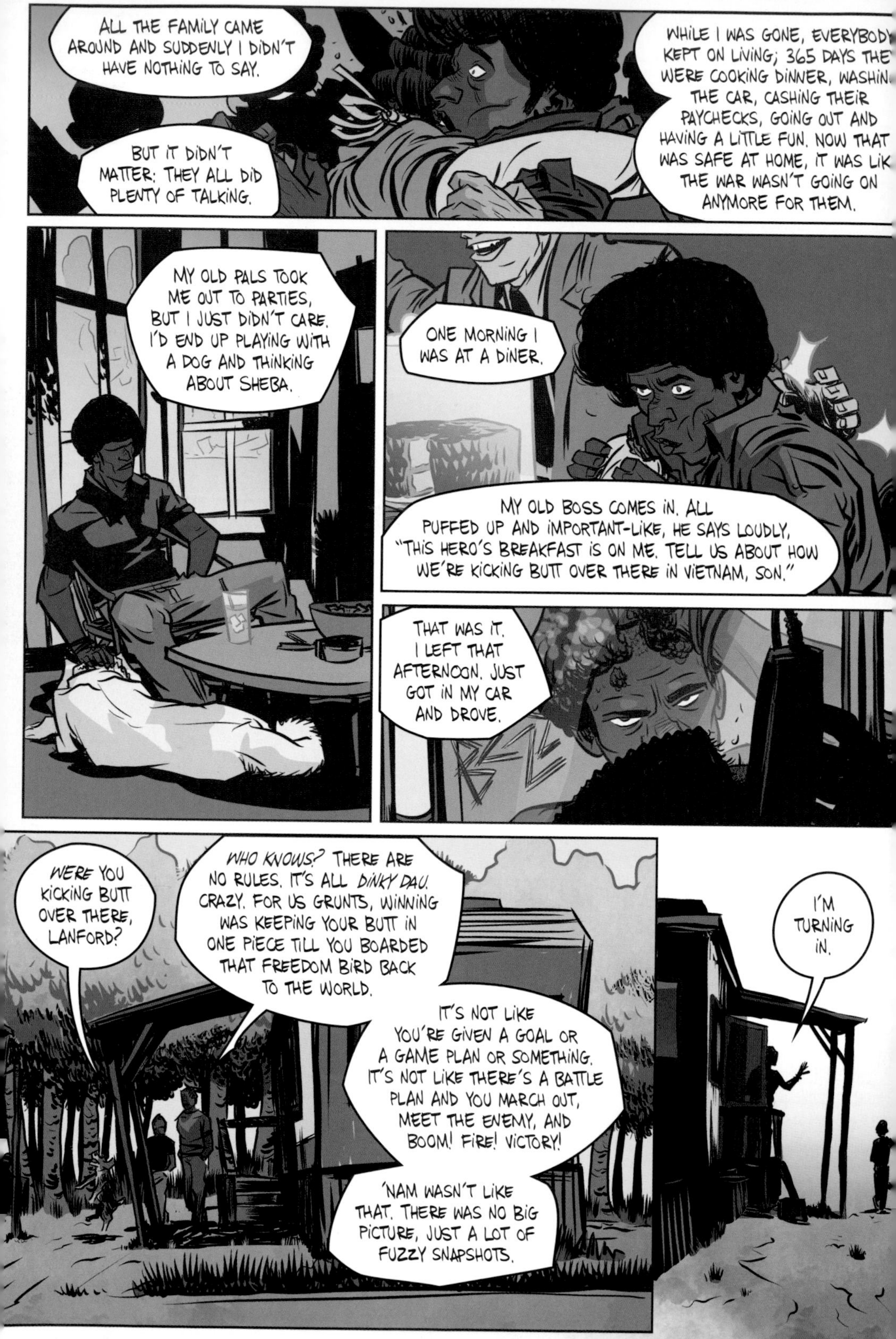
ALL THE FAMILY CAME AROUND AND SUDDENLY I DIDN'T HAVE NOTHING TO SAY.
BUT IT DIDN'T MATTER: THEY ALL DID PLENTY OF TALKING.
WHILE I WAS GONE, EVERYBOD KEPT ON LIVING; 365 DAYS THE WERE COOKING DINNER, WASHIN THE CAR, CASHING THEIR PAYCHECKS, GOING OUT AND HAVING A LITTLE FUN. NOW THAT WAS SAFE AT HOME, IT WAS LIK THE WAR WASN'T GOING ON ANYMORE FOR THEM.
MY OLD PALS TOOK ME OUT TO PARTIES, BUT I JUST DIDN'T CARE. I'D END UP PLAYING WITH A DOG AND THINKING ABOUT SHEBA.
ONE MORNING I WAS AT A DINER.
MY OLD BOSS COMES IN. ALL PUFFED UP AND IMPORTANT-LIKE, HE SAYS LOUDLY, "THIS HERO'S BREAKFAST IS ON ME. TELL US ABOUT HOW WE'RE KICKING BUTT OVER THERE IN VIETNAM, SON."
THAT WAS IT. I LEFT THAT AFTERNOON. JUST GOT IN MY CAR AND DROVE.
WERE YOU KICKING BUTT OVER THERE, LANFORD?
WHO KNOWS? THERE ARE NO RULES. IT'S ALL DINKY DAU. CRAZY. FOR US GRUNTS, WINNING WAS KEEPING YOUR BUTT IN ONE PIECE TILL YOU BOARDED THAT FREEDOM BIRD BACK TO THE WORLD.
IT'S NOT LIKE YOU'RE GIVEN A GOAL OR A GAME PLAN OR SOMETHING. IT'S NOT LIKE THERE'S A BATTLE PLAN AND YOU MARCH OUT, MEET THE ENEMY, AND BOOM! FIRE! VICTORY!
'NAM WASN'T LIKE THAT. THERE WAS NO BIG PICTURE, JUST A LOT OF FUZZY SNAPSHOTS.
I'M TURNING IN.

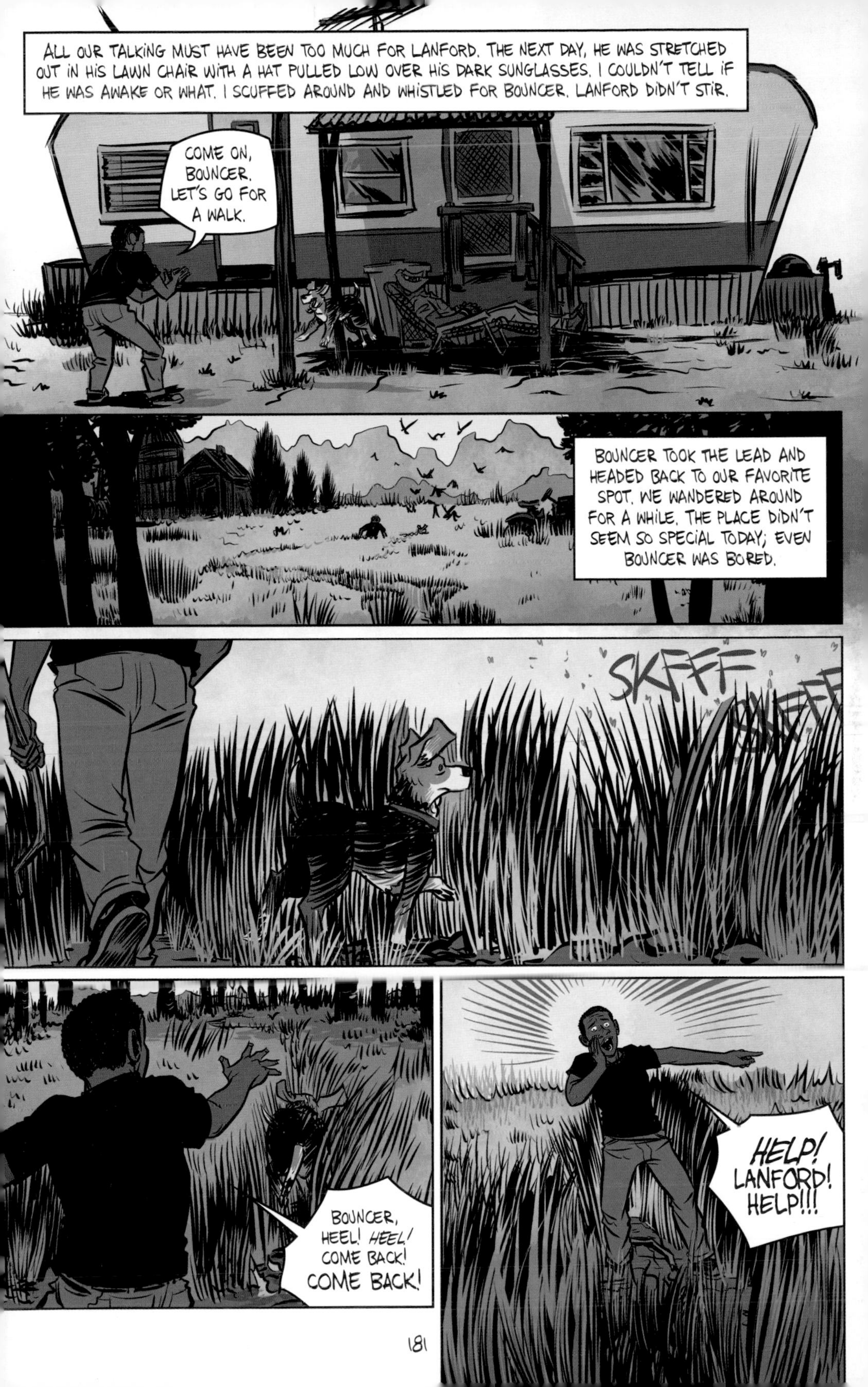
ALL OUR TALKING MUST HAVE BEEN TOO MUCH FOR LANFORD. THE NEXT DAY, HE WAS STRETCHED OUT IN HIS LAWN CHAIR WITH A HAT PULLED LOW OVER HIS DARK SUNGLASSES. I COULDN'T TELL IF HE WAS AWAKE OR WHAT. I SCUFFED AROUND AND WHISTLED FOR BOUNCER. LANFORD DIDN'T STIR.
COME ON, BOUNCER. LET'S GO FOR A WALK.
BOUNCER TOOK THE LEAD AND HEADED BACK TO OUR FAVORITE SPOT. WE WANDERED AROUND FOR A WHILE. THE PLACE DIDN'T SEEM SO SPECIAL TODAY; EVEN BOUNCER WAS BORED.
SKFFF
BOUNCER, HEEL! *HEEL!* COME BACK! COME BACK!
HELP! LANFORD! HELP!!!

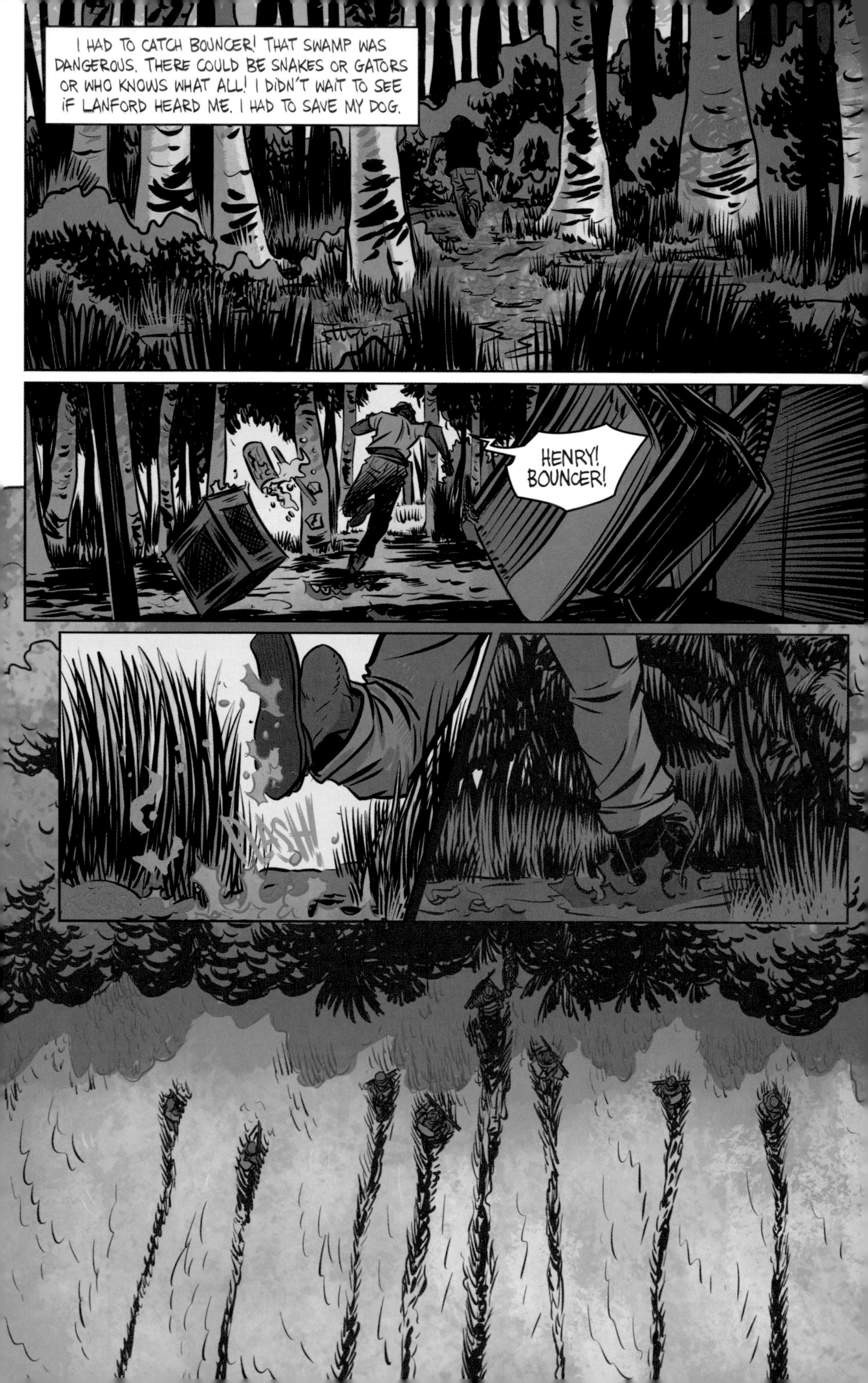
I HAD TO CATCH BOUNCER! THAT SWAMP WAS DANGEROUS. THERE COULD BE SNAKES OR GATORS OR WHO KNOWS WHAT ALL! I DIDN'T WAIT TO SEE IF LANFORD HEARD ME. I HAD TO SAVE MY DOG.
HENRY! BOUNCER!

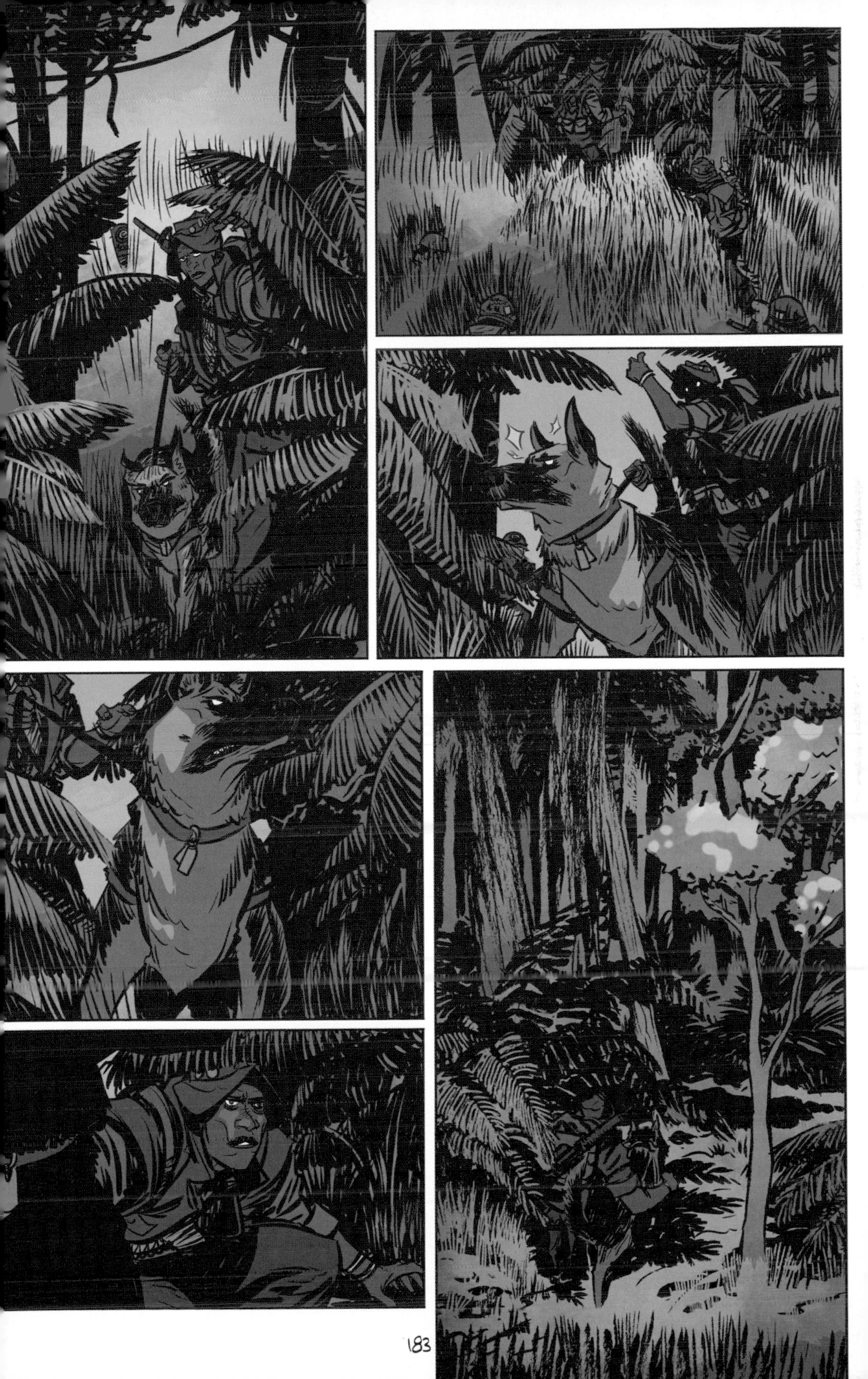

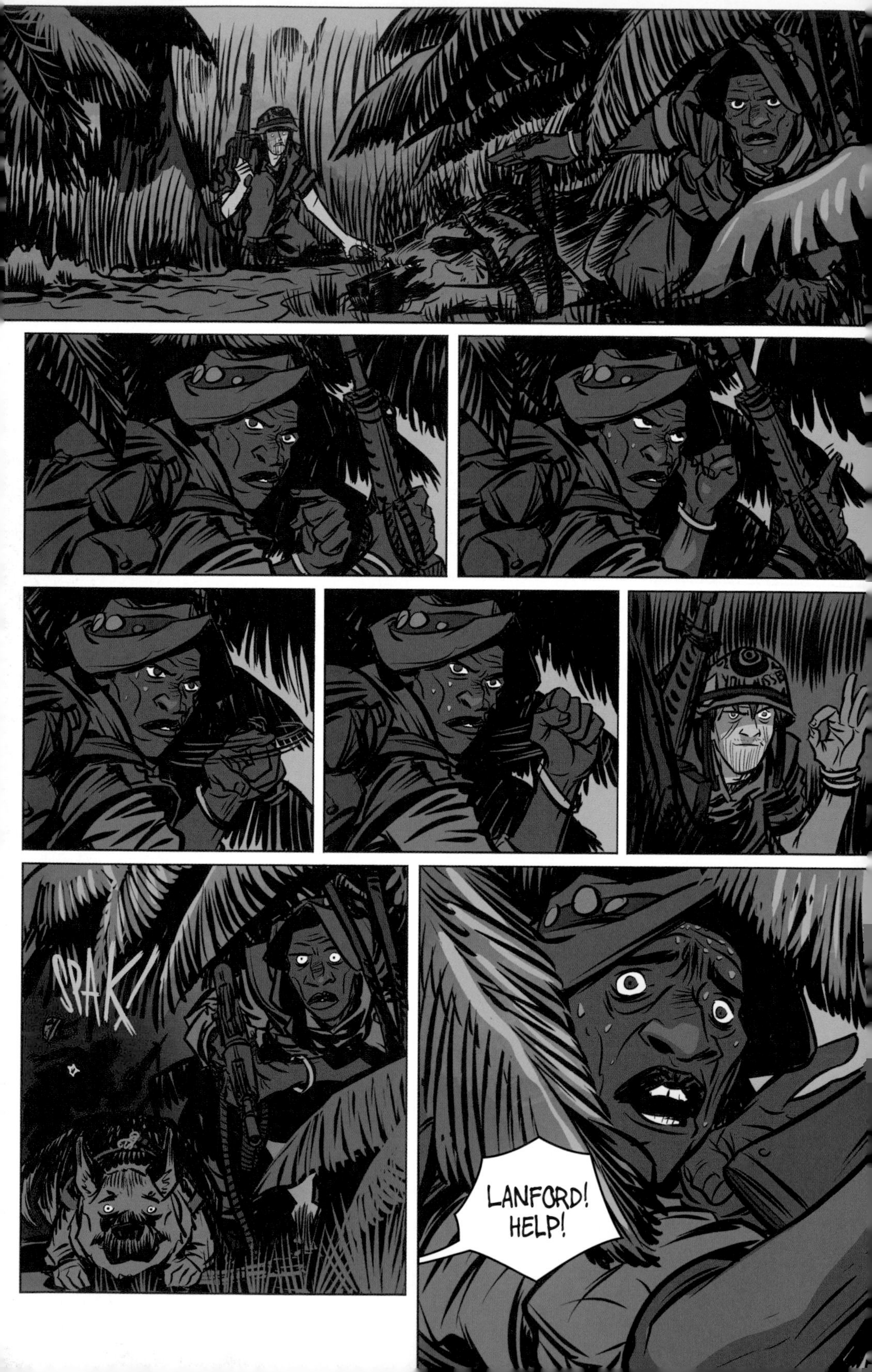
SPAK!
LANFORD! HELP!

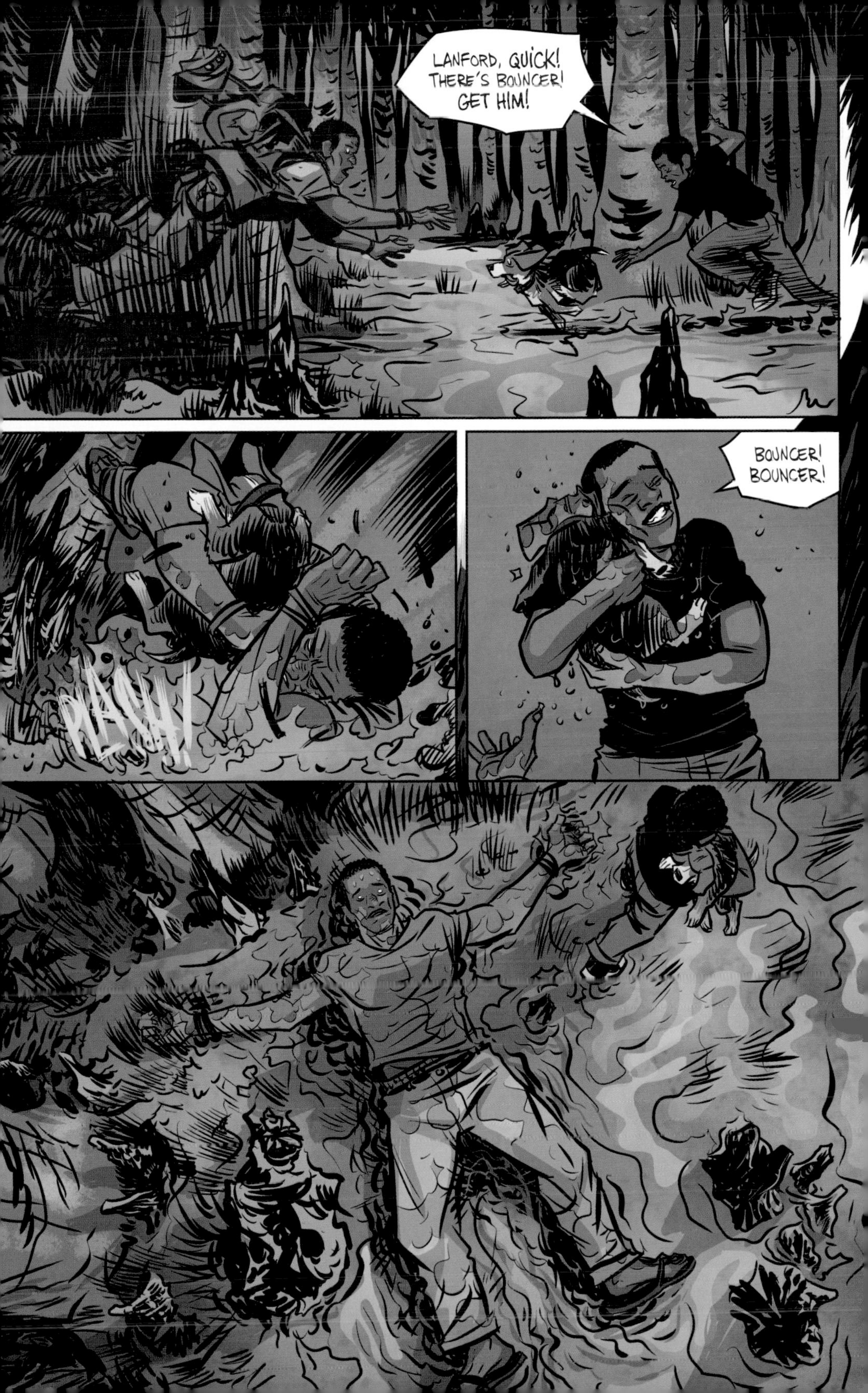
LANFORD, QUICK! THERE'S BOUNCER! GET HIM!
PLASH!
BOUNCER! BOUNCER!

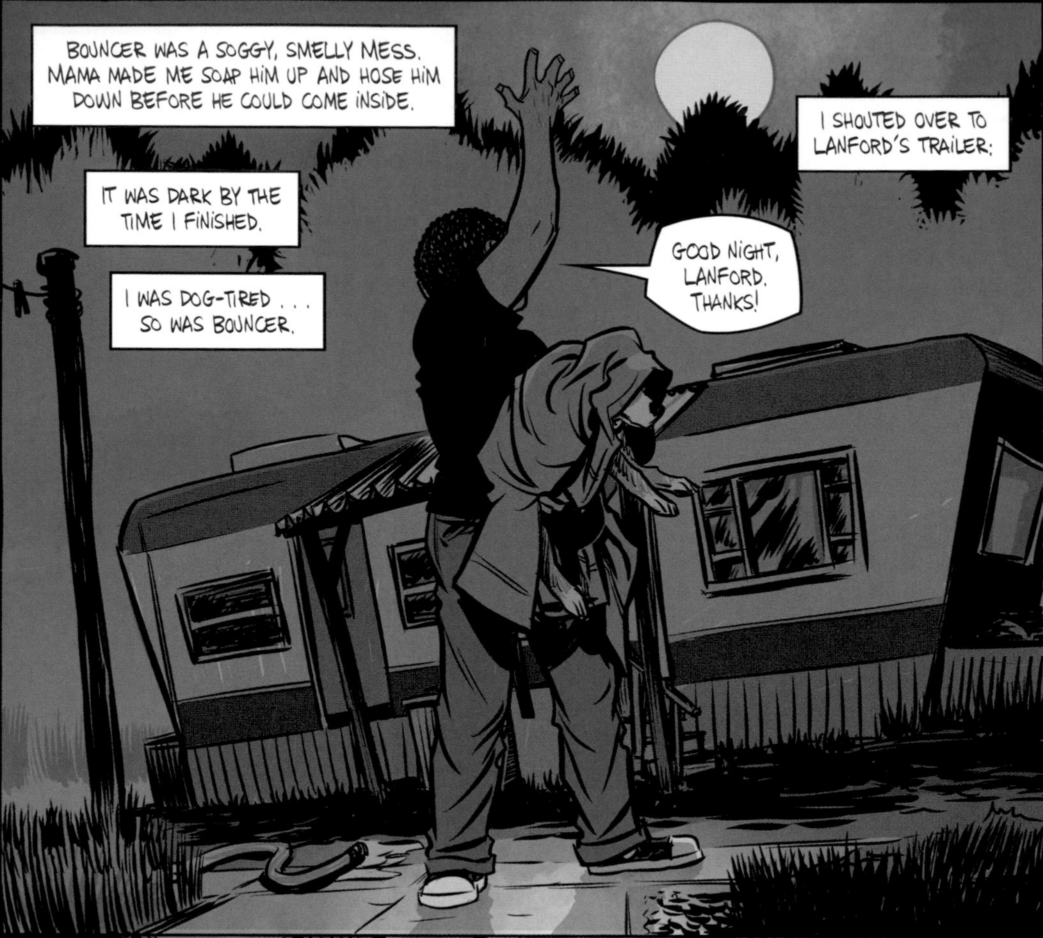
BOUNCER WAS A SOGGY, SMELLY MESS. MAMA MADE ME SOAP HIM UP AND HOSE HIM DOWN BEFORE HE COULD COME INSIDE.
IT WAS DARK BY THE TIME I FINISHED.
I WAS DOG-TIRED . . . SO WAS BOUNCER.
I SHOUTED OVER TO LANFORD'S TRAILER:
GOOD NIGHT, LANFORD. THANKS!

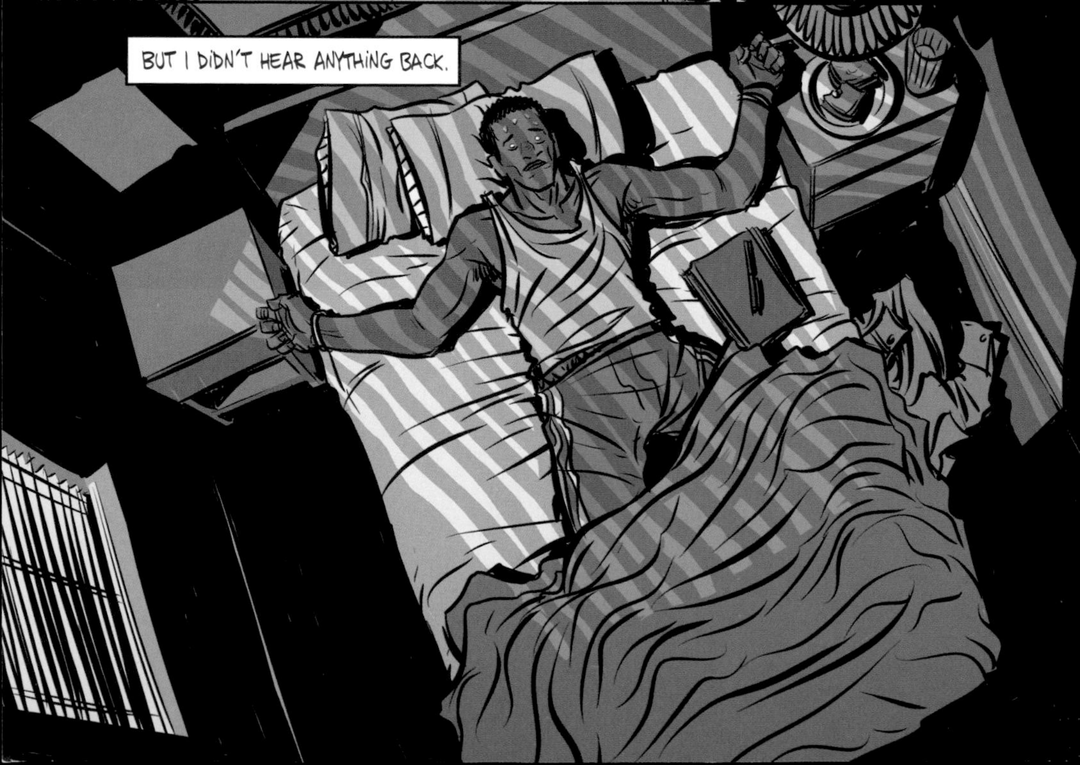
BUT I DIDN'T HEAR ANYTHING BACK.

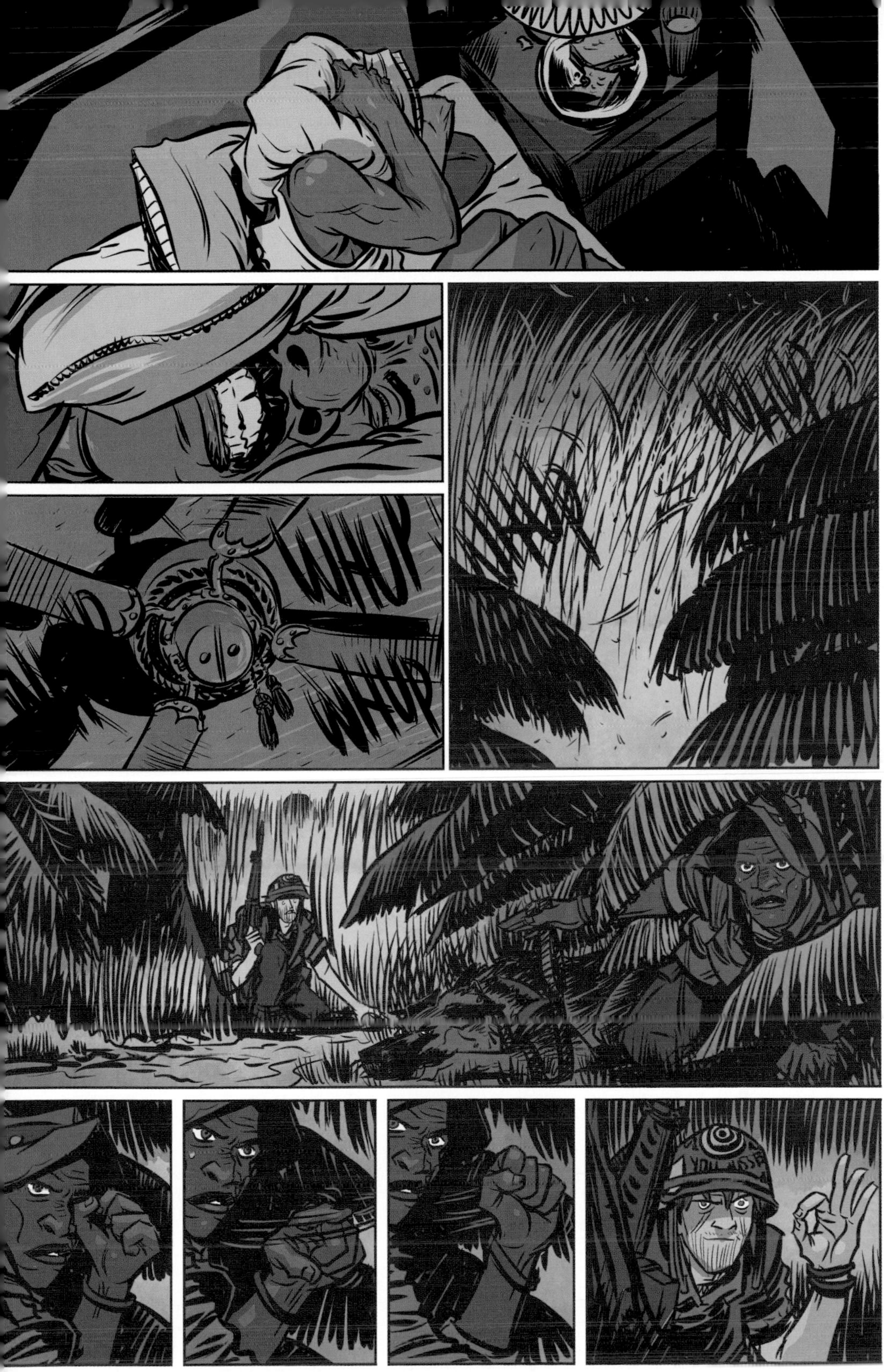
WHUP
WHUP
WHUP
WHUP

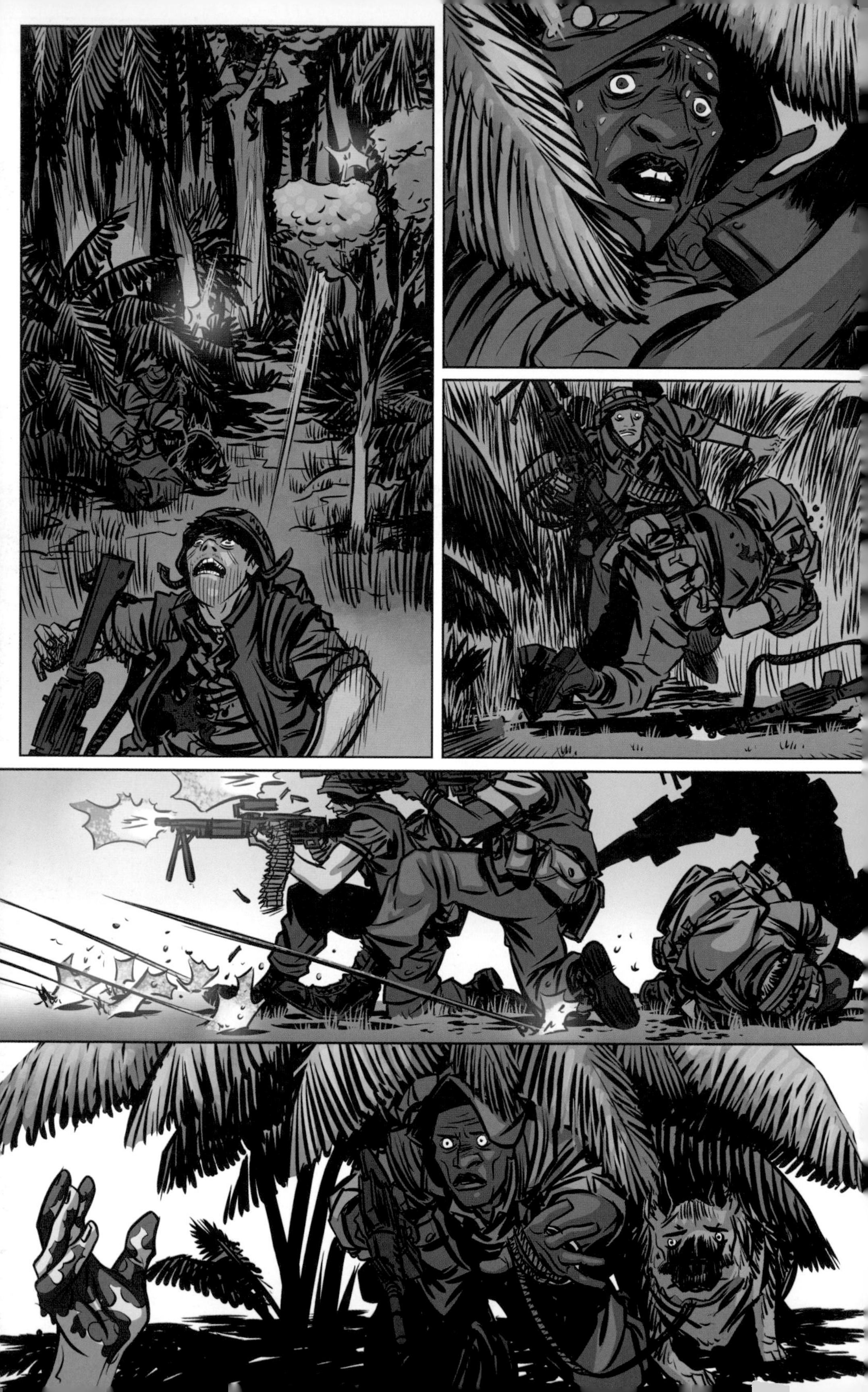

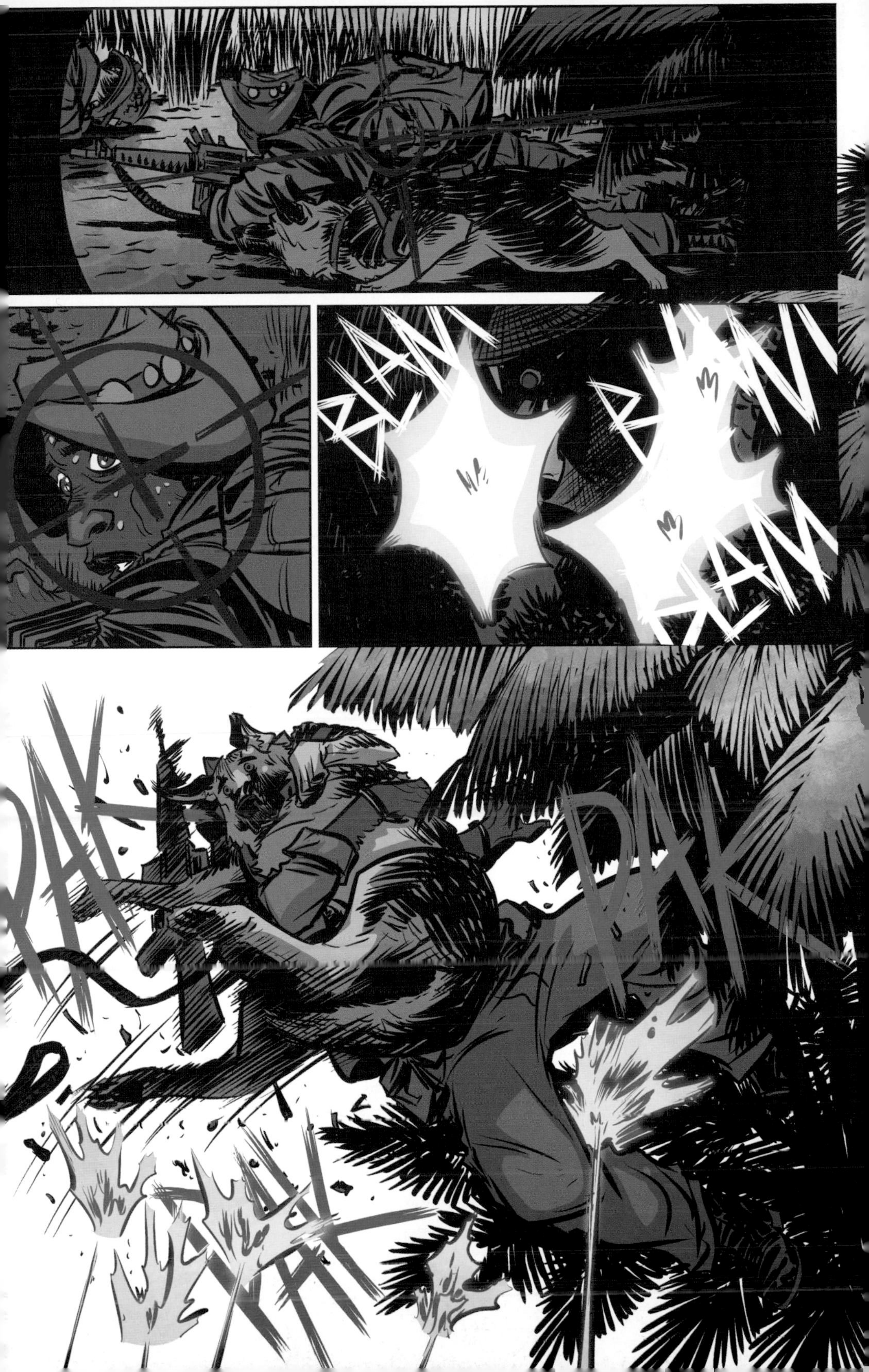
BLAM
BLAM
BLAM
PAK
PAK
PAK

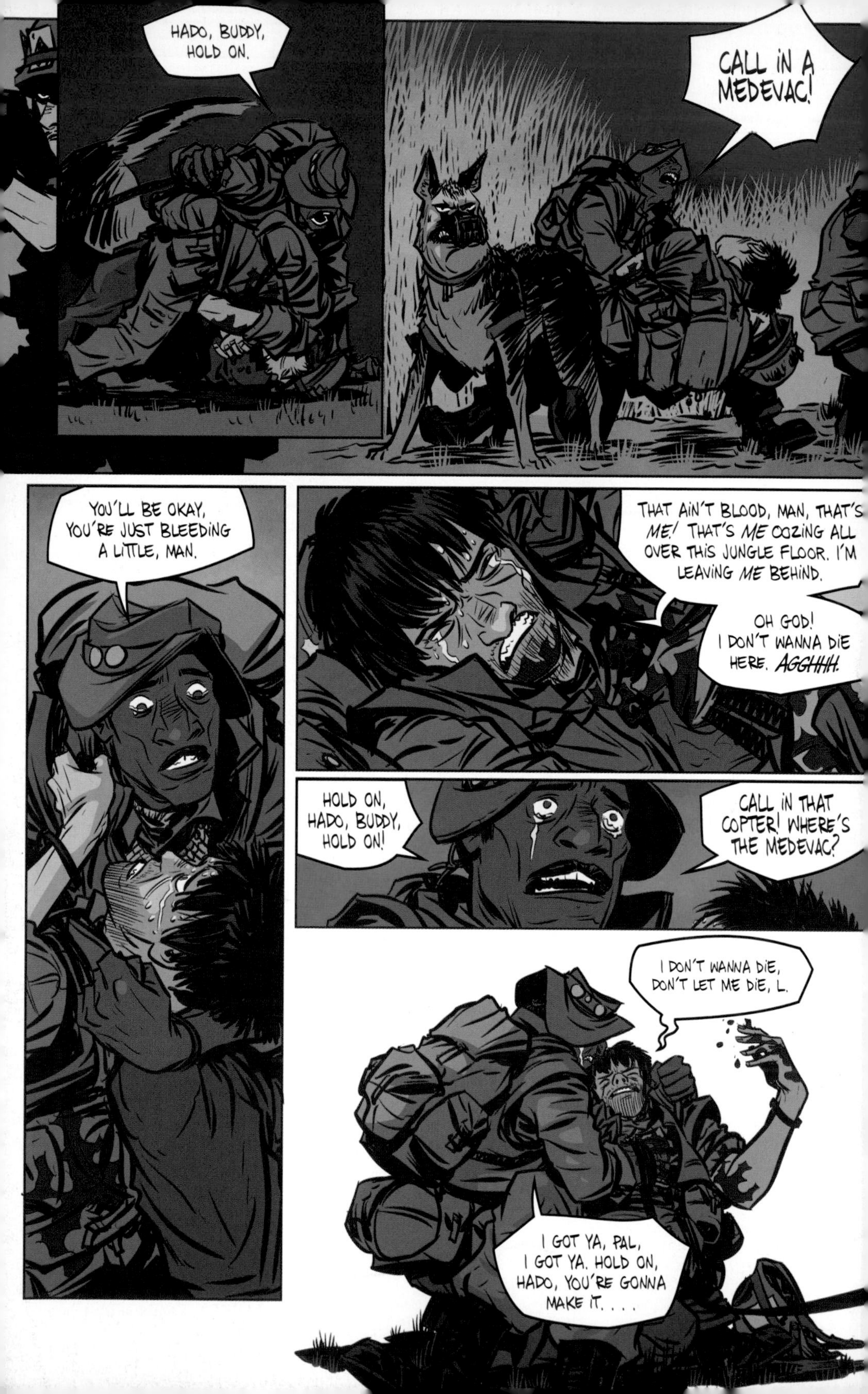
HADO, BUDDY, HOLD ON.
CALL IN A MEDEVAC!
YOU'LL BE OKAY, YOU'RE JUST BLEEDING A LITTLE, MAN.
THAT AIN'T BLOOD, MAN, THAT'S *ME!* THAT'S *ME* OOZING ALL OVER THIS JUNGLE FLOOR. I'M LEAVING *ME* BEHIND.
OH GOD! I DON'T WANNA DIE HERE. *AGGHHH.*
HOLD ON, HADO, BUDDY, HOLD ON!
CALL IN THAT COPTER! WHERE'S THE MEDEVAC?
I DON'T WANNA DIE, DON'T LET ME DIE, L.
I GOT YA, PAL, I GOT YA. HOLD ON, HADO, YOU'RE GONNA MAKE IT. . . .

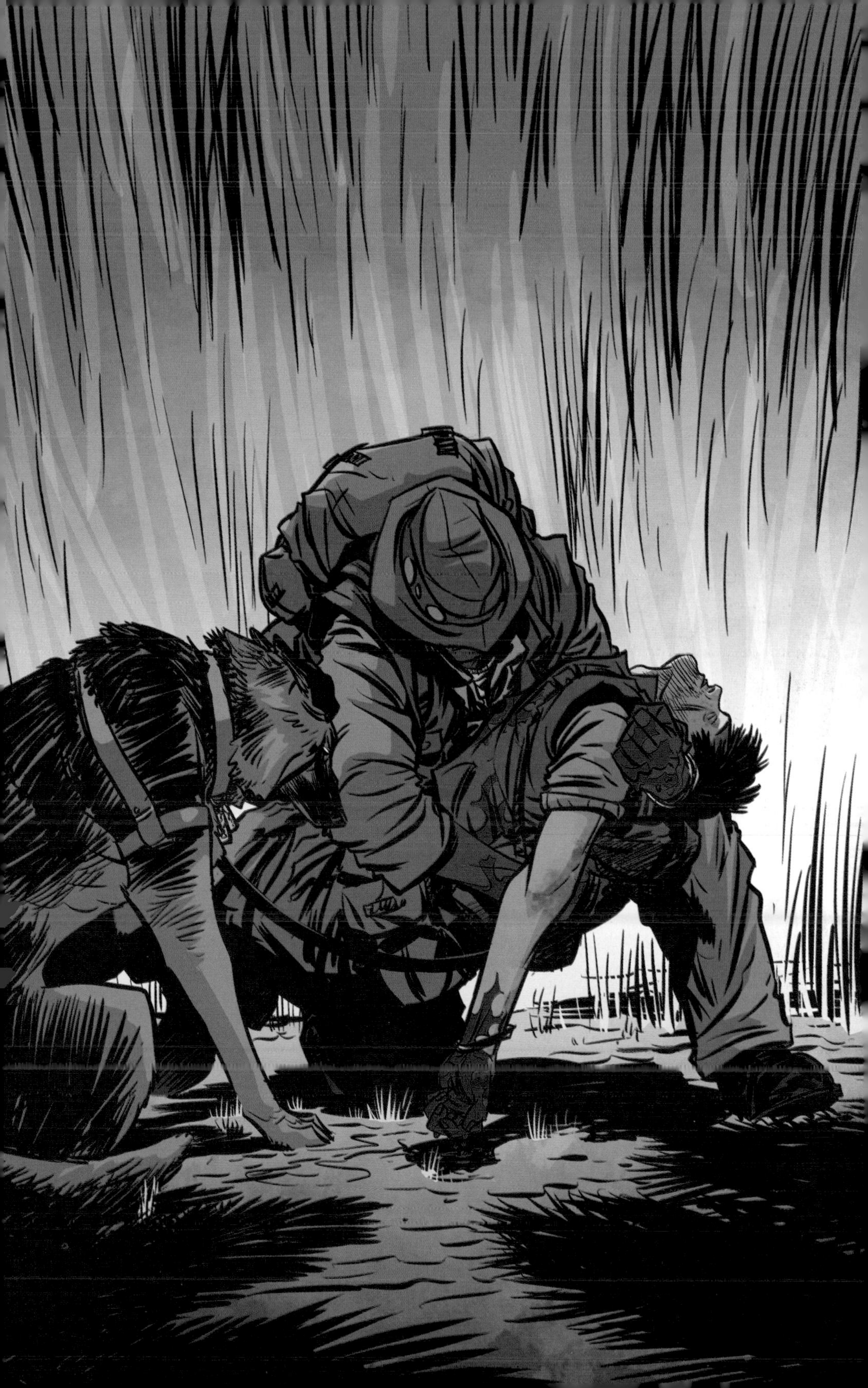

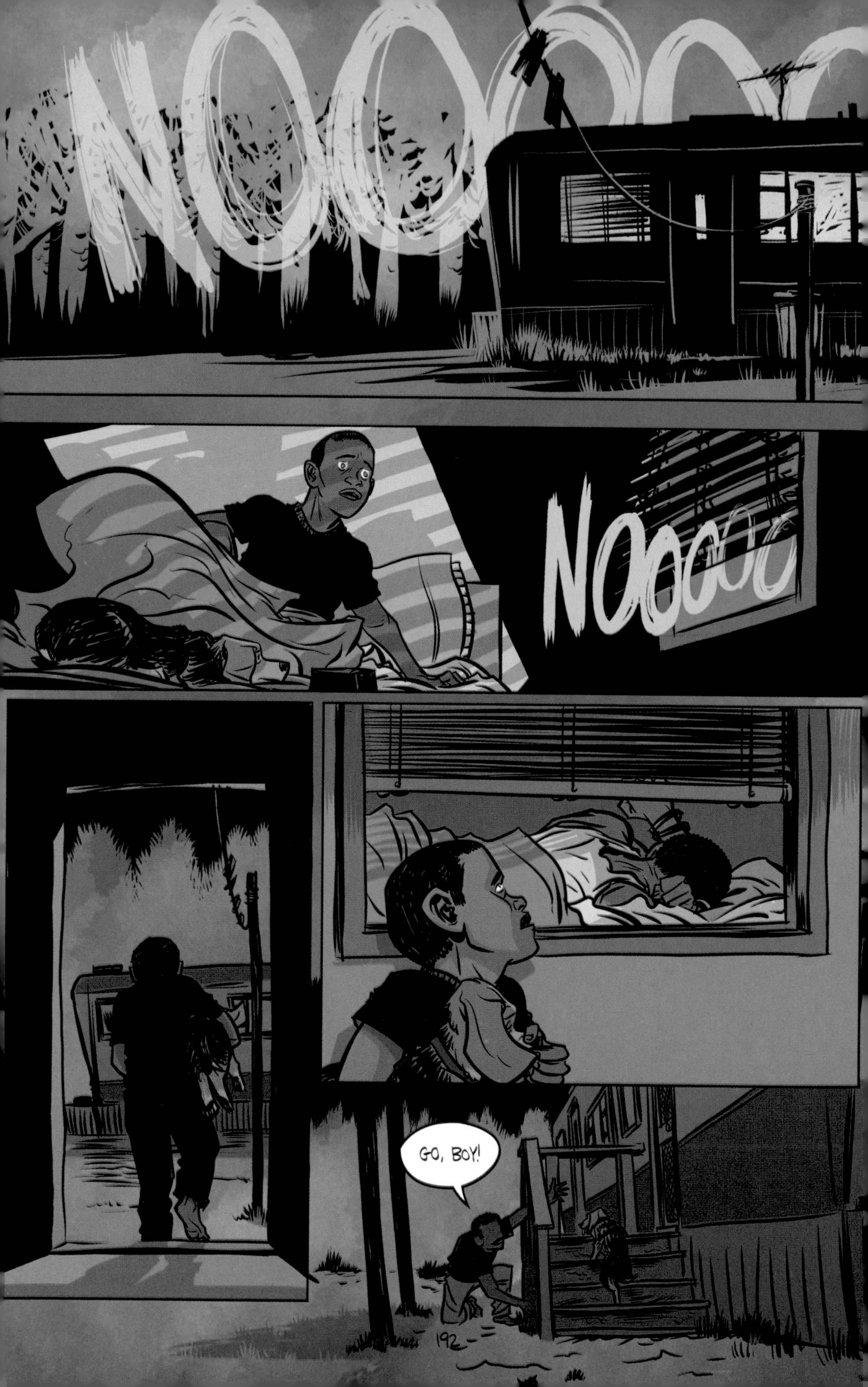
NOOOOO
NOOOOO
GO, BOY!

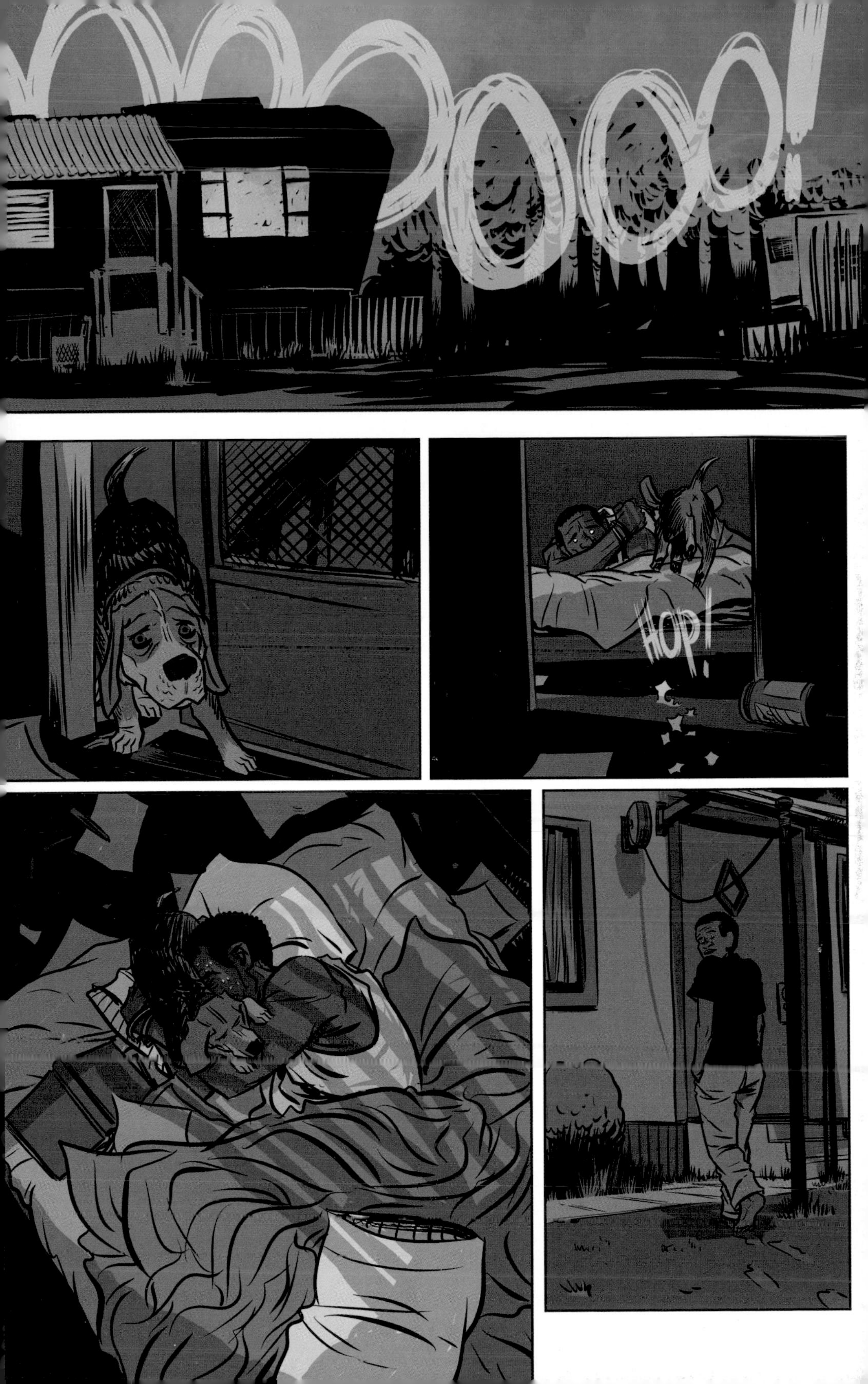
WOOOOOOO!
HOP!

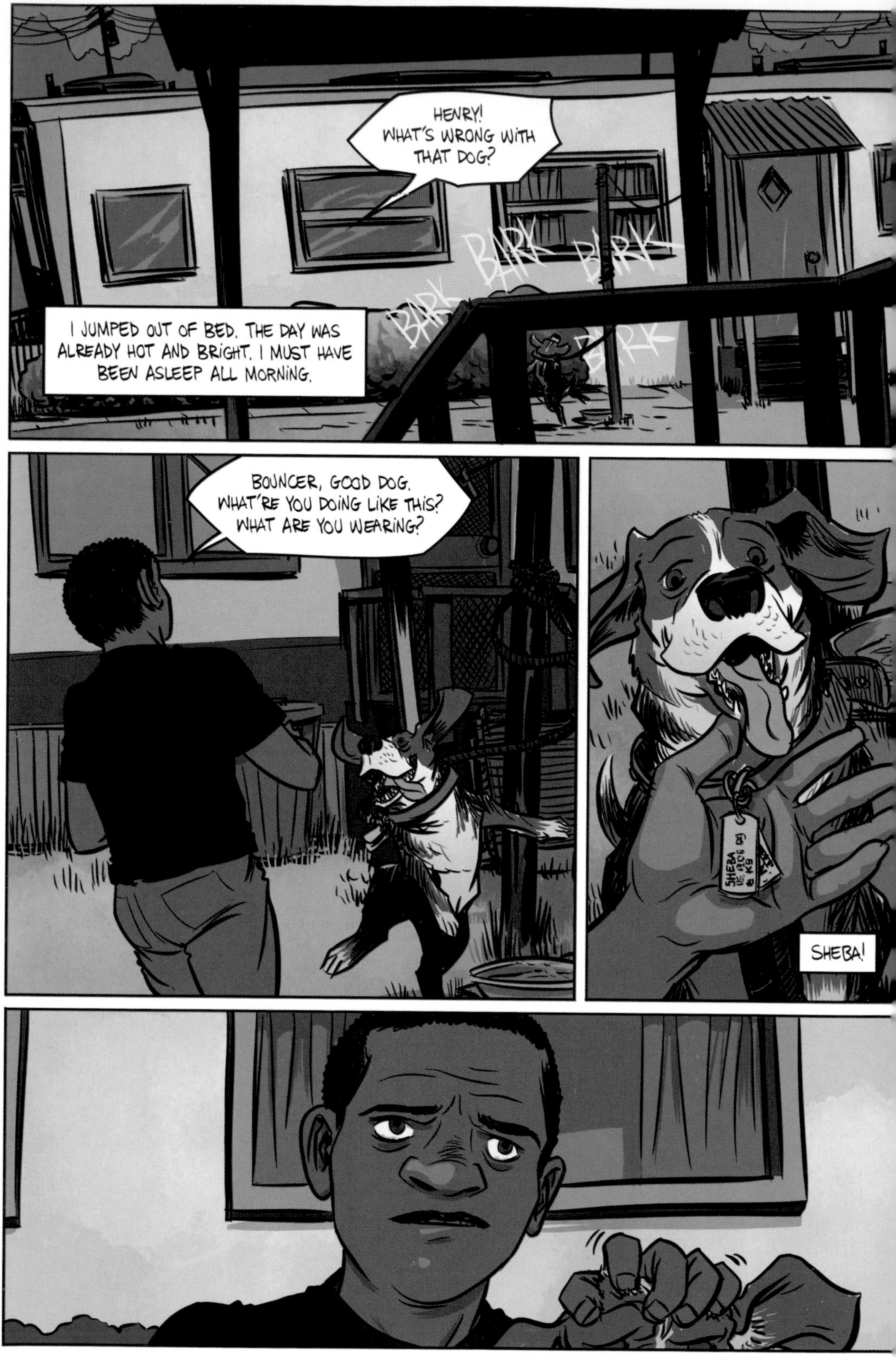
HENRY! WHAT'S WRONG WITH THAT DOG?
BARK BARK BARK BARK BARK
I JUMPED OUT OF BED. THE DAY WAS ALREADY HOT AND BRIGHT. I MUST HAVE BEEN ASLEEP ALL MORNING.
BOUNCER, GOOD DOG. WHAT'RE YOU DOING LIKE THIS? WHAT ARE YOU WEARING?
SHEBA
SHEBA!

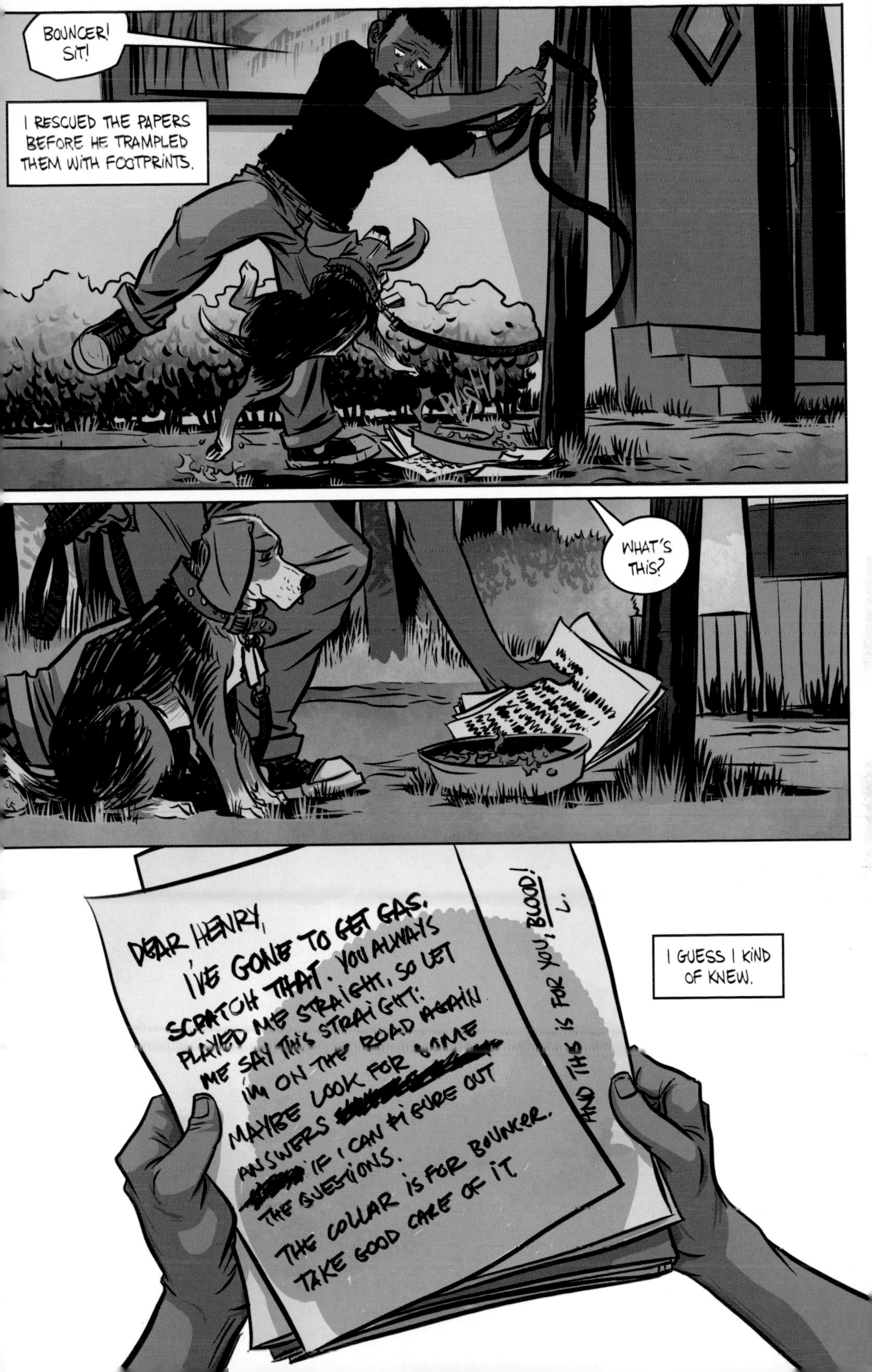
BOUNCER! SIT!
I RESCUED THE PAPERS BEFORE HE TRAMPLED THEM WITH FOOTPRINTS.
PLASH!
WHAT'S THIS?
DEAR HENRY,
I'VE GONE TO GET GAS.
SCRATCH THAT. YOU ALWAYS PLAYED ME STRAIGHT, SO LET ME SAY THIS STRAIGHT:
I'M ON THE ROAD AGAIN
MAYBE LOOK FOR SOME
ANSWERS
IF I CAN FIGURE OUT THE QUESTIONS.
THE COLLAR IS FOR BOUNCER.
TAKE GOOD CARE OF IT.
AND THIS IS FOR YOU, BLOOD!
L.
I GUESS I KIND OF KNEW.

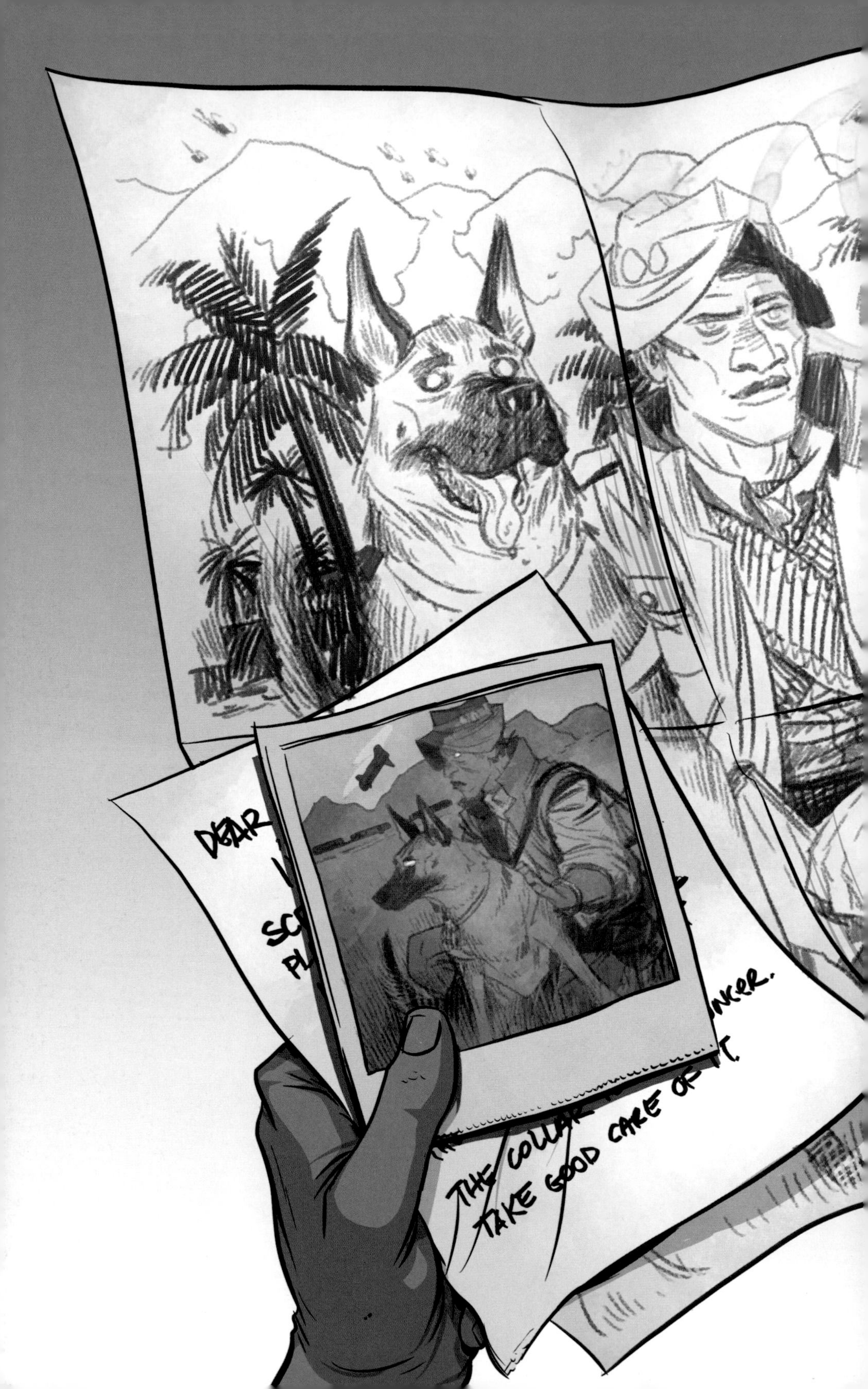
DEAR
THE COLLAR
TAKE GOOD CARE OF

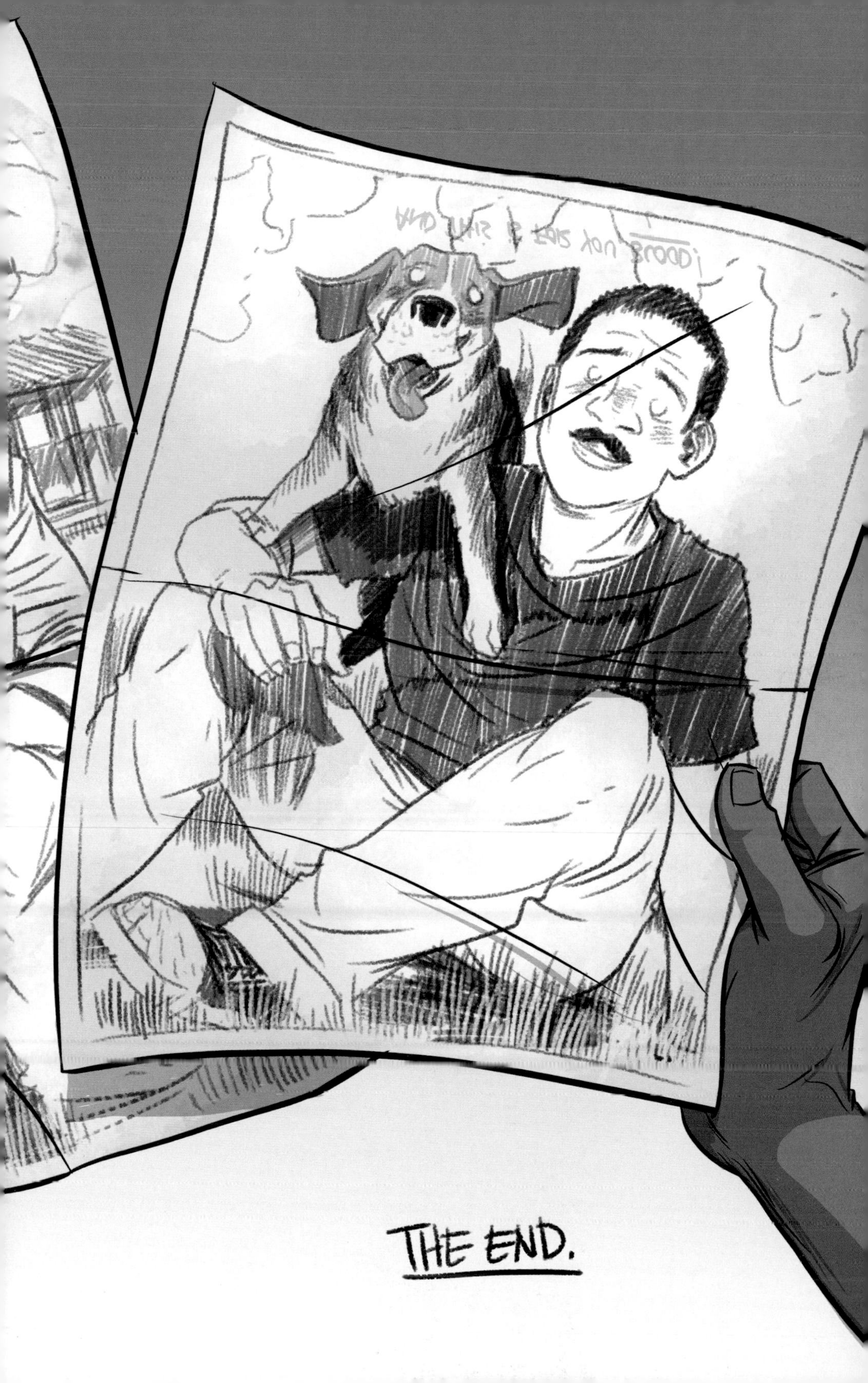
THE END.

AUTHOR'S NOTE

"War dogs have served the nation well." — General Colin L. Powell

Whenever people go to war, so do their best friends. Military forces from the ancient Roman army to the Navy SEAL 6 team that carried out the Osama bin Laden mission in Pakistan brought trained dogs along with them. War dogs have worn spiked armor in antiquity and chain mail in the Middle Ages and armored plates during the Renaissance; in modern times, they've been outfitted with everything from gas masks and goggles to bulletproof camouflage vests with infrared and night-vision cameras to give their handlers the dogs' eye view.

Countless soldiers in countless wars kept dogs as mascots or adopted strays in battle-torn areas. Who knows what good luck these mutts brought their masters in combat? But military working dogs (MWDs) are specially trained to support a war effort; they are canine soldiers — and good ones.

Dogs' superior senses of smell and hearing, their capacity to be trained, and their responsiveness to human beings, especially their handlers, make them ideal for many dangerous wartime jobs. Before mass communication was easy, messenger dogs carried urgent information from one military unit to another, often traveling through or around enemy lines. War dogs carry supplies, ammunition, and medicine. They cross battlefields to alert medics to wounded soldiers who need help. They serve as scout dogs, ahead of the infantry, ever vigilant of the presence of enemy patrols or snipers. They can spot machine gun nests and sniff out bombs, mines, and booby traps. They can flush out enemies from caves or underground tunnels. And, of course, war dogs are the perfect guards, keeping military camps or foxholes safe.

European and American military dog trainers prefer certain breeds, such as German shepherds, Belgian Malinois, Airedales, Doberman pinschers, malamutes, and Labrador retrievers. How military dogs are used depends upon the technology and geography of the war.

World War I raged from 1914 to 1918. It was set off by the assassination of an Austro-Hungarian archduke in Sarajevo, Bosnia and Herzegovina, but that was just the match to the fire. Territorial, political, and military rivalries were already simmering, particularly between Germany and Great Britain, which each wanted to be the world's foremost naval power. More than ten million soldiers and civilians died in World War I, which spread across Europe, the Middle East, and some parts of Africa and Asia. The Central powers, which included Germany, Austria-Hungary, and the Ottoman Empire, fought the Allied powers, which included France, Britain, Russia, Italy, and the United States. And dogs were there: carrying messages, pulling supply carts, killing trench rats, and working as mercy dogs, that is, leading medics to wounded soldiers. Germany deployed about 30,000 war dogs, while 20,000 canines joined the British and French troops. Many of World War I's most famous — and most deadly — battles took place in the trenches on the Western Front, which was the site of an unofficial Christmas truce in 1914.

The world was again engulfed in war from 1939 to 1945. And again, the causes were complicated: There had been a great global economic depression; empires had fallen apart because of World War I; Germany was ordered to pay for war damages and its military forces were restricted to a certain size. Enter Adolf Hitler and the Nazi party. Hitler invaded Poland and the die was cast. Allied forces, including Great Britain, the Soviet Union, France, China, and the United States, fought the Axis powers of Germany, Japan, and Italy. More than 100 million military personnel were called up during World War II, not counting dogs . . . that would have added another million to the ranks (though heavily on the Axis side).

When the United States entered World War II, due to the Japanese attack on Pearl Harbor, there were already American rescue dog teams working in Arctic regions such as Greenland, an essential location for aircraft being ferried over from North America to the Allies. Sled dog teams there saved at least 100 aircrew members over the course of the war.

In the summer of 1942, the U.S. war dog program, called K-9 Corps, put dogs and handlers through basic training; some of those dogs were "civilians," volunteered by their owners. By 1944, U.S. Army war dogs had shipped out for European and Pacific battle zones, where they worked as scouts and sentries. The Marines also had war dog units, and their canines, often Dobermans, saw active duty in the Pacific Islands, meaning these "devil dogs" saw combat. Nearly 10,000 dogs served in the U.S. Army, Navy, Marine Corps, and Coast Guard during World War II. When the war ended, many of these dogs were demobilized. They were retrained, given honorable discharges, and went home with their handlers, back to their original owners, or were given to new owners.

The Vietnam War was fought between the Communist north and the anti-Communist south, both of which wanted to control the entire country and each of which had the aid of world superpowers. U.S. involvement in this conflict (on behalf of South Vietnam) lasted from 1959 to 1975, which took the lives of more than 58,000 American servicemen and servicewomen, and became one of the most complicated and divisive chapters in American history. And waging the war itself was just as complicated.

The Vietnam War was fought in hot, dense tropical jungles and rugged mountains, through rivers, rice paddies, and swamps. The enemy was often unseen and moved around mostly at night. War dogs were essential, and nearly 5,000 of them served in Vietnam in all branches of the military. Sentry dogs guarded bases and supply depots. Scout dogs alerted soldiers to snipers and other ambushes when they went out on patrol. Tracker dogs helped locate injured soldiers or downed pilots. Mine and tunnel dogs helped flush out the enemy or signal booby traps. Despite the fact that war dogs were credited with saving thousands of lives in the Vietnam War, most of them never came home. They were classified as equipment and left behind in Vietnam.

Military dogs continue to be a part of the American armed forces and of homeland security. K-9 Corps are deployed in the United States, at military bases abroad, and in the wars in Iraq and Afghanistan. There are about 2,700 dogs of war on active duty right now — helping thousands more human soldiers make it through their active duties.

Semper fido!

FURTHER READING

BOOKS

Barnett, Correlli. *The Great War*. London: Penguin, 2000.

Burnam, John C. *A Soldier's Best Friend: Scout Dogs and Their Handlers in the Vietnam War*. New York: Carroll & Graf, 2003.

Caputo, Philip. *10,000 Days of Thunder: A History of the Vietnam War*. New York: Atheneum, 2005.

Clarke, William F. *Over There with O'Ryan's Roughnecks: Reminiscences of a Private 1st Class Who Served in the 27th U.S. Division with the British Forces in Belgium and France*. Seattle: Superior Publishing, 1968.

Dean, Charles L. *Soldiers and Sled Dogs: A History of Military Dog Mushing*. Lincoln, NE: University of Nebraska Press, 2004.

Ebert, James R. *A Life in a Year: The American Infantryman in Vietnam, 1965–1972*. New York: Presidio Press, 1993.

Edelman, Bernard, ed. *Dear America: Letters Home from Vietnam*. New York: W. W. Norton, 1985.

English, June A. and Thomas D. Jones. *Scholastic Encyclopedia of the United States at War*. New York: Scholastic, 1998.

Greene, Bob. *Homecoming: When the Soldiers Returned from Vietnam*. New York: G. P. Putnam's Sons, 1989.

Hamer, Blythe. *Dogs at War: True Stories of Canine Courage under Fire*. London: Carlton, 2001.

Josephy, Alvin M., Jr., ed. *The American Heritage History of World War I*. New York: American Heritage, 1964.

Lifton, Robert Jay. *Home from the War: Vietnam Veterans; Neither Victims Nor Executioners*. New York: Simon & Schuster, 1973.

Longley, Kyle. *Grunts: The American Combat Soldier in Vietnam*. Armonk, NY: M. E. Sharpe, 2008.

Putney, William W. *Always Faithful: A Memoir of the Marine Dogs of WWII*. New York: Free Press, 2001.

Santoli, Al. *Everything We Had: An Oral History of the Vietnam War by Thirty-three American Soldiers Who Fought It.* New York: Random House, 1981.

Sheffield, G. D. *The Pictorial History of World War I.* New York: W. H. Smith, 1987.

Wallace, Terry. *Bloods: An Oral History of the Vietnam War by Black Veterans.* New York: Random House, 1984.

Weiner, Tom, ed. *Voices of War: Stories of Service from the Home Front and the Front Lines. Vol 1, The Library of Congress Veterans History Project.* Washington, DC: National Geographic, 2004.

Weintraub, Stanley. *Silent Night: The Story of the World War I Christmas Truce.* New York: Free Press, 2001.

DVDS

Ayres, Lew. *All Quiet on the Western Front,* DVD. Directed by Lewis Milestone. Universal City, CA: Universal Studios, 2007.

Berenger, John, Ellen Burstyn, and J. Kenneth Campbell. *Dear America, Letters Home from Vietnam,* DVD. Directed by Bill Couturié. New York: HBO Home Video, 2005.

Choosing Sides: I Remember Vietnam, DVD. Directed by Michael Moriarity. New York: History Channel, 2005.

Douglas, Kirk. *Paths of Glory,* DVD. Directed by Stanley Kubrick. Los Angeles: MGM/UA, 1999.

Font, Louis. *Sir! No Sir! The Suppressed Story of the GI Movement to End the War in Vietnam,* DVD. Directed by David Zeiger. New York: Docurama, 2006.

Kruger, Diane, and Benno Fürmann. *Joyeux Noel,* DVD. Directed by Christian Carion. Culver City, CA: Sony Pictures, 2006.

Lyman, Will. *Vietnam: A Television History,* DVD. Arlington, VA: Public Broadcasting System, 2004.

Meredith, Burgess. *Vietnam's Unseen War: Pictures from the Other Side,* DVD. Washington, DC: National Geographic Video, 2002.

Nguyen, Xuan Ngoc. *Regret to Inform,* DVD. Directed by Barbara Sonneborn. New York: Docurama, 2000.